FIGHTING
FATE

Also by JB Salsbury

FIGHTING
FATE

JB SALSBURY

Fighting Fate

JB Salsbury

Edited by Theresa Wegand

To Kelly Fletcher,

Who's proven there's hope after unimaginable pain,

You make the world a happier place

in a gadda da vida.

PROLOGUE

Four years ago . . .

Killian

It would take dying to slow my pulse. And I'm not being dramatic. I've tried everything for that last hour and a half; nothing has worked. Deep breathing, prayer, meditation—none of it does squat to calm me down.

My fingers drum against the steering wheel while taillights from the cars in front of me blare bright red. If being asked by the most beautiful girl at Vegas High isn't enough to make my nerves want to rip through my skin and drown themselves, then the added pressure of being late because I'm stuck in traffic sure as heck will.

No, it'll be fine. Even if I am a little late, Axelle will understand. She's not like most girls. I mean, even though my experience with girls is limited to the occasional joke at my expense or tutoring session I get roped into, I never have been able to turn down a pretty girl.

But Axelle is different from the rest. She actually seems interested in me. At first, I thought we were just friends—which was more than I'd ever expect from someone like her—but then she asked me to the dance. Not just any dance, the Valentine's Day Dance.

So tonight I'm going to tell her. I'm finally going to spill my guts that I've been in love with her since the day we met. I never thought I'd have the courage to do it, but *she* asked *me*. That's gotta mean something, right? It doesn't make

1

sense because she's so freakin' beautiful and nice. I mean . . . why me?

I have a four-point-oh GPA, so I know better than to dwell on the *why* and just live in *the holy heck this is really happening.* If Peter Parker can get the girl, why can't I?

I push my glasses up my nose and squint around the line of cars in front of me. The tie I borrowed from my neighbor Mr. Heeber is suffocating, and I'm starting to sweat while the traffic remains at a standstill. I crank the AC on my Mazda 323, and the twenty-year-old thing sputters to life. Maybe I should call the restaurant and let them know we might be a few minutes late. I pull my phone from my center console and see I have two missed calls from Axelle and they're only a minute apart.

I still have eight minutes until I'm supposed to be at her house, so why . . .? My phone vibrates in my hand and I immediately answer it.

"Hello?"

I'm met with silence and then the soft clearing of a throat. "Hey, Killian?"

"Axelle, hey . . ." She sounds off: sad or something. "I'm almost there to pick you up. I'm stuck in stupid traffic."

"Oh, yeah, about that, um . . ." She's whispering. "Listen. I can't go tonight."

My pulse finally slows to a crawl. Okay, so I'm not dead, but with the way my chest feels, I may as well be. "What? I mean . . . why?"

"It's not a good night."

"But you said you got a dress and we picked the restaurant so—"

"I know. I feel so bad. I—"

A man's voice filters through the phone. I can't make out his words, but he sounds irritated.

"Is that Blake? Is he there?"

She sniffs. "No." God, she sounds so tiny.

"Axelle," I whisper. "What's going on?"

"I . . . my dad's back. He—"

"Say good-bye, Elle," the man's voice commands.

"I'm so sorry, Killian. I have to go. Please don't be mad, okay?"

"Okay."

"Bye."

I don't even get the good-bye out before the phone disconnects.

My gut churns with worry. Her dad is in town? She never talked about him much, only to say that she was grateful to be away from him.

It was something we had in common. My dad was a mean son of a bitch, but luckily, he left when I was young. Granted, he left me with my mom, who wasn't much better, but it's easier to defend myself from the verbal attack of one rather than two, so I never complained.

Still, I wouldn't wish any of this on Axelle, and there was fear in her voice. I go with my gut and hit a number on my phone then press it to my ear. My heartbeat kicks faster with every ring.

"Killer, what's up, man?"

"Mr. Slade, I'm so—"

"Enough with the 'Mr. Slade' shit. You're going to have to get used to calling me Jonah."

As if I could ever get used to having the Universal Fighting League's Heavyweight Champion's personal cell phone number programmed into my phone much less actually talking to him.

"Okay, sure. But, um, I just got off the phone with Axelle and, uh . . ." It's freakin' Valentine's Day for crap's sake, and I'm about to pull this man away from his wife. I better not be wrong about this. I push my glasses up my nose; nervous sweat makes them slide right back down. "I don't have Mr. . . . er . . . Blake's phone number, but I figured you would, and I think—"

"Spit it out, Killian."

Damn, he sounds mad. "Axelle sounded . . . off. She cancelled on me tonight, and when I asked her why, she mentioned her dad was there." I'm met with silence. I check the phone to see if we were disconnected. "Are you there?"

"How long ago did you talk to her?"

"I called you right after we hung up. I was in traffic on the way to pick her up when she called and cancelled. I don't have a good feeling about this. I'm sorry. I know it's Valentine's Day and you probably have plans—"

"Don't worry about that. You did the right thing." He quickly catches Raven up on what I told him and she replies, but I can't understand what she's saying. "Killian, you go on over to Layla's, but *do not* go inside. Wait for us in the parking lot and keep your phone on you, understand?"

"Yeah."

"Chances are everything's fine, but we'll be there in about thirty minutes, so just hang tight until we get there."

"Okay, sure, sounds good."

"See you in a bit."

~~~

Time drags on. I'm pacing the lot with my phone welded to my palm.

It's been over thirty minutes, and I'm about to call Jonah back when his truck comes barreling into the lot.

He parks next to my car, and he and his wife Raven hop down from the truck. They both look insanely pissed off, which only ratchets up my panic. That and . . . there's no Blake.

"What's going on? Where's Blake?"

Jonah's jaw ticks. "He's not coming."

"Not coming?" I motion to the second-story apartment where Axelle and her mom are inside with her dickhead ex-husband. "What if he's hurting them up there? How could he not come and help them?"

Raven steps into my line of sight, and I'm struck by the softness in her pretty face. "Killian, they'll be okay. Chances are everything's fine. Let's not freak out until we have a reason to."

I nod. "Okay, yeah, let's go." I move to jog up the steps when Jonah snags my arm.

"Whoa, hang on there, Killer."

I whirl around and glare at his hand on my bicep. Respect flickers in his expression and he lets me go.

Raven takes to the steps. "I'm going to go feel things out."

"This is a stupid idea." Jonah's arms and shoulders are tense.

"We talked about this. If you guys come with me, we might make things worse." Raven sets unwavering eyes on us. "I'm not a threat to Layla's ex."

Jonah growls, and I make a sound in the back of my throat that comes out more like a groan.

"Fine, you have five minutes and then we're coming up," Jonah says through clenched teeth.

She nods and jogs up the steps. I watch until she disappears around the railing. Jonah looks downright deadly in the glow of his phone as he watches the seconds crawl by.

Axelle's only mentioned her dad a couple of times. Her mid-semester move from Seattle to Vegas doesn't say good things about this guy.

Were they trying to get away from him? Was he abusive? God, if he hurts her, I'll fucking kill him.

My hands shake at the thought of him laying a hand on her perfect skin. I pace the parking lot, my eyes darting from Jonah to the direction of Axelle's apartment and back again. Usually, I'd be awestruck being so close to the Heavyweight Champion, the man I've idolized since he had his first fight more than five years ago. His shoulders look like they're about to Hulk out of his T-shirt, and the veins in his forearms bulge against his colorful full-sleeved tattoos, but this is no time for hero worship. I'm just glad he's here. No one, not even the biggest asshole in the world—which I'm sure Axelle's dad is—would fuck with The Assassin.

"Time's up." Jonah takes the steps and I drop in right behind him. "Killer."

I slam into his back and peer up at him, straightening my glasses. "What?"

"Stay here."

"But—"

"Listen to me." He steps down one step, and damn, the guy is huge towering over me. "I don't know what's going on up there, but I do know everyone in that apartment is an adult and can handle whatever's about to happen—all except Axelle. I'm going to get her out of there, and when I do, she's going to need you down here so you can keep her safe. Understand?"

I can't even think clearly enough to understand what he's saying. All I hear is she needs me and I can keep her safe, so I nod and step down.

"Good. Hang tight." He takes three steps at a time until he's gone.

I rip my hands through my hair, the waiting making me crazy. Why didn't Raven come back down before the five minutes were up? Or at least peek out to let us know everything's okay?

Because everything isn't okay.

I go back to pacing. My scalp burns from scraping my nails on it. She's okay. She has to be. And when this is all over, I'm not waiting another second to tell her how I feel, to let her know I've never been more in love with anyone in my entire life. I'll do whatever she asks me to, jump through any hoops she lays out, if it means she'll give me a shot at making her happy.

She claimed my soul from the first time we met, and I can't imagine ever loving anyone the same way I do her. If she'll have me, I'll—

The high-pitched shriek of truck tires speeding around the corner calls my eyes and I skid to a halt.

Black Rubicon.

Blake.

The vehicle jerks to a stop, and he's out and running to the stairs. He's dressed like me: suit pants, button-up shirt, and dress shoes.

I run to catch him. "Blake!"

He freezes, and I flinch at the mix of anger and self-hatred I see in his eyes. "Killian, what's going on up there?"

"I don't know. Raven and Jonah went up, but they made me stay down here. I don't know, Blake. Something's not right. Axelle didn't sound right when she called me. I just . . . She wouldn't admit it, but something's wrong." I press my hand to my heart as it splinters behind my ribs. "If something bad happens, I . . . I can't lose her. What if he takes her back to Seattle? What if he takes Layla and they—"

"Not gonna happen." He hooks me around the neck and makes me meet his eyes. "I'm going up there to get my girls, and no one, especially not some piece-of-shit, abusive ex-dick will stand in my way."

My eyes widen and my hands shake. "Abusive?"

His mouth opens and his eyes soften, but he slams his jaw shut and races up the stairs. "I'm sending Axelle down now. Be ready."

It doesn't take long, and before I know it, she comes bolting down the stairs with a trail of chestnut hair whipping in the wind behind her.

I'm breathing so heavily I'm practically panting with relief. She's okay.

"Killian!" She launches herself off the steps and into my arms.

Raven's standing at the top of the steps, and with a satisfied nod, she turns back to the apartment.

"He has my mom. He's not going to let us go, Kill. We'll never get away." Her body jerks with the force of her sobs. "Why . . . why won't he let us go?"

I bury my nose into her hair and breathe deeply, reminding myself that she's here and safe in my arms. "Shhh . . . he's not taking either of you anywhere."

"I was so scared." Her arms grow tighter around my waist, and my arms shake with pent-up rage and relief. "I was so afraid no one would be able to help us. Blake left, and I thought you bought my stupid excuse for not being able to go to the dance." The more she talks, the harder she cries, as if she's been holding it all back for days.

"It's alright. I knew. I heard it in your voice. I knew something wasn't right."

"Thank you. Thank you, Kill. You saved us. God, what if you guys never showed up?"

"We're here; that's all that matters." Is this what Superman feels like when he saves Lois Lane?

Her body freezes in my arms and she pulls back. Her eyes are red and puffy, but she still takes my breath away. "I have to go back up there."

I hold her tighter. "No way. We're staying down here. Let Jonah and Blake take care of—"

She breaks free and starts running up the stairs.

"Shit! Axelle, wait!"

It takes a fraction of a second for me to realize she has no plan to stop, so I race after her and reach the front door just behind her.

Axelle's dad is in a standoff with Blake, and Jonah is at his friend's back. Not good odds for *Daddy Dearest*, but he doesn't seem the least bit concerned.

"Did she tell you how many guys she slept with the night she got pregnant with Elle?"

Oh no.

Axelle gasps and covers her mouth.

"Oh, come on! Look at me." He points to his face. "She looks nothing like me."

He's right. His blond hair and dark eyes don't match Axelle's coloring at all.

Axelle seems to follow my line of thought and bursts into silent sobs. Raven wraps her arms around her, and I simply stand there, totally stunned and completely useless.

"Me and the boys had some fun that night. Hottest chick in school was drunk as hell at a party." The man's words take up all the oxygen in the room, and the tension thickens with unbridled hostility. "Didn't take much to get her so drunk she passed out. Shit, she probably weighed ninety pounds back then. We had our fun with you, taking turns, filling you up."

"Get Axelle the fuck out of here." Blake's command snaps me out of the horrific story being told.

I grasp at Axelle, but she shoves me away.

"Axelle, please," I whisper. "You don't need to hear this."

Tears fall freely down her cheeks, and she peers over at me with bloodshot eyes. "Yes, I do."

Her father sneers at Layla. "You and your bastard kid."

I watch with revulsion as every word he says chips away a piece of the girl I love. Her shoulders cave, and her face pales with each verbal blow.

"I married you because I thought you were Axelle's dad. If you weren't, why didn't you say anything?" Layla's face is white, her lips quivering.

"What was I supposed to do? Admit that I roofied the hottest chick in school so the boys and me could gang-bang her? I'd end up in jail."

Blake's practically vibrating now. I reach forward and grab Axelle's hand, afraid the worst is coming and offering my support.

Stewart studies Blake through narrowed eyes. "Haven't you been listening, asshole? You don't want her. She's garbage. Even back in high school, no one stepped up. Not one of the guys claimed the baby as their kid. No one wanted them."

Crack!

Some would think the sound came from Blake's fist as he finally shut that piece of shit up by slamming it into the guy's nose.

That may be true, but what I heard was the crack of Axelle's heart breaking.

ONE

Present Day . . .

Killian

The sun beats down on my back as I hunch over my phone. My eyes devour line by line of the latest sci-fi novel by my favorite author, Mikel Vermouch. Aliens have implanted their seed in hundreds of unsuspecting human females, their gestation cycle is half the length of a human's, it's been four months, and shit's about to get ugly.

Voices flood my fictional world, along with the opening and slamming of doors signaling my time is up, and the best part of my day is about to begin.

I shove my phone into my backpack and lean against the picnic table, my gaze zeroing in on a door that leads to her last class. Creative Writing, room E34.

One by one, UNLV college students filter out of the room, and I search for her from behind my sunglasses: a guy shoving a book in his bag, another popping in his earbuds, a string of women I don't even notice beyond their hair color, and then finally . . . I suck in a breath.

Axelle.

Fuck, time slows like some cheesy chick-flick, and I drink in every inch of her—from all that chestnut hair she bitches about being too thick to her baggy tee that droops on one side to reveal the smoothest olive-skinned shoulder, and those dick-hardening yoga pants that hug her ass. I groan as she pulls her backpack straps on, taking the fabric of her shirt on a ride up her slender belly. Gorgeous. I want her.

I tell myself it's possible to live the kind of life I read about in books. The kind where ordinary men can become extraordinary and the geek wins the girl. Even if that girl is more beautiful than anything he could possibly deserve. Somehow the fates would favor him or some dynamic bullshit within would shine through and show her he's a fucking superhero.

Yeah . . . I tell myself it's possible.

But experience has proven it sure as shit is not.

Her eyes find me almost immediately, and she lifts her chin before heading over. Green Converse-clad feet trudge through the grassy commons, and she smiles, watching me watching her. Those thick lips can deliver a slicing word and bring unimaginable pleasure. That's not true. I've imagined it plenty. Hell, that's all I've fuckin' done is imagine it. Any pleasure those lips have brought me so far has been in words only.

She pops on her sunglasses and my stomach plummets. Those blue eyes, so expressive when they light with the fire of her anger, shine with tears, or dance with humor are entertaining as hell to watch.

She stops a couple feet in front of me and props a hand on one slender hip. "You don't have to wait for me *every day*, Killian."

That's true, but you know what they say about old habits. The last three semesters our classrooms were close, and I made a habit of walking her to her car every day after school.

We've only been back in school for a week after Christmas break, and though the spring semester brought more distance between our last classes, that doesn't mean I'm giving up my after-school ritual.

I shrug one shoulder and swing my gaze around the commons, taking in groups of co-eds. "Who says I was waiting for you?"

Her smile slams me in the chest, but I've worked for years to school my response to her, tamping down my physical reactions to appear unfazed. Friendly. Because that's what I've always been—friend zoned.

"Your last class is all the way across campus." One sculpted dark eyebrow pops up over her shades. "You're telling me you come here to sit outside my classroom for thirty minutes for someone other than your best friend?"

Friend. There's that fucking word again.

"Maybe I'm waiting for my girl." Truth. She just doesn't know it.

"Oh, *your girl*." She taps her chin. "Hmmm . . . and who is this imaginary girl, huh?" She points to a huddle of women. "Oh, is it Charlene? She's a book-nerd like you. I could see you two getting along." She flashes a teasing smile then searches the common area and points to what I'm assuming is another girl. I don't know. I only have eyes for her. "Tarryn maybe? She's smokin' hot and dates jocks."

"Jock? I thought I was a book-nerd?"

"You're both." Her smile suddenly crunches up, and she curls in on herself, hissing through her teeth. "Ugh!"

My pulse kicks in worry. "What's wrong?" I stand and move toward her, but she holds a hand up.

"No, I'm okay." She takes a few steps to the picnic bench and sits.

"You sure?" I sit back down next to her, her pained expression not doing shit to relieve my worry.

"Yeah, just cramps." She crosses her legs and lays a hand on her lower abdomen. "Worst. Period. Ever."

Being an only child and having a terrible relationship with my mother, I put talk of girl issues high up on my don't-go-there list of convos, but this is different. This is Axelle, so I swallow my discomfort.

"Right." I reach into my backpack and pull out a bottle of Advil. I shake a couple out and hand them to her. "Here."

She flashes a grateful, but strained, smile. "Thanks, but I don't have—"

I push my water bottle into her hand.

She sighs and thanks me again before tossing the pills back. Her lips wrap around the bottle's mouthpiece, and I have to look away. A sick part of me revels in the fact that I'll be able to have her mouth on mine, even if only through the connection of the water bottle. Yeah, I'm fucking pathetic. Four years of this shit and I still haven't grown a pair big enough to confess my feelings for her.

"How do you always seem to know what I need before I need it?"

"I pay attention." *Because I'm in love with you.*

She hands me the bottle back. "You're too good to me."

Aw, baby, I could be so much better if you'd let me.

Again, my chest cramps. If she only knew how much I hold back to keep our friendship from being awkward . . . I'd give her everything she ever wanted, satisfy her every whim, work my ass off to make enough money to provide for her, and die trying to give her the beautiful life she deserves.

Ever since Axelle came into my life back in high school, I knew she'd own me. She claimed my heart the day I found her in the parking lot: the new kid, kicking and screaming every profanity in the book at her Bronco. As much as I tried to hint to something more than a friendship back then, nothing beyond it ever developed. I knew it was because she was way too good for me, so I spent the next few years bettering myself: got a job and contact lenses and started training with the world's best MMA fighting league. But even bulked up at just under 200 pounds, a good half foot taller than I was when we met, she still sees me as scrawny Killian McCreery.

Someday soon I'll win her over. There's no other option because, no matter what life brings, she'll always own me. So unless I plan on continuing what I've been doing— standing on the sideline while she gives the biggest douchebags on the planet what was solely made for me—I need to work less on my BFF skills and more on my seduction skills. Right, the guy with zero experience is going to win over the most desirable woman in existence. It's fucking laughable.

I run a hand through my hair, pushing back my love-sick thoughts. "Come on; let's get your crampy-ass home." I grab my backpack and pull it over one shoulder to the sound of her giggles.

"It's not my ass, Kill. It's my uterus."

"Ick." I cringe, wrap my hand around the back of her neck, and guide her through the breezeway. "If you're trying to get me to squirm, you win."

"What is it with you big bad fighters, huh?" She peeks up at me with a sly grin. "All that muscle and you can't handle a little talk of the female anatomy?"

"Oh, I can handle the female anatomy." I'm such a liar.

She rocks her hip into me and laughs. "Suuuure, dude."

We get to the parking lot, and I walk Axelle to the little white Ford SUV her mom and Blake got her for graduation. She tosses her backpack into the backseat and sits in the front with her legs out and feet propped on the running board. She manages to make even the most casual things look hot. I lean my forearm against the top of the open door, thinking if she stood up her lips would line up with mine perfectly.

"Listen. So you know it's Clifford's birthday, right?"

Buzz-fucking-kill.

I nod and push past the jealousy roaring in my chest.

"Well, I know what I want to get him for his birthday." She tilts her head as if she's waiting for me to ask.

I don't because I could give a flying fuck about Clifford, her current piece of shit.

"But the thing is I'm kinda nervous, so"—she shrugs one shoulder in that adorable way she does and my resolve caves— "will you come with me?"

I fist the strap of my backpack and force a calm into my voice I'm far from feeling. "I planned on going straight to the training center."

"Pleeeaaase?" She puffs out the full lower lip that has starred in more fantasies than I'd ever be willing to admit.

I clench my fist and try to relax my jaw enough to get a damn word out. "You know I can't miss training."

"Oh come on!" She slaps my stomach, and fuck, I love her touching me. "Why not?"

Still working on becoming good enough for you, baby.

"I mean, really, you're running out of places to store muscle." She playfully pulls up my shirt, and I don't fight her. I know what's underneath, and for now, until I get my first official UFL fight and get my degree, it's my best asset. She motions to my abdomen. "You're already at full capacity."

"Nah . . . I'll find room."

She points to my bicep on display with my arm propped on her door. "Um . . . you look like Popeye."

"Do not."

She laughs and the sound shoots straight between my legs. "Do too! I think you even have an anchor tattoo under here somewhere." She pulls at my shirt again, and I flinch as her fingers brush my ribs. Her eyes flare. "You're so ticklish!"

I drop my arm, back up a step, and point at her. "Don't."

"Don't what?" Ryder, a friend of ours, and the son of the UFL's owner Cameron Kyle, saunters up wearing a Bad Religion shirt and a frown.

"Ryder, tell Killian he should come with me to run a quick errand and then come to Clifford's party tonight. And tell him he'll have plenty of time to work out between our errand and the party so he can have the best of both worlds." She shrugs like it's *just that* simple.

"Or maybe Axelle should skip the party tonight"—I give the guy a fist bump and nod at Axelle— "and hit the gym with me instead."

Ryder's eyes widen. "Dude, never tell a woman she needs to hit the gym, man. That's bad juju. Bitches talk, and before you know it you'll be taken off the fuckable list of every chick on campus."

"Yep, he's right." She swings her feet into her car and shoves the key into the ignition. "You've now been scratched from my list."

I clear my throat, but it makes more of a choking sound. I think she's kidding, but was I on her list? Even if only a proverbial one? Damn, just the thought and . . . I can't feel my legs.

"Oh crap!" Axelle rests her head on the steering wheel. "I think I forgot my phone in class."

I blink away the visual of my name getting slashed from her list. "I'll grab it." I move to head back to room E34 when she stops me.

"No, you stay here and let Ry convince you to come to the party tonight, and when I get back, we'll go run that errand." She pinches my cheek, and I know I'll do whatever she asks. I watch her jog-walk back to her classroom, mesmerized by the sexy sway of her hips and the cute way her left foot kicks out a little, making her gait uniquely hers.

"Breathe, brother."

I peer down at Ryder, who's almost my size, minus about three inches and fifty pounds of muscle. "Does it look like I'm not breathin'?"

He shakes his head. "Dude, just come to the damn party. Better to be there than stuck at home, worrying something's going to happen to your precious princess."

"Fuck off."

"Yeah, you keep that act up. No one's buying it except you . . . and maybe her."

I freeze and glare at his blond spiked hair. "First of all, you're an idiot. Second, if you're at that party tonight and anything happens to her, I'll break all your fingers."

"Come to the party. Have a drink. Hell, meet a girl. Act irresponsible for once; make some mistakes. You live like a priest, man."

"Got shit I wanna do." I shrug. "Partying and *making mistakes* will stand in the way of where I'm going."

He throws his head back, laughing.

My skin itches in irritation. I'd never expect him to understand. He's been practically handed everything his entire life. Whatever. I don't have time for this shit.

"It's one night!"

A growl rumbles in my chest. "I'm not going." I've made the mistake of being around Axelle when she's "dating" someone, and the torture is so bad I'd beg for disembowelment.

"Fine," he moans.

Axelle comes bouncing across the lot with a bright smile and her phone in hand.

"I'll keep an eye on your girl," he mumbles.

"So?" Her head swivels between us. "Are you coming?"

Ryder lifts an eyebrow, and I scowl at him before nodding to her. "Sure. But let's make it fast."

She squeals and wraps her arms around my neck, pressing her soft body deep into mine. Pure fucking heaven. I give her a quick squeeze and back away as I always do. Sometimes I wonder if I didn't break away first how long she would hang on for.

She jumps in her car. "Follow me!"

Ryder grins and shakes his head. "See you kids tonight."

I don't have the balls to say I'm not fucking going. I'll text Axelle later, tell her I fell asleep or training went long. Either way, there's no damn way I'm going to this party tonight.

~*~

Axelle

Shit. Bringing Killian might have been a mistake.

If the look of disgust on his face when he pulled up wasn't a sign, his brooding silence and perma-glare send a pretty clear message.

He doesn't approve of my birthday gift to my current . . . um . . . what is Clifford? Not my boyfriend, but he's more than a hookup. We've been seeing each other for a month now. What we have isn't like a *traditional* relationship. We don't go out on dinner dates or spend the weekends together making meals and shopping or whatever dating people do. But we spend a lot of time together, or rather, I spend a lot of time with him when he's playing video games and hanging with his friends.

An uneasy flutter turns my stomach, but I push away the discomfort. Clifford was hard to win, and he certainly makes the chase fun, never really giving me the checkered flag for exclusivity, but I've never seen him with other girls so . . .

"What do you think of the placement?" The tattooed and pierced-to-hell guy who introduced himself as Tom—which is kinda funny because he looks more like a Gunther than a Tom—holds a mirror up to my face.

"Eye lyle eh."

He scowls. "You can close your mouth to answer."

I close my lips and try not to press my tongue to the roof of my mouth and risk messing up the ink dot. I turn to Kill, who's slumped in his seat, his long powerful legs open and outstretched, arms crossed at his chest, and a chilling glare aimed at the body piercer.

"What do you think?" I drop open my jaw and show him my tongue.

His eyes flash with something tender a second before his eyebrows drop low and he radiates fury. "How are you going to explain this to Blake?" He spits the words from his mouth. "No, better yet, how am *I* going to explain this to Blake?"

My spine stiffens and I scowl back at my grumpy best friend. "I'm twenty years old, Kill. Pretty sure piercings are my choice now, not his."

He tilts his head, and the deadly look in his eyes almost makes me flinch. "It's not the piercing; it's the *why*." He growls the last word.

I roll my eyes. "Oh my God, like I'd ever tell Blake I'm getting my tongue pierced as a gift to a guy."

Tom chuckles. "Lucky guy."

Killer glides—really, it's like he floats—to his feet and stares me dead in the eyes. I catch my breath at the overwhelming intensity of his face. All that dark hair, framing amber eyes, and he has the kind of skin most women would kill for. "Do not ask me what I think about the tongue piercing you're getting to suck your man off on his birthday, Ax, because you know my answer is going to be I don't fucking like it. Not one fucking bit."

My cheeks flame, and I'm not even really sure why. I'm a legal adult. If I want to get my tongue pierced, I can get my tongue pierced. "It's not like that's the only reason I'm—"

"Fuckin' hell." He runs his hands through his hair.

"Are we doing this or what?" Tom holds up his black-rubber-gloved hands. "I've got another appointment waiting."

"Yes, let's do it—"

The sound of a beaded curtain being thrown aside calls my attention, and the last thing I see is Killian's back as he stomps from the room.

"Looks like someone's jealous." Tom positions himself in front of me with clamps in hand.

Jealous? No way. Killer has had plenty of opportunities to accept my pathetic attempts to throw myself at him, and he's always played dumb. He's smart, talented, and lining up to be the next Universal Fighting League superstar. The last thing he needs is an average girl with average intelligence and zero goals in life hanging on his arm.

"Let's get this over with." I open my mouth and squeeze my eyes closed, wishing like hell I had Killian there to hold my hand.

Since the moment my life fell apart, he's been there for me. I've depended on him so much I don't think I can go through more than a headache without him. I don't want to admit to myself that his disapproval is giving me second thoughts about the piercing. It's time I thought on my own, made my own choices and my own mistakes, rather than sitting back and paying for everyone else's.

I stick my tongue out and the cold metal of the clamp declares its intention. I scrunch my eyes and squeal as the sharp sting of a needle pierces my flesh. A quick rush of adrenaline and power races through me.

There's no way Clifford won't fall all over me now.

TWO

Killian

"I swear if I didn't know better I'd think you were juicing." Blake glares at me through the mirror while I crank out a few more curls to finish my set.

"You know I'm clean." I drop the dumbbells on the rack while frustration and guilt war in my chest.

I upped my weight, grinding the hell out of my body to blow off the shit with Axelle. What the hell is she thinking? As much as I wanted to slap her silly for getting her sexy-as-shit tongue speared through, I can't deny the little flick of her tongue with that pink ball she flashed me when she walked out of the piercing room had all the blood collecting between my legs. If Blake only knew the reason for my all-out workout tonight . . . he'd fucking kill me. He'll find out soon enough, and then he'll fucking kill me for allowing it to happen.

All for that fuck-wad Clifford.

The only thing that brought me a little peace of mind was the moment the aftercare instructions were explained. No kissing or oral sex for two weeks. I had to hold back from doing a victory dance right there in the piercing place, but I didn't hold back my laughter.

So much for Clifford's epic birthday present. That greaseball fucker can't even kiss her now. At least . . . not on her lips. Motherfucker!

"We know you're clean." Jonah pops up from the bench next to mine, dropping his weights to the mat and wiping a towel over his face. "But your gains are impressive."

Six days a week in the gym, two-a-days on Saturday, times that by three years . . . what the fuck did they expect? They dangle UFL dreams in front of me. I'm not the kind of guy to brush that shit off. Hell, I've been the UFL's biggest fan since I was sneaking in my living room to watch the fights from behind my dad's La-Z-Boy.

"Thanks . . .?" I move to the heavy bar and drop down beneath it, bracing my hands for the optimal position.

"He's been holding his own with Rex lately too," Blake says to Jonah, like I'm not even here.

I blow out three quick breaths then push the bar off the rack.

"No shit. And Cam said Kill's ready for a fight."

My arms wobble. A fight?

"Heard Webb is ready."

I drop the weight to my chest and push it back up, all while eavesdropping pathetically on Jonah and Blake's conversation.

"Kill would destroy that cocky asshole."

"Cam said by the end of . . ."

The rest of his words are mumbled, and I lean to grab even a hint of what he's saying, which sends the bar careening to the side.

"Oh shit!" Jonah's closest and jumps up to spot me. "You okay?"

I grunt and accept his assistance in getting the bar back to the rack. "I'm good, just"—I'm breathing heavy, excitement and exertion squeezing my lungs— "fatigued."

"No fuckin' way." The sarcasm in Blake's voice is more than obvious. He shoves my legs aside, and I sit up on the bench, staring into his overly surprised expression. "Can't imagine why you'd be fatigued."

I shake my head and move to grab a swig of water before hitting the treadmill.

"Go home, kid." Jonah crosses to me with Blake on his heels.

"Fuck that. It's Friday night. Go have a beer, get laid, *then* go home." Blake grins.

"Can't." I hop on the closest treadmill. "I wanna fight. I wanna be the best." I have to be.

Jonah tilts his head, studying me. "Not a doubt in my mind you won't get that, but that doesn't mean you can never take a break."

I turn up the speed on the treadmill to a jog. "I'm good."

"When Jonah and I were your age, we went out almost every night after training, and it didn't hurt our game one fuckin' bit." Blake leans over my treadmill and pulls the emergency stop.

"Oh, come on—"

"Go!" Blake points to the door. "Boss's orders."

"You're not my boss." But he knows I'd never argue with him or Jonah or any of the guys here. I owe them everything.

"Alright, how 'bout this . . ." Jonah checks the time on the wall. "It's eight o'clock at night, which means Sadie's been put to sleep. It's Friday night, and my wife always has a couple glasses of wine in front of the TV on Friday night, so I'd like to go home and take advantage of that."

Blake raises a hand. "I second that."

Jonah shoves him. "Fuck you."

"Not your wife, asshole! Mine."

"Alright!" I swear if I didn't break them up they'd continue bickering for hours. "I got it. I'll call it a night." I step off the machine and grab my gym bag. My stomach rumbles. Damn, I need to eat.

"And we don't want to see your face here tomorrow," Blake says from behind me.

"But—"

He holds up a hand. "No buts. One day off. Eat the shit out of tomorrow, rest, come back refreshed. Understand?"

"Yeah." I sling my duffle higher on my shoulder.

"Good." Jonah slaps me on my bicep. "Now go act your age, for fuck's sake! Go have some fun."

Right. There's only one place I can go, but it'll be far from fun. At least if I show my face at the party, I'll have evidence I went out, and it'll get these guys and Ryder off my ass.

Two birds, one stone, and the love of my life in the arms of someone else.

Yay.

~*~

Axelle

The music at this party is painful. Not in a so-bad-it-hurts-my-inner-music-critic kind of way, but in an actual rubbing-my-temples-and-begging-for-mercy kind of way.

I get it. It's *screamo*, which as far as I understand means it's emotional screaming—as if there's any other kind—but to me, it's just a lot of whining and screaming. It's like, if hell had a sound, it would be *screamo*.

I try to ignore it and focus on downing my drink so I can tolerate my roommate Mindy as she gives me the play-by-play of her most recent hookup. A football player, or was it baseball? I wasn't really paying attention, but there were balls involved, mostly in Mindy's mouth.

". . . do I call him, or wait to see if he calls me?" Her eyebrows pop above her light brown eyes.

I squint one eye and lean in. "The music . . . I can't . . ." I point to my ears and strain with what little hearing I have left. "Say again?"

She rolls her eyes and hooks my elbow so we're walking arm in arm as she drags me through the living room. We move in front of the large flat screen TV and get heckled by the guys lined up on the couch as they play some stupid war game.

I stumble on my heels to keep up, amazed that her shoes are twice as tall as mine and she walks like she's in Nikes. I bump into a few people playing beer pong and pass through a cloud of marijuana smoke before I'm finally tugged to a stop outside on the patio.

The crisp desert air is heaven, and although the death metal can still be heard out here, it's much more manageable.

Mindy scans the dozen plus people that litter the patio and, once satisfied, turns her eyes back to me. "The short story is that we hooked up, had the best sex of my entire life, but when I left, he didn't say he'd call me." She runs one hand through the front of her blond hair, holding it off her face with a huff. "I mean this is stupid, right? I should just call him."

"I guess." I shrug. "I think it's better to be forward about what you want."

Not that I know shit about shit. My relationship history goes a little something like this.

Girl meets boy.

Girl falls for boy.

Girl lies down and becomes doormat for boy.

Boy wears her out and moves on.

"Hm . . ." She chews her lip. "You're right. I should just call him."

"Yeah, why not?" The backdoor slides open, and a group of female co-eds comes stumbling out.

"Where is Clifford tonight?" the tall blonde with the killer body and face that would make an angel weep says.

She's not the only one wondering. It's his damn birthday party at his own freakin' house and yet he's MIA. My tongue throbs, reminding me of my surprise that will, no doubt, end badly. *Happy birthday! No blowjobs or kissing for two weeks!*

"Axelle, did you hear me?" Mindy follows my gaze to the group of girls.

"No guy can rock a pair of skinny jeans like Cliff. His ass is like . . ." The blonde makes the shape of his ass with her hands, and I have to agree. He's got a nice ass—small, perfect for the rocker/emo thing he has going on, but firm.

Mindy's eyes widen. "They're talking about *Clifford*." She whisper-spits his name like it's a dirty word.

"Yeah, so? He's mine. They can *talk* all they want." I force as much confidence as I can muster, when inside I'm on the verge of tears and I have the vodka to thank for that.

I can fake confidence like a champ. Hell, I learned from the best. My mom put on one hell of a show my entire life up until a few years ago. Then she found her safe place to fall, the shelter of the love of a great man where she can finally be herself.

I'm not there yet.

Not even close.

". . . fingers are so long."

". . . seen the bulge in his jeans? His dick is huge!"

". . . get too drunk to leave and crash here."

Mindy snaps her fingers in front of my face. "Hello?"

I rip my attention away from the gossipy girls and focus on my friend. "Yeah, sorry. What were you saying?"

"Those bitches are after your man."

I shake my head and wave her off with a huff. "I'm not worried about them." *I am. I so am.* "Come on. Let's grab a drink." *And hunt down Clifford before they do.* I grip her hand and lead her to the kitchen, weaving around the giggling girls as we go.

The kitchen, like the rest of the house, is modest, but a decent size. The rental is close to campus, so the owners must know it's going to get trashed, and everything is cheap and easily replaceable.

Ryder and a few of his friends are standing around a bar—or more accurately a stack of Solo cups, various bottles of booze, and a few liters of soda and fruit punch.

I give Ry a hug and stumble a little. His eyes go wide on my feet. "Hot shoes."

"Thanks. When did you get here?"

His gaze slides from my peep-toe heels, up my jeggings, to my translucent black long-sleeved shirt, which I've paired with nothing but a black push up bra. His mouth twists and his eyebrows pinch together. Mumbled words fall from his lips, but I don't catch them.

I lean in. "What?"

"Nothing." The way he continues to scowl at my clothes makes me think he doesn't approve of what I'm wearing.

Self-consciousness crawls over me, making me want to cover up with my arms, but then I look around. Mindy's in a similar outfit, but her jeans are high-waisted, and she's paired them with a barely there crop top. Some of the co-eds outside had on micro-minis and stilettos. What I'm wearing is modest in comparison.

"What're you drinking?" Ryder motions to the booze.

"Vodka and fruit punch." Mindy answers for me.

Ryder's mouth pulls up on one side. "Long time, Min."

Her cheeks flash pink, and she gives him a sultry grin. "Too long."

I practically roll my eyes. These two have been fuck buddies for months, and every time they see each other it's like the flame that flickers between them gets doused with gasoline.

She squeezes in close to talk with Ryder, and I scan the kitchen, looking for Clifford.

Ry hands me a drink, and I take a long pull of the puckery-sweet liquid.

"So, Axelle, how's this semester treating you?" Theo, Ryder's friend and band mate, pushes back his shaggy hair to reveal his piercing blue eyes.

"Great. You were right about History of World Religions. It's a lot more entertaining than I thought it'd be." Theo told me last semester that Professor Conway had a sexual analogy for everything. He wasn't kidding.

He laughs. "Because the emergence of Eastern Religion was like gently prying open the dew-soaked petals of a flower, like . . ."

"Foreplay!" We say in unison.

"Shots!" Mindy hands me another Solo cup, this one filled with clear liquid that burns my nose.

May as well, I'm not driving. I throw back the shot, but it takes me three times to get it all down. I finish my punch and have one more while scanning the area, looking for Clifford. By the time I'm through with my second drink, I'm feeling a little foggy and a lot tired, and I have to pee.

"I'll be right back!" I call to Mindy, who is curled up under Ryder's arm. Guess she's no longer worried about calling the football player.

I wander through the party to the bathroom, but there's a line, so I search for a place to sit and rest. My ankles wobble with each step, and I use the narrow hallway walls to steady myself. I may have drunk too much. Again. I reach the end of the hallway when a sharp sting meets my ass.

"Ouch . . ." My response is delayed, but I rub the burn on my ass and look up into the hungry eyes of my boy—um . . . hookup, Clifford. "Hey, where've you been?"

He grips my hips and pulls me to him, and I have to tilt my head back to see his face. "You drunk yet?"

"Oh, yeah." Stupid alcohol. "Happy Birthday." I smirk and bat my eyelashes; although it doesn't feel as sexy as I'd hoped. "I have a present for you."

He hums and grips my backside hard enough to hurt, or I suppose it would hurt if I wasn't numb. "Does it involve you naked and spread wide on my bed?"

"Umm . . ." I chew my lip.

He nuzzles my neck, and I get a whiff of what I've started calling his party smell. It's not cigarettes or weed; it's something else, like burning plastic.

I pull back and meet his eyes. "Where've you been?" He never did answer when I asked him before.

"Been partying, babe." He jerks his head to get his bangs out of his eyes. "Where've you been?"

"Here." God, I haven't seen him all night, and now it's like we're interrogating each other. I frown.

"Let's go make out." He slides his tongue up my neck to my ear.

"Oh, um . . . I can't."

He stills and pulls back, his hold on me going slack. "What? Why not?"

"Happy Birthday." I stick my tongue out to show him my piercing.

He narrows his eyes on it, and my stomach plummets at his lack of immediate excitement. "Well fuck, guess you won't be using your tongue on me tonight." He studies it closer. "It's swollen. You know you're not supposed to drink while it's healing, right?"

Oh shit. Did I know that?

He sighs. "Oh well, so no tongue action, but I can still get in here." He cups me between my legs.

I pull his hand away, half embarrassed and mostly irritated he'd even grab me like that in public. "Actually, I can't do that either."

His eyes widen and he grins. "Clit piercing?"

"Period."

"Well, fuck." He drops his hold from me completely and steps back. "Happy Birthday to me."

"I'm sorry. I thought . . ." I thought the piercing would be enough, but I was wrong. "Guess we could just hang out. I mean just because it's your birthday doesn't mean you need your dick sucked to have fun."

"Ahh, that's where you're wrong, Elle."

Elle. It's the nickname I give people I don't know well. My full name is something only my close friends call me. Clifford picked up on it once, called me Axelle, but I told him I hated the name and to please call me Elle. It was a lie. I love my name. But Elle helps me to remember there are still boundaries between us.

His gaze follows the group of co-eds from outside as they walk by, the gorgeous blonde sending the major come-fuck-me eyes to Clifford. "Plenty of girls here who'd suck my dick."

Panic rises in my chest. An emptiness I bury deep in my heart flares and pushes to the surface. *Don't leave me.* The whisper in my head is so soft and familiar I can basically ignore it, but my hands slide over his shoulders to lock around his neck anyway. As if my body can't deny what my soul is screaming.

"Stay with me tonight." I press a soft close-mouthed kiss on his lips. "Please."

His bloodshot gray eyes search mine, and he cups my jaw. "Go wait for me in my room. I'll be there in a minute." He slaps my ass and leaves me alone, feeling cheap, weak, and empty.

I peer down at my clothes and I see what Ryder was seeing: the attempt of a desperate girl to win over a guy. I'd never get away with dressing like this if I lived at my mom's house. My stepdad would lock me up for the rest of my life if he saw me in some of the shit I wear to parties.

They don't know though.

They don't understand.

No one does.

Killian

It's times like these that my size pays off.

As I push through the front door of Clifford's house, people see me coming and get the fuck out of the way. This isn't a party of college athletes, rather the opposite. Rockers, druggies, and artsy types. I tower over most of them, and those who are as tall are also gangly as hell, so they step aside.

I'm sure the don't-fuck-with-me vibe I've got going on doesn't help either. I texted Axelle twice to let her know I was stopping by, and she hasn't responded.

The sound of Carcass blasting through the speakers adds another layer to my concern for Axelle. She despises death metal.

I have to wonder if she's even still here.

My eyes scan the room, and other than a few people I've seen on campus, one really nice girl from my bio class, and the stoner guy who always has to take smoke breaks from my lit class, there are no familiar faces.

Good, as soon as I can get eyes on Clifford, assure myself he's not going to bed tonight with my girl in his arms or worse—things of which I cannot imagine without breaking something—I'll be able to go home and crash, with my phone, of course. Because the second she finally does respond I'm going to ream her ass for not keeping her fucking phone on her at all times.

Shit! Has the woman learned nothing from her mom's mistakes?

"Yo! Mr. UFL, what's up?" Theo calls to me from the kitchen where it looks like the final few hands of strip poker are being played.

I fist-bump the guy. "You here with Ryder?"

"Yeah, he's around here somewhere." He looks around then shrugs. "Can I get you a beer or something?"

"No, thanks." I search the area for Axelle. "I'm not staying long."

"Suit yourself." He throws back a shot of something.

"Is Axelle around?"

"Yeah, man, she was just here. Might have hit the can or wandered off to pass out." He laughs.

I clench my fists.

"She was pretty fucked up."

Ryder, that piece of shit son of a bitch!

"I'm sure she'll turn up . . ." His voice fades as I plow through the house, practically flipping over furniture to find her.

Don't freak out, Killian. This isn't the first time you've had to rescue her from a party. She's probably outside or in the bathroom.

I move to the backyard, but she's not there.

I knock on the bathroom door, and three girls stumble out. They try to talk, but I spin on my heel and head for the bedrooms, my blood boiling to the point of fucking murder.

I tell myself this isn't my business. Axelle's old enough to make her own decisions, she can fuck who she wants, and as far as I know, she probably does; although I'd never ask because the confirmation would destroy me.

But she's drunk and Clifford is a dirtbag.

I wouldn't put it past him to take advantage of her.

Dammit to fuck, why didn't I just suck it up and bring her to the damn party? At least then I could've kept an eye on her all night and convinced her to go home when she'd had enough.

I fist my hands in my hair and try to calm my breathing.

No, I need to find her and get the hell out of here.

I bang on one of the doors. "Axelle, you in there?"

"Fuck off!"

I jerk away from the door at the sound of a woman's voice, which is very much not Axelle's.

I knock on the next door, but find it unlocked and cracked open. I peer inside. "Axelle . . .?"

It's as if my mind has memorized every single curve of her body, because even with her lying there on her side, facing away from me, on top of a faded black comforter, I recognize Axelle immediately. She's sound asleep.

"Shit." What the motherfuck is she thinking? Any asshole without a soul could creep in here and— A growl rumbles in my chest as I cross to her. What the fuck is she wearing? My eyes devour her plumped-up breasts barely encased in a black lace bra, the flat plain of her belly that flares into hips wide enough to grab hold of, and her ass— fuck! I rein in my libido and focus on her perfect face relaxed with sleep.

I run a hand through her silken hair. "Axelle, baby . . ." I whisper.

Nothing.

I lean down and a slight hint of sugary booze is on her breath. I resist the urge to taste it from her lips. After all, that would make me the asshole without a soul. I scoop her into my arms; she weighs next to nothing. When I straighten, she startles, but only nuzzles deeper into my chest and inhales.

Is she . . . smelling me?

A long sigh falls from her lips, followed by a soft snore.

My blood heats just as my ribs seem to fill with something warm, something that feels really fucking good. Or maybe that's just having her body so close to mine.

I walk carefully, turning sideways to squeeze out of the doorway without knocking any part of her on the doorframe. The hallway is a challenge, but pulling her tight to my chest, I'm able to negotiate it without cracking her head on the wall. People part out of the way as I head straight for the door, one girl even opening it for me.

"Thanks."

I move to my Jeep that's parked illegally across the street. With the thing stripped down without a top or doors, I easily lay her in the back. I contemplate strapping her in, but decide against it. It's a short drive to her place and . . . shit. How the hell am I going to get her into her place? There are no pockets in her pants for keys, and I didn't see her purse anywhere near the bed. I turn back to the house, but ripping the place apart to find her shit would mean leaving her out here alone.

"Fuckin' hell," I mumble and prop my hands on my hips.

Guess that only leaves one alternative.

THREE

Killian

The closer I get to my place, the more pissed I become.

Why would Axelle put herself in this situation at a party, and where the hell was her fuckhead boyfriend?

She has a B average in her classes—which is impressive seeing as she hardly ever studies—so I know she's not stupid. But something about her personality, it's like being around dumb people making jackass decisions rubs off on her. She hitches her cart to the biggest fucking loser and sits back oblivious while he takes her for a ride.

I pull into the parking lot of my apartment complex and slide into a spot. It's student living and most days the lot is full, but Friday nights are pretty dead around here. The entire complex consists of studio apartments, which keeps things fairly quiet. Hard to have a rager in 500 square feet.

Not that I give a crap. I sleep, study, eat, and shower here. It's paid for with my academic scholarship money, close to school, and anything is better than living with my mom.

Axelle's out cold, her mouth wide open, and damn if her snore isn't adorable.

I pull her out and into my arms. She struggles a little, her hands pressing against my chest.

"Ax, it's okay. It's me."

Her eyes pop open, and she peers up at me then around the parking lot, her eyes landing on my hand that's cradling her legs and gripping her thigh. "Why are we at your place, and why are you carrying me?"

"You mean it isn't obvious?"

She answers with a glare.

"You're nice and fucked up, passed out alone. Better I take you home and take advantage of you in private than allow some piece of shit to fuck you, right?" My teeth grit together as I force back a full-blown angry speech on responsibility.

Her glare tightens and she kicks out of my hold. I allow her to slide from my arms and hold her steady while she finds her balance. She pushes me off. "I'm not that fucked up, Kill. I'm just tired."

I step into her space, wanting to grab her and shake the stupid from her brilliant brain. She backs up until she hits my Jeep, her eyes shining with defiance. "I found you in his bed. Alone. You were so out of it I carried you through the party, brought you outside to my car, and drove you home without you even knowing."

Her mask slips and genuine fear flickers behind her deep blue eyes.

"Let me ask you something." I clench my fists. "How much do you think you would've been able to take before you'd come to, huh? Some asshole's fingers? Maybe his mouth? Or do you think it'd take him shoving his dick inside you to wake you up?"

"Shut up!"

"Stop acting like a rebellious teenager and start taking care of yourself!"

"I only had a couple drinks!"

I cringe and step back, shaking my head. "That's what you always say. Stop lying to me, Ax. Grow the fuck up."

She gasps, but tears shine in her eyes. Dammit. I don't want to make her cry, but she doesn't understand what would happen to me if something bad happened to her. Not only does she mean more to me than anyone else on the fucking planet, but I owe Blake and Jonah my life, and they've made it clear that when I'm around Axelle she's my responsibility. Fuck, if anything happened to her on my watch, I'd beg them to beat my ass, not that I'd have to.

"Where's my purse?" She pats her hips and ass. "My phone?"

I shrug. "No clue."

She chews her lip. "Mindy." Her hand rubs at her forehead. "My purse is in Mindy's car."

"I didn't see Mindy there."

"She's probably somewhere with Ryder or that football guy." A groan falls from her lips. "She has my keys too."

"Come on. You can stay here. Call Mindy and tell her you're safe and you'll be home in the morning."

"Yes, *mother*." She stomps past me and I grin at her back.

This woman and her damn mouth.

Axelle

Fuck, fuck, fuck!

I'm such an idiot. Killian's right. What I did tonight was irresponsible. I know better! But it's not like Clifford or any of his friends would take advantage of me . . . right? A wave of fear crashes over me, causing me to shiver.

"Cold?"

I keep my head down and focus on climbing the stairs to avoid him seeing how embarrassed I am. God, what would've happened if he hadn't shown up?

He chuckles in that deep way that sends ripples through the air between us and practically caresses my skin. "Stupid question, seein' as you're damn near naked," he mumbles.

I whirl around to face him and immediately freeze at the possessive glint in his expression: half predatory, half crazy, and all kinds of sexy. I've been seeing this look more and more lately, and I have to admit it looks incredible on him— all that dark hair, those lips that if they weren't framed in stubble on that powerful jaw would appear almost feminine.

One thing I've always known about Killian is he's beautiful. Now he's powerful, big, and burly, but he's still pretty.

"How can you say that? I'm in jeans and a long-sleeved shirt!"

His eyebrows lift and his eyes dart to my push-up bra.

I growl and continue to stomp up the three flights of stairs to Kill's apartment. Tapping my foot impatiently until he pulls out his key and lets me in, I push into the pristine space and head straight for the bathroom when it hits me.

"Crap."

He clicks on a light. "What?"

"I need my purse." I groan and rub my temples as the beginning of a headache forms. What time is it anyway?

"I have everything you'll need for a night." He drops his keys in a small bowl that I know also contains loose change.

My hand absently rubs my lower abdomen. "No, I don't think you do."

He looks confused until his eyes track my hand. I expect irritation, maybe even anger, but he simply grabs his keys and turns back to the door. "Take a shower. Help yourself to a T-shirt. I'll be back."

"Kill—"

The door closes behind him, and the telltale click of the lock tells me he's locked me inside for my safety.

My heart practically melts. God, this guy, he's too perfect, too good. I can't believe he's stayed by me as long as he has. I haven't always been the best friend to him, and yet, he's never once made me feel like the burden I so clearly am.

I click on the kitchen light and down a big glass of water before heading to the tiny bathroom that smells like soap and bleach. I swear the guy must clean his pad twice a week. I've never even seen water spots on his mirror for crying out loud. Mindy and I are pretty clean as far as college students go, our dirty dishes and laundry pile up, and we could probably mop more than we do. Kill is borderline obsessive.

I hit the water on and strip off my clothes, folding them and placing them in a tidy pile on the small counter space. I take care of business on the toilet before stepping under the hot spray, and immediately the scent of liquor and smoke rushes to my nose before it dissipates. I grab the fancy sports-themed shower gel and lather up my body, thinking about how differently tonight could've gone had Kill not shown up. I wash my hair with his two-in-one shampoo, and every time I close my eyes, I almost fall over. Those drinks Ryder made me were stronger than I thought.

After rinsing, I stand there and let the water beat down on me. Finally, after my body is pruned and exhaustion weighs me down, there's a soft knock on the door before it cracks open and Kill places a paper bag onto the counter.

I turn the shower off. "Thank you."

He doesn't answer, but closes the door. Ripping a clean towel off the rack, I wrap up, peek into the bag and almost burst out laughing.

Inside are small boxes of almost every size tampon in every brand available. I imagine what he must've looked like in the tampon aisle, fingering each box into the basket. Even as the visual makes me laugh, my chest warms with the same heat that his attentiveness has always evoked.

Picking up my brand of choice, I brush my teeth, comb out my hair and—fuck. I forgot to grab something to wear. I pick through my old clothes and cringe at the smell. No, I can't put those back on.

I check out my reflection. None of my girlie parts are showing. Hell, Killian's seen more of my body in my bathing suit. I shrug and head out into the studio to find him sitting at the end of his bed with his head in his hands.

"You okay?"

He turns and something flashes in his eyes, but I don't have time to catch it as he points his eyes to his feet in front of him. "Fine. Um . . . do you need a—?"

"Shirt, yeah. I'll just—"

"I got it." He reaches forward, his dresser about a foot from his face in the cramped space.

A T-shirt flies toward me, quickly followed by a pair of plaid flannel boxers. I scoop them off the floor.

"I'll give you some privacy." He snags a pair of sweatpants and keeps his eyes down while walking into the bathroom and slamming the door behind him.

I exhale hard. He'll never see me as anything more than the pathetic girl with abandonment issues. After all, I'm the girl who had two dads and they both walked away without looking back.

I've always been Killian's charity case.

No matter how badly I've wanted him to see me differently.

Killian

I'm staring at my distorted reflection in the foggy bathroom mirror, willing myself to calm the fuck down. Doesn't help that the limited space of my studio has been infiltrated by her presence. Her naked presence. The shower only liquefied her essence, so now I'm not only breathing in her delicate sweet scent, but it lies upon my skin, coating my body with a sheen of moisture that I consider licking to see if she tastes as good as she smells.

I slam my eyes closed as my dick punches the zipper of my jeans. Calm, breathe, don't fuck this up.

Thing is I've had Axelle over to my place more than any of my friends. We've hung out, watched movies, studied, even had dinner a few times. I had a spare toothbrush she used once when she ate a Caesar salad and was worried about her breath, and she even showered here a few times after we'd hung out at the pool. We've even fallen asleep while watching TV, but she always ends up going home.

Tonight she'll be in my bed until morning.

Wearing my tee.

My boxers.

I groan as my hard-on jumps at the visual of her bare body covered in my clothes.

I turn my head to see her outfit from tonight in a folded pile by my right hand, her bra placed on top, the tag sticking out displaying a proud 32C. I try not to imagine the way her breasts looked spilling out of that bra and, for a split second, contemplate how far down in the pile her panties are. I wonder if they match her bra, if they're the kind that cut up the crack of her ass.

Sick bastard!

Pushing the thoughts from my mind, I brush my teeth and pop out my contacts, making sure to take my time to avoid walking in on Axelle naked. I don't know how long it takes for a girl to slide on a T-shirt and a pair of boxers, but by some rare chance, if it takes more than ten minutes, I want to give her the time she needs, because one flash of her naked body and I'll probably hump her like a dog.

By the time I finish, pull on some sweatpants, and have taken a few minutes to calm my dick down, I push out into the apartment to find Axelle sitting on the bed with the remote in her hand.

I dig my phone from my jeans pocket before tossing them in the dirty clothes hamper and hand it to her. "Call Mindy before you forget."

Her bright eyes find mine, and her dark brown hair looks black as the wet locks fall down her back. She screws up her lips as she always does when she's concentrating, and with a freshly clean face wiped free of makeup and rosy cheeks from the heat of the shower, she looks fucking incredible.

"Oh . . ." She hits a few numbers then hits "end." "No, that's not it." Her face screws up again. "Hmmm . . . six four five eight . . ." She mumbles to herself until she finally presses the phone to her ear. "Mindy, hey, I'm on Killian's phone. I left my stuff in your car." She picks at a loose thread on my bedspread. "Yeah, well that didn't work out. He was busy entertaining. I mean it was his party. No, I'm not mad. I . . ." Her eyes dart to mine. "Listen. Since you're still out and I don't have my key to get into our place, I'm gonna crash with Kill."

I can't hear the questions that Mindy's asking, but the series of yeses and noes makes me think they're about me, and Axelle's trying to answer without letting on. I grab my glasses from my bedside table, grateful for the return of clear vision. I've only been wearing contacts for a couple of years now. Cameron was cool enough to include medical insurance when he hired me in my senior year of high school, so I could finally afford them. Still love wearing my glasses though. Never do enjoy sticking my fingers in my eyes.

"You too. I'll see you tomorrow." She hits "end" and passes me the phone.

"Everything okay?"

"Yeah, she ended up ditching the party for this football player she's been skeezing on. She's staying with him tonight."

"You still tired or do you want to watch—?"

"I know what you think of me." Her mouth is pulled in a tight line, and her spine is straight and rigid. "You don't have to keep saving me."

I blink and my brain scatters to figure out how I missed the first part of this conversation, because that just came out of nowhere. "What is it you think I think of you?"

She sighs and rolls her eyes dramatically. "Please, Kill. I'm the world's most pathetic damsel in distress."

"You're wrong. That's not what I think."

"You said it yourself. I put myself in unsafe situations, and I'm constantly requiring your white knighthood."

I push up my glasses, hoping to cover the twitch of my lips. "My *white knighthood*?"

She glares, but she's grinning so it doesn't count. "You know what I mean."

I scratch my head. "I don't, but let me fill you in on something while we're on the topic of what I think about you."

She sucks in a shaky breath like she's prepping for a verbal smack down.

"I think you've been through more in twenty years of life than most people twice your age. You witnessed your mother being abused, heard her being raped by a man who you thought up until you were sixteen-years-old was your father. Then you find out the man who really is your father took advantage of your mom, knew she got pregnant, and took off anyway." Her eyes tear up, but I can't stop now. She needs to hear this. "Things are looking up for you now. You got a great stepdad who'd fucking kill for you; he loves you so much. You got a baby brother who acts like you're happiness incarnate, and you get to watch that . . ."

A soft whimper falls from her lips.

"You get to watch the perfect family you always wanted, and even though you're a part of it, you still feel like you don't belong. Like you're the outsider looking in. And that . . ." I shrug. "That kills you."

She nods slowly as a single tear falls down her face.

"I don't see a damsel in distress in need of saving. I see a woman just trying to make sense of her life, searching for where she fits in it all. I'd like to be there while she does that, make sure she stays in one piece so that when she does finally grab hold of her piece of happiness, she does it alive and healthy enough to enjoy it."

Her hands cup her face, and her shoulders shake with silent cries.

"Come here." I pull her down to my chest and wrap her up in my arms. She's not a big girl, average height and the perfect weight—fit with healthy curves—but in my arms she feels tiny.

"I don't know what I'd do without you." Her cheek is pressed to my pec and her arm thrown over my gut. "You're the greatest friend I've ever had."

Friend.

I cringe hard at that word.

Fuck, at this rate, the way I keep shoving myself into the friend zone, it's all I'll ever be.

FOUR

Axelle

I don't know which woke me up first, the sound of breakfast being made or the smell of bacon and melted butter. Either way the first thing I see when I crack open my eyes is Killian's back while he works at his tiny stove, mixing up what I hope will be breakfast for two.

I snuggle deeper into the Downey-scented sheets and admire his entire backside: his broad shoulders that pull the thin fabric of a worn T-shirt taut, the mounds of muscle that jump in his back as he moves effortlessly in the small space of his kitchenette, rippling triceps, and the narrow waist that flares into a healthy round ass that holds up his heather-gray sweatpants. God bless squats.

He moves to put something in the fridge and catches me staring. Those whiskey-colored eyes shine behind black-framed glasses, his dark hair falls over his forehead, and the side of his mouth lifts in a crooked grin. "Morning."

"Hey, you sure are busy at this ungodly hour." I stretch and notice his eyes track down to my chest before he whips his head around to focus on the contents of his fridge.

"It's almost nine in the morning, Ax." He shuts the door, and his bare feet slap against the tile as he goes back to whatever he was doing on the stovetop.

"But it's Saturday. Wait . . ." I prop myself up on my elbows, and I don't have to see my hair to know I look like Beetlejuice. I can feel it. "Why aren't you at the training center?"

He scoops something onto two plates. *Score!* "Blake and Jonah forbid it. Said I needed a recovery day." He moves to place the plates on the small table, and I notice then there are two icy glasses of water already waiting.

I smack my lips together, my mouth feeling like I sucked on a sock in my sleep while the tang of metal mixes with the soreness from my piercing. "That's probably smart."

"Come eat." He stands at the table with a shy smile that adds a boyish handsomeness to his intimidating size.

I hop out of bed and hit the bathroom then move to the kitchenette, smoothing down my hair as much as I can manage, which isn't much seeing as I can still see it from my peripheral vision. "Going to bed with wet hair is never advisable. Don't suppose you have a ponytail holder, huh?"

The corner of his mouth lifts as he studies my hair. "I think it looks great."

"Ha! You're such a liar." I take a seat in front of a full plate of scrambled eggs, bacon, and buttered toast. "Kill, this looks so good. I'm starving."

He moves to the small bowl where he keeps his keys and comes back to drop a black ponytail holder next to my plate.

"Oh, you do have one?" A flicker of something really uncomfortable tenses my belly. "How do you have a hair tie in your place?"

He takes his seat and shovels a bite of eggs into his mouth, swallowing and lifting a brow. "How do you think?"

That uncomfortable feeling twists violently. "Oh, um . . ." Wow. A girl. Nice. I mean good for him. I slick back my unruly hair with a little more aggression than is required.

Nice to see he's bringing girls to his place; probably cooks them breakfast too. Well, the ponytail holder is stupid and boring. Probably just like the woman who owns it—

"It's yours, Ax." I dart my eyes to him, but he's focused on his food, chewing. "You left it here a few weeks ago."

My cheeks flame and my shoulders cave in. "Oh, right. Well, thanks for holding on to it for me."

He makes a sound like he heard me but leaves me in silence with my humility while I shovel food into my mouth. What the hell was that all about anyway? He's free to date whoever he wants. The eggs are fluffy and buttery and the bacon just the salty relief required after a night of drinking.

Killian has been cooking for him and his mom since he was a kid. She never took very good care of him, or so he tells me. To this day I've only been around her once, and it wasn't a pleasant experience. He never talks about her, but explains away things like his exceptional cooking skills, stain-removing techniques, and organization by saying he was forced to grow up fast.

"How's the"—he motions to my mouth with his fork—"tongue?"

I swish with some cold water and hold back a groan at how good it feels against my heated mouth. "Sore."

"I have mouthwash. After you eat, you should go clean it."

He's always taking care of me. "Thanks. I will."

He forks a bite into his mouth and swallows; then his jaw clenches hard. "And Clifford, how'd he like it?"

Humiliation burns my cheeks, and I keep my eyes to my plate, even though I can feel him staring at me intently. "I don't want to talk about it."

"Guess him leaving you alone to pass out in his bed tells me all I need to know."

I open my mouth to defend myself, but slam it closed because I have no defense. He's absolutely right.

He scoops up his plate and tosses it into the sink with so much force I'm surprised the thing doesn't break. "I'm gonna hop in the shower, and then we should get you home." The slam of the bathroom door is the last thing I hear.

I'm left alone to finish my breakfast but have lost my appetite.

The water in the shower kicks on, and I take my plate to the sink. It doesn't take long to do the dishes. Killian is a clean-as-you-go guy, so outside of our plates and glasses, there's nothing more to do. Once that's done I make the full-sized bed and plop into a chair, waiting for him to come out so I can brush my teeth, clean my piercing, and change back into my clothes.

The shower seems to go on forever, and the thought of what he might be doing in there makes my skin flush. I rip the rubber band from my hair and pull a higher ponytail on my head to try to get some cool air on my neck. It doesn't help. Eventually the shower shuts off, and minutes later, he strolls out wearing a pair of jeans, bare feet, and no shirt. He's not wearing his glasses, and his brown hair looks black, wet and combed away from his face, as he rifles through his drawers and throws on a tee. The second he pulls it on, I roll my eyes. It's one of his favs, blue, and reads, "That's what I'm Tolkien about."

His gaze lands on the bed. "Thank you."

I think he means for making the bed, but something heavy in his tone has me second-guessing. "You're welcome." I hop up to head for the bathroom.

"Ax."

I stop and turn to him, his eyes heavy with something, regret maybe?

"Never mind."

"Okay." I head into the bathroom to get ready to go home and can't help but wonder if he's holding back as much as I am.

Killian

My stomach's growling again by the time I pull up to Axelle's to drop her off. Her place is much nicer than mine—a two-bedroom apartment in a gated complex with assigned parking spots. There's plenty of lighting in the lot as well as surveillance cameras. Blake insisted after she lived her first year in the dorms that she move somewhere safe, and he made it his mission to find the safest complex near the university.

It worked out that Axelle ended up meeting Mindy her first year. They weren't roommates but lived on the same floor, and both were itching for off-campus living. Money wasn't a factor seeing as Mindy's family are heirs to some heating blanket fortune or some shit. So yeah, my girl is living in luxury, albeit college style, but still her place is sick AF.

I throw the Jeep into visitor parking and walk her to her door. Things have been quiet between us since our talk over breakfast. Fuck, seeing her wake up in my bed, her bare leg thrown over the comforter and all that hair tossed around her face, made me imagine things that are far from innocent. At one point in the night, she curled up to me and slid her palm up my stomach to my chest. I've never felt anything like it. I tried to convince myself she knew exactly where she was and who she was touching, but the truth is she probably had no fucking clue. Most likely she thought she was sleeping with that dick Clifford, which makes me want to slam the asshole's face into a brick wall.

I walk her to her door, and because she doesn't have a key, she has to ring her own doorbell.

A little over a minute later a guy answers. He rubs his hand over his cropped hair and squints into the sun. "Oh, hey . . . um . . ." His eyes dip to his waist where he's sporting nothing but a pair of boxer briefs. "Sorry, I'm . . ." His bloodshot eyes take in Axelle from head to toe, and I almost pull her back to stand behind me, but luckily his gaze comes to me. "Who are you and where am I?"

Axelle giggles. "You must be the football player?"

"I'm the football player, yeah."

"I'm Axelle." She presses a palm against my chest. "This is Killian, and you're at my apartment with my roommate, Mindy."

His eyes light with recognition and he grins. "Oh, Mindy. Right. Shit, okay, yeah." He steps back so we can enter. "My bad. Come on in." He pats his hips where his pockets should be. "And my pants are . . .?"

Axelle grabs my hand and leads me through the living room, snagging her purse off the couch on our way to her room. "Don't mind us. We'll be in here and won't bother you." She closes the door behind us and whirls around to gape at me. "Oh my God, did you see him?"

"Hard not to. He was at the door damn near naked—"

"I know, right?" Her giggles mature into full-blown laughter. "We have to stay in here."

"So what, now we're being held hostage in your room until he leaves?"

"Well, duh! Yeah! This is a pivotal moment. How they handle this awkward morning-after will determine what happens from here on out."

I tilt my head. "You're serious."

"Hell yeah, I'm serious. Think about it. This is the final taste, that last bite that makes you either A. want to go back for seconds or B. makes you want to move on to the next place."

I can't offer agreement. Obviously, I wouldn't know. The fact that she does makes me grind my teeth.

Fuck. Play it cool, Killian.

I sigh and flop back onto Axelle's twin bed, my feet hanging off the end. I remember the day we moved her in and Mindy asked why Ax got such a tiny bed. Blake had said, "It's not tiny, Mindy; it's built for *one* person." He glared at Axelle, sending the very clear message that dudes were not welcome to warm her sheets. If he had any clue, he'd flip his shit.

She drops her purse on her bedside table and fishes out her phone. I watch her expression morph, her smile fall, and her brows pinch together as she clicks through what I assume to be text messages.

"Everything okay?"

Her gaze jerks to mine, and it's as if she forgot I was even there. "Oh, yeah. It's Clifford. Guess he must've been worried about me or something."

"Ha!" Worried. Right. More like disappointed she wasn't left alone and defenseless in his bed.

"You really don't like him, do you?"

I stretch one arm up and prop my head on it. "No, that obvious?"

She laughs. "Yeah, it is."

I shrug. What can I say? Just another dipshit in the lineup of total dicks that compose Axelle's dating life. The good news is none of her relationships have ever been serious. I know she's working hard to fill the void her dad—or dads—left behind, and as much as I want to confess that I'm in love with her, I know she's not ready for it. I've got one shot at winning her, and jumping too soon will make me another one of her hole-fillers. Literally.

"Why are you blushing?"

Fuck. My face is burning up. "I'm not. It's hot as hell in here." Has nothing to do with thinking about filling your ho—

"I'll turn on the fan." She hits the switch on the wall, and then her fingers fly over the keys of her phone. She's texting the prick back, and if I know Ax, she's apologizing for doing nothing wrong.

God, I hate that guy.

The five-tone chime from *Close Encounters of the Third Kind* sounds from my pocket and I grab my phone. I don't even care who's calling, anything to take my mind off Axelle kissing Clifford's ass via text message.

"Hello?"

"Killer, where the fuck are you?" I check the caller ID and see he's not calling from his cell, but from his office.

I sit up at the demand in Cam's voice. The guy has no conversational tone. He could be reading Shakespeare, and it would sound like he's commanding an army. "Blake and Jonah told me to take a day off."

My explanation is met with silence, which makes my palms sweat.

"Wait. What are you doing there? It's Saturday."

"Came in to talk to you, but your training partners seem to think they run this organization." He mumbles something I can't make out before dropping a pretty hefty f-bomb. "How fast can you get here?"

Cam says jump; I say how high and at what velocity. "Ten minutes."

"I'll wait."

"Um . . . can you give me a heads up—?"

The line goes dead.

I tuck the phone back into my pocket, and Axelle's still texting. Now her fingers are really moving, and a hint of anger pinches her usually smooth forehead.

"You think Mindy and Naked Heisman are done out there?"

She peers up at me and smiles. Fuck, she always manages to take my breath away. "No clue."

"I gotta run. Cam's waiting for me."

"Oh, okay. Then sure, just storm on through. I'd keep your head down though, ya know, just in case they're going at it in the kitchen."

I cross to her door and tug her ponytail as I pass. "Talk to you later."

"Wait." She blinks and swallows before setting those piercing blue eyes on me. "Thanks for helping me out last night. I mean I'm sure I would've been fine, but—"

"Don't worry about it. I'm always here if you need me." I motion to the door. "I really need to go."

"Yes, go." She plucks the shirt she's wearing with her fingers. "I'll wash this and get it back to you on Monday."

"No hurry. See ya." I head from her room, keeping my eyes to the floor, and it's a good thing I do because, when I pass Mindy's room, her door is wide open, and I'm assaulted by the hushed whispers of a very heated good-bye.

FIVE

Killian

I knock twice on Cameron's door and wait for him to give me permission to enter. It's cracked, but without Eve or Layla here to let me in, I don't dare presume by barging in.

"Yeah, come on in."

I push inside to find him sitting at his desk, his eyes pinned to a computer screen. His huge hands dwarf the keyboard as he types using his pointer fingers. "If I'm interrupting, I can come back."

He hits me with the full force of his scowl. When I first started working at the UFL, I'd nearly piss myself every time he looked at me, but now I understand that's just his resting scary-badass-do-not-fuck-with-me face. "Sit."

I take the single seat opposite him, and his chair moans in protest as he leans back. "I have an opportunity I'd like to discuss with you. You know Caleb's training over in England?"

"Yeah." He's turning out some kickass fighters and making a name for not only himself but for the UFL.

"We've been talking, and I think it's time you get some fights under your belt."

My pulse jacks up, and I try hard not to grin like a moron.

"How would you feel about a year overseas?"

"Overseas? You're sending me to England?"

"I'd like to, yeah. Hugo Webb is ready. I'd like to promote a UK-versus-USA fight. You go, take a few months to train with Caleb, promote. Opportunity of a lifetime for a new fighter, Kill. We could line up a *few* fights in a year's time. You'd be stupid not to jump on it."

"How is it UK versus USA if I'm training in England?"

"Caleb's always been USA. He'll be your main trainer. Makes more sense to keep you there with him rather than fly you back and forth every four months."

"Three fights in a year?"

"Big-ticket fights."

It's everything I always wanted, just . . . not exactly *where* I wanted. I blink, trying to absorb the offer when my mind screams one name.

Axelle.

"But, what about school? I'm on an academic scholarship and—"

"It's only a year. This semester just started. You drop your classes, get over there, and when you get back, you can pick up where you left off. As far as your scholarship goes, if they can't put it on hold for a year, I can guarantee you'll make enough money fighting for a year to pay for eight years in college."

I run a hand through my hair and wish I could put myself into a headlock for even contemplating saying no. This is all I've ever dreamed of; fighting for the UFL in any capacity is more than I could ever ask for.

"So . . .?" He leans forward, resting his forearms on the desk. "What do you think?"

"Oh, uh . . . can I think about it?" I'm a fucktard!

His narrow glare becomes impossibly narrower, and I cringe when I see a flash of disappointment in his expression. "Make it quick. If you're not going, I've got a line of guys who will." He turns back to his computer, dismissing me.

"Cam, this is a great opportunity. Thanks, ya know, for believing in me. I'll let you know in—"

"Get yourself a passport and pull your head outta your ass so I can put you on a fucking plane to England. I need an answer in a few weeks, tops." His disappointment is suffocating.

"I got it. Thank you." It's all I can say before I stand to leave, and even as I walk out of his office and to my Jeep, all I'm thinking is there's no way in hell I'm leaving Axelle for a year. No. Way.

I'll have to find a different route to achieve my goals, stay local, bide my time, and stick to my plan.

Axelle

Call me when we're cleared to put that piercing to use.

I can't stop staring at the last text Clifford sent me. Even as I run the stupid pink ball along the back of my teeth, my stomach clenches in that all too familiar way. Why can't I just tell him to fuck off? Let him go and move on?

A tiny voice in my head whispers that I need him. That if I can't keep him from leaving then I'm truly destined to be alone. A shiver races up my spine at the very idea of growing old alone. All I ever wanted was someone who'd love me unconditionally, someone who'd commit to me and only me forever and ever.

Is that even possible anymore?

"What are you doing?" My mom waves to me from the front door of her home.

I've been sitting in the driveway, trying to build up the courage to go inside and face the wrath of her and my stepdad. Before I left to come here, I practiced hiding my piercing by having conversations with myself in the mirror. I tried talking with my teeth closed, without moving my lips, and concluded that there's no hiding this thing. The in-your-face approach is the best way to handle this.

"Sorry!" I roll up my window and shut the car off. "I can do this."

She meets me at my car when I hop out and wraps me in a hug. "I swear you seem older every time I see you!"

"Mom, it's been a week."

"I know, but still." She pulls back, but hooks her arm around my waist. "Come on. Jack's inside and the last time I left him alone for too long, he wound up drowning his army guys in the toilet."

I snag my purse and hit the key fob to lock my doors. "Where's Blake?"

"He's on his way. Don't worry." She squeezes me. "He'd never miss dinner with you."

We break apart to climb the few steps up to the front door. Mom and Blake moved from their condo into a very comfortable home in one of the nicer Vegas suburbs. It's a ranch-style home on a huge chunk of land with the biggest backyard I've ever seen complete with a pool, basketball court, and a guesthouse, which Blake turned into a man cave. It's the perfect house for the perfect family. I frown and push through the front door. I really am happy for them.

"Jackie Bear, where is your diaper?" My mom's giggle filters through the high-ceilinged entryway. "God, you're just like your father."

"Ass-ole!" Jack still can't say my name. I sigh as a streak of blond and naked comes racing toward me. "Ass-ole!" He crashes into my shins, nearly taking me off my feet.

"Whoa, buddy!" I scoop him up and he immediately melts into me. "You're a little tank."

He rests his head on my shoulder, and the simple act of tenderness cramps my chest. I never knew it was possible to love someone as much as I love my brother—the kind of love I'd gladly lie in front of a bus for, commit murder if anyone hurt him, the craziest kind.

My mom comes up holding a fresh diaper, her eyes soft as she watches me cuddle Jack. "Here."

I take it from her and move to the couch just as the door that leads from the garage swings open.

"Damn, it smells good in here." Blake's voice booms through the space before he appears from the kitchen and wraps my mom into a hug, his eyes on me. "Hey, kiddo."

"Hey."

"Car running okay? When was the last time you had the oil changed?"

"Yeah, it's great. Maybe a month ago?"

"I'll check your tire pressure after dinner."

"Okay." I put Jack down, his bare bottom flashing the room.

Blake's mouth stretches in a grin that is all manly pride. "He can't help but show off his assets."

My mom shakes her head. "Sounds like someone else I know."

"Dada! Ass-ole!"

"It's Ax-el, son. Ax. El. Stop callin' your sister an asshole."

I secure his diaper and snag his tiny T-shirt that has *Future Heavyweight* written on the front. I pull it over his head and help him pop his little arms through. "Can you say Ax?"

"Ass!"

I tickle him and he squeals. "Ax!"

"Ass!"

"You have a dirty mouth!" I'm laughing and totally lost in my baby brother. "Say Ax!"

"Ass!"

"No, silly! Ax!

"What the fuck is that?"

"Blake!" My mom's voice reprimands him, but her narrowed eyes are zeroed in on my mouth.

I put Jack down, and he scurries off to his train set. Clearing my throat, I throw my shoulders back, which only makes Blake scowl harder.

"Oh this?" I point to my mouth. "I got my tongue pierced—"

"What?"

"Why?"

The *what* was from Blake, the *why* from my mom. And judging by the disgusted look on Blake's face, I'd say he didn't ask *why* because he already knows. "Dunno, just wanted to."

"Oh." My mom has always been good about allowing me to express my individuality with my clothes, my makeup, and hair, but something tells me this particular form of expression hit just outside her comfort zone.

Blake steps forward until he's about a foot from me, and he tilts his head. I love my stepdad. I do. He's the closest thing to a real dad I've ever had, and he'd do anything for my mom and my brother, but he's also intimidating. Especially when he's mad. I try to shrink away as he towers over me.

"Let me see it."

I lick my lips and then open my mouth.

He crosses his arms over his chest. "It hurt?"

"A little."

My mom's hand is braced on her neck as if she's physically holding back her freak-out. "When, um . . ." She nods to my mouth. "Why?"

Blake pinches the bridge of his nose at my mom's question.

"Oh, well . . . I was just bored I guess, and I wanted to try something new, ya know. Killian and I went—"

"Whoa!" Blake's jaw clenches hard. "Killian took you to do this?"

"Oh, no. No, he um . . . I asked him to go and he—"

"So he was there when you did this."

"Yes, he was there, but—"

"And he didn't stop you?" Oh shit, his face is getting red.

"Blake, calm down. He didn't want me to."

"He didn't stop you!"

Now I'm pissed. "Like he could?"

"Of course he could!"

"I'm a grown woman!"

Blake's eyes fly to my mom, who suddenly looks embarrassed. "Did you hear that? *She's a grown woman!*" He lifts his brows. "Sound familiar?"

"You're overreacting! I'm over eighteen and can get anything I want pierced."

He clenches his head between his hands. "Oh, fuck, don't go there."

"Blake! Language!"

"You guys." I force my voice to calm. "It's okay. Honestly, I don't even think I'll keep it for long. Rex has piercings, right? You don't see him any differently."

"He's a fucking pin cushion for a reason, kiddo. What I'm concerned most about isn't your need to express yourself; it's what the hell are you expressing and why." He holds up a hand. "Don't tell me."

"Blake . . ."

Without warning, he launches himself at me and wraps me in a hug. "I love you, baby. You're my girl."

I hug him back. "I know."

"Just want the best for you."

Shame heats my body. "I know that too."

He drops a kiss on my head then claps his hands. "Let's eat. I'm starving."

My mom relaxes, and when Blake leads the way to the kitchen, she hooks her arm in mine. "I like the pink. It's pretty."

"Thanks, Mom." If she knew I did this to get a guy's attention, she'd lecture me for days on how important it is to find someone who likes me for me. That who I am is impressive enough.

But damn, if my own father doesn't even love me enough to stick around, then how can I expect anyone else to? Sure, I have Blake, and he's amazing, but if he didn't have Mom, he wouldn't keep me. Only reason he has me is because Mom and I were a package deal.

So yeah . . . some girls get the man they want just by being them.

The rest of us have to prove we're worth it.

SIX

Killian

"Still can't believe you're passing this up."

Ryder's voice rakes against my nerves as we push out of the classroom and squint into the sun. He pops on his vintage black Ray-Bans, looking like some Sex Pistols throwback as we make our way across campus to the café.

"I haven't decided anything yet." Actually, I have. It's been almost two weeks since Cam made me the offer. A tiny voice whispers I'm making a mistake by passing this opportunity up, but that voice shuts the hell up every time I see Axelle.

"You know how rare this is, man? You're twenty-one-years old, and you'll be representing the UFL USA over there." He shakes his head. "You're a dumb ass if you don't jump on this."

"But it's a year overseas." I hook my backpack straps with my thumbs and weave through the crowds of co-eds lingering between classes. "I've got school and . . ." I slam my lips shut. "I'll get where I want to be another way. It's not like this'll make or break my career."

Ryder stops and his sudden freeze makes me do the same.

"What?"

His eyes narrow. "You're passing this up for *her*, aren't you?"

Fuck yes. "No, I'm passing it up because I have a plan. Finish college, get my first fight, and once I graduate I'll be able to do—"

"You're a fuckin' liar." He chuckles and continues to walk. "Can't believe you're gonna pass this up for a chick. I'd say you deserve to lose your balls for that, but my guess is you handed those over to her a long time ago."

I have no defense or desire to continue this conversation. I focus on the quad, which is bustling with people who're grabbing food between classes.

We spot Theo at a table and head over to say hi. My eyes scan the area for Axelle. She's usually here by now, but I don't see her.

"What's up?" Ryder drops down to sit next to one of the two girls Theo's entertaining.

"Oh, hey." One of the girls leans around Theo to study me. "I know you."

I peer down at her. She's good-looking and has bright red hair that falls over her shoulders in waves and a few perfectly placed freckles across her pale cheeks. "Oh, yeah?"

"Yeah, we had Econ together last year." She lifts her strawberry blond brow. "Dr. Farlow, remember?"

"That's right." She looks vaguely familiar, but we never spoke. "How'd you do in that class?"

"B plus. You?"

"A."

She smiles sweetly. "Nice."

"Killian's never gotten a B in his life," Theo pipes up from across the table. "He's got a 158 IQ."

Her eyebrows pop up to her hairline. "Is that true?"

A flash of warmth hits my cheeks.

"Fuck yeah, it's true," Ryder answers. "Too bad his decision-making is less than genius."

I glare at the guy, grateful no one at the table asks questions about his verbal jab.

"So, are we going out for Valentine's Day or what?" Theo asks the brunette who's been staring at him adoringly.

"Depends." She flips her hair in that way girls do. "Are you going to actually take me out, or is this like the last date you took me on where we hung out on your couch?"

Whatever good mood I'd managed to find fizzles at the mention of Valentine's Day. It's been a bummer holiday since the night Axelle's dad reappeared in her life only to crush her to pieces.

After that, we've always spent the holiday together. It's never romantic. We pass the time by going to the movies, grabbing something to eat, or these last two years we've spent watching Jack so Blake could take Layla out. It's not their favorite holiday either, and between the four of us, we're like the Cupid Killing Squad, all trying desperately to normalize a day that has left us with memories that are far from pleasant.

". . . come with us, Killian."

I shake my thoughts at the sound of the redhead saying my name. "Yeah?"

"Oh yay! It's settled then." She motions to Ry and Theo. "The three of us, so it'll be, what, a triple date!"

Oh shit. "Wait, for Valentine's Day? I can't—"

Ryder slaps me on the shoulder. "Of course he can."

I glare at him and he manages to smile wickedly. Fuckface.

"Great!" The redhead scribbles something on a piece of paper and rips it off, handing it to me. "Here's my phone number."

Ryder snags the paper from her since I make zero attempt to take it. I am not taking this girl out for Valentine's Day.

She stands up and her friend follows her lead. "We have to go, but keep in touch and we'll work out the details." She flashes another sweet smile and then walks off with a confident sway in her hips.

Theo jumps up too. "Hillary, wait up." He chases after the brunette.

I swivel around to glare at Ry. "What the fuck do you think you're doing?"

"Helping you to move on." He chuckles and takes a swig of Red Bull. "It's one night, bro." He tosses me the scrap of paper.

I take it and look at the girly swirl numbers of her phone number. "I don't even know her name."

"Really? You guys had a class together." He shakes his head. "Her name is Brynn. For a genius, you're really fucking stupid."

"Look. I'm not going." I toss the scrap of paper back at him.

Ryder's eyebrows pop above his sunglasses. "You got something better to do?"

He knows Axelle and I spend Valentine's Day together every year, so I don't answer.

He leans in. "Don't worry, Kill. Something tells me her plans are already made anyway, and . . ." He nods to a spot just over my shoulder. "My guess is they don't include you."

I spin around, and all the air is sucked from my lungs. Axelle's across the way and sandwiched between a tree trunk and Clifford. His head is tilted and his tongue's down her throat. I cringe but can't look away.

"You sure you want to give everything up for her, man? 'Cause from where I'm sitting I don't think you're even on her radar."

Clifford gropes her body, his hands sliding around her waist to grab two fistfuls of her ass. I rip my gaze away and stare blindly at the café.

"Axelle's a cool chick. Seriously, I wish things were different. But it's time you start seeing things that're right in front of your face."

Fuck. I push up from the table, ignoring him. "I'm getting some lunch. See ya later."

Axelle

Clifford didn't wait the two weeks I was supposed to abstain from kissing. He swore he couldn't help himself. It's to the point now where I hardly get two words out before he attacks my mouth. I thought this was the reaction I wanted, but now I'm not so sure.

He tastes like cigarettes and coffee, and as gross as that should be, it's not. My first kiss was a rocker kid who was three years older than me. I was thirteen, but in his defense, I looked a lot older. Despite his rough exterior, he was really tender, and his mouth tasted like an ashtray. For me, he set the standard for every kiss that followed.

And other than the smoky taste, Clifford's have yet to meet the expectation.

I mean the fact that I'm even thinking about that first kiss while Clifford's tongue flicks at my barbell is proof positive his kiss is less than earth-shattering.

I press my palms against his chest until he breaks away. He's breathing heavy and his eyes roar with lust. "What . . . what's wrong?"

Sidestepping to get out from between him and the tree at my back, I tuck hair behind my ear and grin. "You know how I feel about PDA."

With one arm, he braces his weight on the trunk, tilting his head to study me. "That piercing makes me crazy."

My cheeks heat and my heart flutters at his approval. "I can tell."

"Can't keep my hands off you." He chuckles. "Hope I didn't fuck up the healing process."

"Nope. I'm a good healer. I think it's okay." Something pulls my attention, and I look over to see Killian headed into the café.

He unknowingly snags the eyes of practically every girl he passes. Even the guys he passes seem to puff out their chests in a silent defense of their manhood. And honestly who could blame them? He's tall, wears clothes that fit him too well, and his body is sculpted to perfection, but that's not even his most attractive quality. It's his humility. He has absolutely zero idea of the effect he has on people.

"You hungry, babe?" Clifford's voice calls me away from watching my friend in all his gloriousness.

"Yeah, do you have time to grab a bite?"

He checks his phone. "No, but I'll walk you down there before I head to class."

I pick up my backpack off the grass, and he throws his arm over my shoulder, making me melt into him.

God, I'm the worst girlfriend . . . er . . . hookup girl ever. In the time I've been with him, I've been thinking of two other guys. Clifford is far from ugly. His light brown hair is skillfully cut in an emo shag, He's slender, not super skinny, but his muscles are longer. Lean. Not like Kill's bulging physique. He's tall, close to six feet, and he dresses like he belongs in a band: small shirts, tight jeans, spiked belt and a wallet attached to a chain.

We head into the café, and even over the crowd, Killian's gaze immediately tangles with mine. He flashes a small smile that dissolves the second Clifford spots him.

"Killian, what's up, man?" Clifford pulls me closer to his side.

Kill's eyes dart between us and then settle on him. "Nothing much. You guys grabbing lunch?"

"I am. Clifford has to go to class."

Killian's eyes stay on me.

"I have class all the way across campus, so I better go."

I rip my gaze from Killian and peer up at Clifford. "Okay, you sure you don't want to grab a coffee or something for the road?"

The side of his mouth lifts and he leans in close. "Oh, yeah, I'll definitely be taking something for the road."

Before I have a chance to turn away, his tongue is in my mouth, flicking like a snake against my piercing. I pull my head back, but he locks me to him with his forearm at the back of my neck. I squeeze my eyes closed and consider taking this stupid thing out if it continues to bring on Clifford's probing kiss every time I open my mouth.

He finally pulls away and again he's breathless. Huh . . . why don't his kisses do the same for me? I don't feel anything. Hell, I may as well be watching *Cars* for the six millionth time with my brother as it has the same dulling effect.

I pretend to swipe at the messed-up lip gloss I'm not wearing, when really I'm clearing the wetness of his mouth from my upper lip. "Okay, well, I guess I'll talk to you later."

He nods to Killian, and for some stupid reason, I can't even look at my friend because I'm terrified to face the disappointment I know I'll see in his expression.

"Yeah, tonight." He squeezes my ass, and I resist the urge to glare. "You're coming over, right?"

"Yes." Most likely to watch him play X-box, but it's better than being alone.

"Later." He spins on his black Converse high top and is gone.

"I'm sorry about that," I whisper and reach into my backpack to fish out some money. "I told him I'm not into PDA, but he's not a very good listener." I laugh uncomfortably and fumble with a few dollars, still avoiding Killian's eyes. "It's awkward and I don't know . . ." Why isn't he talking? Did he walk away and I've been here talking to myself?

I risk a glance and immediately regret it. His dark eyebrows are set low, and he's gripping a water bottle so tight the thin plastic caves beneath the pads of his fingers.

"I'm sorry," I whisper.

I don't even know why, but it had to be said.

He blinks a few times and then sucks in a shaky breath. "You have nothing to be sorry for."

I don't. But then . . . why do I feel like I do? I'd hate to see Killian kissing his girlfriend, if he ever had one. I mean I wouldn't *hate* it, but it's always awkward seeing people make out.

I lick my lips and shift on my feet, vacillating between doing the moonwalk or giving myself a wedgie just to erase the unease in his eyes.

"You getting something to eat?" He nods to the money in my hand.

"Yeah."

"I'll grab a table." He moves past me without waiting for my answer.

Not that I would've said no. And he knows my schedule well enough to know I have thirty minutes before my next class.

I grab a premade turkey sandwich and a grape Powerade Zero then meet Killian outside where he's sitting at a table that's half shade half sun. I grin and shuffle over to him, dropping my stuff on the table just as he takes a bite of his sandwich.

He chews then motions to the other chair. "If you sit there, you'll get both."

I gauge the sun and shade then agree and move my things to the chair closest to him. "You think I'm weird that I like to sit half in the sun, don't you?"

He takes a pull off his water bottle. "You've always been like that."

"Right." I unwrap my sandwich. "*Always* weird."

For the first time since I walked into the café, he grins. "Maybe a little."

"I knew it." I take a bite of my food and smile right back at him. Being with him is always so easy.

"But it's not the sun-shade thing that makes you weird. It's the air-conditioning thing."

I roll my eyes.

"You know blasting the cold air in your car with the windows down kinda defeats the purpose."

"I disagree. It's air *conditioning*. I'm conditioning the air around me, so if it's cold outside, I like to feel the brisk air on my face, but I don't like being cold so—"

"You turn on the heat."

I shrug. "Right. And vice versa."

"Weird," he mumbles before taking another bite of his food.

"So how's work?"

He frowns. "Why?"

"What do you mean why? I'm catching up on your life, making conversation. You know, the thing friends do when they hang out."

He blinks then goes back to focusing on his sandwich. "It's good."

"That's it? Just *good*?"

"Great . . . I guess." Finished with his food, he balls up his trash and moves it to the edge of the table. "You never did tell me how your mom took the piercing."

"Good enough, I mean she kinda freaked at first, but then once it sunk in she was cool. It took a little longer for Blake to come to terms with it."

"Yeah, I know."

My eyes dart to his. "What . . . did he . . . oh my God, Kill, did he give you shit about it?"

He shrugs one shoulder and drops back into his seat. "Nothing I couldn't handle."

I bury my face into my hands, completely humiliated. "Oh God, that's so embarrassing. I'm sorry."

"Like I said, I handled it."

"I didn't mean to tell him you were there. It just slipped out, and then he went off about why you didn't stop me, and I said it's none of his fucking business—"

"You said that?" His eyebrows rise and a hint of a grin ticks his lips.

"Not exactly, but basically."

His grin widens, and a deep chuckle filters from his lips. "I was gonna say I would've paid to have been there when you told Blake it's none of his fucking business."

I laugh and agree. That would not have gone over well.

He smiles sadly. "From the looks of it, I guess Cliff approves."

I study him and a tension strings tight between us, as if a million unspoken words hover in the space between our lips. Mesmerized by the depth of his stare, I'm incapable of looking away.

"Yes," I whisper.

He nods and breaks eye contact. "That's good, Ax. I'm . . . I'm happy for you."

An odd feeling comes over me at those words, because I'm always desperate for his approval, but for the first time, in this case, I don't want it.

SEVEN

Killian

"Get in and out! In and out!" Rex's shouted instructions are called from outside the cage.

I step in, throw a left, pivot out.

"There it is!" He claps. "Again!"

Wade's eyes are focused on me, gloved hands raised. He blinks to clear the sweat from his vision. I know because I'm doing the same.

I step in. Body shot. Pull back.

Wade lands a kick to my ribs.

"Shit." I grab his ankle just in time to take him to the ground.

"Nice!" Rex yells. "Half guard!"

I use the weight of my body to wrap my leg around his. He struggles as I secure half guard. He braces my hip, making so I can't get a tighter hold, then thrusts up. His hands get between us.

"No! Lock 'em down!"

We go back and forth, him gaining an inch, me getting it back. We're breathing heavily and fatigue makes me clumsy. He takes advantage and locks me in a guillotine choke.

"Dammit, Kill!" Rex yells just as I sag and tap.

"Fuck, boy!" Wade jumps off me, grinning. "You're one strong son of a bitch!"

I roll to my back, trying to catch my breath. "Not strong enough." I spit out my mouth guard and stare at the ceiling.

Rex's face comes into view as he leans over me. I expect to see him scowling, but his pierced lip is pulled into a wide grin. "That was some impressive shit, Kill." He holds out his hand. "Get your ass up."

I allow him to pull me to my feet where Wade wraps his arm around my neck. "You're going to destroy the competition in England, bro." He slaps my back.

Fuck. Not this again.

It's been three weeks since I got the offer to go to London, and I haven't told the guys I'm not taking the offer yet. They seem to leave me alone when I say I haven't decided yet. But I find the surest way to stay clear of their shit is to just keep my mouth shut altogether.

Wade lifts his water bottle to his lips before looking to Rex. "Dude, can you imagine getting your first fight overseas at twenty-one?"

Rex studies me with a knowing expression. "No, I can't. It's the opportunity of a fuckin' lifetime."

His words set a thirty-pound weight of guilt in my gut. And no way I can tell them the real reason I'm not considering the move. Or rather, why I'm only considering it a little.

After Axelle and Clifford's little PDA last week, I started to wonder if maybe some space wouldn't be good for us. I even followed Cam's instructions and went straight from school that day to apply for a passport, paying extra for expedited service. I've heard absence makes the heart grow fonder. If that's true, maybe a little absence is exactly what Axelle needs. I, on the other hand, can't stand to get any fonder than I already am. My guess is the next step of infatuation for me comes with a high-powered telescope, her dirty underwear, and a secret entrance to her bedroom.

The Velcro from Wade's glove being ripped off calls my attention. "When do you guys leave?"

My gaze darts to Rex, who is looking on expectantly.

"Leave for England?" I'm stalling. Not my proudest moment.

"No, leave for Dubai." Wade tosses his glove at my head. "Yes, England, jackass."

"Cam's giving me some time, so I don't know."

Wade's eyes narrow. "Time for what?"

Rex interrupts. "Killer hasn't decided if he's gonna take the UK gig yet."

Wade's eyes dart to mine, and his jaw falls loose on its hinges. "Are you insane? Of course you're taking it!"

I shrug and pull off my gloves. "Yeah, I most likely will, but I'm still trying to weigh the ramifications of leaving school for a year."

"Ramifi—no! There are zero ramifications." He tilts his head, studying me like I'm a freak of science. "Why *wouldn't* you go?"

Because I'm in love with my best friend, and if I leave, she might find the guy of her dreams, and I want to be that guy, so I can't fucking go!

"School." School. That's my answer. I'm an idiot.

"Fuck school, man! It'll always be there, but you only have this window of opportunity open now."

"He's right," Rex mumbles.

"It's one year. That's like a fart in time, my friend. You'll never miss it. But you will absolutely miss it when you don't get this kind of offer again and you're stuck in small-ticket fights that pay piss-all because you missed out on your chance to do something awesome."

"You're probably right. I just . . . needed to think about it."

"The fact that you even have to think is worrisome." Wade follows us into the weight room.

"I'll probably go."

"Where are we going?" Mason says from his position at the squat rack.

Wade points at me from over his shoulder. "Boy genius here is considering passing up the UK."

The surfer-looking fighter sets his eyes on mine. "Don't be stupid, Kill. It's only a year."

Only a year.

365 days away from Axelle.

I can do that.

Can't I?

Axelle

When I first started hanging out at Clifford's place, I didn't know what GTA5 was. After sitting in his living room for more hours than I can count over the last couple months, I've learned it's a video game where men get to pretend they're bigger and badder than they really are. They get to role-play the things they'd never have the balls to do in real life.

It's basically a playground for pussies.

"Dude, a hitchhiker." John, Clifford's roommate and all around loser friend, points to the screen. "You gonna pick him up?"

"Yep." Clifford laughs and jimmies his joystick, or controller, whatever they're called. "Then I'm gonna drive him up to the mountains and feed him to the coyotes."

Doesn't say much about society that we now have games that allow him to do just that.

I'm bored and repulsed and need a distraction.

"You guys hungry?" It's after nine and I haven't eaten dinner.

When I got here, Clifford dragged me back to his room with his mouth all over mine. He insisted I put my piercing to use. John came home seconds after we finished and roped Clifford into playing video games, leaving me alone and unsatisfied in his bed.

I shook off the whispers of desire I'd felt when he was telling me how beautiful I was, how talented my mouth is, and how much he enjoyed me. I know it's not love he feels for me, but it's something, and like a drug, I'm addicted to it. When my mouth is on him, or he's inside me, I feel wanted. After years of feeling unwanted, I desperately cling to that feeling of being wanted when we're together.

"I'm starving." John clicks the remote, his tongue hanging out the side of his mouth in concentration.

"Yeah, why don't you go grab us some food?" Clifford doesn't even look at me when he says it, his gaze firmly planted on the big flat-screen.

Better to be useful than to warm this damn chair. I get up and grab my keys. "What do you guys want?"

"Tacos."

"Pizza."

They say it simultaneously, and rather than try to decipher which one to grab, I decide hitting two different places means killing more time and hit two drive-thrus instead of one.

Thirty minutes later I push through the front door, balancing a pizza box and a bag of tacos in my hand.

"Food's here," Clifford's voice sounds from the living room followed by two more that are distinctly female.

Girls.

It's not uncommon for girls to show up here. After all, Clifford doesn't live here alone, and John's a decent-looking guy, for a stoner. Knowing that doesn't keep jealousy from waging war in my chest.

John comes into the kitchen, where I'm pulling out all the tacos and accompanying hot sauces. Clifford is on his heels, trailed by two girls. My stomach turns when I realize it's the two girls who were talking about him at his party. What the fuck are they doing here? I stand back as they all huddle around the kitchen counter and fish out food for themselves.

John takes a bite of a taco and moans. "God, I love you, Elle."

Clifford grabs pizza, and even though he doesn't offer the girls food, he doesn't stop them from taking slices for themselves.

He bites and nods toward me. "Thanks."

"You're welcome."

"Did you get this from Stubby's?" The pretty blonde takes a bite.

"No, I got it from—"

"That place is always so crowded on the weekend," her equally beautiful blond friend says.

"Come on. Watch me kick John's ass on this next mission." Clifford snags another piece of pizza and heads back into the living room.

The girls do the same.

"Kick my ass, yeah, right." John grabs a taco and goes after them.

It isn't until they're all back in the living room that I look down and notice all the food is gone and I'm standing there alone like some fucking servant while they go entertain their dates.

Shame washes over me in a dizzying wave. I can't believe after all I offer him, after everything I've done to make him happy, he'd treat me like some slut whose sole purpose is to keep him sexed up and fed.

If it walks like a slut and talks like a slut . . .

My eyes burn and I grab my keys and purse. This is stupid, and the last thing I need to top off this humiliation is to cry in front of them.

I move to leave and remember my backpack is in Clifford's room. I have to walk through the living room to get it, but chances are those pieces of shit are too involved in their game to notice me anyway.

I stomp through the living room, and other than a quick shout that I'm blocking the screen, they don't seem to notice me. I shove a few books in my backpack, zip it up, throw it on, and then storm back out through the front door. Tears sting my eyes as I shut the door behind me to the sound of them laughing at the game and not a single mention of my leaving.

Thirst for booze to numb the humiliation flares in my throat, and I hope we have a bottle of something at home because risking a hangover tomorrow is better than feeling this.

I climb into my car, fire up the engine . . .

And wait.

Scowling at the front door, I don't move, delaying my escape to see if Clifford comes for me.

Time passes; the door remains closed.

Nothing.

I slam on the gas and head home, beating myself up for being so stupid.

My mom has always said, when someone shows you what they think about you, believe them. It's not what a person says that matters; it's what they show. And although Clifford always says he cares about me, his actions certainly don't show it.

Numbly, I drive to my complex, and when I don't hear Clifford's muscle car pull up behind me, my self-hatred intensifies.

I walk to my apartment in a blur of tears and head straight for the freezer. Pulling out a bottle of cherry vodka, I screw off the cap and tilt it to my lips.

"Whoa . . . rough night?" Mindy's tucked under a blanket on the couch in the dark with the only source of light the flickering of the television.

I cringe as the liquid paints my throat in fire and then morphs to numbness. "I've had better."

She sits up and clicks off the remote, plunging her into total darkness before she turns on the lamp at her side. "You wanna talk about it?"

I throw back another swig of vodka. "Let's see. Do I want to talk about what an idiot I am? How I manage to lay myself down to be a doormat for men who could give a flying fuck about me? No. Not really."

"Don't beat yourself up. It's all part of the learning process."

If only that were true, but something tells me I'll always be this girl—the one who falls backwards for anyone who offers to use his dick on me.

Oh wow, the vodka is kicking in.

I cross to the living room and drop into the overstuffed chair. The icy bottle hangs from my fingers, and I offer it to Mindy.

She takes it and throws back a healthy chug before handing it back. I take another shot.

"Ax, this is what college is for. You get out there, screw whoever you want, however you want, and then when the time comes to settle down, you'll know it. You'll walk into a committed relationship with the knowledge that you thoroughly played the field and exhausted all your curiosities." She sits back with a proud grin.

"It's not that easy for me. I get . . . attached."

"Yeah, that happens," she says sadly.

"The worst part is I'm so sick of being walked on, and yet I continue to put myself through it. I'm lying to myself about what I have with these guys, glorifying it or something, when it's really so simple. I give. They take." I toss back another gulp and start to feel a little better, still pathetic, but at least the burn of humiliation has now been tempered with a warm belly full of booze.

A heavy pounding on our door breaks our reverie.

Mindy's eyes widen on me as she calls, "Who is it?"

"It's Clifford!"

I groan and Mindy grins. "I'll leave you two alone. Just"—she leans in— "remember what I said. Explore all avenues and take it for what it's worth. Experience. That's it."

Detach. Okay. I can do that.

She crosses to her bedroom and Clifford pounds again. "I know you're in there, Elle. I saw your car downstairs."

I wobble to my feet and open the door. "What are you doing here?"

His gaze slides to the bottle in my hand and he grins. "One-woman party, huh?"

I don't answer him, but continue to glare.

He shoves his hands in his pockets. "Why did you leave?"

My jaw practically hits the fucking floor.

He holds up a hand. "I didn't invite those girls over, I swear. They just showed up and John invited them to stay."

"They ate my dinner."

He runs a hand through his hair. "Yeah, that was fucked up. I should've said something. I'm sorry. I get so caught up in those games. I just . . ." His eyes meet mine and I see genuine remorse there. "Can I make this up to you?"

"I don't know—"

"Come on, babe. I drove all the way over here . . ."

Five miles.

". . . apologizing . . ."

Eh . . . weak apology.

". . . and you left before I got to ask you something important."

I blink up at him. "What?"

He steps close so that his feet are now over the threshold and he's standing toe-to-toe with me. "I've been thinking a lot lately, about us, and"—he slides a hand into my hair, cupping my jaw— "I want to take you out."

"Out, like . . . now?"

His lips tilt in a tiny half smile, and my heart softens a little. "No, out as in on a date—for Valentine's Day."

My breath catches in my throat and makes his smile widen. He doesn't realize my shock isn't because he offered to take me out; it's because I hate Valentine's Day.

I swore the night Stewart Moorehead ruined it for me I'd never acknowledge the damn day again. That I'd spend it doing boring shit that would be a big ole fuck you in the face of Cupid.

But maybe Mindy's right.

What's the harm in letting him take me out? If nothing else, it'll be a little reimbursement for all the meals I've bought him and his friends. Who knows? Maybe I'll even have fun and finally be able to replace the horrid memory of that day with something positive.

Something normal.

"So. . . .? Will you go out with me on Valentine's Day?"

I shrug casually. "I guess so."

His eyes narrow. "Well, shit, don't get too excited."

"It's a bullshit holiday."

"I won't argue that, but that doesn't mean we won't have fun, right?"

I nod into his hand.

"Good, now are you gonna let me in so I can take you to bed and return the favor you gave me earlier today?"

That's how it is with us. An orgasm for an orgasm. Although if I were keeping score, I'd say he's leading on the receiving end, but whatever.

Rather than answer him verbally I just turn and head for my room.

Detach and have fun.

Learn what you like.

Maybe I've been approaching this all wrong to begin with.

Never too late to change. Starting now.

EIGHT

Killian

My eyes blur with fatigue as I read about women's rights written by an 18th century feminist for my World Lit class. It's close to midnight, and I'm considering calling it a night when my cell chimes with a new text.

I pull my glasses off, rub my eyes, and then pop them back on to read it.

Hey. Are you up?

Yes.

Got a second to talk?

Sure.

I palm my phone, and when it chimes, I hit "accept" and press it to my ear. "Ax, what's up? Everything okay?"

"Fine, yeah." She's whispering. "What're you doing?"

Pushing up from the table, I take a few steps to my bed and flop on it. "Getting ready to hit the sack. You?"

"Same."

Silence builds between us.

"You sure everything's okay?"

"Oh, yeah, it's just . . ." She sighs heavy and deep. "I wanted to talk to you about Valentine's Day."

My heart sinks into my stomach. "What about it?"

"I thought, I don't know, we always spend it doing nothing and, well . . ."

Doing nothing? As if our time together, even doing mundane things, is nothing to her?

"Clifford made plans for us this year, so . . ."

Fucking fantastic. First, that prick gets her lips and her body, and now he's taking our day. I grind my teeth. "I understand."

"You do?"

No. "Yeah, he's your . . . You guys are seeing each other, so I'd expect you to spend it together."

"Okay, I mean as long as you're okay with it."

"I'll never be okay with you seeing him, Ax." I grip my phone tighter. "As far as I'm concerned, he'll never be good enough for you."

"You say that about every guy I date."

"It's true. You deserve so much more."

"Like who?" she whispers.

My breath catches in my throat. She's asking. I could just say it. I could say, "Like me." I open my mouth, but the words stick in my throat. "Not sure anyone out there is good enough." Not even me, but that doesn't keep me from hoping.

"Oh."

I pinch closed my eyes and wish I could knee myself in the balls for being such a pussy.

"Okay, Kill. I should get some sleep. See you tomorrow."

"G'night."

She hangs up, and I sit staring at the wall with the phone still pressed to my ear.

It's time you start seeing things that are right in front of your face.

Ryder's words flood my mind, and I wonder if he's right. I've been living in a fantasy world with Axelle for so long I've convinced myself of things that may not exist.

How much longer will I go on like this? She'll get married, have kids, and I'll be sitting here on my ass, having passed up all my opportunities at happiness. Then I'll get the privilege of watching her live happily while I drown miserably in my own regret.

NINE

Killian

No sooner does the door from my last class close behind me than I hear someone call my name. I turn to see Brynn wave and speed-walk toward me.

She's a tiny thing, can't be more than five-foot-two, which puts me a whole foot taller. Her pale green shirt sets off her red hair and hangs loose over a pair of tight jeans. Without sunglasses, I can see her eyes are almost the same color as her shirt.

"Sorry to bug you." Looking up at me, she squints into the sun. "Do you have a sec?"

"Sure, what's up?"

She chews her lip and her eyes shift off mine. "You haven't called."

I'm an ass. "Right, uh, about that—"

"It's okay. It's just . . . I started thinking about the way we kinda roped you into the whole triple-date thing, and I wanted you to know that if you don't want to do this you're totally off the hook." Her bright eyes peer up at me, and if I'm not mistaken, I see hope reflected there.

"That's alright, I'm, um . . ." This is good. I need to just do it. It's only one date. "I'm happy to go."

Her eyebrows pop. "Really?"

I chuckle at her shock. "Well, yeah, of course."

She exhales and grins. "Okay, great. So I guess I'll just wait for your call?"

"I'll call you tonight, if that's okay."

"Yes, that's fine."

I point over my shoulder at no one. "I'll talk to Ryder and Theo, figure out what the plan is first."

She nods vigorously.

"Hey, Kill." Axelle comes up next to me, grinning. "You ready?"

Brynn's excitement drains from her face. A flash of irritation fires within me, and it's aimed at Axelle, which makes no sense.

Axelle's eyes move between Brynn and me. "Oh, I'm sorry. Did I interrupt?" She sounds genuinely apologetic.

I clear my throat. "Brynn, this is my friend Axelle."

"Nice to meet you," Brynn says politely with a hint of relief in her voice.

"Nice to meet you too." Axelle swings her gaze to mine. "I can grab a table if you guys aren't finished."

Brynn steps back. "Oh, no—"

"That'd be great." I step closer to Brynn. "I'll be there in a minute."

Axelle's eyes flash with hurt, but she shakes it off and aims a polite smile at the girl. "It was nice to meet you, Brynn." She doesn't even look at me and heads toward the café.

Brynn rolls her lips between her teeth, and rather than continue to stand in the awkward silence, I push through it.

"So it's decided. I'll talk to the guys and call you tonight, only"—I rub the back of my neck— "could I get your number one more time?"

She lifts a speculative brow. "You lost it."

More like I never took it. "I did." I take my phone from my pocket and pull up my contacts. "Here." She enters all her info, and when she's done, I fire off a quick text to her. "And now you have mine."

"Okay, so, I look forward to your call."

"Right, yeah." Before I can think too hard about it, I reach over, hook her behind the neck, and pull her to my chest for a hug. God, the top of her head comes to my nipple, and as good as her female curves feel against me, she doesn't have the same fit I have with Axelle.

I drop my hand and step away. "Talk to you tonight."

Her cheeks flush pink and she takes off to class. I turn to watch her melt into the crowd, my gaze tracking her tiny hips and tight little body, and feeling not even a hint of the zip I feel just being near Axelle.

I turn away, grinning at what a hopeless wreck I am, and catch Axelle staring right at me from across the quad, her jaw clenched.

Yeah, how does it feel, sweetheart?

And although I shouldn't, I feel absolutely sick to my stomach.

Axelle

Oh, no, here he comes. Act cool, unaffected, nonchalant—dammit, who is that girl?

As long as I've known Killian, I've never seen him act that friendly with another girl before. And that girl, Brynn, is just as adorable as her sweet little name.

I clear my throat and take a bite of my sandwich just as he makes it to our table and drops into the seat across from me. He's wearing a yellow T-shirt that brings out the gold flecks in his eyes. I force my gaze away to avoid getting lost in them and read the words *The Book Was Better* scrolled across his broad masculine chest. I consider telling him he needs to start buying bigger clothes when—why is he smirking?

"Why aren't you eating?" *Girl problems rob you of your appetite?*

"I ate a protein bar in class." His phone chimes, and when he reads it, he grins before texting back and tucking it back into his pocket. "I keep meaning to ask you if you ever heard back from your dad."

From one uncomfortable thought to the next. Thanks, Kill.

"No, not yet." I pick at the crust on my sandwich, my stomach rejecting the little I've already eaten. "It's cool. He has a new girlfriend, and she has kids, so I'm sure he's busy with them."

All humor dissolves from his expression. "How long has it been?"

I have no interest in sharing with Killian how pathetic it is that my own biological dad, who made huge attempts to contact me, has now decided, after getting to know me a little bit, that he want's nothing to do with me, so I lie. "Not long." *Three months.*

"Hmm." He squints out at the clusters of college students, but doesn't seem to be actually looking at anything.

Time for a subject change. "Have you talked to your mom recently?" It's a shitty thing to do, flipping the subject from my absent parent to his. Last time he accepted a call from his mom, that I'm aware of, was over the summer, and when he got off the phone, he seemed smaller. She's always been horrible for his self-esteem, telling him he's not good enough, which is part of the reason I think he tries so hard to be the best at everything: the endless search for her approval that will most likely never come.

He flicks at something on the table and shakes his head. "No."

I drop my chin, hating the vibe that's forming between us. "Hey, Kill? I hope you know I—"

"Hey, babe." Clifford pulls out the chair between Killian and me with a loud scrape against the concrete.

Killian leans back in his chair and wipes the concerned look he was wearing clean off his face. Clifford looks between us and shrugs. "What did I interrupt?" He reaches out and grabs my hand.

Killian pins Clifford's hand on mine with a glare, and the ache I felt when he was with Brynn earlier comes back. He doesn't like seeing me with a guy any more than I like seeing him with a girl, and for two best friends, how fucked up is that?

I slide my hand free and put it to use by taking a bite of my sandwich, which smells off. Gamey or something, maybe it's expired. "Yeah, we were just talking about my dad."

"Does he have a fight coming up or something?" Clifford lights a cigarette, and while he's busy doing that, Killian and I share a glance.

Clifford doesn't know about my biological father Trip or my asshole ex-stepdad Stewart. All he knows is Blake "The Snake" Daniels is my adopted, and for all intents and purposes my *only,* Dad.

"Yeah, I think he does."

"Sweet, let me know when so I can get some money on it."

Killian blows out an annoyed breath that Clifford doesn't seem to pick up on.

He takes a long pull from his cigarette. making no attempt to divert the exhale of smoke and it billows directly into our faces. "You have plans for Valentine's Day, Killian?"

I fan away the fumes and stare at my friend, more interested in his answer than I bet Clifford is.

Killian's gaze stays on mine and he nods. "I do."

It's like a kick to the chest, but I push through the unwarranted pain and smile. "With Brynn?"

He grins shyly and nods.

I know that smile. He likes her. God, why does that hurt so bad?

"Nice, well if you're interested, we're having a Fuck V-day party at my place that night."

I jerk my head to Clifford. "What? I thought we were—"

"Oh, we're going out first, but afterward we're having a party." He must see the disappointment on my face because his expression grows soft. "Hey, don't worry. You'll love what I have planned."

The last thing I want to do on the anniversary of that day is be stuck at an obnoxious party with Clifford's stupid friends.

Killian's eyes communicate so much as he stares across the table at me: sadness, sympathy, and maybe some regret.

"Listen, I, uh . . ." I wad up my trash and grab my backpack. "I'm going to skip my next class and head home for a bit. I didn't get a lot of sleep last night, and I'm feeling pretty crappy."

"Sounds good, babe."

Killian pushes up from his seat. "I'll walk you to your car."

"Dude." Clifford stands too, blowing noxious smoke between the three of us. "You act like she's walking around without a burka in Afghanistan. I think she can get to her car okay without an escort."

Killian doesn't acknowledge Clifford's lame territorial display and takes my trash to the can for me. He grabs my backpack like we're some old couple that has been taking care of each other for the last fifty years, and as much as I wish I could tell him to give it back and I can carry it myself, I don't.

I step up to Clifford to give him a hug good-bye, but he dips down for a kiss. I turn my head and his smoky lips press against my cheek. "No kiss, huh?"

Is he fucking serious? "I told you I don't feel good."

"Alright, alright." He throws his arms up. "Whatever."

I turn to Killian, who's waiting patiently but scowling hard at Clifford. As soon as we're out of earshot, he mutters, "That guy is such an ass."

For the first time today, a genuine smile pulls at my lips.

Killian walks me to my car, throws my backpack in the back, and makes me promise I'll text him as soon as I get home so he knows I'm safe.

Always taking such good care of me.

What would I ever do without him?

Maybe that's what I was feeling earlier when I saw him with Brynn. If he dated someone else, I'd lose him. After all, how many girls would put up with how close we are? The occasional sleepover, him dragging me out of parties drunk, leaving to walk me to my car because I'm sick, no girl would be okay with that.

I swallow back bile as it rushes up to my throat.

I can't lose him to someone else.

But I can't allow him to pass up on a chance at happiness with someone else either.

TEN

Killian

"I realize it's Valentine's Day, but I'm not dropping three-hundo just to feed my date." Ryder grunts through his last few reps under the bench press, slams the bar back on the rack, and sits up. "It'd be one thing if she was my woman, but I've made it clear this is a onetime thing with her."

I swipe sweat from my forehead with the towel that's draped around my neck. "And how exactly did you do that?"

He pulls weights off the bar and shrugs. "Flat out told her we'd go out and have a great time, make it an all-nighter if she's interested, but I'm not looking to date anyone exclusively."

"She was cool with that?"

"Seemed to be." He loads the bar with heavier weight. "I figure we'd have a lot more fun if we went into the night, knowing what the expectations are."

I chuckle and head to the pull-up bar. "Yeah, but it kinda robs the illusion of romance. Why not just go and let the date play out?"

"Because it's *Valentine's* Day and girls get weird about this fucking holiday. Everything means more than it is. A date is a promise of commitment. Sex is practically a wedding proposal. And whatever you do, don't buy her a gift. That's the kiss of death for the casual relationship."

I grind through some pull-ups, considering Ryder's words. I hadn't really thought through this date with Brynn and all it implies. I thought we'd go out and have a good time, but at the end of the night, we'd go our separate ways, and if anything, I'd gain a friend out of the whole thing.

But this . . . Shit. I'm not prepared for all this.

I suppose I could take Ryder's lead and have the talk with her tonight when I call her. Let her know that I'm not looking for a relationship right now. But doesn't that imply that she is? She could laugh in my face at my presumptuous attitude.

"So I say we find somewhere fairly inexpensive, but fun. Make it less about fine china and fucking champagne and more about having a good time."

I drop slowly from the pull-up bar, savoring the burn in my lats and biceps. "So we hit dinner and then what?"

He flashes a wicked grin. "Party, what else?"

"Fine by me." As long as I stay busy enough to keep my mind off Axelle spending her first Valentine's Day in four years with Cliff the fuckface, I'm all in.

~~~

After the gym, I come straight home to call Brynn. As I stare down at her name on my phone, my finger hovers over the send button.

I remind myself that I'm not doing anything wrong. Axelle made plans with Clifford before I did with Brynn, but I can't help but feel like I'm going behind Ax's back.

I groan and drop my head into my hand. "Stop being a pussy-whipped little bitch."

Before I can change my mind, I hit "send" and press the phone to my ear, half hoping I get her voicemail.

"Hello?"

No such luck.

"Hey, Brynn?"

"Yeah, hey, Killian, I was hoping you'd call."

"Promised I would."

"I'm glad you did. Ever since we bumped into each other earlier today, I've been thinking about you."

I rub my forehead as panic wreaks havoc on my central nervous system. "Oh . . . yeah?"

She giggles, but it's throatier, heavy with . . . something. "It's embarrassing. I can't believe I'm even admitting it, but yeah . . . It's just . . . I've wanted to get to know you since last year, but I was just too nervous to talk to you."

For a second, I'm shocked by her confession, but then I remember that although I still feel like the biggest dork in school, I no longer look like one. If she only knew that inside this big body hides a scrawny, terrified nerd.

"We're getting to know each other now." God, did that sound flirty? I don't want to give her the wrong impression.

"And I'm really happy about that. What're you doing?"

"Oh, what? Like right now?"

"Yeah." There's a smile in her voice.

"Just got home from training, gearing up to study for a bio test I have tomorrow. You?"

"I just got out of the shower."

I blink and stare at the wall of books in front of me. "Oh." I suck at this. And it feels wrong, so, so wrong, yet the stirring in my blood can't be ignored.

"I need to get dressed. Can you hang on for a sec?"

And now I'm picturing her naked. "Sure?"

"I mean, unless you can think of a reason why I should stay naked?"

Holy shit. Is she . . .? Is this . . .? "Uhh . . ."

"I'm on my bed. Are you?"

I bite my lip and close my eyes.

"I wish you were here—oh my God, Ashley!" There's a rustling of some kind and then mumbling. ". . . knock first!"

This is awkward as hell.

"Killian, are you still there?"

"Yeah, I'm here. Listen. I just wanted to tell you that we're going to Kahunaville tomorrow night and then to a party."

"Oh, okay."

Why does she sound disappointed?

"I'll pick you up at seven. Just text me your address."

"Of course, sounds good."

"So I, uh . . . I'll see you tomorrow."

She hangs up and I stare at my phone for a few seconds. Are women usually this aggressive? And if that's how she is the first time we talk on the phone, what's she going to be like when we're together on a date?

On Valentine's Day.

Shit, maybe we should've had the talk Ryder suggested.

I don't think she realizes she's about to go out with a twenty-one-year-old virgin who is helplessly in love with someone else.

ELEVEN

Axelle

I couldn't look more anti-Valentine's Day if I tried.

Staring at my reflection, I almost laugh at the glam-goth thing I've got going on. If Cupid had an enemy, it would be me.

I slide on my chunkiest black biker-esque heels, complete with buckles and a thick sole, just in case I need to stomp on the pudgy diaper-wearing fairy who's aiming his arrows at everyone but me. The spaghetti strap of my purple racer-back tank slides off my bare skin, and yeah, I'm not even wearing a bra because fuck Valentine's Day.

I grab my full glass of wine off the dresser and attempt another sip, but end up pouring the whole thing out. I'm too annoyed to drink, and that's probably for the best.

Lord knows all I need to make this night a complete disaster is to pour a little liquid anger on my already foul mood.

"I still don't understand why you agreed to go if you hate it so much." Mindy's in the kitchen, sipping her glass of wine, her feelings for the day clearly not turning her stomach. Lucky brat.

"You look great." I grab a bottle of water from the fridge and nurse it, hoping it'll cool my mood.

She does a cute little spin, showing off her bright red mini-dress and super strappy heels. "And my panties match."

"Yay!" *Ugh.*

She narrows her eyes. "Axelle, why do you hate Valentine's Day so much?"

I roll my eyes. "I don't *hate* it."

"Really? So you're dressed like a biker-vampire who looks like she's ready to drain the male race just for the fun of it because . . .?"

"I'm not—"

"You're wearing pants." She pulls up my hand and shows it to me. "Black fingernails, Ax? I mean, if I were a guy, I'd be terrified to get my dick anywhere near that scowl you're wearing. And this?" She motions to my face with a swirl of her finger. "You're taking heroin chic to a whole new level."

"Okay, I get it! You don't approve." I salute her. "Ten-four, boss!"

She sighs and takes a sip of wine. "Poor, poor Clifford. He's in a no-win situation tonight."

"He's taking me to dinner and then back to his place for a party, Mindy. I mean this is far from a romantic evening. I've been with the guy for like three months now, and outside of his bedroom, we've never even hung out alone. So don't make tonight out to be any different from any other night, because for me it's just like last night, but I had to put a whole hell of a lot more effort into getting ready." I'm practically panting I'm so annoyed.

"What time is he picking you up?" The cheeriness in her voice makes her message clear. She wants my angry-ass gone. Not that I blame her.

I snag my keys off the counter. "I'm meeting him at his place. I'm already late. And I won't be home until tomorrow, so the apartment's yours."

"Axelle."

I whirl around, expecting to have to defend myself from another one of her verbal onslaughts, but instead she wraps me in a hug.

"I understand. And seriously, you can do better." She pulls back, and I have to look away from the concern I sense in her stare.

"Have fun tonight. I'll see you tomorrow."

And with that, I'm gone.

A few minutes later I pull up to Clifford's, and the driveway and street outside his place are already packed with cars. Looks like the party started early.

I rest my forehead on the steering wheel and wish I'd never agreed to go out tonight. To think that I could be home watching a movie with Killian, not needing to explain my shitty mood because he already knows everything about me. He'd tread carefully, keep the mood light, and steer the subjects away from anything parent-related. He'd go out of his way to make me laugh, and always before he'd leave, he'd hug me for so long, not letting go until he whispered, "Their loss," as if to remind me that the men in my life have given up the honor of knowing me.

My fingers itch to call him, to beg him to drop everything and spend tonight with me, but the problem is I know he will.

I know, and always have, that if I need him he'd drop everything to be there. And as selfish as I am, as badly as I want nothing more than that right now, there's no way I could do that to him.

Not after the smile I saw on his face when he was with Brynn. If anyone on this earth deserves happiness, deserves to live a life of love and success, it's Killian McCreery.

I drag myself from my car, and already it's as if this godforsaken holiday has sapped me of my energy. As my feet carry me to the door, I prepare for what'll lie within.

Clifford and twenty of his closest friends are huddled around the television, smoking weed, with the music blaring. And when I push through the front door without knocking that's exactly what I see.

Fuck.

"Babe!" Clifford hops up from the couch, throwing his controller to the guy next to him with orders to "Play for me until I get back."

He crosses to me and I take in what he's wearing: his favorite pair of skinny jeans, a Jane's Addiction T-shirt, and combat boots. Nice to see he dressed up. Fucking asshole.

He moves to hug me, but stops just shy of touching me.

"What is it, *babe*?" I snarl and he jerks back. "Is there something in my teeth?"

His eyes narrow. "Are you okay?"

He did *not* just ask me that.

"Am I okay?" My fists clench at my sides. "Did you just ask me if I'm *okay*?"

He nods, but says, "No."

"Good, that's good Clifford, because if you'd asked me if I was okay, it would imply that you don't know why the fuck I'm not okay, and I hope to hell you are not that stupid."

"Oh snap! She got you, Clifford!" one of his friends pipes up from the living room.

"Come on. I think we need to talk." He grabs my arm, but I wrench it from his grip. He throws his hands up and nods down the hallway. "I just want to talk to you, babe, but not in front of an audience."

I flick my hair, which took me an hour to flat iron, and stomp down the hallway to storm into his bedroom. He shuts the door behind us and I whirl on him. "If you don't mind, can we skip the lies and excuses and move straight to the ass-kissing? That's my favorite part anyway."

"What the hell's gotten into you?"

I grin. I can't help it. He really is a fuckin' idiot. "You asked me out on a date tonight." I say the words slow and clearly so he can understand. Maybe I should draw him a picture story, dumb shit.

He blinks and has the audacity to look confused. "Right. And *I* told *you* we we're having a party."

"After our date!"

He props his hands on his hips and sighs while studying his feet. "This is why I don't do the girlfriend thing."

"Excuse me? The *girlfriend* thing? Is that what you think this is?"

He meets me with an unwavering glare. "For me? Yeah."

A laugh shoots from my lips. "Really? Because we've never even been on a date, Clifford. This isn't even a real relationship; all we do is hook up!"

"If that's true, then why are you all up on my nuts about a *date*?"

If that isn't the million-dollar question. I sink my fingers into my hair and grip tight. "I don't know."

"Hey." He steps closer to me, but still maintains some distance in case I might rip his dick off if he gets too close. Probably a smart bet. "I want to take you out to dinner, okay? I'd planned on asking you if you'd like that or if you want to order takeout, but you didn't really give me a chance."

He's right. I didn't. For all I know he could have a limo waiting out back ready to steal us off to some fantastic restaurant and Vegas show.

"You're right. I'm sorry."

He lifts his brows and takes a tentative step closer. I end his trepidation by closing the distance between us and wrapping my arms around his middle. He holds me close and I sink into his embrace. It's not the all-consuming hug that Killian delivers, but it's a warm body, and that's better than nothing.

He presses his lips to the top of my head. "You look so hot tonight."

His compliments usually send me reeling, but tonight it just feels forced. Like the words of a desperate man who just learned he may not be getting laid. "Thanks."

"You hungry?"

I'm really not, which makes this entire fight seem even stupider. Demanding I be taken out to dinner when I have no appetite? I really am a fucking psycho. So I lie. "Yeah."

"Okay, let me grab my shit and we'll get a bite." He pulls back. "Sound good?"

I nod and push out a smile that I hope doesn't look as fake as it feels.

He moves to leave the room, but turns back. "Oh, and babe?"

"Yeah?"

He smiles brilliantly. "Happy Valentine's Day."

Fuck off.

Killian

Talk about flashbacks.

Stuck in traffic on my way to pick up Brynn, memories of the night I was supposed to take Axelle to the school dance flash through my mind. I often wonder where we'd be if Stewart hadn't shown up that night. Even if he'd come just one day later, things could've been so different.

I had every intention of making my feelings for Axelle clear that night, and if she'd returned them, we would be together now. It seems presumptuous to think we'd still be together after four years, but it's not. Because I know I would've done everything in my power to make her happy, and if she tried to leave me, I'd fight to get her back.

But fate had different plans for us, I guess.

And now I'm in my Jeep, wearing a dress shirt and a damn tie, on my way to pick up someone else while Axelle is most likely staring lovingly into the eyes of a complete assface, when she should be staring into mine.

Awesome.

I pull up to Brynn's complex just a few minutes after seven. It takes a little time to find her building and door number, which is probably why she opened the door before I was even able to knock.

"I'm late. Sorry."

She hits me with a brilliant smile. "No worries. We're kind of tucked in the back here; people usually can't find us. But at least now you know"—she shrugs— "for next time."

Next time?

"You want to come in?"

"We should probably get going—"

"No way!" A girl comes barreling to the door, her hair up in some fancy twist thing, but she's wearing a robe. "I've never met a celebrity before."

I study Brynn, who looks a little embarrassed. "Killian, this is one of my roommates, Ashley."

Ah, so this is the one who walked in on her last night. I offer my hand. "Nice to meet you."

She grabs my hand with two hands, and while one holds on, the other travels up the length of my arm. "Nice to meet you too. Whoa, you're really strong."

I try to politely extract my hand from her grip, and after a brief struggle, she lets go.

"Brynn tells me you're a UFL fighter."

Huh? Funny she'd know that seeing as we've never even talked about it. "I am."

"That is so hot." She winks. "Is it true you guys have lines of women waiting to service you after fights?"

I chuckle.

"Ashley!"

"What?" She glares at Brynn then swings her lusty gaze back to me. "I'm just wondering where to take a number."

"Oh my gosh, we're leaving." Brynn pushes past Ashley and grabs my hand to lead me away from her place. "I am so sorry. She doesn't know when to shut her mouth."

I laugh. "No problem." I peer down at her, and for the first time since she opened the door, I notice what she's wearing: a dress the color of bubblegum with a thick black belt and black heels that brings the top of her head to my shoulder. The bottom of the dress is short, but puffy, almost like a bubble. The top doesn't have any straps but is being held up by her ample breasts sporting some serious cleavage.

When we get to the Jeep, I open the door for her, and she smiles behind a veil of wavy red hair. After closing her in, I round the hood and climb inside. An awkward silence fills the space, and I fight for something to say.

"You look really pretty tonight." Seems like an appropriate place to start.

"So do you, I mean, not pretty, but you look handsome."

"Thanks."

I pull away from her complex and wonder if things could get any more uncomfortable. Maybe it's because this is technically my first official date or because I'm so used to being around one particular girl, but if things don't get better, this is going to be a long night for both of us.

~~~

That wasn't as bad as I thought.

As I walk out of Kahunaville hand-in-hand with Brynn, we're laughing at Theo as he imitates Ryder at a concert.

"I don't know how he hasn't snapped his own neck." Theo head bangs the air and sends the girls into a fit of giggles, but earns a swift sock to the gut from Ry.

"At least I don't just sit there bobbing my head like I'm at a Taylor Swift concert."

Theo's humor dissolves. "Dude, don't knock Taytay."

"Where are we going now?" Ryder's date curls up to him like a kitten to its scratching post.

Ryder grabs her ass, making her giggle. "I say we check out the party."

"Yes, let's go have some drinks and dance!" Brynn presses her breasts against my arm, and I wonder if she notices how close she's bringing my hand to between her legs.

I may be a virgin, but I've fooled around with girls in the past. There were two girls in my neighborhood who taught me everything I know. We were all latchkey kids and home alone more than we were with our parents. Throw a couple of teenagers in a room together, hormones raging, and too much free time on their hands, and things are going to happen.

However, it's been so long since I've touched a woman intimately I feel like I'm starting from scratch. And although I'm not desperate to be with Brynn in that way, I'd be lying if I said I wasn't curious.

"Sounds good; follow us." Ryder's date squeals as he leads her to his car by a firm hold on her backside.

"They're so cute together, aren't they?" Brynn says as I open the Jeep door for her.

"I guess, yeah." Even if it's only for tonight.

I settle into my seat and fire up the engine when Brynn's hand lands firmly on my thigh. I stare at it, the foreign feeling of being touched sending bolts of heat between my legs.

"Killian?"

My gaze slides up her delicate arm to her face, which is illuminated by the dash lights.

"This might seem forward, but I get the sense that if I don't ask you'd never make a move." She leans across the center console until our faces are less than inches apart. "May I kiss you?"

I swallow hard and lick my lips self-consciously.

She must see that as the okay to move forward because her mouth presses to mine. Shock blasts through my system at the warm and tender caress of her lips. Her fingers grip my thigh tighter, and a moan rolls up my throat like I'm some sex-starved male craving the touch of a woman.

I close my eyes to blue eyes and chestnut hair that flash behind my lids. *Axelle.* What would it be like to kiss her like this? My fantasies hurl themselves to the surface. As my tongue slips inside the warm cavern of her mouth, I hear Axelle's throaty groan as she receives it.

Blood fires through my veins, and the need to get more, to get *inside* her, dominates my thoughts. I grip the back of her neck and tug her closer to me until the tips of her breasts rub against my chest. My dick punches the zipper of my slacks, searching for the heat it so desperately craves. I rip my lips from her mouth to her throat. Her pulse races, and I need to taste her skin, to lap at her flesh and suck—

"Yes . . . Killian . . ."

My lips freeze against her skin. I blink away the Axelle haze at the sound of her voice.

"*Fuck.*" I'm such an asshole.

She laughs and leans back into her seat. The pale skin of her cheeks and neck is flushed red, and shame washes over me at seeing it. "That was the hottest first kiss I've ever had."

I turn to gaze out the windshield and hope she doesn't see the regret I'm drowning in. I know I should say something, apologize or explain, but I can't even bring myself to speak the words.

"Oh look!" She points to Ryder's Toyota pickup. "They waited for us."

This is good. At least at the party I'll have the distraction of being in a crowded room. As long as I stay away from bedrooms and bathrooms, I should be able to get through the rest of this night without giving into my deepest, darkest fantasies.

TWELVE

Axelle

The good news is I think *this* Valentine's Day is shitty enough to trump my original Valentine's Day.

I never thought anything could top Stewart's impromptu drop in, but leaning against the wall in a dark corner nursing a warm beer and watching my date openly flirt with other girls has done it. *Ding-ding-ding! We have a winner!* The only thing that could make this any worse is if he'd strip them down and fuck them right in front of me.

But only a total meanie-face would do *that*. And Clifford, well, he's just friendly with his hands.

The sarcasm in my head makes me grin, but it's all teeth.

Turns out I was wrong. Clifford did take me out to dinner at the little Italian place down the street. He also invited three of his stoner friends to join us. They ate all the garlic bread, and I swear when I went to the restroom I came back and half my rigatoni was gone.

But that wasn't the highlight of my romantic V-day dinner, nooo. The topper was how Clifford forgot his wallet when the bill came. Oh, and what do ya know, so did everyone else. So I bought those free-loading fuckholes dinner.

They all disappeared and left me on my own once we got back to the house. When they reappeared, Clifford had that weird party smell he gets that turns my stomach.

And if I could escape and go home, I would, but *ta-da!* Guess what? I can't because I promised Mindy she could have the apartment for the night, and just because my holiday sucks big fat hairy moldy donkey balls doesn't mean I'm going to ruin hers too.

However, there is a bright side to all this, and that is that Clifford and I are over.

O.

V.

E.

R.

Done.

I will never so much as smile in his direction again.

One more night of torture I can handle. I'll fake sick, although the way I've been feeling lately I may not have to, avoid kissing and sex, and by the time the sun rises in—I check the time—six hours, I will never have to give Clifford a second of my time ever again.

And it's on that thought that I'm able to tolerate this total disaster of a night.

The same ole screamo is blasting through the speakers, people are chattering obnoxiously, but I've erected a sphere of silence all around me. I'm numb to everything, every look, every attempt at conversation, every single fucking thing.

Even now I'm watching as a girl whispers something in Clifford's ear and he holds her close to him by her hip.

I almost feel sorry for her.

"Take a look over here, sweet cheeks." I bounce my eyebrows and laugh, not that it matters because no one can hear me over the music anyway. "This'll be you in three months."

A dude close to me stares at me like I've lost my mind, but I only smile. This is it. I've officially lost every single fuck I've ever given.

Gotta admit. Feels pretty good.

Grinning like an idiot, I'm a fly on the wall as the party rages on. My feet hurt, but I refuse to go get comfortable in

Clifford's bed. I'm staying right here until the sun breaks and then I'm out.

The front door opens, and all my resolve turns to shit when in walks my salvation.

Killian.

Tears spring to my eyes as anguish and relief strip me of my strength. I open my mouth to call to him, but the words freeze in my throat when his eyes meet mine and scream their apology. Something pulls his attention, and I follow the line of his gaze to the pretty little redhead grinning up at him as if he's the sun in a winter wasteland.

And then I notice it.

He's holding her hand.

Killian

I knew this was a mistake.

When we pulled up behind Ryder, I almost kept driving, but then I thought *why the hell not*? I knew Axelle would be here, and fuck if my heart didn't jump in my chest at the idea of seeing her, but not like this.

She's surrounded by a sea of people and has never looked more alone. It's as if she's invisible to everyone but me. Her face pales, and even with all that black shit around her eyes, I notice them glistening the way they always do when she's fighting tears.

Fuck. What the hell did Clifford do this time?

I rip my gaze from her and search the dick-lick out only to find him playing quarters with a girl no more than a few yards from where Axelle's standing. That sorry sack of shi—

"Killian." Brynn tugs my arm for me to lean down. "Where do you think we'll find the keg?"

My palm itches pressed to hers, and as much as I want to shake her off, I don't want to look like an asshole.

I lean in to speak in her ear to be heard over the music. "Outside would be my guess."

She flutters her eyelashes and grins. "Mind grabbing us a couple of drinks?"

My gaze darts back to Axelle, who hasn't moved an inch, but is no longer looking my way, her eyes now unfocused on the people in front of her. I squeeze Brynn's hand before pulling mine free. "Sure. Give me a second?"

Her eyebrows drop in concern before Ryder's date sidles up beside her. "I need to hit the bathroom, but there's no way I'm going alone."

"We're going to run to the bathroom and meet you back here?" Brynn tilts her head, searching for something in my expression.

"Yeah, meet you back here."

She pushes up on her toes, headed straight for my mouth.

Oh fuck, fuck, fuck.

Thinking quickly, I dip down and press a chaste kiss to her forehead. She drops back, blinking, then flashes an awkward smile before being dragged off.

Once she disappears into the hallway, I turn toward Axelle, whose gaze darts between me and the floor. I push through the crowd and the makeshift dance floor, until I'm standing toe-to-toe with her.

Her outfit, hair, and makeup are the complete opposite of my date tonight. Whereas Brynn is dressed like a sweet temptation, Axelle's look is tempting, but more of the deadly variety.

Her eyes snap to mine and tighten into a glare. "What are you doing here?"

"It's a party, Ax. Why wouldn't I be here?"

She huffs and studies the beer bottle in her hand. "Perfect. Icing on the shit cake that is my night."

I step closer to get her to look at me. "What happened tonight?"

She cocks a hip and stares up at me. "Why do you care?"

I motion to where I saw Clifford drinking earlier. "Awfully generous of you to share your date tonight."

Anger flickers behind her sapphire eyes. "First off, he's no longer my date. He's no longer my anything."

That sends me back a step. He broke up with her? On Valentine's Day? What an asshole! No wonder she looks like she's about to rip someone's throat out.

"I'm sorry. I—"

"Don't be." She shrugs. "I'm not."

"Ax, but today? He had to break up with you today of all days?"

She steps in close, and it's then I notice she's steady on her feet, her beer bottle is full and looks warm, and her breath smells like mint gum rather than booze. She pokes me in the chest. "I broke up with him. He doesn't know it yet, but it's been over for close to three hours now, and I'd leave here, but I have nowhere to go. I promised Mindy the apartment for the night, and I can't go to my mom's house because walking in at midnight will get me the third degree, and I can't fuck their night up either, seeing as Valentine's Day is just as fucked a day for them as it is for us."

Us. My chest warms and I resist the urge to pull her into my arms.

"So I'm waiting until the sun comes up. I'm going to stand right here"—she shoves a finger toward the floor—"until the sun comes up, and then I'm walking away from Clifford and never looking back."

"Did he hurt you?"

"No."

"Don't fucking lie to me."

"Why are you here?"

"I already told you. It's a party . . . and . . ." *I wanted to see you.*

Her shoulders collapse as if the fight has been completely drained from her. "Just leave, Killian. Please.

You guys could be anywhere tonight. Do you have to be here?"

"You don't want me here?"

"It's not that; it's . . ." She steps back to lean against the wall, and I follow and press in close so she has to tilt her head back to look up at me. "Did you have to bring *her* here?"

My blood thunders through my veins at the meaning behind her words. She's jealous. Which means she feels more for me than friendship, right? Is it possible that seeing me with another girl is forcing her to confront her feelings? "You don't like seeing me with her?" She dips her chin, but I catch it with my fingertips and bring her eyes back to mine. "Answer me, Axelle."

Her eyes glisten, but her jaw is hard. "I *hate* it."

For a stunned second, I simply stare, forcing myself to acknowledge and absorb her words. I clear my throat and lean in to speak directly in her ear. "What do you want, baby?"

Her breath catches so sharply it swells her chest, and the tips of her breasts brush against me. A low growl of satisfaction rumbles in my throat, and I flex my fingers against the wall to keep from shoving them into her hair and kissing her.

She hasn't answered my question, but her breathing has sped up.

"I need to hear you say it."

She shoves me back, her head turned to the side, and when I follow her gaze, I see Brynn pushing through the crowd toward us. *Fuckin' hell.*

I run a hand through my hair, trying to calm my racing pulse, and I'm thankful it's dark so no one can see my raging hard-on.

"Oh hey." Brynn pushes up next to me, her smile aimed at Axelle. "I didn't know you'd be here. Axelle, right?"

"Hi, yeah." Axelle shifts on her feet and takes a sip of her warm beer. "I like your dress."

"Thanks." Brynn turns toward me, her eyes questioning. "Did you grab our drinks?"

"No, the line was too long. I'll try again in a bit."

Her hand slips into mine, and my muscles tense when I see Axelle's eyes following Brynn's every move. "Dance with me?" She starts to pull me into the thick of the crowd where people are jumping and swaying to music.

"I don't dance." I catch a quick glimpse of Ax, and my chest crushes at the sad defeat I see reflected in her expression.

Brynn stops and presses the front of her body to mine, her arms reaching up high to grab my shoulders. She grinds her body against me and bites her lip when she comes in contact with my dick. I check on Axelle, hoping she's not watching, but she's gone. Fuck.

I scan the area, grateful I'm a head taller than the majority of the people here, and see a quick flash of dark hair weaving through the room.

I take a step back from Brynn and look her dead in the eyes. "I'm so sorry, but there's someone really important to me, and she needs me tonight. I know this is an asshole move and I wouldn't blame you if you hated me, but—"

"It's Axelle, isn't it."

And here I thought I was keeping my feelings for Ax well hidden. "Yes."

"Do I need to find a ride home?"

"No, of course not. I'll take you home, just . . ." Shit, Axelle's gone. "Let me track her down, and then I'll take you home."

"You guys, you and her, you're just *friends,* right?"

"Yes." *For now.*

She exhales in what seems like relief and then nods. "I'll meet you by the door."

I pull her in for a hug and drop a quick kiss to the top of her head. "Thank you."

I release her and move like my feet are on fire to search for Axelle. Ryder's in a corner with his date, his hand sliding up her skirt. "Hey, have you seen Ax?"

His expression sobers and he stands up straighter. "No, why? Is she okay?"

"I don't think so. She was here, but now I can't find her."

"I'll check to see if her car is still here." His date scowls at me, and Ryder ignores her whines for him to stay. He moves through the house while I check the kitchen and backyard.

We meet back up in the dining room where a heated game of beer pong is being played.

"Wherever she is, she's on foot. Her car is blocked in by four others." Ryder glances around. "I'll check the bedrooms."

"I'll check the bathrooms."

We split up, and I head straight to the bathroom in the hallway where a line of people are waiting. "Excuse me." I push through them.

"Hey, there's a line!"

"I swear I will piss in this hallway!"

I ignore the protests and bang on the door. There's no answer, and when I twist the handle it's locked. I bang again. "Axelle, you in there?"

Nothing.

Shit.

Ryder comes stomping down the hallway, and when we make eye contact, he shakes his head.

I bang on the door again. "Axelle, are you in there? Open up."

I press my ear to the door and hear a toilet flush then a mumbled, "Go away, Killian."

Thank fuck!

"Open the door, Ax, or I swear to God I'll bust this shit down."

"I said go away!"

"Stand back. I'm coming in!"

The handle wiggles frantically before the door swings open to reveal a stunned-faced Axelle. "You can't just kick a door down!"

"The fuck I can't!"

"Are you insane?"

For you, always. "Come on." I grab for her, but she backs up into the bathroom.

"No."

I step inside with her and slam the door behind me. "What the hell is going on with you?"

"Me?"

Anger rips through me, making my muscles tense. "Don't play dumb. You felt it too. I know you did. Then you take off and lock yourself in the bathroom? I burst in here, and you look like you've seen a ghost." I step closer, and in the light, I notice she really doesn't look well. Her eyes are bloodshot, her soft skin is coated with a sheen of sweat, and her lips are dry. "Hey"—I cup her jaw and swipe my thumb along her cheek— "you're sick."

She nods into my hold. "I think it's just the day. I don't know."

"I'm taking you home."

"I already told you I can't go home. I promised Min—"

"With me. I'm taking you home *with me*."

She blinks up at me, relief flooding her eyes with tears. "What about your date?"

"I'm going to drop her off now."

"Killian—"

I press my thumb to her lips. "Don't argue with me. I'm going to leave you here with Ryder until I get back. Promise me you won't leave his side."

She closes her eyes and nods.

"Finally something she won't fight about," I mumble.

"I'm tired of fighting." The soft confession heavy with meaning falls from her lips and curls around my heart.

"Me too."

She leans in and I catch her against my chest, wrapping her up so tight I have to be conscious not to crush her. This is all I've ever wanted, and tonight I'm going to finally make her mine.

Banging on the door snaps me from the warmth of our embrace. "No sex in the bathroom! Some of us have to pee!"

Axelle chuckles, and the sound knocks off some of the tension in my shoulders. I grab her hand, and the way hers grips mine back sends chills racing up my arm.

I open the door to a group of scowling girls, but by the time their eyes trace up my torso to my face, they're smiling.

"We're sorry." I motion to the bathroom. "It's all yours."

I pull Axelle out behind me and find Ryder waiting at the end of the hallway with his date. She has her arms crossed and looks less than happy.

"Ry—"

"Thank fuck." He exhales hard. "You found her."

"I'm taking Brynn home. I need you to stay with Ax until I get back."

Axelle presses in close. "I don't need a babysitter."

"Like fuck you don't, woman!" Ryder snags her arm and pulls her in. "You're a regular Houdini." He grins at me. "I got her, dude. I'll sit on her if I have to."

"Alright." I pull Axelle to me and press a kiss to her forehead before meeting her eyes. "Stay put. I'll be right back."

Ryder's date glares at me so hard I can feel it, not that I blame her. She's Brynn's friend, and it's only right that she'd be pissed on Brynn's behalf. It's time to straighten things out with my date.

I find her waiting at the door when I get there. "You ready?"

"Yeah." She sounds disappointed, and I feel like shit about that.

Again, I should've listened to Ryder and laid out things before they got this far.

We head out to the Jeep and then to her place in silence. I'm formulating the gentlest way to let her down and coming up with nothing I'm proud of.

It's not you; it's me.

I'm in love with someone else.

I never even wanted to go out with you in the first place.

Yeah, we kissed, but I was thinking about someone else the whole time, so it doesn't count.

It isn't until we pull up to her complex and I move to get out to walk her to her door that she stops me with a warm hand on my forearm. "Don't."

I release the handle on my door and sit back. "Brynn, I'm gonna walk you to your door."

She shakes her head and smiles sadly. "No, please don't. That'll just make me want you more than I already do, and I think it's pretty clear that you're not where I'm at."

I stare out the windshield, and after a few seconds, I'm not able to come up with any excuse that won't hurt her. I simply nod. "I'm sorry."

"Don't be. You were forced into this. I should've seen it coming."

"I kissed you; that was . . . misleading."

She shrugs one shoulder. "Maybe. But it was the kiss that gave you away. All that desperation? I can see now you'd been holding onto that kiss for someone else."

"I don't know what to say." *I'm an ass.*

"No need. I'm just glad I know now rather than months from now, ya know?"

"For what it's worth, I think you're a great girl."

She laughs. "Thank you. I'm pretty sure those are the exact words my grandpa uses when complimenting me."

"Shit, I'm so bad at this." I rub my forehead.

"It's okay. No hard feelings." She opens the door and slides out. "I'll see you at school."

"Yeah, see ya."

"And Killian? Just in case you don't already know this, she's into you too."

My jaw falls loose and questions roar in my head, but she slams the door before I can pull myself together enough to ask.

Could she be right?

Is Axelle just as crazy about me as I am her?

I throw the Jeep in gear and peel out of the parking lot.

Only one way to find out.

THIRTEEN

Axelle

"I think your date hates me."

Ryder slides a lazy gaze between me and his date, who's stewing with a girlfriend across the room. "Eh . . . she'll get over it."

"Ouch. Remind me to warn the female population of your sensitivity."

He shrugs and shoves his hands into the pockets of his dress pants. "What's going on with you and Killian?"

"You don't tiptoe around issues, do you?"

He lifts his eyebrows by way of reply.

"I love Killian."

His eyebrows pop impossibly higher.

"Always have."

"You think that might be something you should share with the guy? Put him out of his misery?"

"It's not like that with us."

"Yeah?" He looks skeptical. "And why's that?"

"He's . . . too good." *For me.*

"Can't argue that."

I backhand his bicep. "Seriously, Ry, sensitivity. Work on it."

"What? He is. He's smart, funny, decent-looking, and—according to my dad—he's in line to become one of the best UFL fighters in history. He doesn't drink much, never touches drugs. He's a . . . a . . . ." He purses his lips. "Let's just say the guy is as pure as they come."

"He's a virgin. I know."

He scrunches up his face. "Hard to believe, right?"

"Not really. He's never seemed very interested in girls. He's always been about studying and working hard to become a fighter. I don't think girls were ever really on his radar—"

Ryder bursts out laughing, the sound irritating because I get the impression I'm the joke.

"What's so funny?"

He wipes his eyes, and his bellowed laughter slows to a chuckle. "Wow, you're fucking clueless."

"You know what? If you don't learn to use your filter, I'm not—" I jump as a firm grip clamps down hard on my ass. I whirl around to a slit-eyed and sloppy-mouthed Clifford. "Don't touch me."

His hands fly up and he laughs low and throaty. "Whoa, what crawled up your ass?"

Ryder steps between us, his back facing me. "Clifford, you're fucked up. Why don't you go sleep it off and you and Axelle can talk in the morning?"

I sidestep Ry and meet eyes with my ex. "Don't bother. I'm so over you."

He stumbles back and forth then steadies himself. "You're *over* me? Funny, didn't feel like you were *over* me when you were suckling like a starving puppy from my dick."

I launch toward him, but am caught up by Ryder's shoulder as he wraps an arm behind him to hold me back. "That wasn't me suckling, that was me looking for it, you lip-dick pussy!"

His jaw ticks and he lurches forward. "Not so limp when I was buried deep in your cunt, bitch."

Embarrassment engulfs me in flames, because our war of words is riddled with truths. Truths I'd rather forget.

"You're the biggest mistake I've ever made."

"Wish I could say the same, but all the side pussy and free meals made every second fucking you worth it."

Tears spring to my eyes and track down my cheeks. I'm so pissed at him and even more pissed that I'm letting him make me cry that I lean forward again to claw his fucking eyes out.

Ryder's arms grab me around the waist from behind. "Fuck, you're strong."

Just as the words leave his mouth, the room fills with tension. People who've circled around us part to a demanding presence, and I don't have to see him to know he's here.

And furious.

"Killian, man . . ." Ryder's voice is pleading but unwavering. "Breathe through it, brother."

I wrench my head around to find Killian standing behind us, his shoulders bunched so tightly beneath his pale blue dress shirt that it strains the seams. The edges of his jaw are sharp with tension, and his eyes are pinned to his target.

"Oh great, Mr. Wonderful's here to rescue his girl, huh?" Clifford motions to me with a drunken flip of his wrist. "Take her, dude. Won't see me puttin' up a fight."

"Ryder," Killian growls. "Get her to the Jeep."

"No." I pull free from Ryder's hold and he releases me. "I'm not leaving you. Let's go together."

He doesn't spare me a glance. "I'll be there soon, Ax. Just go."

"Yes, please"—Clifford motions with a dramatic sweep to his front door— "get the fuck out."

I grab Killian's forearm, but he rips it from me, and it's then I notice his hands are shaking.

Ryder must notice it too because he leans in close. "Killian, seriously, don't do this."

"He disrespected her."

"They're just words, Kill," I say. "I can take it."

A flash of sorrow softens his expression, nearly taking my breath away.

"But you shouldn't have to." He pushes past Ryder and me and directly into Clifford's face. "I could destroy you, right here, at your own party, in your own motherfucking living room, but you're not worth the stain you'd leave on your carpet."

"Thank God." Ryder exhales beside me and guides me away and toward the door.

"Whatever, man, just get out." Clifford tries to sound tough, but his voice wavers.

"We're gone." Killian turns to leave, but pauses and turns back. "Eh, I changed my mind."

Faster than my eyes can track, he throws a punch that knocks Clifford to his back.

The room erupts in gasps, and Killian eyeballs a few stoner guys, inviting them to be next. They sink back into the crowd, and with that, Killian turns, grabs my arm, and drags me out the door.

He's like a bull as he moves through the party, pushing people who don't move quickly enough out of his way. Ryder's on our heels, and when we get to the Jeep, Killian picks me up by the waist and puts me in it. "Where's your shit?"

"In my car."

He holds his hand out, and I drop my keys into his palm. "Stay with her." Ryder nods and Killian pulls my purse from my car, hitting the lock and alarm before stomping back.

He tosses me my purse and keys and mumbles a quick "thanks" to Ryder before climbing into the driver's side.

I share a quick look of apology with Ry. He smiles too big for my comfort just as Killian pulls away.

Killian

I snapped.

I felt the second it happened, and now that it's done, I can't pull myself back together again.

By the time I hit the front door of the house, I heard him. He'd called her a bitch, made disgusting comments about her body. What a fucking fool! To think he'd been honored with having the gates of heaven opened to him and he spat on the floor and walked away.

My muscles twitch with the fall of adrenaline. It took every ounce of my training and every sliver of my will to keep from pulverizing that douchebag. I wanted to laugh maniacally in his face and wear his gray matter on my fists like a badge of honor—oh fuck. I need to lay off the Stephen King books.

"Killian, please don't be mad at me."

"I'm not mad at you, but I fucking hate that guy. Promise me you're done with him."

"I am. I never want to see him again."

"Good. I'll go pick up your car in the morning."

"You don't have to do that." She picks at her nails. "I can pick it up myself."

"Not now, Ax. Don't do your tough-girl thing with me when I'm barely holding on to the last inch of my patience. *I'll* get your fucking car."

"Fine," she whispers. "Thank you." A few seconds pass and she fidgets in her seat. "Did you kiss her?"

I flex my hands on the steering wheel and contemplate lying. "Yes." I keep my eyes to the road.

"And . . . how was it?"

"It was . . ." *not you.* "Different."

"Hm." She shifts in her seat, and I can see in my peripheral vision that she's looking at me. "Do you like her?"

I make the left into my apartment lot, find a spot, and shut off the car before turning to face her head on. She's gazing up at me with questioning eyes, so I swallow and confess, "No."

Her lips open but then slam closed. I hop from the Jeep, and when I hear her door shut, I hit the locks. Without looking back, I climb the stairs to my apartment, hyperaware of her presence at my back. I push inside, hit the lights on, and drop my keys in the bowl.

"Make yourself at home. Grab something to sleep in." I head to the bathroom and shut and lock the door before bracing myself over the sink and staring at my reflection in the mirror.

I could've killed that guy. I've stuck up for Axelle in the past, gotten in fights to defend her, but I've never been afraid like I was tonight.

This shit between us has to stop. It's built to a level I'm no longer able to control, and if we don't clear the air between us, I could end up in prison.

My mind briefly flashes back to four years ago, the way Blake lost it on Stewart, nearly killing the guy and landing his ass behind bars. Back then I thought Blake was a psycho, totally out of control. Now I can relate.

And that thought alone is scary as shit.

I pull out my contacts and strip out of my clothes. The hot shower spray is punishing against my skin, but I welcome the burn.

I rehearse the speech I'm going to have to give when I exit this room, knowing that the next hour could change the last four years of friendship we've built. It's terrifying and liberating, and by the time I'm out and dried off, I'm eager to get it over with.

With a towel around my waist, I push out and into the studio apartment. Axelle's sitting cross-legged on my bed with a glass of water between her hands. She's wearing my black UFL tee and a pair of red boxers, her long slender legs looking as smooth as silk against my comforter.

"I'm finished if you need to get ready for bed."

Her eyes widen and slide down my chest to my abdomen and then lower to—*dammit, fuck!* My dick is half hard and more than obvious behind the thin white towel. I whirl around and give her my back.

"Thanks, I'll, uh . . ." I look over my shoulder to see her flustered and fumbling with her water glass as it splashes over the lip and onto her legs. "Oh, shit!" She scrambles off the bed. "Do that."

She scurries to the door, tripping once on her way, but I pretend not to notice and dig out some pajama pants to wear to bed. I hear the toilet flushing then the faucet running, and the door opens again just as I'm settling into a chair at my small kitchen table.

She looks between me and the bed. "Are you not tired?"

"We need to talk, and—no shit—I won't be able to concentrate if we have this conversation on the bed."

Her eyes widen, and she crosses to me with uneasy steps.

I nod to the seat in front of me. "Sit."

She lowers herself and blinks up at me with makeup free eyes, and suddenly she's sixteen again. That's the face I fell in love with, the face I'm *still* in love with.

"Killian, listen, if this is about tonight—"

"Shh, please." I close my eyes and pull together all my strength. "It's not about tonight."

She tilts her head. "Okay?"

"Axelle, I haven't exactly been honest with you."

Her eyebrows pinch and she leans away. "About what?"

I open my mouth then shut it then open it again and—

"Killian, whatever it is, just say it. You can tell me anything, you know that—"

"I'm in love with you."

She blinks.

"I know it probably seems like this is coming out of nowhere, but for me it's not. I've been in love with you since we were sixteen years old, and I keep thinking that what I feel for you will mellow and we can stay friends, but it hasn't. It . . . fuck, Ax, it's only gotten stronger."

Her eyes shine, but I can't tell if the tears are the happy or sad kind.

"Look. I don't expect anything from you. I just can't go on living like this. I can't go another day watching you give these guys your time and your body, when they don't even deserve to breathe the same air as you. And I'm not saying I do, but if you gave me a chance, God, Axelle, if it were even in the realm of possibility that you'd give me a chance, I'd show you every second of every day exactly how you deserve to be treated."

I sit back, rest my hands on my thighs, and wait as I watch her phase through a slew of emotions. My heart sinks with every second that passes and she says nothing until finally I sigh in defeat. I just poured my heart out, laid it at her feet, and she has *nothing* to say. Great.

"You've had a long night; you should get some sleep." I attempt to push back the beginning stages of a headache.

The sound of her chair legs scraping the tile brings my eyes to hers. She closes the space between us, and when her knees hit mine, she pauses. Our eyes lock and my heart pounds in my chest.

And then she blows me away by lifting one leg over my thigh and climbing on to straddle my lap.

I hiss when the warmth between her legs covers my dick. My hands instinctively grip her waist and hold her there, absorbing her heat.

Is this really happening?

Her hands slide up my shoulders to lock behind my neck, and she presses her forehead against mine. My eyes slide closed at the feeling of holding her in a way that is far from friendly. Holding her like a lover.

"Killian, no one has ever loved me the way you do." Her minty breath washes over my face, and my mouth waters to taste it. "You've always been there when I needed you." She rocks her hips against me, and the way her breath hitches from the friction between our bodies makes me groan.

"I want you, so bad, in every possible way." The words tumble from my lips in a plea.

"I want you too." She angles her head and brushes her lips against mine.

So soft, so damn sweet. Better than anything I imagined.

Her tongue traces the seam of my mouth and I pull away.

"I'm sorry. Is this too much? Too fast?" She wiggles to back off my lap, but I grip her ass and pull her back flush to me.

"No, never too much and, after four years of waiting, it's far from too fast." I run my thumb along her closed lips. "But I'm not kissing you as long as you have that metal in your tongue that you got for another guy."

Her cheeks turn the lightest shade of pink and she nods.

I press the tip of my thumb between her lips, nice and slow, mimicking the way I've dreamed of doing it with my fingers between her legs. Her breath catches, and her teeth part to welcome me in her mouth. She pulls my thumb deep with a suction that draws all the blood to the surface; the ball of her piercing toys with the pad.

"*Fuuuck.*" Blood powers through my body, making me throb.

She closes her eyes and continues to suck as I drag my thumb in and out with lazy strokes.

"You're fuckin' beautiful, baby."

She flexes her hips, and the heat between her legs intensifies.

Unable to drag this out any longer, I slide my forefinger between her lips and grip the ball of her piercing. "Open."

She slides her tongue out, and I unscrew the ball, pulling free the barbell and tossing it into the nearest trashcan. I expect her to protest, to make some remark about wanting the piercing back after we're finished here, but instead her eyes flash with understanding and acceptance.

She squeals as I stand, locking her legs around my waist. I carry her to the bed.

Laying her back, I thrust long and hard against her. I might be a virgin, but it doesn't take a genius to know how to move inside a woman.

"I'm gonna kiss you now, Axelle."

"Please," she moans.

"Everything changes after this; you sure you're ready for that?"

Her hands fist into my hair, and her body undulates beneath me. I turn my head with a muttered curse. This woman is going to kill me. And what a sweet fucking death it'll be.

"Killian?"

How long have I waited to hear my name from her lips, heavy with hunger and longing?

"Yeah, baby?"

Her gaze tangles with mine and sparkles with desire. I hold my breath, so scared she'll say something that'll end what we've started. That she'll come to her senses and realize I'm nerdy Killian McCreery from high school and be repulsed.

"I love you too."

FOURTEEN

Killian

Axelle loves me.

The words strike my chest and knock the air from my lungs. I drop my forehead to her neck and fight bursting into tears. She holds me to her, comforting me as if she's aware of the power of her confession. I whisper words of gratitude against her skin, silent praises to God for deeming me worthy of this woman and her love.

She loves me.

My lips move from praises to worshipful kisses, slowly skating up the side of her throat to her jaw. The mild hint of soap mixing with the subtle sweet scent I've come to recognize as hers alone ignites my blood. I pull the smooth skin with my lips as she pants heated breaths against my ear. Closer to her mouth, I pull away to gaze down at her. Tears shine in her eyes and burn behind mine.

With our eyes on one another, I lower my mouth to hers. The first touch of her lips is an explosion that races down my spine. I hum in satisfaction as she opens to me, my tongue delving in to glide against hers—testing then tasting and savoring.

She does the same, kissing me back with an unhurried passion, as if she's committing every new sensation to memory. She tastes like mild honey and smells like wildflowers, and my hunger to gorge myself on her pulses beneath my skin.

With my knee between her legs, I shift to her side, giving my hand full access to explore her luscious body. Her breasts strain against the baggy T-shirt as she arches off the bed, an open invitation I'm not stupid enough to decline.

My fingers quake as I slide my hand up her shirt to her belly. The first caress of her skin is a tease and too decadent to experience by touch alone. I want her on my tongue. It takes the temptation of her skin to pull me from her lips, and she whimpers when she loses my mouth.

"Shh . . ." I grin at her while shifting down her body, pressing kisses to her clavicle and breastbone. "I'm not finished with you yet."

She moans when my lips make contact with her belly button and I flick my tongue against it. How many times I've fantasized about this when she's been in a bikini, running my mouth against the gentle slope of her belly, and now here she is, offering herself to me. It's too good to be real.

Her long, slender fingers pull up her shirt, exposing her bare breasts, and I swear if I hadn't looked away I would've come right then.

"Touch me, Kill."

I smile against her skin. Hearing her call me by my nickname reminds me she knows exactly who's touching her, she's not in some fantasy pretending I'm someone else, and she's begging.

Me.

I cup her breast and circle her nipple with my thumb. It hardens and my dick responds in kind. I do the same to the other breast until a trail of goose bumps skitters across each one.

"Gorgeous, baby." I pluck gently at her nipples, and her legs shift restlessly on the bed. "So fucking beautiful."

I dip down and pepper her breasts with kisses before sucking her nipple deep into my mouth. Her hips jack off the bed, and I hum against her in approval. I'm drunk on every whimper that falls from her lips as I continue to shower her with attention.

She writhes beneath me and rakes her fingernails across my shoulders and back. The sting of her impatience sends me to her lips, where I take her in a brutal kiss. Passion unleashes from within, and my restraint drowns in my desire for more.

She digs her heels into the bed and her knees fall open. I slide my hand between her legs, cupping her over my boxers. The thin cotton fabric is wet and my head nearly explodes.

I rub her into a frenzy, nice and slow then hard and fast, and when she's on the brink of coming, I slip two fingers through the flap and—*oh fuck*. She's silken heat and hungry. I'm never gonna make it.

"Yes, don't stop. I'm close." She grips my head and pulls my lips to hers, thrusting her tongue into my mouth and shattering my restraint.

"You're so fucking hot, Ax. From the first day I met you, I've wanted to do this to you." I share my darkest secrets against her lips between kisses. "I've imagined what it would be like to feel your mouth on mine: how many times we've been at the pool and I've wanted to pull your top aside and taste you."

"Yes, don't stop. Tell me more." Her breath hitches.

"I've touched myself thinking about your lips." I suck on her bottom lip, biting gently before soothing the ache with my tongue. "Fantasized about feeling them all over me."

Her hips meet the demands of my thrust. She's close. So damn close.

"I've wanted this for so long." I slide my fingers from her body. "Can't wait another second."

I rip the boxers to her ankles and toss them to the floor. Without a hint of finesse, I position myself between her legs and wrench her thighs apart. I try to be gentle, but I'm too far gone and I devour her.

Her head slams back against the pillow while her fists tighten into the comforter. I lick and suck from her tender flesh, so desperate to drink her in, to take whatever she gives. Every new sound is a symphony of lusty responses I commit to memory. My mouth commands every whimper, every groan. She cries out my name, and the guttural sound raises goose bumps on my skin. When she comes down, she doesn't push me away as I continue to tenderly kiss between her legs.

"You're going to get so sick of hearing this, but you're spectacular. I always imagined what being with you like this would be like, and that . . ." I shake my head and press a kiss to her inner thigh. "That was unbelievable."

She smiles shyly, her cheeks flushed, and holds her hands out to me. "Come here."

I push up and her eyes widen at the rocket that's punching through my sweatpants. I reach down and make an adjustment, resisting the urge to jack off when she bites her lip, staring at it. "If you keep that up I'm going to have to take matters into my own hands."

She pushes up to her knees, my tee falling over her naked body, which only makes me hungry to strip her bare. She crawls to the end of the bed and pulls herself up against me.

Kissing my neck, she smiles. "As much as I'd love to see you take matters into your own hands? I'd rather take matters into mine."

I suck in a shaky breath as she kisses down my throat to my chest, across my pecs, then lower to— "Axelle, baby . . ." I hook her chin and bring her face back to eye level. "I want that, you know I do, but on my long list of things I want to do with you, that's not number one."

She cocks a head and lifts a brow. "Oh yeah?"

I run her soft hair through my fingers. "Yeah."

"I believe I heard part of your list earlier."

I press a kiss to her lips. "Mm-hm."

"So, what did I miss?" She's grinning and playful, but her smile falls when I cup her face and look straight into her eyes.

"Let me make love to you."

Her eyes widen and her lips part. "But you're a virgin. I mean are you sure you want it to be me?"

Even after everything we've done, after all my confessions, my cheeks still heat with embarrassment. "Who do you think I've been saving it for?"

Her eyes fill with tears. "But you know I'm not a virgin, and you deserve—"

"It's always been yours, Axelle. It's just been hanging around waiting for you to take it. So, will you?"

A brilliant smile pulls her lips and she nods. "Yes, as long as you're sure."

"Never been surer of anything my entire life."

~~~

I wish I could say I went into losing my virginity like a champ. That I Rico-Suaved my way to bed, threw down my v-card with a "Bam!" and dropped the mic.

But as I stand there staring into the beautiful blue eyes of the only girl I've ever loved, only one thought powers through my thick skull.

Condoms.

I don't have any damn condoms.

It's like finding the Holy Grail then discovering it's too heavy to carry. Or having someone hand you the formula to cure cancer, but it's written in a dead language no one can understand. Or discovering you are motherfucking Superman at the same time you're diagnosed with extreme acrophobia!

Axelle's lips are on my neck and her hands dip beneath the waistband of my flannel pants.

I grip her wrists. "Whoa . . . hold on."

My heart is racing and my blood pumping so furiously I might fucking pass out with excitement.

She pulls back and eyes me with concern. "Why are you stopping me?"

"I don't have any condoms." I run a hand through my hair and groan. "I'm sorry. I just never thought this would happen, at least, not so soon, and I'm totally unprepared."

"No worries." She shrugs. "I have some."

Total. Fucking. Boner-kill.

I'm well aware of the men that Axelle has shared a bed with, more aware than I'd like to be, but that doesn't mean the reminder of those men doesn't make me want to punch something or someone, specifically one of the motherfuckers who she's carrying around condoms in her purse for.

She hops off the bed, and I watch her long legs as she moves to her bag. "Should be in here somewhere," she mumbles. "Ah-ha!" She whirls around and holds up a strip of gold-foiled condoms.

"Great."

Her grin falls and she looks between me and the big-fat fuck-you she's holding. "Hey . . ." She crosses to me and tosses the condoms on the bed before wrapping her arms around my waist. "It's just us in this room, okay? Please, don't let my mistakes change the way you feel about me right now. I . . ." She sighs and holds me tighter. "I have my own regrets. I've made so many mistakes. Don't let someone like Clifford—"

"Please, don't say his name."

"—ruin this for us."

"You're right." I rub her back and hold her close. "I'm being a little bitch."

She giggles and tilts her head back. "You said it, not me."

I grin, but it's slight, desire to pick up where we left off dissolving any hint of humor. "You have no idea how long I've waited for you."

"I'm sorry it took me so long." She pushes up on her tiptoes and kisses me with all the passion of a woman in love.

I fist my hands in her hair, and she slides her hands down the back of my pants, her nails dragging along my ass as she pushes the flannel to my ankles. I step out of them while walking her backwards to the bed. When her legs hit the mattress, I reach down and pull her tee off. Her dark hair falls in panels down her chest and over her breasts.

A small voice inside keeps reminding me this is Axelle, the girl I've dreamed about for all those years, the only girl who's starred in every single fantasy I've had since I was sixteen years old. And now she's here, in the flesh, and putting every fantasy I've ever had to shame.

We kiss until we're breathless, hands roaming each other's bodies, not leaving a single inch undiscovered. She grows heavier in my arms as her legs weaken. I scoop her from her feet and lay her down on the bed, her long strong body laid out before me in wanting.

I kiss her breasts, her stomach, her thighs, the backs of her knees, worshipping her with gratitude for all she's giving me.

Crawling up her body, I fork my fingers in her hair and kiss her as if this will be the last time. Her hand travels down my ribs, leaving goose bumps in its wake, and then she touches me. She grabs my dick in her tight fist, and I groan as the tingling sensation shoots up my spine. Her hand moves back and forth, priming me unnecessarily. I've been ready for this for years. I bite her lip and she gasps, releasing me.

I reach for the condoms and rip one off with my teeth.

A sultry grin pulls at her puffy lips, and she takes the condom. "Allow me."

I bury my face in her neck, kissing her while she goes to work. My hips jerk when her fingers brush against me, sheathing me in latex.

Her legs open wide, cradling my hips between them, and her heat is right there. "Killian, promise me you won't regret this. I've never been anyone's first, and I'm so afraid you'll end up hating me for it."

With my elbows bracing my weight, I run my thumbs along her jawline. "You're wrong, Ax. You say you've never been anyone's first." I lean down and drag my lips against hers. "But you're mine." She moans as I rock my hips, rubbing against her. "You've always been mine."

I push tentatively forward, sinking into the heat of her body and grinding my teeth against the gripping pressure as it engulfs me. Inch-by-inch I slide forward until we're fully connected. Tingles spread from my spine to coil between my legs, and the sensation is pure ecstasy.

She bites her bottom lip and arches her back. "You feel so good like we were made to fit together."

"We were, baby." I kiss her gently and move with deliberate strokes. "That's what I've been trying to tell you."

Her legs lock behind my thighs, pulling me deeper. "I love you."

"Fuck." I drop my lips to her neck. "I love you too, so much."

"This is really happening? Us, I mean?" Her voice is so soft, almost scared, as it tickles my ear.

"It's happening. You and me? This is as real as it gets."

Her breathy moans and writhing make it impossible to continue at this lazy pace. I push up on my hands and look down her flat belly to watch the beauty of our bodies connected.

This isn't fucking or even making love. This is something altogether different—bigger and more intense than anything I could've ever imagined. My control wavers and baser instincts roar to claim, to mark, and to possess.

I rear back and slam myself forward.

Her nails grip into my shoulders, and I moan as the pleasure-pain rips through my body. "That's it. Hold on."

I continue my heated and hurried pace, watching as every response plays seductively across her face. Her eyelids are low, lips parted, and she fists my hair as if she'll rip it from its roots. "Don't stop."

"Never." I rock into her again and again, setting an unstoppable rhythm. Tension builds, climbing higher. I grit my teeth and hold it back.

Her legs wrap around my waist. "Kill . . ." she cries out her release. I dip down and plunge my tongue into her mouth as her body pulses around me, tossing me into an orgasm that makes me see stars. She whimpers and swallows my answering growl as we coax each other back from the aftermath of total combustion.

Her body turns to jelly beneath me, and I allow myself to drop my weight on top of her for a few seconds. When I move to roll off of her, she shocks me by wrapping me up in her legs and arms. Even her head comes off the pillow to nuzzle my neck.

"I knew it would be beautiful with you," I whisper against her hair. "Had no idea it would be *that* beautiful though."

She drops back to the bed with a sated smile that I feel in my chest. "If I had any idea things would be this good between us, I would've told you how I felt about you sooner."

I blink and roll to her side. "Wait. You've had feelings for me? Since when?"

"Since I asked you to the Valentine's Day Dance." She covers her face with a hand. "Why is this embarrassing?"

I pull her hand away. "I thought you asked me because we were friends."

"That too, but I guess I was hoping for more."

A flicker of annoyance dowses my post-orgasm haze. "Why didn't you tell me?" To think how much time we wasted, how many assholes I had to stand by and watch work their way through her.

"After that night, Stewart showing up and"—she sucks in a shuttering breath and then lets it out— "all that, I wasn't in the best place emotionally. By the time I finally got around to considering dating, I realized you treated me differently. You were, I don't know, more friendly, almost parental."

I wrinkle my nose at the imagery. From friend to parent. No wonder nothing has ever happened between us.

"I assumed you saw me the way I see myself: broken, messed up, desperate. You're so together, Killian. You deserve someone more . . . like you."

I study the wall across the room for a second then look down at her. "Stewart is an unforgivable asshole. What you went through . . . I wanted to protect you from ever having to go through that again. I guess in looking out for you I may have lost focus when it came to dating you. But I never saw you, and still don't see you, as the person you're describing."

She plays with the hair at my nape. "Don't get me wrong. I know you cared about me, but after that night, it's like something died between us."

"What do you think that was?"

"I don't know." She shrugs. "Hope maybe?"

"You gotta know that was one-sided, Ax. I never gave up hope in us. I'll take responsibility for backing off you a bit, but after that night, you were so weak. I would've been an asshole to pursue more than friendship with you. I should've spoken up sooner, but I'm still not sure you're ready for what I want with you. I'm so afraid that, now that my feelings are on the table, you'll find your piece of this life, grab on with two hands, and have no need for me. I knew that if I wanted a chance with you, if I really wanted a shot at making you happy, I'd have to time it perfectly."

"So I guess Valentine's Day exactly four years later was the perfect time."

"Is it?" I dip down and kiss her. "I want this night to be the start of making new memories, replacing the old. But only if you're ready."

Her dark brows pinch together. "Why wouldn't I be?"

My muscles tense. "Up until a few hours ago, you were with someone else, Ax."

Her body tenses. "I don't love him. I never did love him. With you, it's different."

How I hope she's right.

"Mmm." I breathe in the scent of her skin while kissing her collarbone.

She yawns long and hard then snuggles deep into my chest. "This is going to be great, okay? Us? We're going to be amazing."

I squeeze her close. "Or die trying." I drop a kiss on the top of her head, thinking that nothing has ever felt more right than holding her naked against me while she finds rest. "Go to bed, baby."

She yawns. "I love you, Kill."

I grin into the dark, so big and wide it hurts my cheeks. "Love you too, Ax."

FIFTEEN

Axelle

The sun reaches through the window, stirring me awake. I'm warm and sunk deeply into the biggest comforter ever when I hear the sound of breathing at my back.

I roll over to find Killian, completely naked, and flat on his back. He managed to push the covers down so they only come up to mid-thigh. I grin and greedily take in his muscled frame, wide shoulders, thick arms, and a powerful chest that tapers to his six-pack abdomen and narrow hips. My eyes widen when I study what's between those hips. I blink, amazed at how gorgeous he is and marveling at what happened between us.

He loves me.

This intelligent, kind, and gorgeous man loves *me*.

I suppose I should've seen it sooner. He's been on the front lines of every major event in my life, which is exactly why I thought he'd never be interested in me. I've broken down and shown him my ugly side more times than I can count. He's let me cry and curse him to hell and back, accepting the punishment for all the people who've truly deserved it.

My stomach sinks with guilt, and for a moment, it feels wrong being in his arms. Like I'm taking so much more than I deserve.

I turn away from him and bite my lip to keep from crying. Great, Axelle. In case you haven't already proved it, drive home your psycho by crying in his bed.

He shifts behind me, like he's stretching, and then freezes for a second. I hold my breath, terrified of what he might be thinking and how he'll respond now that all our confessions lie bare in the light of day.

Then he moves.

The heat of his body pushes up flush to my back, and his arm snakes around my waist. He presses kisses as soft as butterfly wings to my jaw and whispers, "So it wasn't a dream."

My chest cramps at the awe in his voice. I squeeze my eyes closed.

He drops his head back to the pillow and makes a sound of contentment. "Where are you at?"

I cover his hand that's splayed over my belly with my own. "I'm right here; thought that was pretty obvious."

He kisses the top of my head. "That's not what I meant. Where are you at with *us*?"

I roll over to face him, tangling my bare legs with his. His eyes shine with wonder and curiosity. Framed with thick black lashes, the view practically stops my heart. "I'm right here, Kill. I'm not going anywhere."

His lips twitch as if he's fighting a smile, and soon he loses the battle and flashes his brilliant white teeth. "Yeah?"

I laugh and bury my face into his chest. "Yeah, it's crazy, right? It's like this is where we're supposed to be." *However unworthy I feel.*

His arms come around me and pull me flush to him. His hard-on wedges between my thighs, but he doesn't make a move to do more than simply hold me. "I wish I could lie like this with you all day. Shut out the world and keep you as my naked hostage."

"Mmm, that sounds nice."

"How about this weekend? We could rent movies and stay in bed all day."

I peer up at him and imagine spending two whole days naked with Killian and nod frantically.

He laughs low and throaty, the vibration of it against my skin awakening my desire. "Good. Now, I have an econ quiz in an hour and fifteen minutes, so as much as I'd love to move this morning along slowly, I'm afraid I can't."

I sigh and press my cheek to his chest. "I have to get my car and get home too. I have a ten-thirty class."

His hands run up and down my back in lazy strokes. "I'll hop in the shower; you get dressed. I'll drop you at your car on my way to class."

I run my lips along his pec, the feel like velvet over steel against my mouth. "Deal."

"We break on three. One . . ." He squeezes me tighter. "Two . . ." He kisses my head. "Three!" He slaps my ass, and I yelp as he jumps out of bed and dashes to the bathroom.

It suddenly hits me that I'm going to be seeing him between classes today, and the excitement of being seen together makes my stomach flip. I roll to my back and press my palm to my belly. "Calm down, Axelle," I whisper to myself. "This is nothing to make yourself sick over."

The shower turns on, and I contemplate heading in there to offer Killian some assistance, but decide that would only make us both late for class. As seriously as he takes his studies, it would be bitchy of me to interfere with his perfect GPA.

So I drag my ass out of bed and pull on the UFL shirt of Kill's I wore last night before he stripped it off me. I bite my lip as memories flood in, his big body moving above me, within me, consuming me. A ripple of need flip-flops in my belly, and the thought that I was his first makes me feel like the luckiest girl in the world.

I tug on my pants from last night, pull a ponytail holder from my purse, and finger-comb my hair into a messy bun. When the shower turns off, I'm making the bed, and when Killian strolls out wearing nothing but a towel around his waist, my mouth goes dry.

He seems totally oblivious to my gawking as he digs through his closet, pulling out clothes and tossing them to the bed. Droplets of water hang to the ends of his chocolate brown hair, some falling loose and gliding down his muscled back. His skin is tan from hours in the sun, unblemished and soft to the touch.

I cross to him and sneak up from behind, wrapping my arms around him and gripping the towel at his waist. "Can I help?"

He sucks in a breath and drops his head forward. "Whatever you want."

I know we're pressed for time, so I can't do *whatever* I want, but I can satisfy some of my craving for him.

I pull the towel from his hips and toss it to the floor. His breathing speeds up. His skin is hot and smells like spicy man soap. I run my nose along his back, inhaling deep, and he shivers. I allow my hands to explore his rippled abdomen, which flexes under my touch. As much as I want to go lower, I know that will put us right back in bed, so I hold him to me, pressing my chest to his back. His hands come to mine in a silent acceptance, and for a moment, we just stand there until our breath is synchronized.

Reluctantly, I let go and step around him, my gaze drawn to the powerful erection standing proudly between his legs. I swallow hard and walk him back to the bed. He drops to sit, a mix of interest and excitement on his face.

"Don't worry. I know we have to get going." I reach for the clean boxer briefs he tossed to the bed and kneel between his feet then slide the soft cotton up his legs to his thighs. Sexual tension strings tightly between us as I reach for his shorts and do the same, the simple act of dressing him somehow just as erotic as undressing him. Finally, I grab his shirt and slide it over his head. He closes his eyes as if he's absorbing the tenderness of being taken care of.

"Stand up." I'm surprised how much my voice shakes, giving away my nerves. It's just . . . this is Killian, *my* Killian.

He complies and I pull his boxer briefs and shorts up, blushing when I struggle to tuck all that is him behind his clothes. I drag his zipper up slowly, and when he's finally dressed, he pulls me into a hug so tight it takes my breath away.

"Thank you. Never thought having you put my clothes *on* would be that hot."

"I was thinking the same thing." My cheeks heat, and I'm glad he can't see my face as I'm sure it's embarrassingly red. "You take such good care of me; you deserve to be taken care of too."

He rubs my back reassuringly. "I appreciate that, Ax, but I do that because I want to. Don't feel like you owe me shit."

But I do. I owe him more than I could repay in a lifetime. "We better get going." I pull away and read what's written on his shirt. "What's *The Overlook Hotel*?"

He plucks at it with his long thick fingers, looking down at it, then swings an amused gaze back to me. "Seriously? You don't know?"

"If I knew, why would I ask?"

"*The Shining*?"

"The movie?"

He rolls his eyes and steps close, tugging my messy bun back so my mouth lifts to his. He kisses me softly, his peppermint breath ghosting against my lips. "No, baby, not the movie. The *book*. Stephen King?" Another kiss and he whispers, "I'll read it to you if you want."

My stomach clenches. "Is it scary like the movie?"

"Scarier." He smiles and it's lazy and crooked and so damn sexy. "Now stop being so sweet so I can drop you off and go ace my quiz, alright?"

"Okay." I pull away and grab my things, already missing Killian, even though I'll be seeing him in a couple of hours.

~~~

My stomach is in knots as I sit in the quad, waiting for Killian's class to let out. I've picked the last of my black nail polish off and pulled a loose thread from my sweater, which I'm now wrapping and unwrapping obsessively around my forefinger.

I mentally shake myself for the nerves. This is Killian, my best friend, who I'm totally in love with and deflowered twelve hours ago. I lick my lips, trying and failing to hold back a ridiculously wide grin. I can't believe this is happening, and more importantly, I can't believe how excited I am that this is happening.

"Ugh." Mindy drops down hard beside me at the table, her backpack falling unceremoniously to the concrete and her face lifting to the sky. "Why am I here? I'm so hung over."

"A wise woman once told me that some of the best nights are followed by the worst days." Her hair is pulled back in a ponytail, but I can tell it's still sporting the curls and hairspray from last night. "Maybe a shower would've helped."

"Woke up too late." She pulls a water bottle from her bag, takes a small sip, and cringes. "Everything still tastes like tequila."

"Ah . . . tequila. The romance liquor."

She grips her head, massaging her temples. "Don't say it. I can taste it when you say it." Her head lulls to the side, her oversized sunglasses fixing on me. "What the hell are you smiling for?"

"I'm not smiling." I so am; I can't help it. After last night, everything seems . . . happier.

She rakes her shades up on her head and squints. "The hell you're not." She drops her sunglasses back down with a groan. "You and Clifford get busy last night?"

"Gross." Okay, maybe not *everything* is happier. "Not even close. We broke up."

Her eyebrows pop up over her shades. "No kidding?"

"He was such an asshole last night." Classroom doors open, signaling the end of this class hour. I don't want to get into the Clifford story when Killian should be here soon. "I'll tell you about it later."

"That's probably best." She groans. "I think I'm still drunk, so I'd probably forget if you told me now anyway."

I search the flood of students as they all swarm the quad, grateful that Killian's taller than the average guy so I'll be able to find him easily.

The first thing I notice is his white baseball hat with the bold letters UFL in red on the front. He's not actively searching for me, but his head isn't down either. He's strutting with a casual confidence that probably isn't even obvious to anyone but me. My heart bangs behind my ribs as he approaches. I push up from my seat, and before I'm even fully aware of what I'm doing, I'm speed-walking toward him.

The second his gaze lands on me he grins in this tilted, shy way that speeds my walk to a jog. His smile widens, and when I jump and launch myself into his arms, he catches me without fail.

Long bands of muscle coil around me, lifting me off the ground. I throw my arms around his neck and nuzzle his throat. His skin is warm and smells like his spicy cologne. I drop secret kisses there. He moans and holds me tighter.

"I missed you," I whisper.

He chuckles and the vibration against my lips is heady. "I can see that."

I pull away, and he places my feet back on the ground as if I'm made of glass. I grin up at him, and he leans in, pressing his lips to mine. All the heat from this morning flares back to life at the firm touch of his lips. I dig my fingers into the muscles of his neck, and his hands cup my jaw, tilting as he slides his tongue against mine. My leg itches to lift and wrap around his hip, to rub against him like an animal. He must sense my urgency, and his fingers sift into my hair, gripping at the roots as the kiss turns demanding.

"Damn, that's hot." The voice of a girl passing by slams us back to reality, and the world around us that had dissolved the second we touched comes back in vivid clarity.

He presses soft kisses to the corners of my mouth and keeps his hold in my hair. His eyelids are lazy and blink slowly open. "I thought PDA wasn't your thing."

I'm breathing heavily, willing my pulse to calm and my thighs to stop quivering. "I don't mind it so much when it's with you."

His lips pull into a beautiful smile, and he turns me to tuck me under his arm. That kiss sapping me of strength and coordination, I lean on him for support as he guides me back to the table.

Mindy's sitting up in her seat, her back not even touching the chair and her lips parted.

"Hey, Mindy." Killian drops his backpack next to mine.

She says nothing.

He looks between us, confusion pinching his dark brows. "She okay?"

I hold him to me with my arm around his lower back, the dips of his muscles and the memory of them flexing as he made love to me last night sending an army of butterflies loose in my stomach. "She's fine, just a little hung over from last night."

"Too bad." He squeezes me. "I'm going to grab a sandwich." He kisses the top of my head. "You want anything?"

"No, I'm good." I release him and take my seat.

He peers down at me, those gorgeous eyes flashing with concern. "You feeling okay?"

"Yeah, why?"

He tilts his head. "Did you eat breakfast?"

"I had a piece of toast, Killian. I'm fine." As much as I love that he cares, his concern is often overdone and pointless.

"It's after twelve. You need more calories or your body is going to cannibalize itself. It'll eat any muscle you have and—"

"Stop." I hold my hand up. "I've heard the speech before. My stomach's been off for the last few days, and it's messing with my appetite." I shrug. "As soon as it comes back, I'll eat."

He doesn't look convinced, but thankfully lets me off the hook. "Mindy? How 'bout a Gatorade?"

Her eyes continue to move between Killian and me.

He grins, like me, interpreting her silence for shock. "I'll take that as a yes."

He heads toward the café, and I enjoy the view of his muscled backside as it moves beneath his shorts. I've checked his body out before when we were just friends, but it always made me feel dirty to do so. Now I stare unabashedly because I have every right to gawk at my handsome boyfriend.

Boyfriend.

That's what he is, I think.

We never officially discussed it, but a confession of love from both parties I think is self-explanatory. I make a mental note to bring it up later when we're alone. That is, if we can keep our mouths off each other long enough to talk.

"You and Killian." The sound of Mindy whispering calls my eyes to her. She's shaking her head slowly. "I can't believe I didn't see this coming."

"Yeah." I try to force some maturity into my voice rather than squealing like a teenager at a Bieber concert.

She swivels her body toward me and leans in. "He porno-kissed you in front of the entire school."

I cringe. "Porno kiss?"

"Hell, yeah, it made me horny just watching, and I'm fighting puking, so that's saying a lot."

She's not the only one. Killian's lips are smooth and strong, and the guy knows how to use them. Every time he kisses me it's like he's making love to my mouth.

"I don't judge, you know that, but has this been going on for a while?"

"No, we've been best friends for years, but our first kiss was last night. I think on some level I've always loved him, and it seems he feels the same."

She slumps back in her seat and smiles. "I'm so jealous. But lucky for you, I love you, so I'm happier for you guys than I am jealous."

I laugh. "Thank you . . . I think?"

"You guys make a great couple, and the chemistry . . ." She fans herself with her hand. "I foresee some epic sex sessions in your future."

A lemon-lime Gatorade is placed on the table between us, and mortification stiffens my spine.

"I hope you told her about us and that Mindy's not foreseeing you having epic sex sessions with someone else." Killian's voice is laced with humor, but the edge in it reminds me of the times I've seen his protective temper flare.

I peer up at him and he scowls as he hands me a granola bar. "Give it a shot, yeah?"

I take it and nibble on the tasteless bark to make him happy. "Mindy was just commenting on our 'porno kiss.'"

He unwraps his sandwich. "What does that mean exactly?"

"It means"—Mindy wrestles with opening the Gatorade until Killian pulls it from her hands and easily cracks the lid before handing it back to her— "that you guys almost risked turning the UNLV quad into an orgy with the heat coming off that kiss, that's what!" She throws back a healthy gulp of the yellow fluid and smacks her lips.

He winks at me. "Can't argue that."

My stomach tumbles, and I'm suddenly desperate to get Killian alone where we can enjoy each other in a more comfortable environment, like his bed.

Preferably naked.

Although the way his T-shirt is stretched taut against his biceps I'd be willing to make an exception and allow him to keep the shirt on.

He leans over and places a soft kiss on my cheek then moves his lips to my ear. "If you want me to be able to get up and walk away from this table without embarrassing myself, you'll stop fucking me with those eyes." He nips at my ear.

The combination of his hot breath, his hot words, and the hot as hell way he bit me, flushes my cheeks.

He chuckles and shakes his head.

"You guys make me sick." Mindy grabs her backpack, and with all the grace of someone who very well could still be drunk, pulls it on and pushes herself to stand. "I'm skipping a class to go home and sleep this off."

"You okay to drive?" The concern in Killian's voice for my roommate makes me fall a little deeper.

"Where were you at eight o'clock this morning when I was staggering to class, huh?" She squeezes his shoulder as she passes. "I'm fine now. Thanks." Her eyes get dreamy and she mouths *he's so sweet*.

He's looking right at me, so I can't respond other than to simply smile. "I'll see you later. Text me if you need me to bring you something. I can grab it on my way home."

She waves her fingers and leaves.

I take another bird-sized bite of my granola bar and watch the muscles in Killian's jaw flex and release as he chews. I've been watching him like this for four years and never thought I was deserving of anything more with him. Not after the night he learned I was the daughter of a rapist.

I know our past doesn't dictate who we are, but I've been so locked up emotionally I didn't even entertain the idea of seeking a meaningful relationship with anyone. I guess that's why I allowed myself to be with Clifford. He treated me the way I expected, in a way I found familiar. To him I was replaceable, and on some level, I think I tried to earn a higher status with him just to prove that I wasn't. Some desperate part of me thought by earning that with Clifford meant I could make up for not getting it when I was a kid.

"See? I knew you could do it." Killian's staring at the empty granola bar wrapper in my hand.

Guess being lost in my thoughts made me forget I had no appetite. I toss the wrapper to the table and take a swig of Killian's water bottle to wash it down.

He gazes across the table at me thoughtfully. "I want you to stay with me tonight."

"Okay."

His eyebrows pop up. "That was easy."

"Did you really think I'd say no?"

"I hoped you wouldn't, but I wasn't sure." He leans forward and takes my hand, pressing my knuckles to his lips. "Can you believe this is really happening?"

"I wonder how many times we'll ask each other that before we finally start believing it?"

He blinks, his finger tracing the underside of my wrist. "It's unreal."

"You know we're going to have to tell my mom and Blake." I laugh. "They're going to love this. I think they've been secretly praying we'd end up together."

His expression is suddenly serious. "They're not the only ones."

My pulse skitters as he presses another kiss to my knuckles, followed by another, his lips parting slightly and leaving the moisture of his mouth against my skin. It's so innocent, gentlemanly, and strangely erotic.

"So you finally fucked her, huh?"

I gasp as Clifford's voice slices through our moment. The only satisfaction I get is seeing the once narrow bridge of the jerk's nose swollen black and blue from last night.

I expect Killian to jump up and get into Clifford's face, but instead he grins and leans back casually in his chair, keeping my hand in his. He squeezes it gently, a reminder that he'll handle this and everything will be okay. "Nothing could ruin this day for me, not even an asshole like you."

Clifford grins, but it's far from friendly. "I understand. That pussy is fucking gold once she finally gives it up."

Killian's posture remains casual, but his grip on me tightens and his jaw ticks.

Clifford's cold gray eyes latch on mine. "Funny thing, she only made me wait days." He swings his glare to Killian. "She withheld her body from you for years."

"Fuck off, Clifford." I grit my teeth, resisting the urge to vault over the table and tackle him to the ground.

"Yes," Killian draws out the word like he's bored, but his grip says he's far from it. "Please, fuck off, Clifford." He pulls my hand to his lips, kissing the underside of my wrist.

My ex shrugs one shoulder then darts his gaze between us. "One thing." He tosses a stack of photos onto the table and grins so wickedly I'd swear his teeth were pointed. "You forgot these at my place."

I lean over the photos, and at first, all I can make out is skin until— "Oh my God!" I rip my hand from Killian's and scramble to collect the pictures from the table.

A shadow falls over me as Killian stands to his full height. I clutch the photos to my chest as he rounds the table with the speed and composure of a predator stalking his prey. He pushes close to Clifford, nose-to-nose, and tilts his head to look right into the cocksucker's eyes.

"This ends now."

"Says who?" Clifford clearly doesn't know when to keep his mouth shut as Kill steps impossibly closer, ignoring the idiotic question.

"Don't fool yourself into believing you can take me, Cliff, because I'm twice your size and you know I'd destroy you." He taps Clifford's nose with his finger, making the guy hiss in pain. "Think I already taught you that lesson last night, but I'd be more than fucking happy to give you a recap."

One of Clifford's friends, who I didn't notice until now, tugs at his elbow. "Security's watching, man. Come on."

For once Clifford seems to use his reasoning and turns away, but stops mid-step to whirl around and face me. He eyes the photos pressed to my chest. "There's more where those came from."

Killian shoves Clifford, making him stumble, but he recovers with a laugh and walks away.

My vision blurs with tears of humiliation. Killian spins to face me, his expression a mix of torment and, if I'm not mistaken, disappointment.

He pries the photos from my chest, but I refuse to let them go. I want him to continue to believe I'm good enough for him, and these photos are more evidence that I am not. In the tug-of-war, a couple fall to the ground where he scoops them up. He peers down at them before I can get them back.

"That sick fuck," he mumbles.

My entire body heats and I snag the photos from him, pressing them tightly to my chest with the others.

"Ax, give those to me. I'll make them disappear."

I shake my head. "No."

"What do you mean no?"

"I don't want . . ." *you to see them.* "I can do it."

He stares at me for a few weighted seconds before grabbing my backpack and slinging it over his shoulder; then he does the same with his. "Come on. We're gonna be late for class."

"Wait."

He glares at me then growls. "We're gonna be late."

I hold out my hand. "I can carry my backpack."

"What?" He grips my hand and tugs me away from the café. "I'll walk you to class."

I dig my heels in and pull my hand from his. "Killian, stop!"

"What's the matter with you?"

"Give me my backpack!"

He huffs and reluctantly slides it off his shoulder and hands it to me. I take it and stash the photos inside it before I slip on both straps and peer up at him. His face is etched in confusion. "You can't keep cleaning up my messes, Kill."

His cheek throbs with restraint, and I wonder what he's calling me in his head, wonder if he's regretting everything that's happened between us. I wait to hear the words, "You two are perfect for each other" or some other reprimand for the photos. Tears burn my eyes, and when one slides down my cheek, Killian's entire demeanor changes.

He steps in close; the warmth of his arms envelop me. "Don't waste another tear on that prick, Ax."

Comfort, I can accept. But he needs to stop trying to fix everything for me.

I relax into his hold and allow my feelings about the photos to leech out of me. "I was . . . so stupid. Clifford swore he'd erase them right after he took them."

I hold him to me and remember his words from last night, his fear about me not being ready for all he wants for us. In order for things to work, he's going to have to allow me to work things out on my own rather than stampeding me and taking over. Just like everyone else in my life.

"He lied. No shocker there."

I pull back and blink up at him. "That's true. I should've seen this coming."

"Don't beat yourself up; this isn't your fault." Killian wipes under my eyes. "Hate the fact that he has these. He's probably passing them around to all his friends—"

"Oh my God!"

"Shit." He grimaces. "I shouldn't have said that."

"You think he has more?"

He shrugs. "Nah, and besides, what's done is done. If I find out he's sharing these, I'll fucking mutilate him." He dries my new tears and takes my hand. "Come on. We're going to be late."

I walk alongside him. "What should I do with these pictures?"

"Burn 'em, shred 'em, bury 'em. You pick."

My heart sinks as I consider how quickly my good mood was turned to shit. And now I have to worry about finding naked photos of me all over campus.

This day just went to hell.

SIXTEEN

Killian

Shredded. Double-bagged. They're shoved to the bottom of her garbage and then thrown in the dumpster outside of her apartment complex, but I'm still sick about those photos of Axelle.

My girl's naked body is being shared with who-fucking-knows-who, and yeah, she may have only *officially* become my girl last night, but to me she's been my girl since day one.

She's dated some real winners in the past, but none of them have pulled a bullshit stunt like this. Clifford is a grade-A morally deprived piece of shit, and I'll do everything in my power to keep him away from her.

I channel my frustration into every hit as I dance around the heavy bag. I'd usually spar with Rex today, but Cameron called him in for an emergency meeting. My guess is they're planning the trip to London. It didn't take long after I passed on the opportunity for them to fill the spot with a fighter out of Chicago. He's making a name for himself up there, has some fights under his belt with a small organization, and just signed with the UFL.

I throw a combo to the bag, pushing back a wave of envy. He might have the dream career opportunity, but I got the dream girl. Besides, opportunities can be made. I plan on working hard to force open doors so that I'm able to provide Axelle with the life she deserves.

She doesn't know it yet, but that's the direction I'm heading—white dress, church bells, house, cars, kids, a fucking dog—all of it.

Feeling eyes on me, I grip the bag to keep it still and turn to find Blake glaring. Shit. Does he know about Axelle?

I wipe sweat from my eyes with my forearm, which proves pointless because my forearm is just as sweaty. "Blake? What's up?"

He takes a couple of steps toward me, and it's all I can do to not double-step back to keep distance between us. I give myself a mental high-five for standing my ground when he stops just a foot or so before me. "What. In the *motherfuck*. Is wrong with you?"

"I . . ." have no idea what that could possibly mean. If he found out I'm in love with his daughter, would he ask me this in response? Probably not. "Don't know?"

"You don't know." He lifts his eyebrows as if that's a question, and I'm completely lost on how to answer.

My eyes wander around as if they're desperately seeking guidance or possibly another fighter just in case whatever is simmering below Blake's surface explodes all over me. "Did I do something wrong?"

"Do something *wrong*?" He drops his gaze and shakes his head before he pins me with a glare. "You sure fucking did." He tilts his head, those arms crossing at his chest and emphasizing his size. "Explain to me why you're not going to be on a plane to motherfucking London with Rex day after tomorrow."

I exhale long and hard and run a hand through my hair, which is so damp with sweat it sticks out on all ends. "I know it seems like I'm passing up something huge, but—"

"Nope." He frowns. "It doesn't *seem* like you're passing up something huge. You are."

"Okay, I'm passing up something huge, but I have a plan, and in order to see that plan play out, I have to stay in Vegas and finish school."

His eyes widen as if I just told him chickens fly out of my ass. "One year, Killer. No one's asking you to change the course of your life; it's one fucking year."

"I realize that, but it's an important year."

His eyes narrow. "Important how?"

I'm in love with your daughter, and she's finally given me a chance. There's no way in hell now that I finally got her I'm going to leave her for a year!

I rip my gloves off and sigh. "Listen. You'll understand soon enough, okay? But please, for now, just trust that I'm making the best possible decision."

"I don't get it. I thought MMA was your life. You're walking away from a chance at making all your dreams a reality and *quickly*. You stay here; it could take years to get a fight."

"I'm willing to wait." *For Axelle, I'd wait forever.*

He blows out an exasperated breath. "Well, fuck." He shrugs. "I hope you know what you're doing, man."

The disappointment in his voice cramps my insides. These guys are my role models, and their approval means everything to me. Surely when Axelle and I tell him that we're together and in a committed relationship, he'll understand why I didn't leave. He may disagree with it, but he'll have to respect the fact that I love his daughter enough to put my entire future on hold to be near her.

And he'll know I'll do whatever it takes to make a good life for us.

~~~

I left the training center a little early to hit the grocery store and grab stuff for the weekend. I got Axelle to agree to spend the weekend with me, and there's no way we'll be leaving the bed.

If I have my way, she'll be in my arms for forty-eight straight hours. We'll have to take breaks to eat, but showering will definitely be a joint experience.

Just imagining her wet and wanting in my shower has me readjusting in my sweats. Last thing I need is to welcome her with a raging hard-on.

I stack the few movies I rented neatly on my nightstand and check the top drawer and make sure the condoms I bought are available for easy access. Once I'm convinced everything is in place, I fall back on my bed and try to relax. I contemplate calling her to find out how close she is, but decide not to add pathetically desperate to her list of reasons why she shouldn't be with me. Right above nerd and below socially awkward.

By the time she finally knocks, I jump off the bed with so much force I hit the wall. *Calm down. Breathe.* I make myself walk at a controlled speed to the front door. When I open it, I'm struck right between the pecs by the most brilliant smile I've ever seen on her.

"Hi." It's such a benign word, but the way she says it, the flash of lust in her eyes, makes me dizzy.

"Hey." We stare at each other, and my eyes rake over her short tee that shows off a healthy section of her slender belly. Her stylish gray sweatpants hang low on her hips and are rolled at the bottom, and she's wearing flip-flops with bright red toenail polish tipping her gorgeous feet. "You look hot."

She laughs, but sobers quickly as her gaze zeroes in on my sweatpants. "So do you."

I contemplate trying to hide my semi-aroused dick, but figure it'll be like this all weekend. The sooner she gets used to it, the better. "Come here."

She falls into my chest, and I slide her bag off her shoulder to the ground before scooping her into my arms. She wraps her legs around my hips, and I slam the door shut, making sure it's locked before moving her to the small kitchen counter. Setting her there, I hold her face in my hands and cover her lips with mine.

A long moan slides up her throat, and I eagerly swallow it as I continue to explore the soft heat of her mouth. She hooks her heels at my ass, pulling me deep into the apex of her thighs and locking me there.

She tastes like bubblegum and mint, and that combined with her delicate scent make me damn near frenzied. I reach for the hem of her shirt and break the kiss long enough to pull it over her head. My eyes widen as I take in her neon yellow bra and her dark nipples that strain behind their lacey cage. "Never seen anything so sexy in my life."

She arches her back in offering, and I pull the lace down to pop one breast free before repeating the process on the other. Licking down her chest, I press kisses to the valley between them while gently massaging her full mounds. I nip across to her nipple and suck the hardened tip into my mouth. Forget eating. I could survive off her body alone. She writhes against me, gripping and pulling at my hair.

"What is it?" I continue to suck at her. "You want my mouth?"

"Yes, Kill, please . . ."

I smile against her skin and kiss back up her neck to her lips. Her mouth is wet and hungry as she sucks my tongue and nips at my lips. I hook my hands under her ass and carry her to the bed. She kicks off her flip-flops. I waste no time and pull her sweats off her legs and—no panties.

I gape at her and she giggles. "Surprise!"

I pull my shirt off over my head with lightning speed, needing to feel the warmth of her naked flesh pressed against me. I fall between her legs, and she wraps me up completely so that her pulse thunders against my bare chest. I reach up to get into my bedside table drawer, but she rocks her hips up and rolls me to my back. "Not yet."

"No?"

She shakes her head and straddles me, her bare body on display above me. I almost orgasm right there.

"No. There's something I want to do first." She kisses down my chest, and the silken strands of her hair brush along my ribs. The muscles in my abdomen flex as she runs her lips down, down, until she's at the drawstring of my sweats. She pulls the tie with her teeth, and I groan and drop my head back. The visual of this woman between my legs, her eyes heavy with hunger, makes me feel like I'm gonna pass out.

She hooks her fingers inside and slides the cotton down. I lift my hips as the fabric feels like broken glass against my oversensitive skin. She backs off the bed to remove them completely, and I kick them free. Her eyes gaze down at me in appreciation, and I shift self-consciously, or maybe it's eagerly, under the weight of her stare.

She settles back between my legs and grips me in her hand. "This is gorgeous, so strong, proud." She licks her lips. "You're huge."

"Stop talking like that." My voice shakes with barely concealed need. "You'll give him a complex."

She bends down so her ass is high in the air and her lips touch the tip.

"Holy—" I bite my lip against the overwhelming sensation.

She slides me between her lips, down the length of her tongue, and to the back of her throat. I revel in every glorious inch. Her head bobs up and down between my legs, and her hair tickles my thighs, adding to the eroticism as her mouth is wrapped tightly around me.

Her tongue licks, swirls, and presses as she pulls my orgasm to the surface. I grit my teeth and concentrate on anything and everything that'll keep me from ending this too early, but it's all in vain.

It's her mouth, her love. Fuck . . . it's Axelle, who's moaning while she pleasures me, and no amount of algebra or quantum physics equations could take my focus from that.

I'm gonna blow.

~*~

Axelle

This is the most turned on I've ever been without being touched.

His abdomen contracts viciously, the balls of muscle in his chest and belly popping up and straining. His hands grip my hair until I feel the sting of his restraint. All of these things just push me on.

I grip him tighter and move faster against him. He brings his knees up, his heels pressing deep into the bed and his thick thighs surround my head. He thrusts along with me, keeping a quickened pace, and just when I think he's about to peak, he reaches down and scoops me under my arms.

"Whoa!"

He drags me up his body, and when I'm settled over his hips, he reaches for his bedside table. He pulls out a condom and rips it open before handing it to me.

"Put it on me. I need to be inside you."

I roll the latex on with shaky hands.

"Hurry, baby." His eyes are transfixed between my legs as I lower myself onto him.

A hissed breath slides from my lips at being filled by him so completely it's overwhelming.

"Just . . . give me a sec." His fingers dig into my hips, seating me so I don't move.

I lean forward and press kisses to his jaw, his throat, his collarbone, and the tension slowly leaves his muscles. Once he's released me enough to move, I do exactly that.

He cups my breasts, and I roll my hips against him. For once, I tower over him, having him under my control. He gives it to me, allowing me to set the pace. I drop my head back on a moan, and with a growl, he flips me to my back.

With his knees on the outside of my thighs he forces my legs together. I gasp at the new position as it wraps me completely around his erection, forcing an added friction between my thighs.

"Mmm . . . I love this."

He's breathing heavily and kisses me. "Yeah?"

"Don't stop."

His motions become frantic as he pounds deep into me, every inch of him gliding against my most sensitive skin in a sleek caress. My upper thighs clench his length, and he circles his hips, once, twice . . .

My back arches off the bed as an orgasm, so intense it makes stars flash behind my eyes, rips through me. I call out his name, fork my hands through his hair, and finally calm when he slams his lips to mine. I devour his mouth and tremble in his arms. His tongue glides along mine in languorous strokes as he coaxes me back down.

"You okay?" he whispers against my lips.

"Never better." I grin, but it's lazy as I'm drained of energy.

He moves and maneuvers my legs apart then guides my foot up to his lower back. I follow with the other until my legs are locked tightly around him. "I love it like this, feeling you all around me." He slides in deep and pulls almost all the way out then repeats it. "I can feel your heartbeat against my chest. Your thighs shake. It's unbelievable, Ax."

"I love you."

He moans into my neck and quickens his pace until he's powering into me. I tilt my hips, and he gasps just before he thrusts one last time and holds himself there. This man, this valiant and honorable man, lies limp in my arms and totally at my mercy.

We kiss until his weight on me causes my legs to go numb. He rolls off and goes to the bathroom to get rid of the condom. I hop up to grab my sweats, but when he sees me, he scoops one arm around my waist and tosses me to the bed. "Oh no, no clothes."

"But how are we going to make something to eat?"

"Naked." He pulls the covers back on the bed and motions for me to crawl beneath them.

I do. "Is that safe?"

He hits me with a questioning smirk. "Why wouldn't it be?"

I shrug. "Oh, you know, fire and private parts."

He frowns and crawls into bed to pull me into his arms. "Good point. Guess we'll have to make sandwiches."

"I can live with that."

"Now that we managed to knock off some of the sexual tension so our brains can work properly, wanna watch a movie?"

I giggle and nuzzle deeper into his chest. "Sure, what do you have?"

He pulls three DVD cases off the bedside table, and my eyes are glued to the way the muscles in his side stretch and tense with the movement. He leans back against the pillows, pulls me back to his chest, and holds them up one at a time. "*Jurassic World, The Martian,* or *Terminator Genisys.*" He fans them out for me to choose.

"Hmm . . . I'm going to go with Jurassic World."

"Good choice. It's hard to say no to a dino flick."

"More like it's hard to say no to a Chris Pratt flick."

"Hey! No lusting after other guys in my bed." He tickles me and I scream for mercy.

He moves to the DVD player that sits on his dresser just below the flat screen. His wide back and full round ass are like a playground for my eyes as they dance over every sculpted mound. When he turns around to head back to the bed, I blush at his brazen nakedness. He crawls under the covers and pulls me into his side.

"You know, for someone who doesn't have a lot of experience being naked around women, you sure are comfortable strutting around in front of me." I've often wondered if Killian's sexual experience was more than he shared. I've never been with a virgin before him, so I can't be sure, but he certainly doesn't move like an inexperienced man.

He points the remote at the screen to get the movie started. "Does my openness bother you?"

Flashes of his bare body assault my mind. "No. Just surprising, that's all."

He hits play and drops the remote at his side. "I guess it's because you're my best friend, Ax. That and I don't have body issues. There's nothing on me I wouldn't be proud to show off to the right girl."

I peer up at him. "Well, aren't we arrogant."

He kisses the top of my head. "Not arrogant, just honest. I'll always be honest with you."

Honesty is something I know very little about, and the mention of it triggers a flicker of panic. "Promise?"

He pulls my chin, his eyes scarily serious. "I promise to give you everything; in all things, you'll always come first." He takes my hand resting on his chest and makes an X over his heart with my finger and kisses my knuckles. "Cross my heart."

I melt deeper into him, and to avoid bursting into tears at the meaning behind his confession, I focus on the screen. Two young boys, brothers I think, are on a boat on their way to get eaten by dinosaurs.

"You'd think they'd have learned their lesson from the first three movies," he mumbles, settling in as his hand holds mine to his chest.

"Right? But then we wouldn't get to watch Chris Pratt in a tight shirt, chasing dinosaurs."

He gasps and rolls on top of me. "What did I say about lusting over other men while in my bed?"

I chew my lip and pretend to remember. "Hmm . . . I'm pretty sure you said it was encouraged."

He buries his face in my neck. "You're a horrible listener."

The heat of his breath sends goose bumps down my arms.

"And you're a jealous boyfriend."

He nuzzles against me and moans. "Fuck yeah, I am." He nips at my skin. "And don't you forget it." He drops his weight between my legs and kisses my throat tenderly, his lips barely a ghost against my skin.

I run my fingers through his hair, holding him to my neck in a firm request.

He chuckles. "You like that, huh?"

I moan and arch my back. The sheet falls below my breasts, and they meet the firm warm planes of his pecs. "Don't stop."

"Thought you wanted to watch Chris What's-his-name?" He smiles against my ear before kissing a path down between my breasts.

"Who?"

Another deep chuckle vibrates against my skin. How is it that the simplest things he does can be so sensual?

He continues his path downward, kissing, nipping, and licking my skin until he settles between my legs.

I'm pretty sure Chris Pratt saves thousands of tourists from being annihilated by dinosaurs, but lost in Killian, I don't watch a single second of it.

SEVENTEEN

Killian

I'm a creepy bastard.

I know I am, and yet, I can't stop staring at her.

I've woken up every couple of hours throughout the night to feel her naked and pressed to me, and each time I was compelled to watch her—just to stare at her face, lips parted, dark lashes fanned against her creamy skin, and all that hair tossed around her face from hours of love-making. She's beautiful.

I always thought if I were lucky enough to get Axelle naked and in my bed I'd spend all night staring at her gorgeous body, and I'm not gonna lie. I did that too. But the most captivating part of her, which surprised even me, is how her expression softens in sleep. It makes me realize just how much worry she must carry around every day. Like she's tiptoeing through each day with the fear that one wrong step will have devastating repercussions.

The thought makes my chest ache.

"How long have you been staring at me?"

I rip my gaze from the curve of Axelle's hip to meet her sparkling blue eyes still swollen from sleep. "You want the truth?"

She reaches forward and puts and X over my heart with the lightest brush of her fingertip. "I only want what you promised."

I shrug one shoulder and hold off the heat I feel rising in my cheeks. "Off and on for most of the night."

"Huh." Her brows drop low.

"You think I'm creepy."

"No, it's just . . . we must've been on opposite shifts then because I've been up staring at you off and on for most of the night."

A slow grin pulls at my lips. "No kidding?"

Her hand slips into my hair just above my ear, and her thumb brushes my forehead. "You look so much younger when you sleep."

I grimace. "That's not good. Are you sure you don't mean I look so much studlier when I sleep?"

She pushes up and rolls on top of me, straddling my hips. "Definitely studlier."

I run both my hands from her hips, brushing the sides of her breasts then settling on her shoulders. "We should eat."

"We just woke up."

"It's ten o'clock."

Her jaw drops open, and her eyes dart to the clock on the cable box. "Holy shit!"

I push up and over to flip her back to the bed. "I'll cook."

With a kiss to her lips, I snag my sweatpants and head to the kitchen to throw together some breakfast. "Eggs and toast okay?"

There's a rustling of sheets, and I turn to see her snuggled deep into the comforter with her eyes on me. "Yes, are you sure I can't help?"

I prop my arm on the top of the fridge door. "Depends. You gonna stay naked if you help?"

She grins. "Probably not."

"Then no." I pull a carton of eggs, whole-grain bread, and butter from the fridge and get to making breakfast. "You should check your phone. I thought I heard it early this morning."

"Oh yeah, good idea." She hops out of bed, and I make it a point to stop what I'm doing, lean back, and enjoy the show as she crosses to her bag and digs out her phone. Once she's back in bed and covered, I get back to work.

Will I ever get tired of seeing her gorgeous body in my place?

No.

"My mom called twice." She hits a few buttons and presses the phone to her ear.

I pour two glasses of orange juice.

"Hey, Mom, I saw I missed a couple calls from you?"

I scramble eggs while she answers questions about school, her car, and gives a few "yeahs" to unknown questions. I'm plating eggs and buttering toast when she finally hangs up the phone.

"Everything okay?"

I'm sorry to see her hop out of bed and reach for her sweats and shirt from last night. "Yeah, everything's fine." She smiles at me, and her eyes widen when she looks at the plate in my hands. "Killian, that's like a dozen eggs. That's not for me, is it?"

I reach behind me and grab her plate with only two eggs on it, then set it down on the table. "Oh, that's better." She grins, drops into her seat, and looks down at the plate. Her nose scrunches up and she reaches for her juice.

I fork a bite of eggs into my mouth and chew. "What?"

"Oh, um . . . nothing." She spears a tiny ball of egg on one fork tine and forces it between her lips. "My mom needs me to babysit Jack today. Blake had some last-minute thing at the training center, and she made a hair appointment. Shouldn't be more than an hour."

"You want me to come?" I shovel more eggs into my mouth.

"Are you kidding? You'd make me the most popular sister in town if you came. Jack loves you. Oh, and we could tell Blake and Mom about us." She nibbles more eggs.

"You worried about how they'll react?"

"Not even a little bit. They love you." She pushes her fork around, rearranging her breakfast.

I nod to her plate. "You become a vegetarian since last night?"

She laughs uncomfortably. "No, it's just these eggs smell funny."

I lean over my plate and inhale. "They smell fine to me."

She purses her lips and sips her juice.

"What time do we have to be at your Mom's?" I finish the last bite of my eggs and stab at hers.

"Not until one." Her voice sounds distant, like she's somewhere else.

I grab her hand and squeeze. "Hey, you want me to make you something else? I have some fruit, or I can make you pancakes."

She grins, but I can tell she's fighting revulsion. "No, I guess I'm just not that hungry."

"You've been like this for a few days now. Are you sure you're feeling okay?"

She shrugs one shoulder. "I'm fine most of the day, but sometimes when I get around food, I get a little nauseated."

"Maybe you got a bug?"

"That's probably all it is." She sips her juice, and I make a mental note to keep an eye on her appetite for the weekend.

I finish her breakfast, and she jumps up to take our plates to the kitchen before I get a chance to. "You're my guest; you don't have to clean up."

She gazes at me from over her shoulder. "You cooked. I'll clean. That's the deal."

I wipe down the counters and dry the dishes she washes. Grabbing the full trash, I tie off the ends. "Why don't you grab a shower while I take this out." I press my lips to her forehead. "The second drawer is all yours. I put the few things you had here in there; hope that's okay."

"That's sweet of you, Kill. Thanks." I watch until she disappears into the bathroom and snag my keys before taking out the trash.

Locking her inside my place while I'm gone for two minutes might be crossing the line from protective to psycho over the top, but now that I have her, I'm not risking losing her to anything.

Axelle

I shut the bathroom door behind me, and now that I'm safe behind the closed door, I grip my stomach.

It took everything I had to remain casual when the truth was, once the smell of cooking eggs hit my nose, I was fighting throwing up. I'm sure I have some stupid stomach bug. I guess I should be happy that the only symptoms so far are a lack of appetite and a little nausea.

I strip off my clothes and turn the shower on hot. My body is sensitive, and if I'm being honest a little sore from last night. The hot water will do wonders to loosen up my tight muscles and hopefully to drown out the smell of scrambled egg.

My throat floods with saliva, and I hold my fingers over my lips and breathe through my nose. What the hell?

Once under the hot spray I feel a little better. I wash my hair, my body, shave with Killian's kick-ass razor—seriously, why is it that they make men's razors so much more effective than women's?

I linger a little longer even after I'm finished until I'm finally feeling back to normal. Turning the spray off, I push out and wrap up in a towel. The mirror is fogged, but I can see the pink glow on my cheeks. Whether it's from last night or the hot shower, I don't know. My guess is a combination of the two.

Reaching for the second drawer, I grin when I find all my things divided into sections of a cool plastic divider tray. Toothbrush, toothpaste, deodorant, there are even cotton balls and Q-tips. I grin when I see a special square filled with black ponytail holders. He stocked up just for me.

Something in the back of the drawer catches my eye. I lean down and see several brands, boxes, and packages of tampons and pads. He kept all those from last month? I cover my mouth to muffle a laugh. He's way too good to me.

I grab my toothbrush and get to work on my teeth. That night after Clifford's birthday, if I'd only known— My hand freezes. Clifford's birthday.

January 11th.

Foam drips from the corner of my mouth.

Today is February 16th.

I yank open the drawer and stare at the boxes in the back as if they hold the answers I'm looking for.

Over a month ago.

I should've had a period by now.

I drop my toothbrush into the sink and do a quick count on my fingers. No, that can't be right. I count again. And again. Then one more time to be sure.

Oh my God.

I'm pregnant.

EIGHTEEN

Killian

I've cleaned my entire studio apartment, which isn't saying much since the place is the size of a matchbox.

I stare at the bathroom door, wondering why the shower turned off over thirty minutes ago and she still hasn't emerged.

I've heard women take a long time to get ready. I'm sure that's all it is.

I study her bag on the floor. She doesn't have her clothes in there, so what could she possibly be doing?

As much as I want to bang on the door and check on her, I resolve not to scare her away with my incessant badgering. It was bad enough that I couldn't leave her alone about the eggs. If I'm not smart, I could easily push her away by loving her too much.

I drop back to the bed and scroll through my phone, returning text messages and checking email.

After several minutes, the bathroom door swings open and Axelle comes out. She's clutching her towel at her chest so tightly her knuckles are strained, and her hair is wet and un-brushed with a few strands around her face already air dry. She stares at me blankly, and it's then I notice how pale she is. And she's shivering.

I launch off the bed and cup her face. "Shit, you're freezing." I run my hands over her shoulders and down her arms; her skin is like ice beneath my touch. "What the fuck is going on?" I vacillate between covering her with my body to keep her warm and standing back to run my hands over every inch of her, checking for injury. Her teeth chatter as I walk her to the bed. I pull the comforter back, crawl under it, and toss her wet towel aside before pulling her to my chest. She burrows into me, absorbing my warmth, and I tuck the blankets in tight around us.

She's so cold her skin burns against mine.

"Talk to me, Ax." She trembles with full body shivers, and I rub her back, trying to get her to calm down. "Breathe, baby."

She takes long full breaths, and slowly her shivering fades. Her body warms enough that her muscles relax, but only minutely.

"Axelle, I'm not gonna lie. I'm freakin' out here." I speak against the top of her head. "What happened?"

She sniffs and her shoulders jump in my arms.

She's crying.

Fuck!

This is the strongest woman I know. I've been to hell with her several times and rarely seen her cry. Whatever happened between the time she went into that bathroom 'til now is big enough to bring her to her emotional knees.

And the selfish part of me is praying to God this has nothing to do with me.

"Shh . . . it's okay. Whatever this is, it'll be okay."

She sobs and shakes her head. "No . . . it . . . won't."

"What happened?" I kiss her head and hold her tighter. "Talk to me, baby."

She calms and hiccups; the moisture from her tears soak my chest and slide down my ribs to the sheet. "I'm afraid to tell you."

"No, baby. You never have to be afraid to tell me anything. I love you."

"That's why I'm afraid. When I tell you, you won't love me anymore."

"Impossible. I've loved you for four years. Nothing will change that." I pull back just enough to see her face, and the sight shreds through me. "What is it?"

She tilts her head back, but doesn't meet my eyes. "I think . . . I mean, I'm pretty sure I'm—"

"What?" My stomach plummets at what I think might be coming. Please, God . . . no. "You're what, Axelle?" The question comes out harsher than I intend.

She coughs and her face twists with emotion. "Pregnant."

I'm gone. It's as if the single word drop-kicked my mind from my body. My arms close in around her, and she bursts into sobs once again. I can hear her, feel her body shaking and the heat of her tears, but inside I'm numb.

Because I've taken enough sex-ed classes to know that Axelle's not pregnant with my baby.

She's pregnant with Clifford's.

"I wasn't paying attention." She continues to cry. "I was so busy I didn't . . ." More tears. "Then I got sick on Valentine's Day, but I thought it was stress."

She blabs on and on, and all I can do is hold her tight as if I'm physically holding us together because I'm fucking dying, thinking these could be the last few moments we'll have together.

"I need to take a pregnancy test to be sure."

"What?" Even my own voice sounds like it's coming from another room.

"I could be wrong."

"So, you're saying you might not be pregnant with that sorry son of a bitch's baby?"

She shrinks away at the anger in my voice, but fuck it! I'm angry. I go back and forth between my instinct to comfort her and the urge to shake her until her head pops off. What the fuck did she think would happen? And how could she fuck that guy without protection? The thought alone makes me fucking homicidal. I shove my hand through my hair and focus on my breathing.

"I need to take a test to be sure—"

I jerk free of her and make sure she's covered and tucked in before heading across the room. "Give me ten minutes. We'll swing by the drugstore on our way to your mom's." I slam the bathroom door behind me, not waiting for her reply.

I stare at myself in the mirror and can see the barely contained rage that ripples through my muscles. Wouldn't that be just my luck that when I finally get everything I ever asked for it all falls to shit.

Axelle

We're five minutes late pulling up to my mom's house. I grab my backpack, which is not only holding a couple of textbooks, but now a brown paper bag filled with three pregnancy tests. Killian wanted me to get five, but I assured him that three would be enough. Not to mention they're expensive and cost me my lunch budget for the week.

Killian slides from the Jeep without looking at me. He's hardly looked at me at all since I broke down in his arms. I was hoping he'd react in his typical way, assuring me everything would be okay and swearing he'd stand by me through it all.

Instead, he's basically ignoring me. Sure he answers direct questions, but other than that, he's been a robot.

I sling my backpack over my shoulder and see him waiting for me at the hood of the car. When we get to the door, he places his palm on the small of my back. It's a barely-there show of support, but I exhale and relax a little because of it.

Opening the door, I can immediately hear Jack throwing a fit.

"Mom?"

"We're in the kitchen!"

I lead the way in to find Jack squirming in his highchair and my mom wiping something off the front of her shirt.

"Hey, guys." She crosses to us, giving me a hug and then moving to Killian. "Jack, look who's here," she says in an over animated voice. "It's Killian, see?"

Jack's bright red face fades to a light pink, and he grins, flashing all his teeth even while tears still fall from his chubby cheeks. "Illie!" He holds his baby arms up.

"Aw, buddy . . ." Killian crosses to my baby brother. "Are you giving your mom a hard time?" He reaches for the latches on the highchair as my mom swoops in and wipes the last bit of food from his hands and face. He pulls my brother into his arms and Jack grabs at Killian's lips. I stand back as he blows raspberries into Jack's neck, and the sweetness of it all makes my eyes hot.

"Crap!" My mom scurries to the sink to wash her hands. "I have to go or I'll be late."

I suck back the crazy emotions swirling through my chest as she comes to hug me good-bye.

Her eyes narrow. "Axelle, are you feeling okay?" She presses the back of her hand to my cheek. "You sick?"

Killian ducks out of the kitchen with Jack, but I don't miss the glare he points in my direction before he goes.

"I'm fine. Just fighting a stomach bug."

"Oh, no." She pulls me in for a hug. "There's some saltine crackers in the pantry and there should be some ginger ale in there too."

"Thanks, I'll give that a try." I drop my bag on the floor and move toward the pantry for show.

"Thanks for helping her out, Killian!" She calls out as she ducks into the garage, the door closing behind her.

He doesn't answer her. Guess it's not only me he's ignoring.

I pull a cup down from the cupboard and fill it with water, downing the liquid as fast as I can before filling another.

I made sure to drink a water before leaving Killian's, and I grabbed another small bottle from the drugstore, so I'm already feeling the pressure to pee. I grab the bag from my backpack and move through the living room to the hallway where the guest bathroom is. I stop for a moment and Killian looks up from playing with my brother. Our gazes meet in an explosion of apologies and whispers of hope.

I nod and mumble, "I'll be right back," then lock myself in the bathroom to learn my fate.

NINETEEN

Axelle

I emerge from the bathroom a lifetime later.

It's not an exaggeration.

From the moment those double pink lines showed up not once, not twice, but on all three pregnancy tests, the old Axelle Rose Daniels died.

I didn't cry or mourn the loss of the old me. If anything, I expected it. If these last four years have taught me anything, it's that anything can happen, probably will, and most likely will suck.

So that's it.

There's no poetic way to say it.

No justifying why it happened.

It's simple.

I've ruined my life.

"I'm pregnant with Clifford's baby." I toss the positive pregnancy tests on the couch next to Killian as he cuddles my brother watching Thomas the Tank Engine.

His eyes dart to the tests, slide up to mine, then focus back on the TV.

And that's it.

That. Is. It.

I scoop up the tests and shove them into my backpack along with the brown paper bag that's now filled with the empty boxes. Without feeling, I drop hard onto a barstool and stare at my mom's Cuisinart.

I don't know how much time passes. I'm unable to move, to talk, to think. All I can do is trace the letters of the word Cuisinart over and over with my eyes.

So when the garage door sounds from my right, I startle.

"Yo, kiddo." Blake crosses to me and puts me in a headlock from behind, kissing the top of my head. "Where's Killer?"

I don't know. "With Jack."

Blake moves to the living room, and I overhear him exchanging a greeting with my old best friend possibly ex-boyfriend. For the first time since I saw those two pink lines, I feel something like pain slicing through my heart and sucking the air from my lungs.

". . . still think you're an idiot to pass that up." Blake crosses to the refrigerator with Jack in his arms. "One year and you'd be a UFL champ."

I blink and focus on Blake just as Killian drops into the stool next to me.

Blake hands my brother a Go-Gurt and sets him down. "Cam explained what Bates would be doing today at the meeting. Had Rex practically jumping on the balls of his feet to get over there."

"Over where?" The question flies from my lips with a tinge of irritation attached to it because it seems like they're talking about something important and yet it's the first I've ever heard of it.

"You didn't tell her?" Blake's eyes are focused on Killian.

He shrugs. "Why would I?"

"Oh fuck, man, I don't know, maybe because she'd talk some sense into your dumb ass."

I swivel around and take in Killian, who has his chin dropped to his chest. "What's he talking about?" I whisper.

He licks his lips, lifts his head, but still doesn't look at me. "It's nothing."

"Nothing?" Blake's arms tense at his sides. "How can you say it's nothing? I mean, 'cause fuck me, I thought you wanted to be a UFL fighter."

"Blake, I do, but—"

"So you pass up the opportunity to fight in London for one year and get a shot at a title fight representing your fucking country?"

"What? When did this happen?" Excitement, pride, and devastation war within, and it's fucked-up combination leaves me dizzy. "You had a chance for all that and you said no?"

He runs two hands over his face and groans. "No, it wasn't like that."

Blake makes a disgusted sound, and I lean in to Killian. "Cross your heart, remember?"

He sighs hard, and then for the first time since this morning, his eyes meet mine. "Yes. Okay? I had the opportunity, but I turned it down. Happy?"

"No, fuck . . ." I shake my head. "No, I'm not *happy*. Killian, you should go."

"I knew you'd say that," he mumbles.

"Because you know it's the right thing to do."

"I don't want to—"

"Why not!"

"Because—"

"Because why?"

"Because of you, alright?"

I jerk away from him with a gasp.

His gaze slides between me and a stunned-looking Blake. "I don't want to leave you, Ax."

I open my mouth to either scream at him for being an idiot or to confess my undying love. I'm not sure, so I shut my mouth and stare.

He tilts his head, only looking at me from the corner of his eye. "A year away, anything could've happened, and"— he sighs— "I didn't want to miss my chance."

Blake's standing back, eyes narrowed on Killian when the front door opens and my mom's hollered "I'm home!" comes filtering into the kitchen.

I duck my chin as frustration bubbles to the surface. Killian never should've made this decision based on me. Guilt settles heavily over my shoulders and I slump into myself. As if I don't have enough to feel like shit about, now I can pat myself on the back for ruining the career of the man I love, who, now that I'm fucking pregnant with another man's baby, I've already lost anyway.

"Hey, guys." My mom moves through the kitchen with a squirming Jack in her arms. She must sense the tension because she sidles up to Blake. "What's going on?"

Jack manages to squirm free and toddle back to his toys in the living room.

Blake slings his arm around mom's shoulder and pulls her in for a hug. "Nothing, Mouse. It's all good." He goes on to ask her how her appointment was, compliments her on her hair, and small talks her to distraction.

The air between Killian and me strains with what needs to be said. My mind tumbles in a thousand different directions, and not one of them leads me to a happy ending.

I've disappointed every single person I love, and they don't even know it yet. I've signed away the rest of my life by getting pregnant, and I'll have to face Clifford, that asshole, and beg him to be part of our baby's life.

And my mom . . . fuck. She'll be crushed. My entire life she warned me against making the same mistakes she did. She swore I was the best thing that ever happened to her but always piggybacked that with a strict "Don't throw your life away like I did" speech.

This is going to kill her.

Nausea sweeps through me, and I brace my forearms on the counter resting my forehead on them and breathing through the tightness in my throat. A warm hand immediately comes to my comfort, rubbing up and down my spine in soothing strokes.

Killian.

God, I'm going to miss him.

"Baby, are you okay?" My mom comes to my side and pushes my hair away to place her hand on the back of my neck.

I nod, but the lump in my throat grows bigger.

"She sick?" Blake whispers the question to Killian, who must reply in a non-verbal of some kind.

"Let me grab you some medicine for your stomach." My mom shifts away.

"No." The single word grates from my throat. I push up and meet Killian's eyes. At first, his expression seems shocked, as if he knows what I'm about to do, but then his face morphs to understanding and finally approval.

"Kiddo, listen to your mom." Blake moves around the counter and presses his palm to my forehead. "Take something and get some rest."

"I can't take anything."

Killian shifts to stand at my back, and the supportive move catches Blake's attention as well as my mom's. They stare between us.

"Why not?" My mom's eyes narrow as she studies me.

I sigh and resign to the inevitable. "Because I'm pregnant."

My mom gasps and rocks back on her heels as if the news was a punch to the gut. "No." Her eyes glisten, and her trembling fingers press against her quivering lips.

The fury rolling off Blake is so intense I'm afraid to look at him. "Explain."

"Pretty sure you understand the mechanics—"

"This isn't a fucking joke, Axelle! Who the hell did it?"

I meet his eyes and wish I hadn't. It's not fury I'm seeing in his green glare; it's unadulterated disappointment. "I'd rather not say until—"

"You'd rather not say?" He scowls at Killian. "You know, don't you? Who the fuck got my girl pregnant?"

My mom places a palm on Blake's chest. "Blake, calm down—"

He swings his glare to her, and his face softens when he sees a single tear trace down her cheek. "Fuckin' hell." He turns toward me. "How could you do this? You fucking know better!"

"It was a mistake."

"You're damn right it was a mistake." He seems to be getting angrier and pushes in front of my mom to stand less than a foot from me. "Who did it?"

"I don't want to say."

"Why not!"

Because I'm embarrassed. Humiliated.

"You've made this man a father and you can't even tell me his name?"

"*I* didn't make him a father, Blake. He was there too."

"Shit, Axelle, does he even have a job? Can he afford to take care of you and this baby? Have you thought about any of this?"

"No," I whisper.

"How are you guys going to do this on your own? You're twenty-fucking-years-old! You can pretty much screw getting an education." He rips his hands through his cropped hair. "God, Axelle . . ." His voice breaks. "I wanted so much better for you."

My mom sobs behind him, her shoulders shaking and tears streaming down her face. Her tears only make him madder.

"Who did this to you!" He roars in my face.

I shy away from his anger just as Killian's hands settle firmly on my shoulders.

"I did."

The entire room goes still. Static blares in my ears.

Blake's head swivels in slow motion to stare blankly at Killian. "What did you say?"

Killian moves from my back to my side and pulls my hand into his. "It's mine. The baby, I mean."

What the fuck is he doing?

I stare up at him and gape.

"I'm sorry. We didn't mean for this to happen, but it did." He squeezes my hand firmly. "I'm going to take care of them."

"Killian, no—"

"Blake, I've loved Axelle from the day I met her. I want to marry her and start a family. This is sooner than I expected, but it doesn't change what I want."

"You got my *daughter* pregnant," Blake growls through clenched teeth and takes a step forward.

"She's pregnant, yes, and I'm in love with her."

I jump to my feet. "No, Killian's not—"

"You son of a bitch!" Blake's fist whizzes by me and cracks Killian in the jaw.

His hand is ripped from mine as he falls to the ground.

"No!"

Blake follows him down and straddles him. His arms fly, but he's not punching him as much as he's slapping Killian's face. He doesn't even put up a fight but allows Blake to punish him for my mistake.

"Stop!" I race to Killian, drop to my knees, and shield him with my body. One of Blake's palms smacks my upper arm, but it's nothing more than a quick sting of pain.

"Blake, no! You're going to hurt her!" My mom pulls at Blake, and he easily hops to his feet.

Killian's cheeks are red, and the space below his left eye is already turning a sickening shade of purple.

"Look what you did to him!"

"He deserves worse!" Blake looms over us, his eyes no bigger than slits and filling with tears. "I trusted you with her!"

Killian pushes up to sitting and rests his arms on his cocked knees. "I love her."

"If you loved her, you'd protect her!" Blake wipes his eye with a thumb.

I push to stand and put myself between Blake and Killian. "He does protect me! That's all he's ever done since I've known him! God, he gave up a dream opportunity to be close to me, Blake! This isn't Killian's fault—"

"He should've taken care of you."

"He did!" I motion to Killian, who's on the floor with his head between his hands. "He still is! Killian is not this baby's father! He's taking responsibility for me, and you hit him for it!"

All eyes go to Killian.

"Can't you see what he's doing? He's protecting me even now."

"Killian didn't get you pregnant?" Blake's shoulders slump a little and tension falls from his muscles.

"No, up until two nights ago, I was dating someone else."

"Dating someone? Why didn't you tell us?" my mom says between sniffles.

"He wasn't someone I was proud of, and it turns out . . . I was right not to be."

Blake scrubs his face with his hand. "Fuck." He moves to Killian and offers him a hand. "I'm sorry, Killer."

Killian glares between Blake's hand and his face and finally grabs hold and allows Blake to pull him to his feet. Blake grabs an ice pack from the freezer and wraps it in a clean dishtowel then hands it to Killian, who accepts it graciously and presses it to his cheek.

"Da-da?" The tiny whispered word comes from around the corner where Jack is peeking in with wide and teary eyes.

Blake jumps and moves to his son. "Hey . . ." He scoops him up and cradles him to his chest. "I'm sorry, bud.

Everything's okay." He continues to soothe Jack by taking him out of the kitchen and back towards the bedrooms.

My mom looks between Killian and me and then follows behind Blake to disappear down the hallway.

Silence expands between us until I can't stand the awkwardness for another second. I brace myself and face him, pulling up every bit of strength I have left just to meet his troubled gaze. "You shouldn't have done that."

"I meant it. All of it. I want to take care of you."

"Yeah, well, take a number." I fist my hair in my hands and attempt to sort my thoughts.

"What's that supposed to mean?"

"It means that it's time I started taking care of myself." I should've done it years ago, but I was so wrapped up in feeling sorry for myself I allowed everyone else to feel sorry for me too. "God, I'm such a mess."

He reaches out and covers my hand with his. "Ax, you don't have to go through this alone."

"Yes, I do." I sigh and turn to my best friend, his swollen eye a painful reminder of why I can't accept his offer. "Killian, you made a mistake by falling in love with me. If you're smart, you'll take the European thing and go. I have nothing to offer you if you stay."

Killian

Damn.

That hurts.

I'd rather take a thousand hits from Blake than hear her utter another word in that blank tone that's heavy with finality.

I just offered her my life. I stood before her parents and laid claim to that fuckface Clifford's baby. I would've raised the kid as if he or she were my own because that baby growing in her belly is half Axelle, and, for me, that's more than enough.

I'd work my ass off to get fights, do whatever it took to provide for her and our baby. Yeah, I laid all that shit out there and she rejected me, threw the idea out as if it wasn't as desirable as the alternative.

A life attached to Clifford.

"What we had these last couple days . . ." I move to her and cup her cheeks. "We can have that again."

She shakes her head in my hold and closes her eyes. "Everything's changed."

"Not the things that matter. I'm still in love with you."

Her hands come to mine, and for a moment, I see our future unfold: her baby in my arms as I stare down with the love of a father and our lives intertwined forever. I could have her, all of her, take care of her as long as we both shall live.

She gazes up at me with tears in her eyes. "I have so many regrets, Killian, but this, this right here, will prove to be my biggest. I've taken a lot of help over the years; you've been there through all of it. I won't let you sacrifice your future for me." She steps back. "Go to Europe."

My vision shatters. "I don't want to. I want to stay with you." Desperate to hold her close, knowing I'm about to lose her, I pull her to my body. "Marry me. Let me have you and this baby. Please."

She grips my shirt at my chest, clinging to me. "I can't. As much as I want to, I can't take the easy way out this time."

My throat gets tight and my eyes burn.

"You saw what I went through with Stewart, how much it fucked me up finding out that the man I thought was my dad really wasn't. I can't do that to this baby. I refuse to do it."

"No one will ever know."

She pulls away and peers up at me with a shaky smile. "Of course they will, and if not in the next few years, they will eventually. And when the kid is sixteen and trying to figure out where he or she fits in the world and finds out you're not the biological father . . ." She shakes her head. "No, I have the power to make things right for this baby, and I'm going to do it."

I push back and put distance between us, disgust rolling through me. "So you're going back to Clifford? You and him going to take a crack at it? You'll be his barefoot little wife waiting on him hand and foot while he's off fucking half of Las Vegas?"

"Of course not!"

"Then what's your plan?"

She blinks. "I . . . I don't know. I just found out I'm pregnant two hours ago!"

"So that's it. You're putting an end to what we have?"

She wraps her arms around her waist. "I won't be responsible for ruining your life."

I throw my arms out. "You're not listening! You *are* my life! All I've ever wanted is *you*!"

"That's not true. You're a UFL fighter, Kill. What do you think would happen if I took you up on your offer to take care of us, huh? Five years down the road when you're still busting your ass to get fights and missing training because the kid is sick? Or what if I want to get my degree, and you end up being Daddy Daycare so I can take college courses. You'd grow resentful, and knowing you, you'd carry it around never saying shit, until one day you'd be forty and looking at me and you'd realize then I wasn't worth it."

"Bullshit! Don't put your insecurities on me, Ax. I'll always think you're worth it. The only person around you who doesn't think you're worth it is you!"

A tear drips from her eyes. "And Stew and Trip and Clifford, and a string of other guys who let me go without a fight."

I spit out a laugh and shake my head. "And yet here I am. This whole time I've been here fighting for you every fucking second of every damn day, and you're the one who's letting me go."

Her face crumbles and she cries. "Don't you see? Whatever you think I am, I'm not. You'll see it eventually; they all do."

I bury my hands into her hair and force her eyes to mine. The heat of our breath mingles as our lips are mere inches apart. "Then don't let me go, Axelle." I press a soft kiss against her lips, tasting the salt of her tears. "Please"—I close my eyes and pray she hears— "don't let me go."

Her hands come to my wrists and hold me there. Seconds pass and she continues to clutch me to her. "I love you, Killian. Nothing will ever change that."

Hope explodes in my chest until all too soon she steps back out of my hold. "No," I whisper.

She shakes her head and tears fall from her jaw to her shirt. "Don't hate me."

I want to say I could never, but as a single hot stream tracks down my cheek, something dark expands in my chest. A billowing riot of outrage, heartache, and defeat swells until something inside me breaks. I can almost hear the audible snap as everything I've been holding back rushes to the surface and I see Axelle through new eyes.

She no longer resembles the girl I fell in love with, the woman I've come to adore. Now she's just a girl who broke my heart.

And fuck her for that.

Numbly, I move through the kitchen and past her. I'm not surprised when she does nothing to stop me. I pass through the living room and to the door with my head down. I don't know if Blake and Layla are nearby, but it doesn't matter. I have nothing to say to them.

I open and shut the door calmly, move to my Jeep, and fire up the engine. When I back out of the driveway, I'm hit with the scent of her perfume that still lingers in the vehicle, and just as I'd do to air out any smell, I roll the windows down.

Pulling my phone from the center console, I hit my contacts list, find the name I'm looking for, and hit "send."

"Killian . . ." The growled greeting hits my ear, and again I feel nothing.

"What time does my plane leave for London tomorrow?"

Cam grunts. "It's not. You turned it down, remember?"

"I had a change of heart." *Or death of heart.*

"Sorry. Spot's been taken."

"Right." I turn left to hop on the freeway. "I want it back."

"Fuck," he mumbles. "When did you get so fucking stubborn?"

"Just give me a time, Cam, and I'll be there."

"You get a passport?"

"I did."

He blows out a breath and, after a couple beats of silence, says, "United. Flight leaves at seven twenty tomorrow morning."

"Tell Rex I'll meet him at the gate."

I hit "end" and toss my phone to the passenger seat.

Still, I feel nothing.

TWENTY

Axelle

Drawing a figure-eight pattern in my Cocoa Puffs doesn't make it taste any less like glue. My mom's been trying to induce my appetite all morning, but it's all been for nothing. We both pretend it's the pregnancy, but the sad smiles and sporadic hugs she's been giving me make me think I'm not as good at covering up my true feelings as I'd like to think I am.

I didn't go back to my place after Killian left yesterday. There's no way I'm ready to face Mindy—admitting my stupidity to three people was enough for one day—and my mom insisted I shouldn't be alone. I wanted to scream that she was wrong and people needed to stop telling me what to do, but I was too emotionally exhausted to fight. I slept most of the remainder of the day away, and considering how much I slept, I was surprised I was able to sleep well last night. It was almost as if my body forced my brain to abandon ship in order to protect it from going down alongside my heart.

The bad part of sleeping for thirteen straight hours through is waking up rested at five o'clock in the morning. The moment my eyes opened all systems were back online and replaying the last twenty-four hours in vivid detail. How quickly life can go from unlimited possibilities to being stripped of all possibilities. No matter how many times I replay yesterday's events, I can't bring myself to regret the decision I made.

I had to let him go.

Taking him up on what he was offering would've been the most selfish thing I could've done. And frankly, I'm sick and tired of being selfish.

I'm tired of the guilt, tired of feeling like shit all the time.

Because behind all this heartbreak and sadness there's a flicker of good; for the first time in as long as I can remember, I'm actually proud of myself because I did the opposite of what felt good. I did what was right.

Even if it meant crushing my soul.

"You really need to eat something." My mom slides a plate of fresh cut cantaloupe beside my uneaten bowl of cereal. "It's not good for you or the baby." She bites her lip and her eyes fill with tears.

I cover her hand with mine, my eyes filling right along with hers. "I'm sorry, Mom."

She shakes her head and pulls herself together with a shaky smile. "Don't be sorry. Some of our biggest mistakes end up being our greatest blessings." She kisses my forehead and moves to the kitchen sink to wash dishes.

I suck a few pieces of fruit into my mouth, and the sweet juice bursts on my tongue. Finally, something I can eat. I make my way through a few more pieces when Blake comes in and drops into the seat next to me. "How're you doing today?"

I shrug. "Good, I guess."

He seems conflicted about something, but gets over it quickly. "What's the plan?"

"Ha, like there's a plan."

My mom sips her coffee. "One day at a time."

"I think I need to go talk to Clifford." My stomach bottoms out at the thought of telling him I'm pregnant. I can't even imagine how he'll respond to the news. I'll give him the option to be involved and pray he accepts responsibility. This baby deserves to know his or her father—deserves better than I had.

Mom purses her lips. "I don't know if you're ready for that."

Blake nods his agreement. "Take some time. You need to—"

"Stop!"

Their eyes widen and dart to each other as if to say *what did we do?*

"I'm sorry. I . . ." I rub my forehead and try to relax. "I appreciate your support, but you guys have got to stop trying to tell me what to do, okay? Your hearts are in the right place, but I have to make these decisions on my own. I'm going to talk to Clifford today."

My mom flashes a thin smile as if she's holding back what she wants to say, which I know has to be hard, but I appreciate her respecting my wishes.

Blake makes a sound like he's sucking on his teeth. "What time you wanna head over there?"

It's Sunday. Chances are he'll be home, most likely sleeping in. "The earlier the better. If I wake him up, I'll be able to catch him while he's still sober."

Blake groans but receives a sharp look from my mom that shuts him up. "Alright." He claps his hands. "Get showered and we'll head over to Cliff's place to wake his ass up."

I whirl around to face him. "No way. I'm doing this alone."

He lifts a brow.

"I'm serious!" I groan and fix my eyes on him. "Did you not just hear what I said? Besides, I can't show up to drop this kind of bomb with my professional fighter dad at my back."

His shoulders tense. "That's exactly how you should show up."

I whip around. "Mom!"

"Blake, maybe you should—"

"Mouse, you met this guy?"

She rolls her lips between her teeth.

"Exactly. You wanna trust some fuckhole who she needs to talk to early while he's 'still sober'"—he uses air quotes—"when we have zero idea how he's gonna react to this news? Tell me that's what you want, Mouse."

She twirls her hair so fast the end of the strand whips around to make a little blond tornado. "He's got a point."

I drop my head into my hands. "You guys, please, be rational."

"He'll wait outside, right, Blake?"

"Fuck, yeah." He shrugs. "I'll wait outside."

I glare at him. "Promise."

"Yep, promise."

There's something unspoken going on between the two of them, but I've been in this position enough times to know I won't win this fight.

"Fine. I'll grab a shower and we'll go."

"Wonderful." Blake smiles, but it's all teeth. "Looking forward to it."

Dammit to hell.

Killian

I'm weaving through crowds of people as they put their carry-on luggage back together after passing through security. I dropped a duffle bag at curbside check-in, containing everything I'm bringing with me, gym clothes for every season and my toothbrush. It's not nearly enough for a year in London, but my plan is to spend every waking minute training, and I don't need much for that. My backpack hangs off my shoulders, heavy with my laptop and a few of my favorite books I couldn't stand to leave behind.

The rest of the things in my place I'll never see again.

Including Axelle's bag filled with her things left over from our night together.

Again I try to muster up something, anything.

But I'm dry.

I just can't care.

Not anymore.

"Whatddya' know?" Rex's voice sounds from my left. I turn to see him leaning against a wall beneath our gate number. He's wearing a black Ramones T-shirt, jeans, and black Converse with a white pair of Beats hanging around his neck. His hair is sticking out at all angles, but it doesn't look like he just rolled out of bed. No, this fucker's smiling like he hit ten gallons of caffeine. "Guess you changed your mind?"

"I did." Or it was forcibly changed.

His smile falls and his eyes narrow on my bruised cheek. "You train yesterday?"

I press the sensitive mark with my fingertip and cringe. "Yeah." I can't look him in the eye. Fuck, I hate lying.

"Who got one in on you? Wade?"

"Nah . . ." I swallow, reliving the moment, the hatred and hurt blazing in Blake's eyes seconds before his fist slammed into my face. "Blake."

"Damn, wish I'd been there."

No, you don't. Hell, I wish *I* hadn't been there.

He slaps me on the back. "Stoked you decided to come, man. I wasn't looking forward to making this long-ass flight on my own."

"Don't get too excited. I'm shitty company."

"Eh, I hate flying, so shitty company is better than no company." He holds up his airline ticket. "First class and I plan on drowning my nerves in a dozen mini bottles of booze. Plan is we drink 'til we pass out then wake up at Heathrow."

For the first time in eighteen hours, I smile. It doesn't feel right, more like someone is pulling on the corners of my mouth for me, but at least it's something. "Now you're talkin'."

I lean a shoulder on the wall next to him, and he pulls out his phone, checking email, hitting news sites, and catching up on sports stats while I remain blessedly numb at his side. The great thing about dudes is they don't feel the need to fill every available second with sound. Guys can sit for hours without even acknowledging each other, whereas it seems women get awkward if a few silent seconds pass. Then it's "Are you okay? You're so quiet. Why aren't you talking?"

My line of thinking brings a dull ache to my chest that I choose to ignore. It isn't long before a voice comes over the loudspeaker, announcing our flight is boarding. We line up with the other first-class passengers and herd ourselves through the door to the jet way.

A sudden urgency compels me to turn around, as if I left something behind. My feet pause, and I turn around to a flash of chestnut hair. My pulse kicks. Maybe she changed her mind. I lean around to get a better look and frown into the face of a very pretty girl with brown eyes and pale skin.

I force a return smile then follow behind Rex to the jet way.

I make a vow to myself right then. That will be the last time I ever look back.

She made her choice.

And now I've made mine.

Axelle

My hand shakes as I press the doorbell at Clifford's house. It's not cold outside, but I feel a chill, standing here in the shade. I try to shove my hands into my pockets then groan when I realize my mom's leggings don't have pockets, so I roll them into the bottom of her sweatshirt. Without clean clothes, I had to borrow some of hers. Thankfully, we're the same size.

I turn back to see Blake leaning against his Rubicon, arms crossed over his chest, muscles bulging, and looking every bit the bad ass fighter that he is. Maybe Clifford won't notice him. I can slip inside and we can have our talk, and Clifford will never know that imminent death sits just beyond his yard.

I knock on the door a couple more times. Clifford's and his roommates' cars are here, so I know they're home. I'd love to turn around and walk away, but I'm afraid if I don't get this over with I'll never work up the courage to come back and try again.

The door finally opens and John pokes his head out, blinking puffy eyes. "Elle? What're you doing here? It's fucking zero o'clock."

"Yeah, sorry about the timing, but I need to talk to Clifford." My feet shuffle restlessly. "It's kind of important."

The door opens more to reveal his pale pudgy body clad in nothing but white boxers. "He's sleeping." He yawns and scratches his balls.

I take extreme interest in the security light above the door. "Could you wake him up? I wouldn't ask if it weren't important."

When he doesn't answer immediately, I allow my gaze to cautiously slide back down to him, and he's staring with wide eyes just over my shoulder.

Which could only mean one thing.

"Fuck," I whisper.

"Mornin', Olaf." Blake says from over my shoulder. "Look. We hate to bust up the threesome between you, Christof, and Sven, but you need to wake up your friend."

I resist the urge to turn around and shove Blake as John stares openly at him.

"Now."

The command seems to spur the guy into action, and he recedes into the dark house, leaving the door open.

"And while you're at it put some fucking clothes on!" Blake yells with one hand to his mouth. "Creepy little shit."

I turn to Blake and glare. "You promised you'd stay at the truck," I whisper-yell.

"No, I promised I'd stay outside." He motions to where he's standing. "I'm still outside." His face become serious and he sniffs. "What the fuck . . .?" He pokes his nose inside the house. "You've gotta be kidding me."

I lean around his big body, trying to figure out what he sees that I don't. Other than the trashed living room of three college burnouts, I see nothing. "What is it?"

He sets his cold green eyes on me. "How many times have you hung out in this house?"

I'm taken aback by his question. I can't count, so I guess. "I don't know. Twenty-ish?"

He rubs his forehead and groans. "Did you know they're smoking crack in there?"

"What!" Crack? I'm not even sure I know what that is. I mean I've heard about it, but I've never actually seen it or been offered it. I always thought crack was for hardcore drug users, not partying college kids.

"Stick your nose in there and take a whiff."

I lean in, but he snags me right back. "Wait. I don't know if that's a good idea."

I gaze up at him confused, and he looks a little embarrassed. "The baby."

"Oh . . . right."

"It has a"—he rolls his finger through the air, searching for a word— "synthetic smell, ya know? Like plastic."

My eyes widen. "Yes, I know. I've smelled it on Clifford before."

"Ah hell . . ." He grips the back of his neck with both hands and looks up to the sky.

I know what he's thinking. It's not bad enough that I got pregnant by a jerk but by a crack-smoking loser jerk. I know that's what he's thinking because I'm thinking it too.

"I swear to God, John, if there's anyone but a naked J. Lo standing on the other side of the door, I'm gonna beat your ass." Clifford's voice booms just before the door swings wider to reveal him.

I'm grateful he's wearing jeans and a wrinkled shirt, rather than his roommate's au natural look. He glares between Blake and me, not acting the least bit intimidated, then stops with his eyes on me. "What do you want, Elle."

I feel more than see Blake's shock from my side at his calling me Elle. He's a smart guy; I'm sure he's figured it out.

"I'm sorry to wake you, but we need to talk."

He runs a hand through his shaggy hair. "And this shit couldn't be done over the phone or at a decent fucking hour?"

"Watch your tone, Kurt Cobain."

Clifford doesn't react to Blake, but rather acts like he's not even there. "So? I'm up. What is it?"

I scratch my neck as anxiety pricks at my skin. "Do you think we could talk in private?"

He groans as if I'm putting him out and swings open the door for me to come inside.

"Nope. She's not going into your crack house, bro."

Clifford jerks and his eyes flash to Blake with a flicker of panic.

"You two talk out here. I'll wait by the truck." Blake drops a kiss to the top of my head and stalks back to the Rubicon, resuming his position at the hood.

I lick my lips. "Look. I don't know how to say this, so I'm just gonna say it." I meet his eyes to gauge his reaction and then let 'er rip. "I'm pregnant."

I don't know what I expected, shock, maybe anger. But I do know that I never in a million years would've expected laughter.

Clifford doubles over, his hands braced on his knees as hilarity shakes his shoulders.

I watch him for a few seconds, wondering if maybe he really is still drunk. When he doesn't stop, I turn to see Blake, who looks about a half-second away from charging Clifford and beating every last chuckle from the guy's body.

"Did I say something funny?"

"Oh fuck . . . that's some good shit." He stands up and wipes his eyes. "Nice try."

"This isn't a joke, Clifford. I'm serious. I'm pregnant."

He shrugs and grins. "It's not mine."

My chin tucks in offense. "Of course it is. You're the only one I've been with."

"Yeah? Prove it."

"I . . ." I shake my head. "How would I do that?"

"Is this about the photos? Some kind of payback or something?"

"No, I'm . . . God, I just thought you should know."

"Why? So I'd marry you?"

"Eww. That's not what I want at all."

"Then what do you want, Elle? You come over here claiming I knocked you up and I'm supposed to what? Fall to my knees and confess my undying love?"

My eyes heat. "I guess I thought you might be interested in knowing your son or daughter."

He shrugs like I just told him the weather. "You thought wrong. First, I don't believe you because the only times we didn't use protection I pulled out."

I roll my eyes.

"Second, I think you're pissed about the pix I dropped on you and your boy toy and you're trying to get revenge. And third, you have no proof. You got an ultrasound? 'Cause

I know guys who've had girls claim to be pregnant and it turns out they're not."

What kind of woman would lie about being pregnant just to lockdown a man?

He steps in close. "You saw me with another girl and flipped out. I get it. You're jealous and pissed off. But I'm not stupid enough to fall for this, Elle."

"This was a mistake," I whisper.

"Aww, see? She does have a brain." He laughs and the door behind him swings open to reveal a gorgeous blonde I recognize from all his parties.

She's wearing a tiny silver dress, heels hooked with two fingers, and there's dark around her eyes from what I'd guess to be last night's makeup. Clifford hooks her around the waist and tilts his head, slamming his lips on hers.

I stumble back, my hands tangled in my sweatshirt to keep them from wrapping around Clifford's neck.

Blake pushes up behind me, wrapping his arm around my shoulders. "Time to go, kiddo. I think you got your answer."

Both Clifford and his date stare down at me while Blake drags me to the car.

"What did she want?" His date snarls at me while speaking to him.

"Nothing important."

It's the last thing I hear before they disappear back inside and slam the door.

Nothing important.

TWENTY-ONE

Killian

"Killer . . ."

My cheek stings and I'm jostled in my seat. "Hmm . . ."

"Wake up, dude. We're landing."

I force open my eyes and give my brain a second to catch up to my surroundings. Circular window. Tray table. And my mouth tastes like week old tequila and blue cheese. "Water."

Rex hands me a bottle of water and rubs his temples with a groan. "Look out. My head might explode."

I down the small water bottle and lick my lips. "How long was I out for?"

"No clue. Last thing I remember was being cut off by the flight attendant; then it was lights out."

"Were we"—I search my foggy memory— "pirates . . . at one point?"

Rex's eyebrows drop low in confusion, and then a slow smile spreads across his face. "Yeah, I was Captain Phallus, Lord of the Deep, and you were—"

"Captain Flaccid, Ruler of the Impototonuis." I punch the asshole in the bicep. "Fuck you very much for the title, dickhead."

He rubs his arm, groaning and laughing at the same time. "You weren't complaining when you were using your swizzle stick as a sword in search for the rare jewel viagranite."

I burst into laughter, and even though my head feels like it's being pounded by a jackhammer, it feels good to laugh. "Can't imagine why they cut us off."

I flag down the flight attendant for two more waters, and when he delivers them, I catch the look of irritation that flashes in his eyes. I accept the waters politely and gratefully and suck them back. The passengers seated around us shoot weary glances in our direction.

Safe to say we didn't make any friends on this flight.

~~~

By the time we move through customs, it's after midnight London time. Having slept for somewhere in the vicinity of six hours and it being around five o'clock at night in Vegas, my stomach growls for some grub.

"Any chance London has a Denny's?" I hike my duffle further up on my shoulder, following Rex through the glass doors that lead outside. Freezing air hits my face to knock off the lingering hangover. I'm grateful I followed Rex's advice to pull out a sweatshirt earlier. It's cold as shit.

"I'll ask Caleb." He squints against the freezing wind. "Fuck. I hate being cold. Gonna have to change my pirate name to Captain Shriveldick."

I cough out a laugh and burrow deeper into my UFL sweatshirt. "He'd make a better sidekick to Lord Flaccid."

He stops and glares at me. "I'm not your *sidekick*, dude. I'm the Batman to your Robin."

"There's no way Shriveldick trumps Flaccid. Think about it. Flaccid still has size, but lacks strength. Shrivel is . . . Well, he lacks everything."

"Fuck that! Shrivel—"

"I thought the good ole US of A was sending me a couple of fighters, not two numbnuts discussin' the attributes of their tiny peckers."

Rex and I both turn toward the country twang to find Caleb standing there with his arms spread wide in greeting.

"Hole-ee-shit." Rex infuses a very unnatural sounding country accent to his voice. "How the fuck are you, man?" He wraps the big blond in a back-thumping hug.

"Can't complain much." He releases Rex and swings his gaze to me. "Fuckin' A, you grew, boy!" He reaches out and shakes my hand. "Last time I saw you, you were"—he holds his hand up to his chest— "yay high."

Rex slaps me in the chest. "Kid's been working his ass off."

He looks me up in down. "I can see that." He flicks a finger toward my eye. "Who gave you the shiner?"

My heart thuds at the reminder. I push the unwelcome feelings back. "Blake."

Caleb grins. "Very nice."

"Any chance we can finish this get-to-know-ya somewhere with a heater?" Rex's gaze takes in our surroundings. "And less wet."

"Welcome to London, dude. Get used to it." He nods toward a navy blue car the size of a roller skate with four doors. "I'm over there."

My brows pop high. "That?"

"How the hell do you expect us to fit in that thing?" Rex stares at the wheeled dot with curiosity.

"We're in London, brother." He slaps Rex on the back. "This Vee Dub Golf is considered a full-sized vehicle."

I rub the back of my neck, already feeling the muscle cramps that will surely follow being crammed into the backseat. "Not sure the name implies full-size."

"You two spoiled American pussies would rather take a cab? 'Cause I'm telling you the taxis here aren't any bigger." He motions to a line of small black cars.

"I'll ride in the back." I pop the hatchback and toss my shit in, Rex coming up beside me to do the same.

We climb inside the car, and I'm surprised how spacious the interior really is. I still have to sit at an angle to accommodate my legs, but that's mostly because both Rex and Caleb's seats are cranked back so they have plenty of legroom. I make a note to call shotgun next time.

"Any chance there's a twenty-four-hour diner close by? It's dinnertime in Vegas, not to mention the kid and I are battling a little brown-bottle flu."

Caleb pulls out and—oh shit—I have to turn away because driving on the wrong side of the road *and* on the wrong side of the car is freaking me the fuck out. "Nah . . . only thing here open twenty-four hours is Mickey D's."

"Killer, you down to top this body torture off with some fast food?"

"When does training start?" I ask Caleb.

"First thing tomorrow morning."

"Fuck." I shrug and my stomach growls its answer. "May as well."

"No barfing tomorrow, ya hear?" Caleb makes a left turn, and the first few sprinkles of rain hit the windshield. "We've been scaring the shit out of everyone here, telling them that Killer from Team USA is coming in ready to destroy. You've got a rep to uphold."

Rex chuckles and grins back at me before facing Caleb. "He won't disappoint. Trust me. The kid is ready. A little hangover and a heart-attack meal won't change that."

While staring out the window, all I can think is I hope to God he's right.

Fighting is all I have left.

Failure isn't an option.

~~~

"Wake up, princess." A sharp sting on my cheek pulls me from sleep. "Come on. I'm only here for a few days, and we've got shit to do."

214

I crack one eye open and stare at Rex, who's standing on my bed, wearing his training clothes and a shit-eating grin. "What makes you so perky this morning?"

"First of all, it's the afternoon."

I rub my eyes. "No shit?"

"You slept like a corpse. Why didn't you set your alarm?"

"Don't have one."

"Your phone, jackass."

My gut tumbles. "Didn't bring it."

He looks confused.

"Figured I'd just get a new one." And I didn't want the brutal reminder of Axelle not calling me or the temptation to contact her.

"Okay, I'll make sure we get you one today. Now wake the fuck up and smile." He holds his arms out wide. "This is the first day of the rest of your life, man. How the hell can you not be fucking stoked about that?"

I snag my glasses off the bedside table and yawn.

"Get dressed and I'll meet you downstairs." Rex hops off the bed and crosses to the door. "Hope you got a good night's sleep. Today is going to be brutal."

He slams the door behind him, and I groan and drop my head into my hands.

The truth is I slept like shit.

After we hit McDonalds, Caleb brought us to what will be my home for the next year. From the outside, it looks like part office high-rise, part fishbowl. With card access, a gate was opened that led to underground parking and an elevator. It wasn't until we were inside the elevator and Caleb slid the card into the "lift" as he called it, that I realized we were headed to the top.

A split-level penthouse.

If I weren't so tired and half stupid from the whirlwind of the last couple days, it would've hit me then that little Killian McCreery was now residing in a penthouse in

London, fighting for UFL USA. And even after a fitful night's rest, dreams of Axelle's beautiful belly swelling with new life growing inside it, her wrapping that sweet body around me and telling me that she loves me and our baby . . . Damn, I'm far from rested.

But I'm awake.

And it's sinking in.

I cross toward the floor-to-ceiling windows and pull back the sheer white curtains—another thing I didn't quite appreciate about this place when I got here. Everything is either white or black. The carpet of my modest-sized room is white and peppered with sleek black furniture and a white overstuffed chair. It's like living on a chessboard with a kick-ass view.

Gray clouds break up across the skyline, and below is the bustling city of London. But that's not all. There's water.

Caleb explained last night that this part of town was called the Docklands, which makes sense. From what I can tell, it's industrial with waterways and docks for large ships probably making pick-ups and deliveries. It's fucking cool as shit.

I can hear Caleb and Rex laughing downstairs, where the main living space is complete with a state-of-the-art home theater, an open kitchen with fancy-ass appliances, and a dining room fit for royalty. The three bedrooms are upstairs, each with their own private bathrooms, which are bigger than my studio back in Vegas. That Jacuzzi tub will come in handy after those long training weeks.

I cross to my bag that I tossed at the foot of my bed when I stumbled to it last night. Grabbing some clothes, I allow myself to indulge in a fantasy. I pretend Axelle is here with me, I imagine her sky-blue eyes alight with excitement at living in such luxury. She'd giggle at seeing the bidet and the separate urinal in the marble-floored bathroom. My fingers tingle as I imagine sliding them into her hair, looking deep into her eyes until her humor fades as I promise her every luxury I can afford for the rest of her long and beautiful life.

My chest cramps violently at the realization that these things will never happen. She made her choice, and I thought I made mine when I stepped onto that plane, but it's as if my heart needs the constant reminder. As if the last few beats of my love for her are refusing to simply die, but would rather suffer from a long drawn-out process that has me in knots.

I drag my body under the shower spray and close my eyes. "It's over, Killian. The sooner you get that through your thick skull, the better."

I shove all those feelings, all the hurt and the love, deep into the darkest corner of my soul and lock it there behind brick walls. I've made the choice to spend this year in London, working on my fighting career, and I intend to do just that.

No more pain and no regrets. No friendships and complications.

From here on out I'm a fighter.

That's it.

TWENTY-TWO

Axelle

By the time Monday rolls around, I'm ready to get the hell out of my mom and Blake's house and back to my apartment. After confronting Clifford yesterday, Blake insisted I stay with them. I'm sure it was my crumbling into a sobbing mess in my mom's lap that spoke to my instability. The more I cried, the more my mom cried, and between the two of us, we could've hydrated Nevada with our tears.

When we dried out, Blake made us dinner, and I fell asleep on the couch with my head in my mom's lap. I don't remember how I got into my bed, but I do remember Blake's voice telling me everything would be okay, so my guess is he probably carried me there.

My mom slides a bowl of fruit in front of me while holding my baby brother, who just woke up. "What time is your first class?"

I pop a grape into my mouth. "I missed it. I think I can make my afternoon classes though. But . . ." My stomach sours and I threaten to heave. "I have to get my car from Killian's."

I'm grateful I have my keys with me. Since we were coming to babysit Jack on Saturday, I brought them so I'd have Mom's house key just in case I needed it. The problem is the bag I brought with me for our little weekend sleepover is still in his place, and since I don't have a way to get into his studio without him there, I'm forced to see him face to face.

Ever since Clifford practically spit on me, I've been entertaining the idea of taking Killian up on his offer. If we raise this baby to know that Killian is his dad, but not his biological father, there will be no surprises. As much as I'll hate to one day have to explain to him or her that their father was in no shape to be a dad, I believe with all my heart that Killian's love would cushion that blow. But what would Kill be giving up?

Guilt spills like liquid lead over me, and I slump into my seat. I love Killian. I can't expect him to make sacrifices to take care of us.

I always dreamed about what my life would've been like had my mom been strong enough to walk away from Stewart back when I was born. If she'd braved it and raised me alone, I never would've had to bear witness to her abuse. And now here I am considering making the same choice, leaning on a man—albeit a wonderfully loving and gentle man—to avoid having to face the consequences and hardships of my own mistakes.

No, I have to do this on my own—if only to prove to myself that I can. Then and only then will I have anything substantial to offer someone like Killian.

I love him.

I will always love him.

And if we're meant to be together, we will be, regardless of whose baby I'm carrying.

Right?

"Blake's taking Jack for a couple of hours. I can take you to Killian's when you're ready." My mom sets her worried eyes on mine as if she's following the direction of my thoughts.

"Thanks, Mom."

She comes around the counter and drops onto the stool next to mine. Her deep brown eyes are bloodshot from yesterday, or it's possible she was crying even this morning. I hate that I've done this to her. "Listen. I want you to know I understood what you said the other day about doing this on your own, but without a job, you'll need to accept a little help."

She's not telling me anything I haven't already made myself sick trying to figure out. I could drop out of school and get a job, but who'll hire a pregnant woman taking maternity leave just a short time after being hired? And then what? I go back to work to make just enough money to pay for daycare? What about diapers, rent, electricity?

"I know. I just don't know what to do about that. I'm tired of being a burden on everyone."

"You've never been a burden. I know what it's like to have to depend on others when it's the last thing you want to do. I married Stewart for the same reason. You don't have to do that, Axelle. Blake and I would love it if you moved back home."

"Mom, no, I can't. You guys have a great thing going on here. I'd only—"

"No." She shakes her head. "Don't finish that thought. Your lease with Mindy is another four months. Take your time, consider your options, and make the decision that's best for you, but know that we're here to help you through this."

She and Blake have been paying my rent in exchange for me watching Jack when they need me or take a trip out of town. The tradeoff is in my favor since they only need me about once a week, but I can't ask them to continue to pay for my rent once this baby is born. And what am I going to do? Live with Mindy while she's banging football players on the couch and I'm up all night with a baby?

"Okay, Mom."

She sighs heavily. "We'll come up with a plan as things mellow. In the meantime, you should make an appointment with your doctor."

"That's right." I rub my temples. "I need to do that." So much for my *I got this* attitude. I can't even remember to do the simplest things on my own.

Her soft touch runs up and down my back. "One day at a time."

"Am I going to be able to do this, Mom?"

She presses a kiss to my head. "You're never alone. We'll always be right here if you need us."

"You realize I'm making Jack an uncle, right?"

She sucks in a breath.

I tilt my head to study her. "And you'll be a grandmother."

Her eyes widen, but she wrangles in her shock and smiles shakily. "That'll take some getting used to."

~~~

"Are you sure you don't want me to go with you?" My mom's hand grips mine from the front seat of her car as I stare at the back of Killian's Jeep.

He's home.

"He's missing class. He never misses a class," I mumble to myself, trying for the life of me to sort out what I'm seeing.

"These last couple of days have been hard on everyone." Her eyes stare thoughtfully at the back of his car. "He's probably just taking a day to come to terms with everything."

"I should just grab my car and go." I can't face him now. He'll ask about Clifford, and I'll have to tell him how he blew me off, claiming the baby wasn't his and that I was trying to corner him into a commitment.

And then what? Will he offer to get back together? To raise this baby together? I press my palm to my lower belly. If he did, would I have the strength to say no?

"Come on. This is silly." My mom swings open her door and slides out. "This is Killian we're talking about. He's your best friend, Axelle. He wants what is best for you. Stop acting like he's the enemy here."

I open my mouth to defend myself, but she shuts the door before I can. I watch in horror as she crosses to the stairs, and before I can think better of it, I'm bounding up the stairs behind her.

"Mom, wait! What if . . .?" I roll my lips between my teeth to keep from being heard because, damn, for a little woman, my mom is quick.

I'm out of breath by the time she reaches Killian's door and knocks. My pulse rockets even higher with nerves, and I lean against the wall to keep from passing out.

Male voices come from behind the door, and butterflies burst behind my ribs as it swings open.

"Oh hey, Layla."

I step to my mom's side at the sound of Ryder's voice.

He stares between us, confused. "What's going on?"

I peek around his shoulder and see Theo with his hands in a box, staring back at me.

"Ryder, um . . . is Killian around?" My mom seems just as confused as I am because it seems like they're moving Kill's things.

"No, he's in London."

"What!" The word flies from my mouth with such force Ryder slices his gaze to mine.

"You didn't know?"

Tears prick my eyes, but I hold them back. "No, I had no idea." He didn't tell me he was leaving so soon. I thought I had more time. He didn't even say good-bye.

"When did he leave?" My mom presses in close as if to hold me up if my legs give out.

"Yesterday. I guess he changed his mind about the London gig, called my dad, and hopped on a plane with Rex first thing. He asked me to sell all his shit, but Dad said pack it up and store it. We'll put his Jeep in storage too until he gets back." He shrugs, but his eyes fix on mine.

I can't imagine Killian told Ryder about my situation, but he saw us leave together Valentine's night and probably assumed we'd be together. The fact that Kilian left without telling me makes it pretty obvious to everyone where things stand between us.

I clear my throat, eager to get out of here before I burst into tears. "I need to grab my things." I push past Ry and see my bag in the same place I left it. My gaze slides to the bed, and my chest clenches to see it's already been stripped and disassembled.

Pulling my bag up, I go to the bathroom and dump the contents of my drawer into the bag. I quickly glance in the shower and see his things are gone, another reminder that he truly has left to the other side of the world.

I pass by the bowl of change and see the keys to his Jeep and his phone. My heart stutters as I stare at the device. Ryder must be watching because he sidles up next to me. "Guess he forgot it. I told my dad I'd send it to him, but he said it's just easier for him to pick up a new one over there."

Reaching out, I grab it and hit the button that brings it to life.

The screen lights up to an image of our faces, a selfie we took in front of the Eiffel Tower at Paris on The Strip. It was during Christmas break and Vegas was having a cold snap, so I was dressed in a big coat with a fur collar, and Killian had on a hooded sweatshirt and a black beanie. Our cheeks and noses are flushed pink, and he's smiling casually while I'm laughing hard at the story he'd just told me.

Did you know a woman once jumped off the real Eiffel Tower to commit suicide, landed on a guy's car, and they ended up getting married?

I swore he made that up, but he insisted it was a true story.

His future wife fell from the sky right onto his car. They don't call Paris the City of Love for nothing. People line up at the base of it now just waiting to get clobbered by their true love.

I laughed. He snapped the picture.

We posted it on Instagram, along with selfies of us on a gondola at The Venetian and in front of the Statue of Liberty at New York-New York with the hashtag #worldtravel. It was stupid, and no one actually believed we were traveling the world, but for two people who'd never even been on a plane, for just that night, it sort of felt like we were.

"You ready, Axelle?" My mom smiles sadly at me, most likely having been witness to me staring at Killian's phone.

I nod and set the device back down by the bowl of change.

He left his phone here on purpose. That's obvious. He's sending a message, cutting all ties. As much as it hurts, I can't deny that it's probably for the best.

With a wave good-bye to Ryder and Theo, I keep my head down to hide my tears as I scurry out the door and to my car. My mom makes sure I get in okay, and once I'm out of sight, I pull over onto a side street and bawl.

TWENTY-THREE

Killian

One month in London and I've managed to fall into a robotic routine. I wake every morning at five and jog The Thames Path along the river. I throw down a mostly tasteless breakfast and shower then head to the training center with Caleb. The training center here is a quarter of the size of the one in Vegas, more like a storefront than a warehouse, but only five miles from home. Just like back in Vegas, I train with different members of the UFL UK team, but all under the supervision and expertise of Caleb. I've met so many new people it took weeks for me to remember all their names.

There's Laise, pronounced like Lacey, the Scotsman who rivals the likes of Jonah Slade in size and ability. His overgrown beard and shoulder-length hair give him an ominous look inside the octagon, but he has the temperament of a kitten when he's outside it.

Then there are the three local British fighters: Liam, Henry, and Jay who encompass the MMA trifecta: Liam's ground game, Henry's stand up, and Jay whose takedowns are better than Rex's (not that I'd ever admit that out loud).

And finally there are the French siblings, Olivier and Fleur, a brother and sister who're so bad-ass their blood type must be BA positive.

It's Ollie who stares at me now as I annihilate the speed bag. His eyes are narrow and assessing. My arms and back, legs and core, all strain with fatigue as the Frenchman lifts a brow at me. I step back and pop off my earbuds. "I don't care how many times you ask. I still refuse to autograph your dick."

His mouth lifts in a one-sided grin, and he scratches his shaved head. "Hilarious, Harry."

I control the urge to sock him in the gut. Just one time these assholes saw me in my glasses and they've been calling me some variation of the young wizard's name ever since.

"Caleb wants you at grappling." His French accent is weak and mixed with the Londoner accent he's picked up since he's lived here most of his adult life. "And you should know you hit like my little sister."

I laugh and pull off my gloves to wipe the sweat off my forehead. "Is that supposed to be an insult? Because your sister's quick as shit."

"That's what I mean. Your arms are fast; it's like . . . like . . ." His eyes widen. "Magic!"

I grab my shit and make my way over to the grappling pads. "You guys really need to come up with some new material."

He follows right behind me. "Tell me, Potter, how long did it take until Hermione let you Slytherin, huh?"

He laughs at his own joke, and I can't help but chuckle too. The guy is creative. I'll give him that. "Did you know Merlin was a Slytherin?"

"You're off your trolley."

"I'm serious. *The* Merlin was taught personally by Salazar Slytherin."

"You nerds done?" Caleb calls from the mats, waiting with Liam. My first fight is in three weeks against Hugo "Spidey" Webb. He lost the welterweight title his last fight and is looking to make a comeback, and I'm not going to let him earn it on my back.

"Liam's been watching Webb's tapes." Caleb motions to the stocky Brit. "Let's run through some ground game and defensive moves."

Fine by me. Pride isn't something I'm comfortable feeling. I'd like to think I'm a constant work in progress, that there's always room for improvement. But the last two grappling sessions I had with Liam I came out on top. Hopefully, he has something new for me today.

"You ready, old man?" I toss my towel away and grin at Liam.

He snarls and flashes his chipped front tooth, which adds a ruthlessness to his already intimidating mug. "Fuck yeah, you little tosspot."

These guys and their slang. British insults are the cutest damn things I've ever heard. "Aw, that's sweet."

He growls then lunges, and just like every other day, we move through takedowns, submissions, and escapes.

The weeks go on like this, training every day and going back to the penthouse every night to wind down, make dinner, and read or watch a movie.

As fast as the weeks fly by, the weekends do the opposite. Saturday and Sunday drag along at a slow crawl. I train lightly those days, and I've managed to do some sight-seeing, but it makes for an isolated experience. I hit the pubs with the guys at night, which is fun. The UFL UK has a decent amount of groupies, so no matter where we go, we end up with plenty of company.

I've never been the guy who's always surrounded by groups of friends. Being an only child who grew up to be a somewhat—oh, who am I kidding—a total nerdy adult, I've only ever had one friend, who I refuse to let myself think about. So, although being the center of attention isn't something I'm used to, I gotta admit it's not half bad. It's on that thought that Liam hooks my neck from behind.

"Oh come on!" The female voice with a thick French accent sounds from just off the mats. "No chance you'll beat Webb if you're sleeping on the job, Harry!"

"She's right, HP." Liam mumbles in my ear and laughs before releasing me.

Fleur, all five-foot-three inches, stomps across the mats and props her hands on her narrow hips. Her big hazel eyes blaze with irritation, and her dark blond ponytail falls over her sculpted tan shoulder. "What the fuck is wrong with you, Potter?"

"Nothing." I shrug and get to my feet, getting a sense of victory when I stand a whole head taller than her.

"Did you hear that, cowboy?" She glares at Caleb, who rolls his eyes. "He says nothing, but he let himself get choked out by Liam."

"I didn't *let* myself; he just bested me." Okay, that's not exactly true. I may not have been as focused as I should've been.

"Oh . . . he bested you." She smiles, and every time she does, I'm always amazed she chose fighting over something more fitting like modeling. She has an innocent beauty about her that reminds me of a young Kate Moss, except with more muscles. She steps back and crouches, opening her arms in a fighting stance. "Let's see if you can best me, Potter. After all, I'm just a teeny girl."

"Oh fuck . . ."

"He's shafted."

The surrounding fighters continue with their mumbled comments as they back off the mats.

Even her brother Olivier says, "Watch your balls, HP. She doesn't fight fair."

I sigh and shake my head, staring down at her. "You don't want to do this, little flower."

"Don't I?" She lifts a sculpted brow. "Make me regret it."

I keep my eyes on her as she circles me; her eyes study me as if she's calculating where to strike first.

Her legs step with practiced fluidity; they're short but toned and lead from a pair of long MMA training shorts to end with bare feet and bright red toe nails—*umph!*

Her shoulder hits my gut and arms wrap around my middle. Her leg sweeps at my feet, but I step back to avoid her kick.

No matter how many times we train together, it always amazes me how much power she can pack in her small frame. The guys call from all around us, taunting and cheering, which is ridiculous. The girl weighs next to nothing, so I fold over her, reach around her waist, and lift her off the ground.

"Gah!" Her legs kick, and in one swift move, I flip her to her back and hold her arms above her head.

She digs her heel into the mat to try and flip me, which makes me laugh.

A weak growl rumbles in her throat as I tangle my legs in hers and lock her down with my hips.

"I win."

Her eyes narrow, but I see something else there. It's in the way her pupils dilate and her lips part. Even under her loose T-shirt, I can feel her back arch to press her breasts against me. I hiss out a breath and drop my chin, pretending it's exhaustion and not the uninvited rush of lust that's heating through me.

Shit! I don't want this.

I shove off of her and hop to my feet, more than a little troubled by my body's reaction to her.

Not that it shouldn't react. I mean the girl is gorgeous and the soft curves of her body pressed to mine would elicit a reaction out of a dead man, which is basically what I am—dead—at least on the inside.

The slow clap from Caleb calls my attention.

"Very nice, Killer. You've managed to takedown a hundred-pound female. Now let's see if we can work you up to a one-hundred-seventy-pound professional fighter, m'kay?"

His teasing tone is just what I need to clear my head. "Then let's stop standing around bullshitting and train."

I reach out to help Fleur to her feet and she laughs. "I have to give it to you; those were some impressive moves, Killian." She used my real name, and genuine admiration fills her voice.

"Thanks."

"Do you have plans tonight?"

My eyes dart around to the guys, but they're all huddled together, talking fight-night strategy. "No." Unless a date with my e-reader counts.

Her eyes light up and her expression goes soft. "There's a place I want to show you."

I shake my head. "Oh, I don't know. The last time I went out drinking with you I was hungover for three days."

She cocks a hip and crosses her arms at her chest. "And that was my fault?"

"I don't remember much, but what I do involved you dancing on the bar—"

She slaps my gut. "Enough, please, don't remind me. Anyway, it's not a pub; it's a place for dinner. You'll love it, I promise."

The excitement in her expression is hard to say no to, so I simply nod. It's dinner. I can do dinner.

"Great. I have my car, so we can go straight from here."

"Killian!" Caleb motions to the center of the mats. "Let's try this again."

Fleur slaps me on the upper arm. "Have fun. I'll see you later."

Dinner with a friend is doable. Granted she's female and gorgeous, but this is strictly platonic. And besides, I have one year in London, and I'm soaking it up for all it's worth.

~~~

We finish up training around five, and I shower and throw on some clean clothes. For a second, I wish I had something a little nicer to wear. After all, I have no idea where Fleur is taking me, and the last thing I want to do is show up looking like a hillbilly. If there's one thing I've learned in my short time in London, it's that appearances are important.

With no other choice but to go in my Adidas workout pants and UFL sweatshirt, I push out of the locker room with my bag slung over my shoulder.

Fleur must've been waiting because she jumps up from one of the modern red chairs that sit in a formal lobby between the men's and women's locker rooms. I breathe a sigh of relief when I see her in a pair of black leggings, a red UFL sweatshirt, and bright red rain boots. She's obviously showered, her hair falling down around her shoulders, and her eyes are a little brighter and lips a little darker as if she's wearing makeup, but still casual.

"You ready?"

I nod. "Sure. I'm starving too. Hope wherever we're going isn't one of those old Londoner places that only serve jellied eels and warm beer." I shiver.

"Ahh . . ." She tilts her head. "You went out with Jay then."

"I did." My first week here he took Rex and me out for a traditional London meal. I swore if this was what I had to eat for a year I would surely starve to death in weeks.

She rocks into my arm, and the playfulness of it makes my chest hurt from missing an old friend. "Don't worry. Olivier and I fell for it to. I can't even look at Jell-O anymore without vomiting."

I chuckle. "I'm suddenly not so hungry anymore."

"You will be once we get to where I'm taking you." She motions for me to follow her out to the street where it's pouring rain.

She hits her key fob, flashing the taillights of a red Vauxhall Corsa. We jog through the rain and climb in, shaking the moisture from our hair.

"Let me guess . . . your favorite color is red?"

She laughs. "Good guess."

I try not to flinch as we drive through the rain on the wrong side of the road, which is getting easier but still manages to make me tense, and not being in the driver's seat only makes it worse.

We chat about the upcoming fight, and it turns out she's a UFC Wikipedia like I am, so soon we're talking about fights that happened when we were kids, assuming she's around my age, which I'm guessing she is.

"Oh, close your eyes!" She reaches over and tries to put her hand over my face.

I hold her off and turn my head. "Okay, okay, they're closed."

The vehicle makes a right and then, shortly after, a left until it comes to a stop.

"Okay, we're here." Her voice rings with that high pitch girls get when they're excited.

I open my eyes and lean forward to peer out the windshield. "Is that—"

"Yes! Come on!" She jumps out of the car, and I follow her through the rain and to the front door of a 1950's style diner.

From the outside, it looks like something you'd see in Vegas: a long silver structure with a rounded top styled after an old food trailer, and a big neon sign. Once we push through the front door, I grin so wide it hurts my cheeks.

"No way."

She claps her hands excitedly. "Do you like it?"

The entire place is exactly like something you'd see in Vegas, from Elvis's voice coming from the big blue-and-red-lighted jukebox to the black and white photos on the walls. The waitresses are wearing poodle skirts, and the waiters all look like some variation of Buddy Holly. With the scent of fry oil, burgers, and Velveeta cheese permeating the air, it's just like home.

"This place is great." I peer down at her, and she genuinely seems proud of herself.

"You've been here a month and never talk about home. I figured you might be homesick." She swings an arm out. "Thought this might help."

I take another glance around and grin. "And no jellied eels."

She laughs and drags me off to a booth in the back. "Nope. Not a single jellied eel in sight."

The waitress who takes our order could be a Lucille Ball impersonator, all except for her accent. We place our orders, and I study the American license plates that take up an entire wall. One from almost every state. I find Nevada and the plate reads *HI RLR*.

"So . . ." Fleur leans back and squints. "What's your story? How did you end up fighting for the UFL?"

"I've always been a fan. Then when I was fifteen, I was at the airport with my mom picking up my uncle, and there was a guy who—fuck, he took up the entire room. He was at least a foot taller and a foot wider than anyone else, and when I took a closer look, I realized it was Jonah Slade."

She slams her palms on the table, eyes wide. "The Assassin!"

I grin at her enthusiasm. "The one and only."

Lucille Ball drops off our Cherry Cokes, which I'm sure Caleb will kick my ass for tomorrow, but I've gone a month without soda, and I can't come to this old-timey diner without having one.

I take a long pull and groan when the sweet fizz hits my tongue.

"I would die; that guy's a legend! So what did you do?" She's talking fast, making her French accent heavier than usual.

"I walked up to him . . ."

She gasps.

"I told him I was a huge fan, started spouting off his fight stats like a nervous idiot, and asked him for his autograph. He was really cool, and even though I probably weighed ninety-five pounds back then, he encouraged me to give fighting a shot."

"Just like that? The Assassin says give it a shot and now you're a fighter?"

I laugh and push back the ache forming in my chest. "Not exactly. About a year later, I met a girl."

"Ahh . . ." She rubs her hands together. "Now we get to the exciting stuff."

"I don't know how exciting it is." I try not to remember how amazing it was. "She was the new kid at school. I found her in the parking lot screaming at her car." The day I met Axelle is as clear as if it just happened. She was cursing up a storm, totally unaware that I was watching her, and even with the voice of the devil himself pouring from her lips, she looked like an angel. "She needed a ride, and it turned out her mom was the administrative assistant to the UFL CEO."

She shakes her head and whispers, "What are the odds?"

"I ran into Jonah and he remembered me, and it turned out the girl's mom was dating Blake Daniels."

"You're shitting me!" She stares at me in awe. "So here you are, helping out this girl, and you find yourself just chatting it up with *The Snake* and *The Assassin*. You jammy bastard."

"I think they felt sorry for me or something. I don't know, but they offered to let me come in and help out around the gym. One thing led to another and here I am."

"Wow." She takes a long pull off her straw. "You owe that girl a bit of gratitude, huh? Does she have any idea she super-started your career?"

"We've been . . . are . . ." I rub my forehead. "We were best friends ever since."

Fleur doesn't seem to catch my fumble. "What a great story."

"How about you? Why did you become a fighter?" And not a model or an actress?

"Simple really." She stirs her soda with her straw. "Olivier practically raised me. He loved to fight, and since our mum worked crazy hours, I had to tag along."

"Why did you guys leave Paris?"

She shrugs a shoulder. "Olivier got the offer to come here and train, and there was no way I was going to let him leave me behind."

"You ever miss it? Miss your friends back home?"

She leans forward, her forearms crossed and resting on the table. "We try to go back and visit family as often as we can. I grew up in an MMA gym, so I didn't leave behind a load of mates or anything. I find I get along better with blokes anyway."

I can see that. She's easy to talk to, and if it weren't for her looks, I'd probably forget she was even a girl.

My phone vibrates in my pocket and I pull it out to check the caller ID.

Ryder.

This is the fourth time he's called in as many days. I hit "decline" and shove my phone back in my pocket.

"Was it not important?" She tips her chin, indicating my phone.

"No, just someone from back home." I take a sip of my Coke. "I'll call him back later." It's a lie. Talking to Ryder means risking information on Axelle, and in order to stay numb, I can't think of her.

"Do you miss your American friends?"

I clear my throat and lean back. "I don't talk to them much." I drum my fingers on the tabletop, feeling a little exposed. "I've been really busy and focusing on my fighting. I don't have time."

Stupid fucking excuse.

Thing is, I haven't spoken to anyone about what happened with Axelle. Not even Caleb. The only person I do stay in touch with is Cameron, and he's never even alluded to knowing the why behind my sudden exodus from Vegas.

If any of them do know that I pledged my fucking life to her and she kicked me to the curb, they're kind enough to save me from the humiliation and not bring it up.

TWENTY-FOUR

Axelle

"It's been nine weeks since your last period?" Dr. Schwartz scribbles something down in the folder.

"That's right." *Nine weeks.*

The number runs through my head because it seems like just yesterday I was peeing on pregnancy tests.

My OB goes on to explain that the baby is growing; although I'm not showing yet. The morning sickness should kick in, but I actually feel better than I did last month. I suppose that's because I'm settling in and coming to terms with everything. She assures me not to worry, that all women are different, and unless I get extreme cramping or bleeding, that "normal" is relative.

"We can do a transvaginal ultrasound if you'd like?"

"Is that um . . . internal?"

"Yes, the fetus is still too small to be seen on an external ultrasound, so we'd insert a wand vaginally—"

"Oh, ya know? I think I'm good."

It was only weeks ago that my pregnancy finally sunk in. Knowing there's a life growing inside me is one thing. Clifford's rejection of that life is another. Seeing the baby with my own eyes, well . . . I don't think I'm ready to handle that. At least, not on my own.

"And the father?" Maybe it's the big "S" I marked on my marital status, or my lack of engagement ring, but she peers up at me with sympathy in her eyes.

"He's, um, he's not in the picture anymore."

I thought with the way Clifford blew me off that day at his front door that he'd never want to speak to me again. I couldn't have been more wrong. Not only is he still speaking to me, or rather at me, what he says when he does forces me to run off campus in tears.

His precious Xbox must no longer hold his interest, and messing with me has quickly become his most exciting game to play. It hasn't been so bad that I can't handle it. And no way am I going to ask for help on this one. Besides, nothing he can say will make me hurt any more than I already do.

Dr. Schwartz closes the folder and nods. "What we'll do today is take some blood to determine your blood type, Rh factor, and antibody screening. You said your last alcoholic beverage was six weeks ago?"

"Yes, before I realized I was pregnant, and only a beer. Probably not even a full one. Is that bad?"

She shakes her head. "No, it's common for women to engage in social drinking before they realize they're pregnant. Smoking?"

"No, although the baby's father, he um . . ." I lick my lips and struggle to get the words out. I don't want this doctor to judge me, and what I have to say sounds horrible. "I think he used drugs. Bad ones."

Her eyebrows pinch together. "Okay, but you have no contact with him now, correct?"

"No, none at all." Except for the occasional harassment at school, but I keep that to myself.

She makes another note in my file, probably something like "stupid loser having sex with a druggie." Not that I'd blame her. That's fairly accurate.

A blood draw later and a quick stop to get a Very Berry Smoothie, and I'm on my way back to my apartment. It's Thursday and I have a ton of homework, which should keep me busy until I pass out from exhaustion.

Mindy pops her head out of her bedroom as soon as I get home. "Hey, where were you?"

I drop my purse in the kitchen and meet her in the living room. "Doctor's appointment."

"You sick?" Her gaze roams over my face as if she's looking for physical evidence, and I'm glad I thought to take off the cotton ball on my inner arm from the blood draw.

"No, just tired, so my mom thought I should see a doctor." I take a slurp from my smoothie, filling my mouth with the tart goodness before I spill my guts to my roommate.

I know I need to tell her eventually, but every time I get close, I freak out, afraid of how she'll react. I'm getting enough lectures from the people in my life and have zero desire to add Mindy to the list.

"First she makes you take the vitamins and now the doctor?" She laughs. "Guess she doesn't remember how tiring college life is, huh?"

"No, I guess she doesn't, seeing as she never went to college; she had me when she was *sixteen*." I don't know why I feel so defensive.

"Oh, right." She twirls a strand of her blond hair. "I think I knew that. Anyway, you want to catch a movie tonight?"

"Can't. I have too much homework."

Her eyes narrow. "Since when do you care about homework?"

"It's time I start putting forth more than minimal effort." This'll be my last year at UNLV, and whatever grades I get will have to propel me through life as a single mother. Fuck, that's depressing.

"You miss him."

I pop the straw from my mouth and force myself to swallow.

"It's okay to just admit it, Axelle. He's your best friend."

I cough to clear my throat, but the lump that's been there since Killian left remains. "Of course I miss him."

"Why don't you just call him?"

"I already told you I don't want to bother him." And there's the tiny little issue of him not giving me his number. "This is a huge deal for his career, and he doesn't need distractions."

She tilts her head. "Since when is friendship a distraction?"

"Look. He didn't bring his phone for a reason—"

"Didn't Ryder give you his new number?"

"Yes, but that doesn't change the fact that he didn't give me his new number. He doesn't want to talk to me, Mindy."

"That's so weird." I suppose it would seem weird, seeing as she doesn't know all the facts.

"Besides, he hasn't called or texted me, and I'm right here with the same ole phone number I've had since high school."

"So that's what this is about. You don't want to make the first move."

"Move? What, like we're dating?"

"Aren't you?"

"No, Mindy." I push to stand. "Stay out of it, okay? Whatever is or isn't going on between Killian and me is no one else's business." I stomp off to my room, fighting tears.

"Axelle, wait—"

I slam the door behind me and lock it just as the first tear falls.

I've been telling myself the same lie since he left—that he's not calling or texting me because he's too busy—but I know that's not true. Not a day in four years of friendship has he ever been too busy for me.

Blake told me he's alive and well over in London, that he's training for his first official UFL fight. Cam's throwing a big party at the training center where we'll all watch it. I'm torn between being excited and terrified because seeing Killian on the big screen will be the first time I've seen him since he turned his back and walked away. I don't know how I'll feel seeing him again, but if it's anything close to how I feel now, then it might be better if I don't go. No one needs to see me have a total nervous breakdown.

I pull my phone from my pocket, drop to my bed, and curl onto my side to scroll through social media. Killian has a professional Facebook page that hasn't been updated since a week before he left. I hit the Instagram icon and go directly to his page. His last post was a photo of him and Ryder at the Training Center, dripping in sweat after running for an hour on the treadmill. My finger hovers over the "Photos of KillerMC" tab. I've only allowed myself to hit this button one other time, and there were a few new photos posted of him by other people. Most of them were in a bar, and in all of them Killian was smiling. It hurt so badly to see him happy without me. I swore I'd never stalk him again.

And here I am.

With a deep breath, I close my eyes and hit the button.

Peeking through one cracked lid, I see . . . what? I sit up and stare at my phone in my lap. There are several new pictures of Killian.

I hit the first one and crank my head back in shock.

It's Killian, his face damp with sweat and his hair hanging down over his forehead. The shot is taken from a side angle and Kill's not looking at the camera, but down as if he's thinking or catching his breath. The caption on the photo says "Determination at its finest with @KillerMC," and the photo was posted by "PetiteFleur," who, according to her profile picture, is a woman. Not just any woman, a *gorgeous* woman.

I go back and hit on the next photo of Killian. He's smiling big with his head slightly thrown back as if the photo was snapped just after the punchline of a joke. His eyes are dancing even in the still shot, and the caption says, "Making @KillerMC laugh makes my day." And sure enough, the photo was posted again by PetiteFleur. A sick feeling rolls in my gut when I see the last new photo posted of Killian is of two people together. With a shaky finger, I touch it, and when it goes full-size, my heart sinks into my stomach.

It's him. And her. Their faces are pressed together cheek to cheek, and she's doing bunny ears behind his head. The caption reads, "Showing @KillerMC around London is like seeing it for the first time. #luckygirl."

So that's it then. He's moved on.

That's great. It's exactly what I wanted for him, a chance to be happy, and from the looks of it, he seems . . . I hate to even admit it, but he seems happier than he ever seemed here in Vegas. How could he not be? He's dating a girl who doesn't need to be held while she cries for days because her father rejected her. He'll probably never find himself in a situation where he needs to punch her biological father for ambushing her at a hospital. He'll never have to drag her drunk ass out of a man's bed to keep her from being molested or raped.

After stalking her IG page, I see she's also a fighter. So they probably train together, play together, and sit around and talk about fighting until they're blue in the face.

My God, her real name is Fleur for fuck's sake. She's perfect for him. And I'm grateful for the selfies she's posted of herself in her skin-tight spandex workout clothes, because knowing she has a flawless body to match her model face is as fucking comforting as a *habanero* enema.

"Dammit!" I toss my phone to my bedside table and bite my quivering lip.

If this is what I wanted for him, why does it hurt so fucking bad?

I want him to be happy. I just wanted him to be happier with me.

TWENTY-FIVE

Killian

Another snap sounds.

I glare at Fleur. "Would you stop with the pictures already?"

She cocks a hip and glares right back. "I am documenting your first UFL fight. You should be thanking me."

I can't help but grin. Fleur has become my closest friend in London. Sure she has her nipping-puppy-at-my-ankle moments, but it only seems to add to her charm. We've spent nearly every weekend together, sightseeing, grabbing a meal or two, and catching a film here and there. She's been a great distraction from the pressure of my first fight.

She's been a great distraction from a lot of things.

"Back off, Fleur." Ollie shoves his little sister aside. "Annoying, *une petit merde!*"

She punches him in the gut, and although I can tell the hit hurt, he smiles.

I hit "play" on my iPod and close my eyes as *Eminem's* "Mosh" blasts through my earphones. I move to an unoccupied part of the room and try to forget I'm at Wembley Arena in London, England, prepping for my first fight with the UFL. I pretend this is no different from any other day, that my shorts aren't covered in sponsor logos, that my entire team who's been there to support me from the second I got off the plane isn't huddled together, strategizing.

In this moment, it's just me and the music.

My muscles tingle with energy, loose from warming up. I throw punches to the air. Left—right—left. Combination. Left—right knee. Opposite. Elbow—knee. With my eyes closed, I imagine Hugo Webb's game. Dodging, ducking, spinning. I see the entire fight behind my lids and move through it the way I want it to play out in the octagon.

I open my eyes and find Caleb standing in front of me, his arms crossed over his chest. I drop my headphones to around my neck. "Is it time?"

A slow grin pulls his lips. "Depends. You ready?"

I bounce on my toes, keeping my muscles warm. "I'm ready."

He drops his arms and steps into my space. "You prepared to represent the US, kid?"

I nod, his words igniting my passion even more.

"You ready to get out there and drop Hugo Webb?" He's yelling now, getting me amped up.

"Fuck yeah."

"Fuck yeah!" He nods. "Then it's time, brother."

I huddle together with my team, Laise at my right, Caleb at my left, Liam, Henry, Jay, Ollie, and Fleur to complete the circle.

"We've done all we can to get our boy ready for his first fight," Caleb says, and the team mumbles in agreement. "Now we let him loose to cause damage." The team agrees again in strings of curses. "Father God, I pray you'd protect our fighter tonight and give him a warrior spirit to destroy the enemy. Amen!"

Everyone chants, "Amen," and we break.

"For you." Caleb holds out his phone to me, as if whoever's on the line has been listening for a while. I grab it from him, knowing immediately who it might be.

"Yeah?"

"Killian." Cameron's growled voice is laced with pride. "Big night, son."

"Yes, sir." My heart races faster; somehow hearing Cam's voice reminds me that not only will my fight be seen by my crew here in London, but by my UFL family back home.

Including Axelle, if she's watching. It's the only time I give myself permission to think about her, but not in the way I'm accustomed to. There's no pathetic, heartsick longing, only pride that if she is watching she'll get to see what her influence created. Beyond everything else, I want her to feel the satisfaction that she made a difference in my life.

"We're all here cheering you on." There are voices in the background, both male and female, but I can't focus on that now. I have a fight to win.

"Appreciate the opportunity, Cam. I won't let you down."

"I have no doubt about that. Now get out there and kick some ass."

"Will do." I hand the phone off to Caleb, and the door swings open to reveal a stocky guy with a headset mic and a clipboard.

"You're up!"

My team surrounds me from behind. We follow Caleb out the door and down a long corridor where a crowd of thousands can be heard from beyond it. We wait for our cue to enter, and the excited energy bouncing between us is palpable.

A hand reaches up to remove my earphones from my neck and my iPod. I pull my eyes away from the stadium to see Fleur diligently removing my music. At my quick nod of thanks, she doesn't smile back, her fight mask clearly in place just like all the other members of our team.

The lights go dark.

My pulse pounds behind my ribs.

The ticking sound of *AC/DC's* "Thunderstruck" rings through the arena and the crowd explodes.

Caleb turns to me and scowls. "It's go time."

"Fuck yeah, it is."

I lead my crew into the arena filled with screaming fans for my first UFL fight, hoping like hell I don't fuck it all up.

Axelle

Is that really him?

I squint to focus on the television in the lobby of the UFL Training Center. Cameron has a projector set up in the main training room where he's cleared away most of the mats and equipment, and a catering company has replaced them with tables, chairs, and enough food to feed a small country.

Thankfully, he also has the fight pumping into every television in the place, including the small lobby where I can recline on a comfy couch and watch the fight without an audience.

Killian walks—no, walking is too tame. He prowls through the crowd to the octagon like a man who's done this a thousand times. I recognize Caleb closest to his side, but everyone else is a stranger to me.

All except Fleur.

I've never met the girl, yet I've stalked her on every available social media site, which makes me feel like I've known her for years. I know she drinks wine, red mostly, that she indulges in reality television, and that she hits a French bakery for chocolate croissants that remind her of home.

Her brother, the tall blond with the light brown eyes is Olivier. He fights in Killian's weight class and has only lost one fight out of seven. Fleur hasn't had an official fight yet, but that's only because the female UFL team hasn't quite taken off in the UK yet. See. We're practically best fucking friends.

Killian rips his shirt off and my jaw falls wide open. Holy hell, he's grown. I mean he's always been big, but he's more defined now. His muscles seem to stand out more than before. I growl as the camera shot moves to Hugo Webb as he enters the arena. He dances around and plays to the crowd. What a cocky asshole! I hope Kill destroys him. He points to Killian and laughs, making the crowd erupt in a series of cheers and boos. Blake always told me the fighters with the biggest show have the least amount of talent. I hope he's right.

The shot goes back to Killian, and my entire body warms upon seeing him. He looks prepared, confident, as if every single day of his life has been in preparation for this moment.

My chest swells with pride. "I'm so happy for you, Kill. You deserve this more than anyone."

"You know he can't hear you, right?"

I jump at the sound of Ryder's voice. His crooked grin and barely concealed laughter make me want to backhand his pretty face. "Of course I do, idiot."

"You're talking to a television in a room alone, and *I'm* the idiot." He drops down on the couch next to me, his eyes on the screen. "Damn, can you believe he made it?"

"Yes. Absolutely. He wouldn't give up until he did."

"I don't know about that," he mumbles. When I look over at him, he pulls his eyes from the screen, and I see sadness in them. "He would've given it up for you."

I hurry and look away before Ryder can read me. "No, he wouldn't have. He's smarter than that. And besides, I wouldn't let him."

The fight commentators go through Killian's and Hugo's stats where we learn that they're nearly perfectly matched in height and weight, but that Hugo has a little longer reach on Kill.

Killian's expression is cold, and I recognize the look of him being in the zone. Hugo flaps his arms to rile up the crowd, but none of it seems to faze Kill.

"Fuck, you guys beat me to it." Jonah drops down on a chair close to us, leaning in over his knees to study the television. "Need a little privacy to watch my boy's first fight. Loud as hell out there and—"

"Shhh!"

Jonah grins at me, popping both dimples. "Guess I'm not the only one."

"Dammit, you assholes." Blake drops into a seat opposite Jonah. "Didn't think anyone would be in here." He squints at the television. "Killer looks fucking lethal. Hope they have an EMT close by. Something tells me Webb's gonna need—"

"Oh my God, *shhhhhhh!*"

Blake's eyes widen at my outburst and Jonah simply chuckles.

The announcer does his spiel, but I'm deaf to most of what he says because I'm stuck on Killian. He's shaking his arms out, rolling his head, and staring at Hugo as if he could knock him out with mind power alone.

The ref directs them together and gives them the "fight fair" speech. Killian lifts his fists to touch knuckles, but Hugo tells him to fuck off, which I can see by reading his lips and his pretty obvious hand gesture.

A slow evil grin spreads across Killian's lips, flashing his black mouth guard, and my heart pounds in my chest, and heat pools between my legs.

He's deadly and powerful and . . . I miss him.

With a swipe of the ref's arm, the fight is on.

"Get him, Killer!" Jonah's nearly out of his seat, glued to the screen.

Killian remains calm while he and his opponent circle each other. Hugo taunts Kill. I can't tell what he's saying, but his lips are flapping. Killian remains focused.

Hugo swings. Kill dodges the hit and goes back to circling.

"He's waiting for his in," Blake says.

"Yeah, he could take that clown down, but he's waiting for an opening to jab."

250

Ryder and I share a quick glance, not fully understanding the conversation between Blake and Jonah.

Hugo swings and connects with Killian's face, but he bounces right back like he'd never been hit.

"Come on, Killer! Take the shot!" Blake's standing up now.

I chew my lip, hoping Killian isn't getting stage fright. "Come on, Kill. Hit him," I whisper.

They circle each other, Hugo's taunts getting wilder.

"He's gonna drop his hands," Jonah says.

I don't know who he's talking about, but tension between Jonah and Blake strings tight as they hover close to the television.

"That's it." Blake says. "He's waiting for him to—"

Hugo drops his hands.

Killer swings.

Connects to Hugo's jaw.

The guy drops.

"Holy fuck!"

"Knock out!"

Blake and Jonah are yelling in unison while the roar of cheers from the training center are almost deafening.

Ryder tackles me from the side as I watch a startled Hugo stagger to his feet only to fall again.

"He did it!" Ryder shakes me from my shock. "His first fight and he knocked the guy out in thirty-seven seconds!"

Jonah's hands are in his hair. Blake's are propped on his hips, and all of us stare at the screen with grins so big we can hardly contain them.

"He did it." My voice shakes with the powerful emotions swirling inside me. "I knew he could do it."

The announcer holds up Kill's hand, and I can't help but laugh at the mix of joy and shock on Killian's face. Something tells me he thought he'd have to work a little harder for this win.

Caleb wraps him in a hug and says something in Killian's ear that makes him nod. Then Kill disappears behind bodies as his training crew surrounds him in congratulatory hugs.

All of them, including Fleur.

She winds her way through the bodies and presses her front to his. The camera zooms in, and I don't miss the way all the guys back off a bit to give them space. In what seems like slow motion, I watch as Killian curls his upper body around her. I swallow hard when he closes his eyes. Time freezes as I bear witness to the intimate embrace.

The volume comes back as they rip apart and Killian pulls a shirt on over his head and pops on a hat when a mic is shoved into his face.

"Knockout in thirty-seven seconds, Killer. Can you walk us through that fight?"

He looks almost embarrassed. "Yeah, uh . . . I thought he'd come at me more aggressively, so I was waiting for him to charge, but . . ." He's still breathing heavily. "He never did, so I waited for a clean shot."

"Everyone thought you'd go for the takedown. Is there a reason why you didn't?"

"I expected the fight would end up on the ground, but I wanted to keep it a standup as long as I could." He chuckles. "Guess it worked."

"It certainly did. Excellent fight. I predict we'll be seeing a lot more from you."

"I hope so." Killian's eyes come to the camera, and I flinch at the intensity of his stare. It's as if he's looking right at me, right through me.

"Killer McCreery, the UFC's next superstar . . ." The announcer goes on, and Killian lifts his fist to his chest.

With his thumb up, he traces an "X" over his heart.

Cross my heart.

He brings his fist to his lips when someone pulls on him from behind.

Was that for me? Was that *our* cross your heart?

My pulse pounds, and just as I'm about to grab my phone and text him to confess how much I miss him, how I love him and will wait for him until he comes home, he gets knocked into by a blur of dark blond hair.

Fleur.

She hops into his arms, and he wraps her up tight, smiling down at her. I watch in horror as she tilts her head and presses her lips to his.

I suck in a breath, and the camera shot moves to the commentators, cutting me off from the view of Killian and his . . . his . . . girlfriend?

"Kiddo?" Blake looks down at me, concern pinching his features. "You okay?"

I sniff and realize a few tears escaped my eyes. "Of course." I push back my shoulders, which only makes Blake scowl. "I'm so happy." I force a shaky grin. "I'm really happy for Killian."

All three men in the room study me like I might be unstable, and I'm grateful Blake's the only one of the three who knows about my *condition.*

I blow out a breath and stand, patting my pockets for my keys. "That was some fight. I uh . . ." *need an excuse to leave.* "I'm tired. I'm gonna go ahead and head home."

Blake steps closer. "Axelle—"

"Could you tell Mom I'll call her tomorrow?" I make my way to the door. "Please?"

Blake nods and Jonah and Ryder watch me with curiosity.

"Great, um . . ." I lick my lips. "Awesome fight. I'll uh . . . I'll see you guys later."

I whirl around and beeline to my car, barely holding back the torrential downpour of tears.

TWENTY-SIX

Killian

My life changed dramatically in the span of thirty-seven seconds.

I walked into that octagon a nobody and walked out a fucking rock star. I have a publicist, an assistant, and an accountant. I don't even have to talk to them, and they all manage my shit behind my back.

I've got a bank account filled with money, a new wardrobe that won't even fit into my closet, expensive sunglasses that I'm ashamed to say I fucking love, and it's only been one week since the fight.

For the first few days after the fight, I couldn't even walk on the streets of London without getting stopped for a photo and autograph. The front doors of the training center were littered with paparazzi every morning when I arrived and every evening when I left. Caleb even had black-out curtains put in because they were snapping photos of us training.

All for me?

Seems ridiculous and at the same time gratifying.

I've done interviews, photo shoots, but the most shocking of all is the women. They show up at our penthouse, stop me on the street. There was even an actress who went through my publicist to see if I'd be interested in a date. If someone had told me six months ago that I'd one day be turning down some of the most beautiful women in the world, I'd have told them they're insane. And if things aren't crazy enough, Cameron's already lined up my next two fights, warning me I'm being catapulted into superstardom.

It's everything I ever imagined being a UFL fighter would be and so much more.

I'm fresh out of the shower and digging through my plentiful wardrobe when my phone rings. It's probably Fleur asking where I am. I was supposed to pick her up for dinner and a movie ten minutes ago, but I had a telephone interview that ran late.

I pull a pair of charcoal gray slacks from my closet, snag my phone, and hit "accept."

"If you're calling to bitch because we're gonna miss the movie, I swear I have a valid excuse."

"No. Fucking. Way."

I freeze, staring at the rainbow of dress shirts hanging in my closet.

"I thought for sure you'd died and the only reason I'm seeing your photos all over the Internet is because your training crew was pulling some kind of *Weekend at Bernie's* shit."

"Ryder, it's been awhile."

"Ha! Ya think?"

He's pissed. I guess I can't blame him. He can't possibly understand what my life has been like.

I toss a navy-blue shirt on the bed next to my pants and grip my towel around my waist. "What can I say, man, I've been—"

"Swear to God if you say busy I'm hanging up. That's what people say to people they don't like. I'd rather you just tell me the truth."

I pull out a black belt, socks, and search for a pair of shoes. I don't have time for this shit. "That is the truth."

I'm met with silence.

"I'm focusing on my fighting." It's the excuse I use with myself; surely Ryder will believe it too.

"Bullshit."

Frustration pricks at my skin. "Look. I really have to get going. Did you call for a reason?"

"I've been trying to call you all week to congratulate you on your fight. Although, it seems from all the media coverage, you're getting plenty of that, so I can see why you don't need to hear it from me."

My hand freezes on a pair of black Ferragamos. "You watched the fight?"

He laughs humorlessly. "Of course I did, asshole. We all did."

We all. As in . . .

Walls crumbling.

Chest aching.

I scramble for a way to end it. "I appreciate that, but I'm out the door—"

"I heard. Late for a movie."

"Right."

"But too busy to text me back."

"What're you, my wife?"

He sighs. "I get it, Killian. You're moving on. You've got a new life, new friends, new girl . . ."

Girl. He's obviously believing the rumors. My mouth moves to correct him, but the memory of Axelle and Clifford kissing flashes behind my eyes, and I slam my lips together. Maybe it's best they believe I moved on.

"I'm just sayin' it sucks—"

"Believe what you want." I run some sticky shit through my hair.

"Whatever, man. I'll let you go."

"Ryder, hold up."

He doesn't say anything, but I don't hear him hang up.

"How's um . . ." I wonder if she's announced her pregnancy, if her belly is starting to swell, if Clifford got his shit together so he can take care of her. I fist my hand in my hair, begging myself not to ask, struggling to hold up the barriers, but feeling the words bubble up from my throat anyway. "How's Axelle?" I haven't said her name in so long, and yet saying it now feels more natural than breathing.

"Why do you ask?"

My stomach tightens with offense. How the fuck can he ask me that? She's my best friend, *was* my best friend. Fuck him.

"Never mind—"

"I'm not interested in playing telephone between you and Axelle. You wanna know how she is; you clear your schedule long enough to call her and ask her yourself. You should know I didn't have the heart to sell all your shit, so I put it in storage along with your Jeep. Dad said the UFL would cover the cost."

I rub my eyes as guilt floods in. "You didn't have to do that."

"No shit. Have a nice life."

The phone line goes dead, and I stare at the ceiling, feeling sick to my stomach.

Not only did I just lose one of my best friends, but I didn't get jack shit as far as information on Axelle.

But she's not my problem anymore. I wanted her to be my problem. She wanted nothing to do with that. What more could I do?

You could've remained in touch, asshole.

And watch her throw her life away for a loser like Clifford? No fucking way.

This was the best thing I could do for both of us.

Just because it feels like my soul is dead doesn't mean leaving her wasn't the right thing to do.

Axelle

It's hard enough trying not to think about someone when he's on the other side of the Atlantic Ocean. What makes it damn near impossible is when that person becomes famous and everyone at school won't stop asking me about him.

"What's it like being friends with Killer?"

"Does he eat raw eggs for breakfast?"

"You should've dated him; then you'd be famous. Wait. Why didn't you date him?"

I've come up with some standard issue answers that seem to shut people up for the time being, but some of the questions make it hurt to breathe.

"Did you know his girlfriend is, like, French royalty?"

"Have you heard he's proposing?"

"Is it true he bought her a Porsche?"

I had to stop Internet stalking him the day after his fight when I saw a photo of him kissing Fleur and the caption read, "A Killer and his Queen."

I cried for hours, blaming pregnancy hormones, of course.

"Hey, Axelle, wait up!"

I turn around to see Brynn speed-walking toward me with a smile stretching her lips and a mane of strawberry billowing in her wake.

It's not her fault she's pretty. I'm in faded black sweatpants and an oversized tee and flip-flops, feeling like Nanny McPhee, ya know, before she got pretty.

"Sorry to bother you, but . . ."

Three.

Two.

One.

"Do you know how I can get ahold of Killian?" She flashes a bright smile, which only manages to deepen my frown.

"Of course I do. Why?"

"I tried to call him, but it says the number is no longer in service. I've been messaging him on Facebook, but he hasn't messaged me back." Her gaze darts around as if she's making sure we aren't being heard. "Can you tell me how to reach him?"

I tilt my head and study her overeager expression. "No."

"Wait. Are you guys, like, you know, together, because I thought—"

"Not that it's anyone's business, but, no, we're not."

"So . . .?"

"So you think because we're not dating that I should just pimp him out to anyone who asks?"

Her expression falls, and for the first time, I see a hint of irritation in her glare. Finally, woman. Backbone! "He's my friend too."

"Really? Then why didn't *he* give you his number?" The question sours my stomach because clearly he didn't give me his number either.

"I . . ."

"Exactly. I'm sorry, Brynn, but I'm not comfortable handing out his info."

"Okay, I understand." Her shoulders slump, and I immediately feel like a huge bitch.

"Listen." I sigh hard. "Ask Ryder, okay? I'm sure he can pass along a message to Killian for you."

Brynn nods and walks away. I internally scold myself for being rude. My stomach aches, and I'm sweaty, and all I want to do is go home and sleep.

Feeling heartless, I walk with my head down to the café to grab a cold water, hoping it'll help end the blazing inferno inside my body, when I trip over something. I drop the spiral notebook in my arms to try to get my hands in front of me to catch my fall, but I'm not fast enough and land hard on my shoulder.

"Shit!" I push to sit, and my face flames as the sound of muffled laughter surrounds me.

"Are you okay?" A guy reaches out his hand to help me up.

"Yeah, thanks." I wave him off, holding on to a sliver of my pride, then gather my things before pushing back up to my feet.

"Oops." A deep male chuckle sounds to my right. "You should probably watch where you're going."

I groan. Clifford, that ass, tripped me.

I turn to face him, frustrated I wasn't paying attention and allowed this to happen again. "It's not your fault; it's hard to avoid tripping over piles of shit when they're as big as you." Even as my tough-girl defense falls from my lips, humiliation burns in my chest.

He glares and gets close enough to whisper. "How's the baby, huh?" His eyes track down to my belly and back. "Funny how, what, two months later your stomach is still flat."

"You made it clear you don't care, that I was *nothing important*, so why don't you leave me alone?"

"Don't want to." He reaches to touch my hair, but I duck away and head to the café.

"This isn't over, Elle!" He yells from behind me.

That's okay, two more months until the semester is over, and then I won't have to face him on a daily basis.

I shove my middle finger into the air and hope to God he sees it. For a second, I fear he might come in behind me and continue to harass me, but when I grab a water and find an empty seat inside with the blessed air conditioning, I'm grateful to see he's gone.

My phone vibrates in my pocket, and I pull it out to see I have a text from my mom.

Last minute, I know, but can you watch Jack tonight?

Last minute, like that matters. I have zero social life.

I text her back.

I can do that. What time?

I take a few swigs of water, feeling a little better.

Seven until late. Maybe midnight?

No problem. I'll bring my school stuff and sleep there.

Thank you, honey! See you then.

Free dinner, a warm bed, and my baby brother? Sounds like the perfect cure to my shitty day.

~~~

"There's veggie lasagna in the oven." My mom's heels click across the hardwood floor as she grabs her clutch, and I smile, watching Blake watching her. Eyes wide, lips parted, that subtle awestruck gaze. It's the same look Jack gets when staring at a doughnut.

I don't blame Blake for still being gaga for Mom. She's smokin' hot. His feelings for her give me hope that I might not end up alone, that a great guy could fall for a single mother.

"You cooked veggie lasagna?"

"Of course not." Blake scoffs. "I did."

"Where were you when we were living off cereal and peanut butter?" I laugh and poke my head into the living room to see Jack playing with his toys on the floor.

"I was waiting in the wings." He flicks lint from his dark gray button-up dress shirt. "Gearing up to blow your minds with my culinary flair."

My mom's warm palm cups my cheek, and her eyes roam over my face. "Are you feelin' okay?"

I turn my face away from her touch. "Mom, you worry too much."

Blake comes alongside her and stares down at me. "She's right to; you look tired."

"That's because I am." And heartsick over losing my other half to a gorgeous model-looking fighter, but they don't need to know that. Pregnant by a fucking asshole who purposefully tripped me at school. There's nothing in my life that *doesn't* make me tired.

"Jack's ready for bed. Feel free to crash out as soon as he does." Blake hooks me around the back of the neck, pulling me in for a hug. "Hate leaving you with him if you're tired, kiddo." He releases me to be hugged by my mom.

"It's okay, really. I'm looking forward to a good dinner then flopping on the couch and watching Nickelodeon."

My mom holds my face between her hands. "We won't be far away. If you need us, just call, okay?"

"No need. We'll be fine." I pat my mom's hand and go into the kitchen to dish up my dinner.

Mom and Blake give Jack kisses good-bye then head out to the garage. "I'm arming the alarm, so no opening doors." Blake hits the four-number code and I salute him.

"Yes, sir."

He grins— "Smartass"—then heads out.

Jeez, the guy is seriously over protective.

I drop open the oven door and grab hot pads to pull out the bubbly lasagna. As I move to stretch over the oven door and place the lasagna on the stovetop, my lower back cramps. The dish drops hard to the burner, making a loud noise.

"Ass-ole?"

"I'm okay, Jack." I bend over slowly and pull the oven door closed then rub the monster back spasm that seems to wrap around to my front.

I cut out a square of the cheesy, veggified goodness and take it out to the living room. Setting my dinner down on the side table, I dread asking the question I already know the answer to. "What do you want to watch, Jack?" It's seven o'clock, which is his bedtime. Whatever we put on, he'll fall asleep watching, so at least I won't be subject to too much torture.

"Cars!" He holds up a toy car and smiles with his little white teeth. He mumbles something then makes car sounds as he comes to me in his one-piece pj's with the words, "I'd Flex, but I Like this Onesie" written on the front.

Crawling up onto the couch, he snuggles up to my side as I queue up his favorite video. He smells like baby soap and that naturally mouthwatering scent that babies have. I hit "play" and wrap an arm around him then shovel a bite of Blake's lasagna into my mouth. Damn, the man can seriously cook.

I shift to try to get more comfortable, my back still spasming, until I find a position that buys me some relief.

Less than twenty minutes into the movie, I'm staring at an empty plate and a sleeping little boy. I slip out from under him and take my plate to the kitchen to rinse when my cell vibrates in my pocket.

I pull it out and it's Ryder's name on the caller ID. I peek in on Jack, who is gone to the world, so I hit "accept" and drop onto a stool in the kitchen.

"Hey, Ryder."

"Hey." He sounds a little bugged.

Shit, I should've probably warned him Brynn would come sniffing around looking for Killian's contact info.

"Crap, you're calling about Brynn." I rub my forehead. "I meant to warn you she'd be—"

"Brynn? What about her?"

"I ran into her at school today. She was looking for Kill's new phone number, but I didn't feel comfortable giving it out. If she told him she got it from me, he'd probably be pissed I had it, and anyway, I thought she could just let you know she's looking for him and you could pass it along."

"No, I haven't talked to Brynn today. If I had, I would've told her to leave him alone anyway."

"That's probably smart. I figure his phone's probably already blowing up with women calling him and begging for autographed pairs of his dirty boxers."

He laughs and the sound makes me smile, which takes my mind off the dull ache in my gut. "Nah . . . Kill doesn't have dirty boxers to give away. He tosses them and wears a new pair every day. Probably makes his butler go out and buy him the ten-thousand-thread-count kind."

I'm not smiling anymore because whatever humor was in Ryder's voice is gone. "What happened?"

"What—?"

"Don't bullshit me, Ry. You're clearly pissed at Killian. Why?"

He exhales hard. "I shouldn't have called you. I just didn't know who else to tell."

"Tell what?" I press my palm to my lower abdomen. "Is he okay?" Please, don't tell me the engagement rumors are true.

"Okay is debatable."

"Stop messing with me." My back and abdomen cramp. "I'm freaking out here."

"I talked to him."

I jerk upright and stare blindly across the kitchen. "And?"

He makes a frustrated sound. "He's changed, Ax."

"Changed? How?"

"I've been calling and texting the guy since he left, and he's never gotten back to me. The only reason I got him on the phone today was because he answered, thinking it was someone else."

That doesn't sound like Killian at all. He's the most loyal friend I've ever had, and even though he's basically famous now, he's not the type who buys into his own hype and gets arrogant. No way. Not Kill.

"He's busy. I'm sure it's not personal."

"He said as much, but I don't buy it. Who's too busy to send a text? Fuck, that can be done at a stoplight."

He's got a point. "Fame is all so new to him; it'll take some getting used to. You know Killian's never been the most popular kid in school; now he is. Give him some time to soak that in and be that guy for a little w—" I double over as a cramp squeezes my lower body. "While." I spit out the last word through clenched teeth.

"John-Mayer syndrome, I get it."

Sweat breaks out across my forehead. "Right, that's all it is—" Oh God! My back and womb squeeze hard, feeling like they're crushing my spine between them. I groan and move the phone from my ear. Shit, shit, shit! This is bad.

". . . you there? Axelle, talk to me! Are you okay?"

"I'm not feeling well. I—*argg!*" I drop the phone on the floor and double over hard, just as a gushing heat coats my inner thighs. "Oh no, no . . ."

Ryder's yelling through the phone. I can't hear what he's saying, but I know he's panicking.

I grab my phone and breathe through the pain. "Ryder, listen . . ." Another cramp squeezes hard enough to take my breath away. My eyes water, and I look down to see my light gray sweatpants soaked in bright blood. "Call Blake, okay? Tell him . . . just tell him that . . ."

I think I'm losing the baby.

~~~

From my bed in the dim light of the spare bedroom, I stare at my mom, who's talking on the phone with Dr. Schwartz.

"She took a shower and has a heating pad, yes." My mom looks over at me with sympathy. "I'll bring her in tomorrow. Thank you."

Luckily, Ryder called Blake the second I asked him to, and within five minutes, they were home. I was afraid to leave the kitchen and go to the bathroom because I wouldn't be able to see Jack from there, so I was curled up on the kitchen floor when they came in.

Blake wanted to take me to the hospital, but my mom calmed him down, saying, "It's a miscarriage; she'll be okay."

He wasn't convinced and demanded the number to my OB. Another five minutes later they verified what mom had said.

I'm losing the baby.

"The doctor said to take you to the hospital if you get a fever or if the bleeding gets worse." She runs her fingers through my hair. "I'm sorry, honey."

I sniff back tears. "What if it was something I did, ya know? I don't think I drank enough water and—"

"Shh . . . your doctor said this isn't uncommon. For whatever reason, the baby wasn't healthy enough to grow." She nods and continues to stroke my hair. "She'd mentioned that the father's lifestyle might have something to do with it, or it could've been any of a bunch of different factors that have nothing to do with you."

That makes sense. Who knows what drugs the guy was using and what all they were doing to his sperm?

"I can't help but feel like I lost something important. Really, really important."

"You bond instantly with your baby on some primal level, even if you're not fully aware of it."

I wipe a wayward tear from my cheek. "I didn't realize how much I loved him until I lost him."

Her smile quivers. "He was a boy, huh?"

"Maybe." Or maybe the loss I'm feeling is for my best friend. Because not having him here when I need him most amplifies the hole in my heart he left behind.

"It'll be okay, Axelle. I promise. You'll bounce back and finish college, get married, and have as many babies as you want."

"How's our patient?" Blake stands in the doorway, keeping his distance while lending support.

Mom turns toward him. "Better. Did you get Jack back to sleep?"

He nods. "Out like a light."

"What did you tell Ryder?" The last thing I want to do is explain that I miscarried, seeing as he never even knew I was pregnant.

"Told him you got sick to your stomach but that you're feeling better and resting."

"Thank you."

"You girls have everything you need in here? Want me to bring you some water?"

Mom looks down at me. "That'd be great."

"You don't have to stay with me all night, Mom."

"I know, but I want to." She climbs under the covers and pulls me to her chest. "You'll always be my baby, Axelle, and right now I just want to hold you."

I snuggle in close, absorbing the warmth of her touch.

Blake places two glasses of water on the side table and then kisses me on the forehead and Mom on the lips. "I'll be right across the hall if you need me."

"We know." My mom holds me closer.

"Blake?"

"Yeah, kiddo."

"Please, don't tell him, okay?"

He doesn't need me to say his name to know who I'm talking about. "Think he'll figure it out on his own when nine months come and go. You sure you don't think he should know?"

I shake my head. "You know him; he'll worry. He might try to come home, and"—my heart shatters— "I don't want to be his reason for coming home."

Blake studies the floor for a few beats then nods. "Alright, I won't tell him, but I'm going to be honest here and say I think he needs to know. You're the most important person in his life, Axelle. When he finds out we all kept this from him, I don't think he's going to be happy about it."

"I'll cross that bridge when I get there. For now, the only people who know about the pregnancy are Clifford, who didn't believe me anyway, Killian, and the three of us. I'd like to move forward, pretending these last two months were a dream, and go on with my life."

"It's your call, sweetheart," my mom murmurs.

"My lips are sealed, kiddo. Now you two get some sleep. Love you."

"Love you too," we say in unison.

And shortly afterward I fall sound asleep in my mom's arms.

TWENTY-SEVEN

Two months later . . .

Killian

There's got to be one hundred fifty people in the small Irish pub we've taken over for the night. Having met the maximum occupancy hours ago, the manager closed the doors to the public, but a crowd gathers in the street, celebrating along with us.

My second win.

Another knockout.

This one in fifty-eight seconds.

Liam pushes his way through the crowd around me and shoves a pint into my hand, spilling dark beer over my knuckles, not that I care. "Drink up, mate!" He yells to be heard over the voices of hammered fans and music. "We're back at it on Monday!"

"I'm ready now!" I tilt the glass to my lips, losing my balance a little but being held up beautifully between two women who've been acting like gutter bumpers to my drunk ass all night.

"You killed it tonight!" Caleb grins, pride and respect shining in his eyes. "Fizzouli didn't know what hit him."

"They don't call me Quick Kill for nothing!" I hold my arms out and knock one of the girls by accident. "Oh shit." I turn to her and cup her face awkwardly. "I didn't mean to hit you."

A trill of laughter falls from her lips, and she leans in close. "You didn't; you swatted my boob."

My eyes fall heavily to her chest. "I'm so sorry."

She cups her breast. "She forgives you."

"No accent." I pull my focus from her chest. "You're American."

"Yes." Her expression softens. "I'm from Denver, but I go to school at Kings."

"Nice." I turn away from her probing stare; that ache in my chest that comes when I'm around women is dulled from beer, but undeniably there.

"I saw your fight!" Her breath skates along my ear. "You're really good!"

I peer down at her and grin. "I know."

Another string of giggles falls from her lips. She's a pretty girl, really pretty. "Oh! Here!" She pulls out her phone and holds it up. "Let's take a selfie."

"I'll take it." Caleb grabs her phone and stands back a little. "Kill, pick her up."

I groan, but comply and set down my beer. I scoop the woman up and into a cradle hold. Her arms wrap around my neck, and she presses her lips to my cheek. Shocked by her show of affection, I laugh, and Caleb snaps the photo.

"Thank you! My friends are gonna freak when they see I partied with you!"

"No problem."

Another girl, I presume the one who's been on my right all night, pulls out her phone. "Can I get one?"

Then another standing off to the side yells, "Me too!"

I look at Caleb as he laughs and holds out his hand to take the next phone. "Step right up, ladies. One at a time, and please respect the guy and keep your hands to yourself." He's cracking up laughing as each girl hands over her phone and shows off how she's ignoring his warning.

Photos are taken with hands up my shirt, on my ass, and a couple of girls pulled my shirt up and had Caleb take a shot of them licking my abdomen. Thank goodness I'm drunk, or I'd probably get hard from all the groping. It's not my fault. I don't even want any of these women. It's scientific—stimulus, response.

"My turn." A curvy woman steps up to me with a sultry sway to her hips, her body talking dirty as she sidles up to me.

Caleb holds up her phone. "Say cheese!"

I grin, and just as the flash pops, her hand cups my dick. "Cheese!"

"Whoa!" I jump back, laughing, not because it's funny as much as uncomfortable. "That's enough photos for me."

Fleur pushes through the crowd, shaking her head and grinning. "Women are worse than blokes!" Her eyes fix on Little Miss Grabby Hands. "Go on now. The poor guy needs a break."

She winks at me then grabs her phone from a purple-faced Caleb, who's laughing so hard no sound comes out.

"Nice to see you're getting a kick out of my misery." I shove him back, and if there weren't a wall of people behind him, he would've fallen to his ass.

"Dude . . ." He sucks in a breath and wipes his eyes. "This is every man's dream. You can't tell me that having the entire female population worship you isn't awesome."

A slow smile pulls at my lips. He's right, but it's not the women; it's everything. It's the other fighters who look at me the way I look at my UFL idols, it's the kids that stand dazed when I walk by, and it's the way heads turn when I enter a room.

I've never been *that* guy.

I spent twenty-one years of my life a loner. Went through four years of high school never really being seen by anyone. Popularity was never a goal of mine because it seemed too far from my reach, too impossible to ever attain.

And here I am, the most popular guy around, and I wish I didn't like it. I wish my intellectual side would shun fame and expose it for the shallow hero-worship that it is.

But nope.

If I can't have the life I dreamed with the girl I love, this ain't a bad second.

Axelle

Staring out the window of my classroom with the warm sun on my face, I wait for the fifty-minute class to end.

The weather is warming up, and as much as I'd love to go find a nice spot in the grass to study, I can't. Mindy is in class for another hour, and Ryder's class isn't out for another forty-five minutes, which means I'd be alone.

Being alone in the quad is like putting a big fat target on my head.

So I have two options: go to the library or go home.

Neither is an outdoor option.

"Hey . . ." A voice whispers next to me.

I turn to the kid that sits at my left, Brandon or Brendan. I can't remember.

He holds his phone up, and a photo of Killian holding his shirt up with two women crouched down licking him is plastered on his screen. "You know this guy, right?"

I move my eyes from his phone to his face. "Yes, I used to." Although the man I knew wouldn't be caught dead in that kind of position with two women.

"I've been following him on social media; the guy is a playa'," the kid whispers.

Yeah, well, he didn't used to be.

"Did you see his fight the other night?"

I turn back to him and huff out an annoyed breath, hoping he gets the hint. "I did." I'd never miss one of his fights. I learned my lesson though, and as soon as it's over, I avert my eyes until the interview. He did the same thing he did last time, crossing his heart, and all the pain of losing him came rushing back.

Luckily, this time I was at my mom's, watching Jack, and was able to cry and feel sorry for myself with the only audience being my three-year-old brother.

"He's unstoppable." Brandon, or whatever, leans back in his chair and continues to scroll through photos, getting the attention of the guys around him. I catch their whispered words, like, "Damn, she's hot," and "Lucky guy probably got triple-teamed," but it wasn't until the "She's sucking his . . ." that I finally had enough.

I shove my binder in my backpack and throw it over my shoulder as I step down the lecture hall steps and to the door.

That's the great thing about college. You can just get up and leave without excuse, without having to explain that your ex-best friend has turned into a womanizing prick. I try to close the door quietly behind me to keep from disrupting the class any more than I have, which takes some effort since my muscles are tense with frustration. It isn't until I'm out in the fresh air that I take a calming breath then stop dead in my tracks.

There, sitting on the picnic bench that Killian used to wait for me on, is Clifford. Great, and with class still in session, there's no one around to witness his cruelty.

I spin on a heel and speed-walk to the breezeway that leads to the parking lot and my escape. My heart beats wildly in my chest, but I don't hear him following me, so I try to force myself to breathe. I'll be okay. *Just keep your eyes open and get to the car.*

Once my shoes hit the asphalt, I risk a look and peek over my shoulder. He is behind me. Shit. He's keeping a good distance though, slowly meandering in my wake.

Whirling my backpack to my front, I fish out my keys and peek behind me again. He's stopped at the curb where the lot meets the sidewalk, and his eyes are boring into mine. A slow grin crawls across his face, and if this were some kind of mafia movie, it would be the last thing I'd see right before my car exploded.

Thankfully, Clifford isn't in the mob.

I hit the key fob for my SUV, and my breath catches in my throat.

My car exploded, alright; although not in a burst of fiery flames and shrapnel. That would've been better.

No, my car is plastered in photos.

And it doesn't take a genius to figure out what they're of.

The sound of students filtering from classrooms calls my eyes away from the hideous pics, and sure enough, people appear from everywhere.

"Shit." I race to my car and scramble to remove the photos, but they're stuck. Like really stuck. I pick at the corners with my nails, my hands shaking as the rumble of engines firing up sounds all around me. I rip one off and move to the next, but my gosh, there has to be nearly fifty of them. "Come on. Come on . . ." Tears sting my eyes, blurring the images of flesh on flesh, as I frantically rip photos from my car. Giggles erupt from a group of girls passing by, then comments from a group of guys, and no one offers to help.

Tears are streaming down my face now, and I pull as many pictures off as I can. I throw them into the back of my car and decide as the parking lot fills that it's best to get the hell out of here and work on this away from prying eyes.

"There's more, ya know?"

I shriek at the sound of Clifford's voice and find him there with his hands shoved in his pockets and a satisfied grin on his face. "Why are you doing this to me?" I hiccup on a sob and hope my tears appeal to what little, if any, humanity remains in him.

"You fucked with me first." He steps closer. "Turnabout is fair play."

"I didn't fuck with you, Clifford! I was pregnant, but I lost the baby."

He clicks his tongue then tilts his head. "Of course you did."

It's pointless. "Even if what you're saying is true, I didn't ruin your life. I let you off the hook, walked away. You're trying to destroy me."

"You're destroying yourself by sitting here arguing with me when you should be hitting all the community boards."

I swivel my gaze from him to one of the large corkboards in the common area by the parking lot. A group of people crowds around it, and when one of the guys turns to look at me, his face twists in pity.

Clifford posted these photos on the community boards!

Leaving my car door open, I sprint to the board, feeling the sting of tears on my cheeks. I get there just as my lit teacher Mr. Decker shoves his way to the board. His face pales. "That's enough; everyone back away." He rips down the photos and then pushes people back. "I'm serious; you all need to back away. Now!"

The crowd thins, and Mr. Decker pulls the last of the photos from the board to add to the stack in his hands. "Miss Daniels, I think we need to talk."

A muffled burst of laughter moves past us, and I look up just in time to see the back of Clifford's head disappear into the breezeway.

TWENTY-EIGHT

Seven months later . . .

Killian

Having spent my entire life in Las Vegas, I've never experienced a white Christmas. Sure, I'd heard the song, know all the words, but never really thought there was anything magical about one, that is until now.

There's something about a city, from the slush-ridden streets to the tallest skyscrapers, covered in the cold white stuff that makes me feel like I'm living in an old black-and-white movie.

Staring out through the front window of an over-priced restaurant, buzzed on expensive booze, I think about Axelle. Neither of us had ever traveled. She lived in Seattle, which is one more city than I've experienced, but like me, she'd never been anywhere else. She would love this: the history, culture, all of it. Sorrow attempts to disrupt my holiday buzz when I realize she's a mom now and her chances of ever getting to lay eyes on the view before me are slimmer than ever.

My chest cramps every time I think of her. And when I don't think about her, she manages to come up. Every old story I tell, every memory of the UFL camp in Vegas, all of it is wrapped up in her.

Just the other day I overheard Caleb talking to Blake on the phone. I didn't mean to eavesdrop, but we were both in the kitchen, so I may have listened a little more intently than I should've. From what I could tell, it was something about a Christmas card that was sent. It was when Caleb had said,

"Yeah, that's one hell of a good-looking baby, man," that I nearly choked on my sandwich and decided to finish my meal in my room. There's not a doubt in my mind that Axelle's child is just as beautiful as she is. I worry about her, about the toll being a young mother with that fuck Clifford would take, but she has a family and people to support her.

I haven't had the balls to talk to Ryder since the last time we spoke, and other than the occasional talk with Cameron, I stick to my training partners here in London. It might make me a pussy, but it's better this way.

"I'd like to make a toast!" Laise struggles to push up from his seat, his three-piece charcoal gray suit, big-ass beard and longer hair making him look like David Gandy and William Wallace's love child. "To the best fucking UFL team in the world!"

I hold up my beer and cheer, probably a little too loudly, but fuck it! It's Christmas Eve and I'm feeling all kinds of merriment.

Laise sets his eyes on me. "To Killer, who after last week's fight is still undefeated with now *three* knockouts under one minute!"

Caleb shouts and the rest of the team follows suit.

"And to big decisions." He stares at me thoughtfully. "We'd love to have you stay, brother."

Fleur's hand rests gently on my thigh as if to confirm his words. I want to look at her, to reassure her in some way, but I can't. I can't stand the hope that I find in her hazel eyes every single time we're together. The confusion that pinches her brows when she tries to read me.

"Salud!"

We all throw back a healthy gulp of whatever we're drinking and get nods of approval or dirty looks from those dining around us.

Fleur rocks her shoulder into mine. "I can't believe you might only be here for another month."

She really is beautiful, especially tonight. Her hair is long and wavy around her face, framing those wide eyes that look almost green against her red dress. Her full lips are painted the same candy-apple shade, and her skin looks so soft.

And staring at her as she peers up at me with such longing, I can't help but think of the one girl I wish so desperately was in her place.

It makes me sick to think by spending time with Fleur I'm leading her on in some way. Sure, we've shared the occasional kiss, and yes, not all of them have been innocent. I blame myself for that.

"The contract's been offered, Killian." Jay leans back in his seat, sipping a scotch neat. "When do you think you'll decide?"

I shrug and look around the table, feeling suddenly suffocated by my tie. "I think I'll go home first, talk to Cameron and my US team."

"Blimey, if they've got any sense, they'll convince you to stay." Liam throws back almost a half a glass of red wine.

"Liam, don't be daft. You'd have to be mental to walk away from training partners like that." Fleur looks around the table. "You know he gets to train with MMA gods, right?"

Caleb and I laugh. It's true that Jonah, Blake, and Rex have secured their spots as the top MMA all-stars, but they're far from gods.

Fuck. I can't believe I just thought that.

I've worshipped every step they've taken my entire life up until, well, up until I started fighting. What does that mean?

"Why don't you guys come with us?"

My head jerks to Caleb as he sits back in his fancy-ass chair, wearing his fancy-ass suit and grinning wide.

The entire table is silent.

"Are you serious?" I'm not sure I'm comfortable with the idea of having all my London family mixing with my US family, but I can't pinpoint the reasons why.

"Fuck, yeah, I'm serious." He shrugs. "Let's bring them home for a week. Let them experience Vegas and all it has to offer."

Ollie looks at his sister. "We'll never come back."

She laughs and shakes her head. "I don't think we will."

"Paris first," Ollie says. "We've been so busy training this guy"—he nods to me— "we haven't been home in a year."

Laise holds up his glass. "I love Paris!"

"So it's settled." Caleb lifts his glass. "Paris, and then we're bringing our ragtag team home."

Another raucous explosion of cheers and expletives is followed by Henry's belted, "Happy Fucking Christmas!"

Shortly afterward we're asked to leave.

~~~

The cab ride home is mostly a silent one as Fleur sits next to me, her hand wrapped tightly around mine. The boys wanted to hit the pubs, but I'm in no mood to party. I'm drunk, conflicted, and feeling weaker than I have since before my first fight. Fleur gets enough of the rowdy-boy shit in her every day and insisted she was tired, but something tells me there's more to our sharing a cab than she let on.

"When we get back to mine, do you fancy coming in?" *There it is.* Even in the dark, I don't miss the hope in her eyes.

I rub my forehead, trying to sort out the best way to answer. Truth is I'd love the company, but I'm missing home and hammered and probably not much fun to be around. "I don't think you want to hang out with me tonight." I chuckle, the booze making my lame rejection seem hilarious.

The taxi comes to a stop. "That'll be forty pounds."

"Bad company is better than no company." She tugs on my hand. "Come on. I'll make you some tea."

Not in the mood to argue, or possibly too drunk and lazy to try, I pay the cab and allow her to pull me from the seat and up to her front door. Snow covers the ground, and I know I should be feeling the bite of the chill in the air but remain numb.

She pushes open the door, and we stumble inside the two-room flat she shares with Ollie. She rubs her arms over her coat and adjusts the wall heater as I slump to her couch at an angle with one knee on the cushions.

"I hope you like Earl Grey," she calls from the stove, banging through cupboards.

"That's fine, thanks." I allow my eyes to slide closed, and with the liquor making my defenses flimsy, I allow myself to do the unthinkable.

Get lost in memories of Axelle.

Her legs locked on mine, skin on skin, holding us together so fiercely her muscles shake. *"I love you."* She spoke those three words against my mouth, the sweet heat of her love breathing life into mine.

I ran my nose up her neck, getting drunk off her scent. *"I love you too, so fucking much."*

She was scared. I remember her voice trembled as she whispered in my ear, *"This is really happening? Us, I mean?"*

I would've given anything for her to see herself through my eyes. If I had to gouge out my own and rip out my beating heart, I would've done it gladly if only to make her understand. *"It's happening. You and me? This is as real as it gets."*

The couch dips beside me, and I lazily open my eyes to Fleur. "Hey."

Her hand caresses my cheek, and I lean into her touch, accepting her comfort.

"Tea." She hands me a squat teacup, and I push myself up a little to take a few sips.

"Thanks."

She places it on the table, and it hits me that she's always taking care of me. It's a strange role reversal from what I'm used to. With Axelle, it was always me taking care of her. Being on the receiving end of someone's kindness is nice but also makes me feel a little guilty. I wonder if this is what Ax was talking about the day she told me to go to England, if my years of looking after her gave her more to feel bad about rather than the comfort I'd tried to give.

"You don't have to do this."

Her hand glides up my chest to loosen my tie. "I like doing it."

"Fleur." I still her hand at my neck. "I can't. I'm sorry."

She flinches slightly and moves her hand from my tie to the back of my neck, her fingers pressing in to loosen the tight muscles. I've been so fucking tense, and the way her fingers roll against my neck makes me groan.

"I wonder, just for one night, will you let me be her?"

My eyes are closed as she continues to massage my neck. "Who?"

Her fingers stiffen against my collar. "The girl you can't stop thinking about."

My gaze snaps to hers, and her hand moves up to cup my jaw.

"I want to know what it's like, Killian." Her eyes search mine. "I wouldn't expect anything, just . . . We can pretend I'm her."

"God . . . no." I try to push away from her, but with my back to the couch I don't get far. "That's wrong. I—"

"Who's to say what's wrong? I know you miss her, and I want to know what it feels like to be loved like that." She moves closer, erasing what little distance I'd managed to put between us. "It'll stay between us. Just for tonight, we can give each other what we both want. I can give you her, and you can give me you."

Booze-fogged, I'm tongue-tied and struck dumb. "I'm drunk, Fleur. Whatever you think you saw is just me being out of my mind and missing someone."

"It's not just tonight. I've seen her on your mind a lot. The cross you do on your chest after every fight." She makes a fist over her heart and then the X before bringing her fist to her lips. "That's for her?"

Usually I'd lie, but I'm so sick of pretending. I swallow, my eyes burning. "Yes."

She leans in and peppers kisses along my jaw. I know I should push her away, should jump up and storm out and let the freezing outdoor temps cool the fire of arousal I can't seem to shake. The scent of her expensive perfume swirls my senses, and my body responds to her touch, hardening with need. "Fleur, we can't." The words come freely, but I lack the strength to move because every single touch brings me back to Axelle.

Her hand glides down my chest to slip her fingers between the buttons. "Let me be her, Killian."

The offer is so sweet, so damn tempting, to close my eyes and get lost in Axelle's body, even if only in fantasy. The delicate touch of Fleur's lips meets mine, and I give in to the illusion. My hands fork into her hair, tilting her head to gain deeper access. She tastes of red wine and sweet tea. I push the rich flavors from my thoughts and pretend it's the Jolly Rancher taste of Axelle's lip gloss.

"Where are you?"

Her soft giggle sounds in my ear. "Thought it was pretty obvious. I'm right here, Kill. I'm not going anywhere."

She's here, her luscious body pressed against mine. "Yeah?"

Her breathy moan ignites my blood. "This is right where I'm supposed to be."

I cup her breasts, flicking the nipple with impatience. "I miss you, baby. I miss you so fucking much." My voice cracks, and I swallow her answering whimper.

I flip her so she's beneath me, her tiny form fragile and writhing. The skin on her inner thigh is like the smoothest silk against my palm as I slide it up to cup her over her panties. "Don't leave me, Axelle."

She gasps.

"Please, baby . . . don't push me away again."

Axelle

"Wake up, sleepyhead. Santa came." I run my hands through Jack's thick blond hair until his eyes blink open. "Hey, Merry Christmas, buddy."

He yawns and pushes himself up from his racecar toddler bed. "Santa came?" His scratchy little voice is laced with excitement.

"He did. You wanna come see?"

He nods and throws his arms around my neck, his four-year-old-body clad in red-and-green camo pj's his Uncle Braeden sent him for Christmas. "Did he bring me a Nerf N-Strike Elite Rhino-Fire Blaster?" He punctuates his question with another yawn.

I nuzzle his little neck. "I think you'll have to unwrap them all to find out."

As we step into the living room, the Christmas tree lights bathe everything in an ethereal glow. His eyes pop wide open, and he wiggles out of my arms. "Santa came!"

He races to the tree, and I grab the coffee I made when I woke up and settle on the couch with my legs tucked beneath me.

"Whoa . . ." Blake comes in, dragging his feet, wearing his red pajama pants and UFL T-shirt. "I thought I heard elves out here." He swings his eyes to me. "Merry Christmas, kiddo."

"Merry Christmas." I nod to the kitchen. "Coffee's made."

"Thank God." He moves slowly to the kitchen when my mom comes barreling out of the hallway with her hair pulled back in a high ponytail and her Christmas shorts and tank top on. Yeah, we're the cheesy Christmas pajama family. It's a beautiful thing.

"Did I miss anything?" She drops to her knees next to Jack as he pulls every single present from under the tree.

"Mom, look what Santa brought!" His face is so bright and cheery, not a single trace of the tired kid I brought out here just seconds before.

"I see. Now don't forget to only open gifts with your name on them, okay?"

"J-A-C-K. Here's one!" He pushes it behind his back. "This starts with A." He shoves it back under the tree. "J-A. Another one!"

Blake returns from the kitchen with two mugs. He hands one off to my mom and kisses her lightly. "Merry Christmas, Mouse."

They're so cute I could puke.

Blake drops down beside me. "You sleep okay?"

"Yeah, too good. I thought I'd sleep in and miss Christmas."

"Your room warm enough?"

"Yes, *Dad*." I shake my head and take a sip of coffee.

He grins. Big. "Just making sure you're comfortable in your new home."

My smile falls a little. It wasn't by choice, necessarily, that I ended up living back at home with my mom and Blake, but I can't deny it was the smart thing to do.

Or more importantly the safest thing to do.

I can't complain.

Things could be worse.

Things could *always* be worse.

TWENTY-NINE

One month later . . .

Killian

"It's bigger than I thought it'd be."

I dart my eyes to Caleb, who's blinking up at the Eiffel Tower.

"It's called the Eiffel *Tower*, cowboy." Laise grins through his beard and 'stache. "What were you expecting?"

"I don't know. I've seen it on TV and in pictures. I guess I wasn't expecting the base of it to be so . . . *wide*."

"That's what she said," I mumble.

Caleb's head whips toward me. "Holy shit. You just delivered a Daniels' line like it was nothing."

I shrug, grinning at the iron masterpiece before me. "I did, didn't I?"

He slaps me on the shoulder. "The old man would be proud."

My chest warms at the thought. Truth be told, regardless of how I left things with Blake, I miss the guy. It'll be good to go home and see them, talk with Cam, and announce my plan to come back and fight in London for another five years.

It makes sense. My career is at its peak. I have a great team. Leaving would be like backsliding.

"Killian, come here!" Fleur waves me over to where she's standing with a guy I've never seen before.

It took weeks for things to normalize between us after our night together. I felt so horrible about what I'd done I confessed my history with Axelle to Fleur as if I was lying on a psychiatrist's couch. Just what a woman wants to do, listen to a guy go on and on about another woman.

I'm such an asshole.

No matter how many times I've apologized, she insists it's not necessary. She swears she seduced me and knew exactly what she was getting into. I suppose that's true, but I never should've let it happen. The good news is we both value our friendship too much to allow my moment of instability to screw it up.

"What's up?" I look between her and the guy who, now that I'm closer, is more like a kid.

"This is Rene; he's a huge fan."

I reach out and shake his hand, which is a little clammy, and if I'm not mistaken, he's shaking. "Nice to meet you, Rene."

The kid rambles off a string of French, and although I have no idea what he's saying, I can sense his enthusiasm.

"He says he has never missed a single one of your fights, and that your fight against Lyon was the most impressive under-one-minute fight in UFL history." She cups her mouth to whisper. "He's kind of obsessed."

Flashbacks of when I was this kid's age, looking up to Jonah at the airport and spouting off his fight stats, flicker in my mind. If I'd only known then the future that awaited, my fate hanging in the balance and depending on that one seemingly random connection . . . I set eyes on the kid, his grin contagious. "Thank you. I appreciate that. You ever consider becoming a fighter?"

Again he and Fleur go back and forth, and she turns to me. "He said, 'Yes, but it's difficult because his parents think he should study to be an engineer, saying it's a safer route.'"

"I know the feeling. Someone once told me I was too smart for sports."

She translates.

290

I pat the kid on the shoulder, and his eyes widen and move to where I touched him. "Don't give up on your dreams, okay?"

He nods as the translation is completed and then holds up a black Sharpie marker, shaking it and pointing to his shirt.

"He wants you to sign his shirt."

"Sure." I grab the pen, and he turns around and offers me his back.

I don't have to think of the right thing to write. I already know. It took one sentence to inspire me. I think the same can be done for this kid.

Rene,

No one dictates your future but you.

--Quick Kill McCreery

I'm finally able to pass along the one piece of advice given to me by The Assassin to someone who needs to hear it.

Rene turns back around and holds up his phone, indicating he wants a photo. Our little interaction has attracted some attention, and people gather around, snapping photos. Rene and I get a quick selfie, and he hugs me before running off to a group of waiting teens.

This is why I should stay—for kids like Rene. I had The Assassin, and there were days in high school that I'm not proud of where I contemplated putting an end to the bullying and the suffering. It was the promise of seeing another UFL fight that helped me hang on most days. Then it was Axelle, but she's gone.

The crowd closes in, snapping photos and asking questions in French. I hook my arm over Fleur. "Think we better go before the paparazzi show up."

She wraps her arm around my waist, and we motion to the other guys who've congregated close by that we're headed to our car.

"Anyone up for an early dinner?" Liam waves to our drivers, who've been patiently waiting for us to finish up at the tower. "Our flight to the states leaves at the butt crack of dawn."

"Sounds good to me." I usher Fleur into the backseat, turning one last time to get a glimpse of the tower, but the incessant snapping of cameras has me climbing into the car sooner than I'd like.

In twenty-four hours, I'll be flying high over American soil.

And I'm scared to death what going home will bring.

Axelle

I love my job.

Granted, it's the kind that requires a uniform, but I don't mind that as much as I thought I would. I work for a great company, one that prides itself on loyalty, hard work, and commitment. It's more like a family, really.

Actually, for me, that's exactly what it is. Family.

And for the first time in my life, I'm proud of who I am and what I do. I've worked hard to get here, and I've earned my position. The interview process alone would've inflamed all my old insecurities. God knows my boss isn't the most sensitive man in the world. But I'm not that insecure girl anymore. I faced adversity, fell in its wake, and dragged myself to my feet to move forward.

I filter through my work shirts embroidered with the company logo and settle for the blue one. I like the way it brings out my eyes.

Sliding that over my head with a pair of workout leggings and one of my three pairs of color-coordinated Nikes, I grab my bag and head to the kitchen to grab a bite before I go.

"Goooood morning, family!"

"Oh!" My mom slams her cell phone into her lap with a forced smile. "Morning!"

I narrow my eyes. "What are you hiding?"

"What? Nothing." More of that fake smile.

I pin Blake with a glare. "What's going on?"

He sucks on his teeth, seeming to struggle with how to answer my question. "Just, uh . . ." He slams his lips shut.

I peek over at Jack, who has his nose buried in a bowl of cereal, his mop of golden hair ruffled from sleep. I swear when you give that kid food he forgets the world around him even exists.

"Jackie Bear, help a sister out."

He blinks up at me as if seeing me for the first time. "Huh?"

"Ugh, you're no help." I motion toward him and his trough. "Continue."

He goes back to his cereal, and I turn back to Mom and Blake.

I nod to her lap. "Something interesting on your phone there, Mom?"

"Oh, this?" She holds it up and then makes a *psht* sound with her lips. "I was just noticing the . . . weather?"

"Is that a question?" I cock a hip, raise my eyebrows, and she squirms in response. Yep, something is definitely up.

Blake chokes and clears his throat.

"Mom, I know you're hiding something, and if you don't tell me what it is, I'll worry all day. Just tell me. Whatever it is, I can take it."

Blake mumbles, "She'll find out on her own eventually."

"I'll find out what?"

She pinches her eyes closed and shoves the phone at me. "Here."

I approach cautiously, snag the device, and hit the screen.

My breath catches in my throat.

It's a photo from an online news article. Killian and Fleur are walking together, his arm slung over her shoulders. He's leaning in deep to whisper in her ear, and whatever he's saying makes her smile.

But that's not the worst part. After all, seeing them together isn't new to me.

The worst part is the view behind them.

They're in Paris.

Walking away from The Eiffel Tower.

And the caption on the story reads, "UFL Superstar Killian McCreery Bringing his Love Back to the States."

There's an article that follows, which details his week-long stay in Paris. The journalist alludes to the fact that he was there to meet her parents and is now bringing her to Vegas to meet his and possibly get hitched at one of the quickie chapels here in town.

I finish the article, take a deep fortifying breath, and hand the phone back.

"You okay?" Blake's eyes are settled on mine with concern.

"It hurts a little, but yeah, I'm okay." I grab a handful of blueberries from a bowl on the table. "He's not the Killian I knew anymore, and this new Killian seems happy." I shrug. "That's all I ever wanted for him."

My mom stands and wraps me in a hug. "Is that the truth or is that for our benefit?"

"It's the truth. I'll always love Kill, but I don't know him anymore. I mean the Kill I knew wouldn't wear Gucci loafers and Armani suits. I'm not saying he doesn't look good, but . .

." He does; he really, *really* does look good. "That kind of guy would never be interested in someone like me anyway."

"That's a load of bullshi—uh . . ." Blake's eyes dart to Jack, who is still blissfully buried in his breakfast. "That's not true. And from what I hear, the media is blowing this relationship out of proportion. Caleb says they're just friends."

"Who kiss?"

Blake shrugs.

"After every single fight?"

He seems less confident, but still shrugs, this time only one shoulder. "It's possible."

"So the article said he's coming home. When?"

Mom and Blake share a meaningful glance, and then she turns to me with sympathy written all over her face. "They got in last night."

My eyes widen and my pulse speeds. "They're here? Now?"

"Yeah, and you should be prepared because—"

I hold up my hand. "Mom, please, don't worry about me. I promise whatever happened a year ago is in the past. We've both moved on. I'm really happy about where I am in life, and I think it's safe to say he is too."

Blake sighs and doesn't look at all convinced. "If you say so, kiddo."

"Right. Well, I better get to work." I grin and race out the door and straight to work, fighting my nerves the entire way.

THIRTY

Killian

Feels good to be home.

I'd forgotten how much I miss the heat until I felt the dry sixty-degree weather when we walked out of the airport at an ungodly hour. We managed to get to our hotel with only a few camera flashes, and after twelve full hours of sleep and room service, I'm feeling mostly human again.

"I swear to God if you embarrass me I will kick your arse." Ollie's been warning his sister about her fangirling since we touched ground, and he's driving the point home now that we're walking through the parking lot to the UFL Training Center's doors.

"I am sweating like a pig, but I can't tell if it's nerves or because it's fucking hot here." Fleur holds tight to my arm as if I'm her life preserver in rough seas.

"Seventy-two is nothing. The summers are brutal." I ruffle her hair. "Stop being such a girl."

Caleb ended up crashing with Rex and Gia, and Laise, Henry, Jay, and Liam all hit the bars and gambling once they got to their hotel last night, so none of them were answering their phones when we tried to get them to come along.

Opening the doors, I'm hit with the blast of air conditioning, the sound of metal music pumping through the speakers, and the familiar scent of sweat and rubber mats. Yep, smells like home.

"Hey, Vanessa." I greet the receptionist and grin as she takes me in appreciatively.

"Welcome home." She hits a button on the phone. "Layla, can you let him know the kid is home?" She rolls her eyes at whatever Layla says then hangs up. Apparently, the year I was away didn't mend fences between the two women. "Congratulations on your fights. Seems like just yesterday you were here washing towels and cleaning toilets."

Fleur and Olivier chuckle at my side.

"Thanks, Vanessa. I appreciate you bringing that up."

She smiles and jerks her head toward the main training room. "Head on back. They're expecting you."

I thank her and move with Fleur still welded to my arm.

She leans in close. "Who's expecting us? Oh my God, is it *The Assassin?*" Fleur's grip on me tightens to the point that my hand starts to go numb. "Because I will die if—Holy Mary, Mother of . . ."

We step into the main training center, which is at least triple the size of the one in London. Her and Ollie's gazes swing from one end of the room to the other, jaws hanging open.

"There's *The Fade*." Ollie points discreetly to the heavy bags where Wade is working with a fighter I've never seen before.

It seems like there are a lot of faces I haven't seen before. "There's Rex."

We head over to the mats where Rex is working with a flyweight. We stand back until he spots us and grins. "There he is." He says something to the guy he's working with then crosses to us with a smile on his face. "Quick Kill McCreery." He shakes my hand and pulls me in for a back-slapping hug. "Welcome home, brother." He swings his gaze to Fleur and Ollie, greeting them with handshakes. "Happy you guys could make it."

"This place is amazing." Ollie studies the poster-sized photos on the walls, each depicting a different fighter, both past and present.

Fleur remains tight-lipped, her anxieties seeming to get the best of her.

"Is Caleb here?"

"Yeah, I think he's in Cam's office, planning for your future, world domination, shit like that." He slaps me on the shoulder. "Make yourself at home; give your friends the tour."

"Alright, thanks."

Fleur has let up her grip on my arm a little, but as soon as we start making our way to the stairs that lead to Cam's office, she tenses up again.

"Oh my God, oh my God, oh my God . . ."

"What?" I follow the line of her sight and see why she's freaking out. My lips break into a smile so big my jaw aches.

"Fuck, here she goes; she's going to go off on one," Ollie mutters and drops his eyes to the floor.

The second Jonah spots me his face breaks into a grin that pops both dimples and shows all his teeth. He shakes his head and moves toward us.

"He's coming! He's walking over here. Oh my God!" Fleur presses her body so tightly to mine I'm surprised she doesn't wrap herself around my waist.

"Fuckin' A." Jonah opens his arms wide and swallows both me and Fleur, since she's become a permanent fixture on me, in a hug. "Killer, man . . . so fucking proud of you, brother."

I wish I could say I took his compliment like a man, but tears burn behind my eyes, and it's all I can do to say thanks without bursting into tears like a pussy.

He pulls back and sizes me up. "I knew you had what it took."

I shrug one shoulder, feeling suddenly shy and vulnerable, something I haven't felt since I stepped out of the octagon after my first fight. "You gave me the chance. I owe you for that."

"Nah, you worked your ass off. You earned your chance." His eyes track to Fleur, who's staring up at him in wonder and adoration. "You wanna introduce me to your friends?"

I blink and shake myself from the daze of his approval. "Yes, Jonah, this is Fleur and her brother—"

"Assassin, I'm a huge fan. I've been obsessed with you since your first fight, and your career has inspired me"—she catches a shaky breath— "so much."

Jonah holds out his hand to shake hers. "Thank you. That means a lot."

She stares at his hand with wide eyes, and then finally all the blood rushes back to my arm after she releases me. I expect her to shake Jonah's hand, but Ollie groans when she engulfs his entire forearm in her hands and stares at it.

"Fuckin hell, Fleur." Ollie studies the ceiling as if he's looking for patience that's been stored there.

"Your arm is so much bigger in real life," she whispers. "And your tattoos . . ."

I laugh, and when Ollie glares at me, I cover my mouth.

"Um . . . thank you?" Jonah looks at me and shrugs.

"She's a huge fan." I cough on a laugh.

He smiles down at her uncomfortably then pries her hands off him. "How about an autographed UFL shirt."

She gasps and looks up at him. "Yes, please, who me? Of course I want that."

He jerks his head toward the locker room. "Give me a minute. I'll go grab one."

"Thank you." She reaches for him again, to shake his hand maybe, but he jerks back in time to avoid it and heads to the locker room. "Assassin, it will be one of yours, right?" She calls to him, but he continues his path. "A dirty one is totally fine!"

"Oh, come on, Fleur!" Ollie groans.

She cups her mouth to be heard over the distance. "Seriously, though! If it's dirty, that's fine with me. I'd much rather prefer—"

"Fleur, shut up!" Ollie silences her with a hand over her mouth. "I told you not to embarrass me."

My eyes are watering from withheld laughter as Ollie and Fleur argue in French. These two are constant comedy.

"Killian?"

I turn toward the calling of my name and see Layla smiling up at me. The hilarity I was feeling dissolves, and my heart thuds in my chest.

"Layla, hey."

She moves in for a hug. "So happy you're home." There's a heaviness in her voice that makes me think maybe she's not as happy as she'd like to be.

"I'm happy to be home." A couple of awkward seconds linger between us as if she's waiting for me to ask about Axelle, or maybe she's hoping I don't.

"Listen. If you're looking for Cam, he's in the conference room."

"I don't want to bother him—"

"You won't. He's waiting for you." She looks over at Fleur. "Hi, I'm Layla, Cameron's assistant."

"Right, sorry." I rub my forehead, trying to bring my brain back online after the complete one-eighty. "Layla, this is Fleur and her brother Olivier."

They exchange greetings, and Layla mentions their beautiful accents, but I can't shake the feeling that something about the exchange is making her sad.

I try to ignore it, grateful that I have a few days to pull myself together before I reach out to Axelle. I have to prepare myself for the possibility of seeing her and Clifford as one big happy family, and the certainty of seeing her as a mother.

"Well, fuck me stupid."

Fleur snorts with laughter and Ollie chuckles.

Layla rolls her eyes. "Blake! Not in front of guests."

Blake comes up beside her and pulls her to him. "How the hell did I fall in love with a woman with such sensitive ears? She gives me shit, yet she talks like a trucker when we're alone."

She rocks her hip into him. "Behave. Fleur and Olivier, this is my husband, Blake Daniels."

Fleur tenses beside me, obviously recognizing who Blake and Layla are, or better yet who they are to Axelle.

"Killer." Blake holds out his hand and I shake it. "Good to have you back."

Seeing as the last time we were together he gave me a black eye, things are less than comfortable between us. "Thanks, Blake."

"Haven't missed one of your fights." The pride in his voice swells in my chest. "Always knew you could do it."

I nod, afraid that speaking will give away my delicate emotional state. I expected it to be difficult seeing them again. I didn't expect it to be—

The door next to us swings open, which surprises me at first because it's an old office that was used for storage.

A guy saunters out wearing nothing but a pair of loose workout shorts and a lazy and very satisfied smile. Judging by his size, he's a fighter, but he's also new. "Damn, woman, you've got the magic touch." He rolls his shoulders back. "God, I love you. Are you sure you won't marry me?"

"Easy, asshole." Blake growls.

Blake's reaction sends my gut tumbling, as if my body is trying to tell me something I should already know. Then I hear her.

And just like that the earth beneath me shifts.

"Oh, Trick, you don't love me." She appears in the doorway, and I swear to God I fucking choke on my own heartbeat. "You just want me for my hands."

It's her. It's really her, and I never thought it possible for her to get any prettier than she already was, but here I am staring at the proof.

Suddenly, I'm sixteen again.

Gazing upon the kind of beauty I'd only read about in books.

Her hair is longer, pulled back in a sleek chestnut ponytail that reaches her mid-back. Her skin, at least the little I can see with her dressed in leggings and a polo, looks even softer than my dreams imagined over this last year.

She must feel me staring because slowly her smile falls as she turns her head toward me.

When our eyes meet, it sends lightning through my veins.

Everyone dissolves around us. An A-bomb could go off and I'd never know it because locked in the liquid blue gaze of this girl, this *woman* who I've loved for as long as I can remember, nothing else exists.

"Kill . . ."

I bite my bottom lip, suddenly at a complete loss for words.

"Oh look!" Layla says, but I can't pull my eyes off Axelle. "There's Jonah."

I feel the people around us shift, as if they're walking away, but not before Fleur's voice is at my ear. "Will you be alright?"

Axelle rips her gaze from mine, and I could cry from the loss of it, but it zeroes in on Fleur in a way that makes me feel like I need to stand between them.

"I'm fine."

I register the absence of her presence and take a hesitant step toward Axelle.

Her eyes dart from Fleur's retreat to me.

"I missed you." I cringe as the pathetic, but true, words fall from my lips.

She grins; it's small and sweet and so fucking gorgeous it hurts. "Really?"

I blink at the disbelief in her voice. How can she even question that? "Yes."

She nervously tugs on the front of her shirt, pulling it tight across her breasts, and my mouth waters at the memory of their taste, the feel of them in my hands, the—

Wait. I point to the embroidered logo on her chest. "UFL?"

"Yeah, I work here now."

The room, the guy stumbling out . . . My mind slowly connects it all. "Doing sports therapy or . . ."

"Massage." She draws her shoulders back in a sense of accomplishment. "I got my license last month."

She was a business major. "What about school?"

She licks her lips and looks around as if to see who might hear. "It's a long story. I dropped out shortly after you left."

The baby. Of course. I'm sure finishing up college while pregnant isn't ideal. "Right, that makes sense."

Her breath shakes with a deep inhale. "You . . ." She motions to me, her eyes roaming over my designer clothes that I never felt ashamed of until now. "Wow . . . you're looking very . . . successful."

I step closer to her, and the urge to pull her in my arms and feel her, remind her that behind the designer labels I'm still me, is overpowering. She takes a retreating step as if she can read my intent and then holds up her hands. "Massage oil. I wouldn't want to ruin your nice clothes."

Rejected. I cross my arms over my chest to keep from touching her. "How's everything else?" *Clifford. The baby.*

"Good." A high-pitched squeal calls her eyes away from mine, and I stare at her profile as she squints off into the distance. "Wow, your girlfriend *really* likes Jonah."

Girlfriend? I whip my head around to see Fleur wrapped around Jonah's leg and Ollie trying to pull her off as they argue back and forth in French. Luckily, Jonah doesn't seem too pissed off, and Blake's laughing so hard his face is bright red from it.

I turn back to Ax. "Fleur and I—"

"Axelle, beautiful, are you ready for me?"

I instinctively step in front of her and glare at a half-naked fighter.

She leans around me. "Give me two minutes, Jose?"

"Sure thing, mami." He narrows his eyes at me. "Hey, I know you." His eyes brighten. "You're Quick Kill, yeah?"

"Yeah, and you're *Jose*." Fucking talking to my girl like she's some piece of ass.

My girl? She could be married, but I didn't notice a ring. Maybe she takes it off to do massage. Dammit, there's so much I still don't know.

"Jose?" Axelle says again. "Two minutes and then you can fawn over the superstar all you want."

I turn back to her, not at all comfortable with her tone. She said superstar like it's some joke.

"Killian, it was really great to see you, and I'm so happy you're doing well."

My chin tucks in to my throat. "So that's it?"

"What's it?"

I blink, shocked after everything we've been through that she can so easily blow me off. "It's been a year. I thought . . ." I rub the back of my neck, hating the fact that I want to beg. "Forget it."

"Okay." She smiles sweetly, not a hint of regret in her expression. "I'll see you around." She waves Jose over.

"Wait." I move in close without even thinking about it. "Can I call you?" This is wrong. She's my best friend, and it's like there's a canyon between us.

She doesn't answer immediately, which seriously pisses me off, and then nods. "Sure, I'll give you my number."

I glare at Jose, who's studying us like he's watching mold grow. "I have your number."

"Ha . . . could've fooled me."

"What does that mean?"

She shrugs. "I'm surprised you have my number, seeing as you never use it."

I open my mouth to defend myself, but slam it shut because I don't have a defense. She's right.

She disappears into her massage room and comes out with a card. "I have a new number anyway, as of a couple of months ago." She passes the card to me.

Axelle Daniels

Massage Therapist

Not married. I breathe a sigh of relief as hope floods my chest.

"I tried to call you," she whispers. "After you left, I called."

"I left my phone." Because I was afraid of what one more word from you would do to me.

"I know. I saw Ryder packing up your stuff, and your phone was there."

"You told me to go; I was just following orders." I cringe at the hurt that flashes in her eyes. I run a hand through my hair and wipe the slight stick of hair product on my jeans.

Those blue eyes score through me as she lets me sit in my own self-hatred.

"I gotta go." She smiles sadly and then waves Jose into the room, closing the door behind him.

Closing them in together.

While I stare at the door and contemplate breaking the fucker down.

She acts like everything that happened between us was my fault, like I'm the one who walked away, when she knows damn well she shoved me into this life without apology.

Not that I have a right to be upset, leaving was the best thing I could've done for my career. From the frigid way

Axelle's welcomed me home, I'd say leaving was the best thing for her too.

Why the hell does that hurt so bad?

~~~

I pull my phone out of my pocket and head for a quiet corner away from Fleur's incessant screeching. I quickly add Axelle's new number to my contacts, storing the important information from her card.

I scroll through my contacts for a different number, and once I find it, I hit "send."

Ryder answers after only a few rings.

"See what I did there, asshole? Phone rings; I pick it up. It wasn't even that hard. You should give it a shot sometime."

"You're still pissed."

"Yeah. So you're obviously calling for a reason. Dad said you were coming back. I'm assuming you want your shit. I gave the key to your storage place to my dad. He's got all the info."

"That's not why I'm calling. I need to talk to you."

"No."

I groan and drop my chin. "Really? So that's it."

"I'm headed into class right now—"

"I'll meet you on campus."

"Are you kidding? That'll cause a fucking mob."

He's probably right. "What about—?"

"Meet me at my pad in two hours."

My muscles release the tension I didn't even know I was holding. "Thanks, man. I—"

The line disconnects.

He agreed to hear me out, which is more than I expected.

I shove my phone into my pocket and slide down the wall to plant my ass on the concrete floor. And for the next two hours, I stare at that massage room door. Ollie and Fleur are busy picking Blake's and Jonah's brains and have moved on to the full tour without me. People come by to say hi, Cameron stops to welcome me home, but my gaze is glued to that door, not willing to miss another chance to lay my sights on her. When she finally does come out, her eyes flash to mine then narrow before she takes in another fighter.

She seems to be really good at what she does. Every fighter that leaves that room does so with a smile and a dazed look in their eyes. Not that I blame them.

I know what it feels like to have her hands on me. I've experienced firsthand what it's like to be drunk on her attention. It's the closest thing to heaven.

THIRTY-ONE

Killian

I called a cab and had it pick me up at the backdoor of the training center to avoid being followed by photographers. The entire ten-minute drive to Ryder's I spent rehearsing my speech. Once I'm finally at his door, I've forgotten everything I've rehearsed and settle for simply apologizing for being a shithead friend.

I fidget while waiting for him to open, wondering if I should at least hold my hands up to protect my face just in case. Nah, I'll leave them down. He's earned the potshot should he feel the need to give it.

He opens the door and doesn't even meet my eyes. "Come on in." He turns away and flops on the couch, not a hint of the hostility I was expecting, which makes me worry. Anger would mean he at least cares, but his I-don't-give-a-shit attitude might mean any number of *I'm-sorrys* won't do jack crap

He looks about the same—worn jeans, black belt, Docs, and sporting a black and red Ataxia shirt. His hair is still bleached blond, a little shorter than it was a year ago, but still sticking out at all angles.

I cruise through his pad to the bar and prop my ass on a stool. "Thanks for hearing me out."

He's holding onto a pair of drumsticks, absently slapping out a beat on his thigh. "You mind getting to whatever it is you want to say?"

This is awkward as hell. It's been so long since I've had to explain myself to anyone. And bringing up all this crap from the past makes me feel weak, another thing I haven't felt much of in the last year.

"You were right; I lied to you."

His eyes dart to mine and his drumstick thumping stops.

"I was busy in London, busier than I've ever been, but I avoided your calls."

"Why?"

I blow out a breath and lick my lips, not liking the taste of humility on my tongue. "Because I was weak. I was afraid if I talked to you I'd hear about Ax, and I couldn't handle hearing about how she'd moved on."

"You should've just told me that."

"I should've, but that would've been bringing her up, and honest to God, Ry, I couldn't. I couldn't even think about her name without wanting to jump on the next flight home."

"I thought you two were good that night you took her home from the party, after you gave that Clifford fuck a new nose. I thought things were solid between you two."

Even a year later, knocking that asshole for disrespecting Ax is still gratifying to think about. "I did too. Axelle and I made some important decisions about our relationship that night. We were together, ya know?"

He nods. "I figured as much, but then you took the London gig."

I blow out a breath and nod back. "I left, but only because she didn't give me any choice."

He frowns. "That doesn't make any sense. She needed you."

I whip my gaze to his, anger boiling in my gut. "I wanted to stay. I wanted to take care of her. I offered to be there for them. She didn't want me."

His eyebrows pinch together. "You know she ended up having to drop out of school, right?"

"Yeah, she told me that when I saw her today." I shrug, the news coming as little surprise. I figured the baby would force her to have to take time off school.

"She had to get a restraining order."

Time comes to a grinding halt.

The pause button hit on all my internal organs.

No breathing.

No blinking.

I think even my pulse froze. "What did you say?"

"He fucking tormented her, man." He glares at me.

Still on pause. "*What?*"

"Clifford." He throws his hands up. "Dude, are you fucking listening to a word I'm saying? He bullied the shit out of Axelle after you left. He put up naked pictures of her on all the campus boards . . ."

Lungs back online and pumping.

". . . fucking tore her up on social media . . ."

Eyes blinking.

". . . broke into her apartment and trashed the place . . ."

Pulse pounding.

"He'd make sure to catch her walking through campus so he could trip her and she'd fall flat on her face."

Fury.

I push up so fast the stool crashes to the ground. My fists clench at my side as adrenaline bursts through my veins. "Why didn't anyone fucking tell me!"

He jumps off the couch, seeming just as angry as I am. "I fucking tried! You were too *busy* being famous to give a shit!"

I fist my hands in my hair. "What the hell, Ry! You know I would've come home if I'd known this shit was going on!"

"We didn't even know it was going on until it got so bad she couldn't hide it anymore. Then she made us promise not to tell you."

"Why the fuck would she do that?"

"Oh, I don't know, asshole! Why don't you pull your head out of your ass long enough to think about it?"

Think about it? I can't concentrate on shit outside of breaking Clifford's neck.

Unless . . . "The baby." It had to be because of the baby, right? God, he tripped her when she was carrying his fucking child! Anger rips red hot through me.

"What baby?"

Annnd I'm back to pause.

"Axelle's baby."

His face twists in confusion. "Axelle doesn't have a baby."

Hold on. I rub my eyes and try to shake the feeling of being part of some sick practical joke.

"When I left"—I shake my head, trying like hell to make sense of all this— "she was pregnant when I left."

"No . . ." He frowns, shakes his head, blinks, and then . . . "Oh shit."

"What?"

He drops back down the couch and rubs his temple. "She got really sick a couple of months before she dropped out. They told me it was a stomach bug. When she came back to school, she seemed a little, I don't know, depressed or something. I just assumed she was still feeling like crap. Then Clifford started messing with her and . . . *shit*. I didn't know." He peers up at me. "She must've lost the baby."

"When? Do you remember when all this happened?"

"Yeah, it was the time I called you. I called her later that day to talk to her about what a piece of shit you were and . . ." He leans forward, bracing his elbows on his knees. "Fuck."

My chest feels like it's about to explode through my skin.

He tilts his head and stares right through me. "She got sick on the phone. I had to call Blake and . . . damn, poor Axelle."

"I should've been here," I mumble to myself. "I never should've left."

"Nothing you could've done, man."

"She told me to leave and I listened. Why did I listen?" I pace the length of the room. "She needed me, and I didn't even leave her a number to get in touch with me."

"She had it."

I freeze and whip my gaze to him. "What?"

"I gave it to her. She had it."

"Why didn't she—?"

He laughs, but the sound is more sad than happy. "She told me you're too smart to give up your future for her."

"She's wrong."

"That's what I said." He huffs out a breath. "Then she said, even if you'd tried to give it up, she'd never let you."

"She didn't. She made me go to London. I should've stayed in touch. Fuck! I should've grown a pair and stayed in contact."

"What's done is done, brother."

"It's not done." I stare intently at him. "This shit is far from fucking done."

Axelle

"Make sure to double up on your water tonight. I went pretty deep to loosen that spasm in your lower back." I wash my hands and hear the gentle hum of Cameron's breathing. I turn away from the sink, wiping my hands. "Cam, wake up."

His big body jerks on the table, and I quickly turn my back on him again. It's not uncommon for some of the guys to doze off during a massage, but some of them tend to jump up when they wake, and being naked under the sheet has created a very uncomfortable situation more times than I can count.

"Sorry, kiddo." The sheets rustle behind me followed by a groan. "You loosened up my back." The awe in his voice makes me grin. "It doesn't hurt anymore."

I make my way for the door so he can get up and dressed. "Don't forget to drink plenty of—"

"Water. I know."

The sated sound of his voice fills me with pride. Cameron Kyle is never relaxed, at least, not that I've ever seen outside of the massage room.

My fingers hesitate on the door lock. After my short talk with Killian, he stayed, staring at me between clients. Then he was gone. I want to kick myself for wishing it, but a large part of me wants him there when I walk out.

I hold my breath and open the door. My eyes scan the warehouse-like gym, but there's no sign of him.

He's gone.

No sign of him or his girlfriend and the man he came here with.

Girlfriend.

The word spoils in my gut.

Why does she have to be so beautiful? And her accent! French is called a romance language for a reason. When she spoke, it was like sex dripped from every syllable. I bet she whispers all sorts of naughty things to him, and it drives him wild—*no!* No. I refuse to torture myself any more than I already have.

Cameron shuffles from the room and smiles. "Hiring you was the best thing I've ever done."

I stand a little taller under his approval. "Thank you for giving me the chance."

"You've got a gift, kid." His eyes regain their focus. "How much longer you stayin' tonight?"

"An hour."

"Looks like most everyone's gone home, so I'll walk you to your car when you're ready."

I bite my lips and hold my eyes to keep them from rolling to the sky. I realized fighting the whole bodyguard thing was not only a huge waste of my time, but also a waste of energy. I can barely walk to the bathroom without a damn escort, thanks to Clifford. Asshole. "I'll come get you when I'm ready."

"Good." He slaps me on the shoulder with fatherly approval then ambles off to the locker room.

Finished for the day, my back and arms ache. Too bad there's not a masseuse for the masseuse. I strip the sheets from the table, disinfect, and restock my products then head to the women's locker room to change into my workout clothes.

I realized just a few weeks into my new career that lifting weights to strengthen my muscles and stretching them out after my shift lessens the soreness. It's a pain in the ass when all I want to do is go home and crash in front of the television, but I know once I'm done I'll be grateful I did it.

It'll also help for me to work through my conflicting feelings toward Killian. In some ways, I'm happy he's back. The urge to run into his arms and never leave is nearly irresistible. But then I remember how he took off without a single phone call. For a year, he severed all ties. Now he shows up in his designer clothes with his fancy-talking friends, and I've never felt more distant. We used to be so much alike, or at least I thought so. This new UFL star Killer "Quick Kill" McCreery I don't know at all. Sure, there was a flash of the old him in there somewhere, but it felt like this last year had built an impenetrable wall between us.

One we'll never get through.

I peel off my black leggings and pull on some spandex shorts along with a bright orange tank that says "Woman Up." I redo my ponytail, making this one higher and tighter, then grab my phone and earbuds. I have three missed calls and four new texts, all from what I recognize as Killian's London number.

I pop in my earbuds, hit "play" on my high-energy workout playlist, and then open the new text while moving through the training center to the weight room.

We need to talk. Call me.

Then another one two minutes later.

I'm sorry. Please, call me.

And thirty minutes later.

Can we get together? I need to see you.

And finally.

I talked to Ryder.

My feet become cemented to the floor. "Shit." Ryder must've told him about Clifford. Heat rises to my cheeks.

I've been told a bazillion times that it's not my fault, that I have nothing to be embarrassed for, but it's all bullshit. I made horrible choices and faced the consequences. I've paid for my sins and pulled myself up to start fresh. I'm sure Killian is looking for answers, but I've put the past behind me.

I take a fortifying breath and continue on to the weight room. When I shove through the weight room doors, I find the object of my thoughts rooted to a weight bench. His hair and skin are damp with sweat, and his eyes firmly fix on me.

"What are you doing here?" The question comes out like an accusation.

He slides his gaze slowly from my shoes, up my legs, lingering on my shorts before moving to my chest, neck, more lingering at my lips, and finally settling on my eyes. "What does it look like I'm doing?" His voice is husky and a shadow of anger tinges his face.

"Oh my God, are you *waiting* for me?"

He chuckles and drops his chin to stare at the floor. "Don't do that."

I step further into the room as the heat of frustration spreads through me. "Do what? Call you out? First, you sit outside my door, staring, no, *glaring* at me between clients, and now you're here after hours and alone, waiting for me like some kind of stalker—"

"Don't!" He shoots to his feet, wearing a sleeveless shirt. I can see the muscles of his arms flex. "Don't you fucking dare compare me to *him*." He spits out the three-letter word like it's a four-letter one, and I cringe, not needing clarification to know who he's referring to. "You should've told me!"

My face burns and tears sting the backs of my eyes.

His fists flex and un-flex as if he's not even aware he's doing it. "I've been in here for hours, trying to work this off, and—*fuck!*" He tosses his sweaty towel so hard it makes a whipping sound through the air. His stony expression softens, and the sorrow in his eyes breaks me. "Why didn't you tell me?"

"I was afraid—"

"Of what?" He tosses an arm out. "Of him?" He beats on his chest with a closed fist. "I never would've let him hurt you. Never!"

"No, not him, I was afraid that if I told you how bad things were you'd come home."

He narrows his eyes. "Of course I'd come home. You were always mine to protect, you know that." His shoulders slump as if all the fight has been knocked out of him. "*He* knew that I left, that you were vulnerable, and he attacked." He reaches under a bench and flips it upside down. "*Fuck!*"

I jump back, startled by his anger. "That's just it. You would've walked away from your dreams to clean up my mess. I couldn't let you do that."

"That's not your decision to make, Axelle. You took my choices away from me where we were concerned." He closes the space between us and cups my face in his hands, lifting my chin to meet his gaze. "I love you, don't you see that? I've spent my entire adult life loving you." His hands gentle. "Nothing has changed."

My eyes slide closed at the beauty and pain of his words. "Everything has changed, Kill."

He shakes me gently. "No. Don't say that. How can you say that?"

"We're not the same people we were a year ago."

He swipes my cheekbone with his thumb. "Maybe we're better."

"I live with my parents, Kill. You're an international celebrity, and I'm twenty-one years old and working at my very first job, ever."

"You had a rough year; that's understandable." He shifts uncomfortably on his feet. "So you, did you . . .?" He licks his lips. "You lost the baby?"

"Yeah." My heart still aches when I think about it; my mind often drifts to all the unanswerable *what-ifs*.

His arms wrap around me, my cheek presses against his sweaty shirt, and as much as I should be a little grossed out by it, I'm not. I wrap my arms around his middle and allow him to hold me close because, for those few seconds our bodies are pressed together, it feels like he's right. That nothing has changed between us.

"You never should've gone through that alone," he whispers against the top of my head, pulling me from the place we were just a couple of nights before he left for London.

I step back and out of his arms, needing the space to think straight. "I didn't. Mom and Blake were there." I lean back on the weight rack, but Killian rights the weight bench he tossed and offers it to me. I sit on it, and he takes the one just a couple of feet away. "I thought that was it, ya know?

318

That I'd lost the only connection I had to Clifford and he'd leave me alone. The only problem was he didn't believe I was really pregnant to begin with."

Killian's brows drop low and anger boils behind his eyes.

"When I told him, he accused me of lying, like I was trying to sucker him into a relationship." I laugh at the absurdity of it now. "I lost the baby before I really started showing, so naturally it seemed to confirm his assumptions and the harassment got worse."

"Why didn't you go to the cops?"

"Because I was sick of being everyone else's problem. I got myself into the mess. I wanted to get myself out. I was also humiliated. Half my professors now know what I look like naked, thanks to the photos Clifford posted all over campus.

"I didn't tell anyone, not even my mom. Then one night when I was babysitting Jack and Mindy was out, someone broke into our apartment. He cut up my bed, my clothes, broke everything, didn't steal anything though. I called the cops, and they didn't find any suspicious fingerprints. But he left one of those pictures on my nightstand. I told the cops about it, which was"—my entire body blushes with the memory— "so embarrassing."

"Did they lock the fucker up?"

"I couldn't prove that the photo came from him rather than from one of the many I found and picked up at school. I told them I didn't keep the ones I found at school. I destroyed them as soon as I'd found them. They said they believed me but they couldn't prove it and suggested I get a restraining order." I shrug. "Once Blake found out . . ." I cringe, remembering his fit of rage. "You can imagine."

"How is this asshole still breathing?"

"Get this . . ." I lean forward, elbows to my knees. "You can't kill someone for harassment. Go figure."

The corner of his mouth twitches.

"There he is . . ." I point to his mouth. "I see you in there, Killian McCreery."

He covers his face with one hand, peeking through his fingers. "Oh no . . . is my nerd showing?"

"A little." I giggle.

"That's not good. Ya know I have a rather studly reputation."

"Oh, don't think I missed it. Your"—I do air quotes—"*reputation* takes up half the state of Nevada."

"Aww, Ax, baby." He grins all crooked and cocky and breathtaking. "Jealousy isn't your color."

I fake pout. "That's not the color of jealousy, Kill. That's disgust."

His jaw drops in mock offense. "Oh yeah?" He holds both arms up and flexes. "How's this for disgust."

I lean back and yawn, exaggerating by patting my hand to my mouth. "Excuse me, whew. I just suddenly got *so* bored."

He coughs out a laugh, and I grin at how good it feels to have him back like this, realizing now how much I missed it.

His smile falls, and his amber eyes become thoughtful. "I want to see you again. What are your plans tomorrow?"

"I'm booked tomorrow from ten to four."

He frowns. "All day, huh?"

"We can meet for breakfast."

He shakes his head. "I can't. I promised Fleur I'd take her to hike Red Rock Canyon, and I have to be back in time for a nine o'clock meeting with my publicist."

Yep, I was right; everything has changed.

And his girlfriend. God, Axelle.

I jump up from the bench and press my fingertips to my forehead. "I'm so stupid."

He must sense my change in demeanor and stands up too. "Hey, maybe we can get together after you're done? You said four, right? I can—crap. I have a meeting at three-thirty. Who knows how long that'll last?"

I wave him off, backing toward the door. "Don't worry. We'll, uh . . . We'll figure it—*oh!*" I scream when the door behind me opens and slams into my back.

"Fuckin' hell, Axelle." Cameron grabs me by my shoulders to steady me. "Are you okay?"

I rub the ache in my back, my eyes darting between the worried eyes of the two men before me. "Fine. I'm fine. Perfect timing though, I was just coming to get you."

"Already?" Cam's glare tightens. "You sure you're okay?"

Killian's gaze tangles with mine for a few seconds, confusion working behind his eyes.

"Of course. I'm great."

And then, as if I'm being chased by zombies, I run to the locker room, grab my shit, and meet Cameron in the lobby.

I'm looking over my shoulder to see if Killian is still here, when Cam's phone rings.

"What?" He opens the door for me to walk through it. "Yeah, I just talked to him." I point to where my car is parked, and he nods for me to lead the way. "I agree. I think it's a smart move." He stands there while I throw my bag into the back, and I wave him off as I climb into the driver's seat. He doesn't leave though; they never do, insisting on standing guard until I'm safely out of the lot. "I just signed an indefinite lease on the penthouse in London." I freeze, eavesdropping on the conversation. "Yep. Killer's meeting with his publicist tomorrow to handle the announcement. He'll head back next week."

It isn't until Cam mouths *you okay?* that I realize I'm staring blankly at him. I force a smile and slam my door.

Killian's going back to London.

I'm losing him again.

THIRTY-TWO

Killian

I have a headache from bouncing my eyes between my phone and the plate of Asian fusion food in front of me. It's been over twenty-four hours—forty-two to be exact—since Axelle and I had our face-to-face in the gym. I went back to my hotel that night and texted her that I appreciate her filling me in on the last horrible year of her life and that I was sorry for blowing up. I also said I looked forward to seeing her again. And either she never received that text or she flat out fucking forgot because I haven't heard from her or seen her since.

I took Fleur, Liam, and Jay hiking at Red Rock the next morning, got back in time to meet with my publicist at the hotel, and raced to the training center to catch Axelle. She wasn't lying when she said she was booked all day with massages, but this time she never came out of her little room. From what I could tell, she was ordering the last client to issue in the next. I had my late afternoon meeting at the training center, and by the time I was finished, she was gone.

"Figure if you stare at it long enough it'll grow wings?" Liam lifts his brows, his eyes dancing between mine and my phone, which is face up just inches from my plate.

Fleur flicks her water straw at him. "Mind your own business, Liam."

"No." I pick up my phone and shove it into my pocket. "He's right." She's obviously ignoring me, and she's nuts if she thinks she can avoid me forever.

Fleur leans in to me. "She'll call; just give her some space."

I don't understand. I thought Axelle and I had a pretty good talk, but she's not giving me even a hint of how she's feeling. Unless you count her ignoring me, then I'd say she's sending a pretty clear message.

"What time is the press conference?" Liam shoves a bite of food in his mouth.

I throw my napkin on the table and lean back. "Tomorrow at four thirty."

"Four thirty?" He looks disappointed. "But it's Saint Valentine's Day, and rumor has it American girls are horny and willing on this day." He shoves out his lower lip. "I was hoping to be drunk and the meat in a girl sandwich by then." He tilts his head. "Any chance they can reschedule it?"

Valentine's Day. Fuck. "No, dumb ass."

"It's the big announcement, yeah?" Disappointment etches Fleur's voice. "Any chance you want to let us in on what you'll be announcing?"

"They swore me to secrecy." I hook my hands behind my neck and lean back, staring between my loud-mouthed friends. "Didn't want it to leak to the press before the conference."

"Oh come on, we're mates." Liam grins. "I won't say a word."

"So when you're covered in naked strippers and drunk on scotch, you won't slip and give away the secret?"

"What exactly do you think I'm gonna say? 'Take my boxers off and oh, by the way, Quick Kill's going back to London to fight with me because I'm the best middleweight on this side of the equator?'" He purses his lips. "I see your point. That could definitely help me pull a bird, but I guess I'm stuck relying on my accent. Did you know I say one word and American girls drop their knickers and fall on their backs?"

Fleur laughs. "That's what happens when you follow them to the toilet and watch them pass out."

"You're such a fucking comedian."

"I'm just saying how do you know it's your accent?"

"Well, it's not his face," I mumble.

"Fuck off." He checks his phone. "Speaking of . . . I gotta run. I'm meeting the boys at some place called Zeus's." He slams back the rest of his drink.

"You're going to a strip club? It's two o'clock in the afternoon."

"So." Liam stares at me and then at Fleur. "You want to come with?"

She gazes up at me, reads something on my face, and then nods. "Gah . . . fine."

Liam lifts his chin toward me. "You got this?"

"I got it." Cameron gave me a company credit card for entertaining my London brethren.

Fleur squeezes my shoulder as she leaves. "Hang in there, okay?"

"Will do, boss."

She smiles sadly, and as soon as they're far enough away, I check my phone.

Still nothing.

Dammit, Axelle! I didn't want to do this, but she's given me no choice.

I search my contacts and hit "send."

"UFL, this is Vanessa."

"Hey, Vanessa, it's Killian. Listen. I need to ask you for a favor . . ."

Axelle

I went a year without speaking to Killian, and those three-hundred sixty-five days were nothing compared to the two days I've gone ignoring him. I wish I could say I was doing it because I'm immature and selfish. That would be the easiest way to explain away how I'm feeling.

Unfortunately, it's much more complicated than that. My heart and mind are all mucked up together, and I can't make sense of any of it.

On the one hand, I want to spend every single second with Killian before he goes back to London. I'd ignore sleep if it meant I could stay up with him all night, laughing at his stupid jokes and watching the way his face lights up when he talks about his fighting.

But then there's the other hand: The one that rises up without fail to protect me from getting hurt. The one that pushes people away before they can leave. The hand that tells me I've lived without him before and I can do it again. This is the same hand that holds me back from returning his texts and his calls.

How do I explain that I can't get close to him only to lose him again?

". . . Tatyana sneaks in his bed at night." Mason, the fighter currently on my table, face up, grimaces while I work a tight muscle in his arm. "We don't mind, but I think Felix was excited about finally having his own space."

Every time he gets a chance to talk about his two adopted kids, he does. His face even lights up when he tells stories about how they misbehave, which is beautiful to witness.

I move up his bicep to his shoulder. "She's probably so used to her brother being there it'll take some time for her to feel safe without him. Eventually, I'm sure she'll grow out of it."

"Part of me hopes she doesn't." He hisses as I rub deep into a knot. "I like that they're so close."

He falls silent as I work the kinks from his muscles, having to occasionally remind him to breathe. When I sense the he's nice and loose, I check the time. "That muscle in your shoulder took longer than I thought." I move to the sink and wipe my hands on a clean towel.

"*Mmm* . . . feels one hundred percent better. Thank you."

I get so much satisfaction from knowing I'm able to help these guys out. They put their bodies through all kinds of torture during training, and it's nice to feel needed.

I shrug, turn around, and smile. "Just doing my job."

He sits up, and I fight the urge to laugh at his hair, which is sticking out all over. I contemplate sending him behind the shoji screen to get changed as I did with all my clients yesterday to avoid seeing Killian, but I could use a little break from being holed up in this room.

"I'll step out while you get dressed."

He nods, his face still a little groggy.

Stepping out, I close the door quietly and blink while my eyes focus to the bright light of the training center. I jerk in surprise when I see Killian standing there in nothing but a pair of workout shorts and flip-flops.

I stare wide-eyed at his impressive build and remember the way each muscle felt against my body. I shake off the ghost of lust that rushes through me. "What are you doing?"

He tilts his head, and the corner of his mouth lifts. "I'm here for a massage."

"No." I step back, shaking my head. "You can't. I mean . . . I can't. We . . ." I clear my throat and square my shoulders. "I'm booked. Sorry."

With powerful hands propped on his hips, he stares straight through me. "You had a cancellation."

"Says who?"

"Vanessa."

"I don't believe you."

"Ask her. Your four o'clock cancelled."

Shit. I rub my forehead and snap my eyes to him when he moves in.

He closes the distance between us and scowls down at me. "You think you can ignore me and I'll give up; you're wrong."

I swallow and open my mouth to protest, but nothing comes out, so I slam it shut and swallow again.

Get it together, Axelle! You massage fighters all day; this one is no different.

My subconscious screams that he's *so* different, but I ignore it.

"Fine." I check my wristwatch. "You've got an hour."

His confident smirk turns too sexy for comfort. "That's plenty of time, Ax."

The door opens behind us, and Killian steps away, giving back my air. I suck in a deep breath, as if entering the room with Killian will be the equivalent of ducking my head under water.

"Killer, man." Mason and Killian share a man hug. "You're blowing up the UK scene."

"Cameron sends me across the pond to kick ass; I'm gonna kick some ass."

Cocky much?

He slaps Killian on the back. "Nice to see your training team worked the modesty out of you. The press will eat that up."

Killian's eyes find mine, and whatever he sees makes him lose some of his bravado. "Yeah, well . . . it's all about the show, ya know?"

Mason stares at him for a few silent seconds before nodding. "You're makin' us proud. Looking forward to the big announcement tomorrow. As much as I hope you'll be here in Vegas, I think it would be stupid for you to leave London at the height of your game."

"Can't argue that." Killian's gaze drops to the floor, and a hint of my old friend is reflected in his frown.

He ping-pongs from the old Killian to the new as if he's fighting who he used to be, and that pisses me right off.

"As much fun as this little convo is . . ." I tap my watch. "We're eating into Killian's massage time." I hold my hands up. "Not that I mind. If you guys want to continue, I'll go get an iced tea or something." I lift a brow at Killian and he smiles.

"No way." Mason throws an arm over me. "You don't want to miss even a second of this girl's hands. She's incredible."

"Oh, I know she is." He winks.

Really, Killian? Who are you?

I duck out of Mason's hold and slip into the room, ripping the sheets off the table and replacing them with fresh ones. The door shuts and locks behind me. I rein in my reaction while every nerve in my body is aware we're alone together in a dimly lit room.

I avoid his eyes and turn toward the sink. "You, um . . . you can leave your shorts on."

"Really?" His voice is closer now. "I thought I was supposed to get naked?"

"You—" My voice cracks. "You can, but I think it's best if you keep your shorts on."

"Why, Axelle?" He chuckles. "It's not like you're not intimately familiar with what's under them."

I drop my chin and brace my weight on the counter as flashes of his naked body zap through my brain. *Dammit, Axelle! Be a professional for God's sake!*

"Fine." I move to step out of the room. "Get naked. Get under the sheet. I'll be back—"

"Not so fast." He snags my arm as I pass by him. "Something tells me if I let you walk out that door you won't come back."

I lift my chin in defiance. "Guess that's a chance you've got to take." I struggle to pull free of his hold, but he doesn't release me.

His eyebrows drop low. "Talk to me, Ax," he whispers. "What did I do?"

Yeah, that's a fantastic question. What did he do? Other than leave to London for a year without saying good-bye and coming back a totally different person.

Defeat washes over me, making my shoulders slump. "Please, Kill. Don't make this harder than it already is."

"Make what harder? I thought we had a good talk the other night, but ever since, you've been MIA."

I jerk my arm free, and he steps away to give me some space, but I don't miss the fact that he steps in front of the door, most likely to block my escape. "Don't treat me like some stupid groupie."

"Groupie—?"

"Did you tell Fleur about our talk?"

He drops his gaze and rubs the back of his neck. "Yes."

"Does she know you've been calling and texting me?"

He peers up at me. "She knows."

"So . . ." I study the walls that feel like they're shrinking around us. "Your girlfriend is fine with you chasing me down."

His face registers confusion for a few beats, and then his eyes widen and he laughs. "Ax, you think . . . wow." He shakes his head, grinning. "That's been your issue? Fleur is *not* my girlfriend."

What? "Since when?"

"Since ever." He moves in closer. "You need to stop believing everything you read."

"What about what I've seen, huh? Are you trying to tell me all the kisses and photos of you two cuddled up are fake? I've *seen* you guys kiss. Many times." The memory makes me nauseated.

"We've kissed, sure, but she's French. That's what they do."

I cross my arms at my chest. "So you're telling me the two of you have never hooked up?"

He recoils, but stands his ground.

"I'll take that as a yes."

He looks genuinely apologetic. "I had *one* moment of weakness."

"A moment *of weakness?*" *God, since when did he become a womanizing pig?*

Anger flashes in his eyes. "She knew exactly what she was doing, and I explained—"

"Oh, God." I cover my ears. "I don't want to hear about all your European sexcapades."

"Yeah? Why not?" His jaw ticks. "We're just friends, right? Or hell, maybe we're not even that anymore, so why does hearing about me and Fleur upset you?"

"Because this isn't the Killian I know. I lost my best friend one year ago; he left and didn't even say good-bye. And now you're back, but you aren't you, Kill." A lump forms in my throat, and I turn away from him to organize bottles of oil and creams.

"Ax, it is me." He pushes up behind me, his hands braced on either side of my hips, his lips at my ear. "I'm right here. You say I've changed. I won't deny that. But I'm better, right? I never felt worthy of you, never felt like the kind of man you could be proud of, one who could take care of you." His nose runs the length of my neck and I shiver. "I'm that man now."

"I liked—no, I loved the old you." My thoughts spiral as he brushes his lips against my earlobe. "I missed him for an entire year, and I'm afraid I lost him forever."

"No." He pulls at the tender skin of my neck with his lips. "I'm here." His mouth, lips, teeth, and stubble continue their delicious torture, and I lose all my strength and lean back into his chest. "I tried so hard to forget you, but I couldn't. I didn't want to want you, but you're in my blood. I can't shake you."

"Why didn't you call?"

"I thought I was giving you what you wanted. You were pregnant, and I knew you had shit to figure out. I walked away, hoping I could forget you, but I couldn't." He nuzzles my throat. "You were my first, Axelle."

I blink my eyes open, stilling at his words. "But not your last . . ."

He drops his forehead to my shoulder. "No."

I turn around and face him head on, needing to see his face, and I regret it the second I see the shame and embarrassment in his eyes. "I haven't been with anyone since you, Killian."

"Fuck." He exhales hard, steps back, and runs a hand through his hair. "I didn't know."

"I think we just have to accept what is." I wipe under my eye, forcing tears back where they belong. "We had our shot; it didn't work."

He shakes his head. "Don't do that. Don't push me away. We can have that again, make it just like it was before."

"Sometimes you just have to accept the fact that things have changed. I have a great job, I'm saving to get my own place, and I'm paying my own insurance and chipping in with the bills at home. It feels . . . Kill, it feels so good. I'm standing on my own for the first time in my life."

"I want a chance to know who you are now. I want to know everything about you. I want to be the one you lean on again."

"That's the problem, don't you see?" I pound my chest with my fist. "I'm not the girl who needs fixing anymore. There's no more messes for you to clean up. What we had wasn't fair to you—you taking care of me and me secretly loving you but so damn scared that if I made one wrong move you'd leave and I'd be forced to take care of myself."

"Watch it, Axelle." His expression turns deadly. "Don't say it again."

"Huh?"

"That's the second time you've said you love me, and if you say it again, I'll take you"—he motions to the massage table with a quick jerk of his head— "right there. Right now."

Blood pounds through my veins and I throb everywhere. "I—"

"I'm serious, Ax." He pinches his eyes closed and drops his chin. "I've been waiting for a year to touch you again, to taste you. I'm walking a fine line right now."

My legs turn to jelly at the husky sound of his voice. "You wouldn't."

His eyes snap to mine. "Oh, I would. I've never stopped loving you, never stopped dreaming of a future with you. Not a single fucking day. You still love me."

I sigh because he's right. Of course I love him; that's not something I could turn off. Trust me. I tried. "I always have."

"Stop." His voice cracks.

"It's true. I—"

His big body slams into mine, and his mouth crashes against my lips, taking away every last bit of my voice and rational thought.

THIRTY-THREE

Killian

I'm home.

But it's not a casual arrival.

It's a smash-the-door-down-and-light-the-fucking-place-on-fire kind of arrival.

Axelle tastes even better than I remember; the light sweetness of her lips mixed with the peppermint of her tongue makes me ravenous for more. Whatever doubts I had about her feelings for me are put to death by the passion behind her kiss. Her hands rip through my hair, fingers dig into my neck, pulling me deeper under her spell.

I grip at her polo and push it up to expose her breasts. She backs up a few steps, and my lips chase hers until she stops when her ass hits the massage table. I push her bra up to join her shirt, and the heavy weight of her breasts welcomes my touch. "I missed you."

She groans as I run the pad of my thumb along her nipple. "This is wrong."

"Shhh." I dip down and flick the firm peak with my tongue. "It's right. It's always been right."

Her delicate hands glide up my chest and around my neck, holding me to her as I shower her breasts with attention. "Kill."

I growl in approval at the hungry way she says my name, then cup her between her legs. "You want me here?"

"I . . ." She shakes her head, but her body arches into my touch.

"I need you to say the words. I need to hear you."

"Yes." The single word comes out on a heated breath.

I slide my hands into her tight pants and push them, along with her panties, down to her ankles. That one word pushed off the last of her reservations, and she eagerly toes off her shoes and kicks her clothes off her feet as I remove the shirt and bra. I pull the elastic band that holds her hair back, and her silky hair falls free over her shoulders.

"I dreamed about you, about how you'd look after a year without seeing you. The dreams were incredible and yet not even close to how beautiful you really are." I scoop her up to place her back on the table, and she parts her legs in invitation. My gaze devours her from the way her dark hair splays across the white sheets to the tips of her blue-painted toes.

"Killian, I want this, but—"

I smother her lips, cutting off her protest before she can talk herself out of it. Whatever her objection is to us being together, her body doesn't agree as is evident when I move to the spot between her legs.

We moan in pleasure together until she's writhing against me. I need more, need to be deep inside her, losing myself to her.

"Ah, fuck."

"What?" Her chest is rising and falling with the power of her breath.

I drop my forehead to her chest, kissing her breasts. "No condom."

"I'm on the pill."

My eyes dart to hers.

"After the . . . um . . ." She shakes her head, and I drop a soft kiss to her lips.

"Are you sure it's okay?"

"As long as you're clean."

"I am." I lick at her bottom lip. "I wouldn't come near you if it was even a question. You know that, right?"

Her fingers dance through my hair. "Yes, I know that."

We sink into the pleasure of each other's lips, and she reaches between my legs to touch me over my shorts.

I hiss as the heat of her palm presses against me. "Missed those hands."

"They missed you too." She strokes me into a frenzy, and before I know it, I'm naked and crawling onto the massage table.

She welcomes me between her legs, and the second we make contact we both suck in a breath as her heat envelops me. I grit my teeth and edge in slowly, terrified of hurting her, and the sensation is beyond imaginable. Little by little we come together completely, her chest pressed to mine so much I can feel her heart pounding against my ribs.

I slide my arms beneath her back, my hands coming up behind her to grip her head. I ease out and in with intentional strokes, savoring every lick of pleasure she coaxes from me.

"Yes." Her chin tilts to capture my lips, and I kiss her with the intensity of a man starved for a year.

Our movements turn feverish in an explosion of emotion from a year of being apart. This isn't the slow connection I was hoping for, but we're too lost in each other to go slow, giving in to the passion that burns hot between us. Her breath hitches with every thrust until she cries out so loud I cover her mouth with mine. She bites and sucks on my lips as I work her through her orgasm, only sending my own to crash in behind hers.

She locks her heels at the backs of my thighs as I ride out my release and nuzzle her neck to keep my own moans from carrying out of the room.

My head is light with euphoria that has more to do with the woman than it does the mind-blowing finish. "You're perfect, everything . . ." Emotions pull me in every direction, and I drop my forehead to her neck. "I needed this."

She sighs and releases her lock on my legs. "You needed . . . this."

There's a coolness in her voice that turns my blood to ice. I pull back and stare down at her, but she's looking away.

My gut clenches and my chest aches. "What?"

She wiggles beneath me, and I push back to my knees so she can get up and off the table. "I made a mistake."

"What?"

"I can't do this." She pulls her clothes off the floor and scurries behind a folding wall, hiding her naked body from me.

"Do what? Have sex?" My gut churns with anger. "Because it's a little too late for that, sweetheart."

Her breath hitches behind the thin paper divider, and I grit my teeth, wishing I could take it back. I scoop my shorts up off the floor and slide them on, searching for the right combination of words that will diffuse the explosion I feel coming.

She steps around the screen, fully dressed, smoothing her hair back into a ponytail. "*That* is exactly why . . ." She turns to face me and there's fire in her glare. "You need to go."

I stand firm and shake my head. "No way."

Her jaw falls open, and she shoves her finger toward the door. "Go!"

"No."

Her glare sharpens, and I could swear I hear a purr-like growl rumbling in her throat. "What are you doing?"

"I never should've listened to you when you told me to go." I step into her space. "I'm not going to let you push me away again. Not now. Not ever."

"You don't get a say in what I do."

"I do now."

She stomps a foot, and if I weren't so pissed, I'd laugh. "No, you *don't!*"

"Have you not been listening? I am *in love with you*—"

"Don't do that!" Her eyes glisten with tears.

I want to touch her, to pull her to me and hold her tight until she understands, but I can tell by her rigid stance that's not what she wants. "Axelle Rose Daniels." I take a step closer, pleading with her to hear me. "I love you."

"Stop saying that." She shrinks back and her lip trembles. "Stop saying you love me when you're leaving for London next week."

My pulse speeds, but my blood feels like mud in my veins. "How would you know that? No one's supposed to know—"

"Cam said—"

"I'm not sure if I'm leaving."

She blinks up at me. "So, you're staying? In Vegas?"

"It depends."

"On what?"

"I thought I've been making this clear. It depends *on you*. If you'll give us a shot, I'm staying to take it. But if this is all we have left, me holding on while you're kicking me off, Ax . . ." I shake my head, unable to complete the thought let alone say the words. "I'll fight for us, but I'll need you to fight too."

"You love the damsel in distress. I'm not her anymore."

"I love *you*."

She huffs. "I'll drive you crazy with all the reasons why we won't work out. I'll push and push, and one day I'll push you past your limit. You'll walk away from me, Killian. I know you will."

I reach to pull her in my arms, to prove to her with my body what I'm trying to communicate with my words, but she shrugs me off and pushes past me.

"Axelle, I won't." I make the X across my heart. "I promise."

She smiles sadly. "Promises don't mean anything. They're just words. You'll walk away eventually. They all do."

And with that last parting jab, she's gone.

I guess that's her answer.

THIRTY-FOUR

Axelle

"Are you sure you don't want to be here?" My mom's voice sounds in my ear, intensifying my guilt. "If you hurry, you'll make it in time to catch the announcement."

"I'm sure. I have a feeling after our talk yesterday he wants nothing to do with me, and I can't be there when he announces he's leaving." It'll destroy me.

Not that I'd blame him though.

I'd acted like an immature idiot yesterday after we had sex. I ended up stomping straight to my car and calling Vanessa, asking her to cancel my last two appointments, claiming I was sick.

Which was true.

I felt like crap after the way I'd treated Killian.

From the moment we met, he's been my biggest defender, my protector, and after all he's done for me, I put him in the same category as men like Stewart, Trip, and Clifford.

If he doesn't hate me, he should.

I hate myself enough for the both of us.

I half expected him to call or text last night, but he never did. I finally ended up texting him at midnight, apologizing, begging his forgiveness, and asking him to give me another chance. My finger hovered over the Send button when I remembered something he'd said after we'd had sex, as he so callously put it.

I never should've listened to you when you told me to go.

If he'd stayed, he wouldn't be "Quick Kill" McCreery, whose face is gracing the covers of magazines, websites, and every sports network from here to the UK. So do I love him enough to follow through and do what I know is best for him? Or do I hit "send" and allow the one person who's managed to fill the emptiness every man has ever left behind walk away from his dreams.

For years, he loved me and protected me so I could spread my wings and find my way. I owe him no less. He deserves to be successful, and I'll have to be content to watch it from afar with the knowledge that for a brief moment in time I had it all. I had his love, his devotion, his time. I owned his heart.

It was on this thought that I didn't hit "send."

"So if you're not coming to the press conference, what will you do?" There's fear in my mom's voice, probably from years of watching me drown my problems in booze and random guys.

"I'll walk around The Miracle Mile shops. Probably grab a bite to eat. Don't worry about me."

"I'll always worry about you." She sighs. "But especially on . . . *this* day."

I'm grateful she doesn't say the dreaded V-word. "I'm good. I promise." My own words flash through my head. A promise is just a word; it doesn't mean anything. True in this case, because I'm far from good. "I'll see you at home tonight."

"Okay, love you."

"Love you too, Mom."

I hang up and shove the phone in my purse. The sun is out and warms my shoulders as I pass by shops and restaurants, running my gaze along it all but not seeing what's in front of me. Instead, my friendship with Killian plays like old home movies behind my eyes.

"Hey . . ." The kid pushes his shaggy brown hair off his forehead. "I'm Killian."

I'm sweating, holding my hair off my neck, and panting to catch my breath after the string of curse words I just spewed here in the high-school parking lot. "Elle."

He pushes his black-rimmed glasses up his nose and studies the broken down Bronco piece of crap. "I don't mean to be presumptuous. You seem like a capable female, but I can't help but notice your Millennium Falcon seems to be on the fritz."

"My what?"

"Star Wars humor." A blush colors his cheeks and he grins. "Do you need some help?"

I chuckle. I can't help it. The guy is adorable. "Yeah, I could use a ride."

"Sure." His eyes, the color of iced tea, fix on mine. "I can do that."

I trusted him immediately, and not one time did he ever give me a reason not to. He was the safest boy I ever knew. Even scrawny with his thick-rimmed glasses, I knew he'd do everything in his power to keep me safe. He guarded me and my heart with all the ferocity of a fearless warrior.

The group of guys I recognize from school surround the table Killian and I are sitting at. They're holding up their phones, laughing, just like they have been from the moment I walked in the coffee shop.

Killian's been growing tenser, and now that we're surrounded, his hands are balled into fists, and he's staring down at his coffee in front of him.

"Elle, right?" The biggest guy gets so close I lean away to keep him from touching me. "You're new."

"Yeah."

Killian looks up at me from beneath his eyelids.

"I was wondering . . ." His friends at his back all choke on their laughter. "You wanna go out with me?"

"Oh, um . . ." Usually I'd be flattered that the most popular guy in school asked me out, but the way he's

snorting on his withheld amusement proves this isn't a genuine invite.

"Back off, Watkins."

My eyes flick to Killian at the threatening tone of his voice.

The kid, Watkins, ignores Killian's command. "I just figured . . ." He turns the phone screen to me, and there in full color is a photo of my mom. Topless.

I gasp and my cheeks flame.

He grins. "If your mom's this quick to get naked, my guess is you are too."

The guys all dissolve into a fit of giggles, and like a flash, Killian is up. He tackles the dude who's twice his size to the ground.

I swing into a bakery and grab a muffin and a water then search for a place to sit. I spot a table across the way that's half shade and half sun. A shaky smile breaks across my face as I imagine what Kill would say to me if he were here.

"You're so weird."

"Newsflash. You're not exactly perfect either, buddy."

"Guess that makes us the perfect pair."

I'd love it when he'd say that because that's all I ever wanted to be. His perfect match. But then my life would come crashing down around me, reminding me of my insecurities. How could someone like Killian, someone so good and pure, stay with someone like me? I'd chase him off eventually.

Killian steps close, towering over me. "What do you mean Trip's not calling you back?"

My neck flushes with embarrassment. "It's no big deal." I shrug and act unaffected. "He's probably just busy."

"How many times have you tried to get in touch with him?"

"Not many. Maybe five." Fifteen. Eight texts, four phone calls, three emails.

"Five times and he hasn't gotten back to you?" Killian spits the words through clenched teeth.

I hate it when he looks at me like I'm one of those puppies from that commercial about abused pets with the music that always makes me cry. "It's okay, Kill. I've gone twenty years without him. What's a few more?"

What's a few more . . .?

Killian's about to leave for five years, and I'm sitting here doing nothing to stop him. I preach that I want to have more control over my life, that I want to take my fate into my own hands, and here I'm reminiscing about my feelings for Killian while at the same time letting him go.

My spine stiffens. If I want to stop being treated like a damsel in distress, I need to stop lying around waiting to be saved.

I nearly trip, untangling my legs from the table and chair, and then race the few yards to the street. My arms flail to wave down a cab, and I jump in before he's even to a complete stop.

"You in a hurry?"

"Yes! I need to get to the UFL Training Center as fast as you can drive."

He pulls out into traffic and spots me from the rearview mirror. "That'll cost extra."

"Fine, I don't care. Just please, I don't have a lot of time."

Killian

"Mr. Kyle, can you explain why the UFL is sending fighters from the US to train in the UK?"

Cameron sucks his front teeth then leans into the mic, glaring at the poor reporter who asked the question. "It's not rocket science, Phil. As I said before, it's like a foreign exchange student program. We send a guy over to train and set up a few fights; they send a guy our way."

Poor Phil clears his throat, and if I had an ounce of humor in me, I'd laugh. "Um, I understand that, but I guess my question is why?"

"Because I can, Phil. Because it's fun. Because why the fuck not?" Cam purposefully directs his eyes to the opposite side of the room. "Next question."

I peer down the table at my London camp then turn to see most of my Vegas camp looking on with anticipation. The great thing about today's announcement is that, no matter what I decide, I know the guys and girl I fight with will approve. They've all expressed their support, and as difficult a decision as this was to make, their backing me up has made it a little easier.

I've had to accept the fact that I can't love Axelle enough for the both of us. It's possible that what she thought was love for me was only her appreciating me, that the years I spent holding her up and keeping her together made her feel like she should love me.

She doesn't need me anymore.

The thought makes me as sad as it does proud. I'm happy for Axelle, for her new found independence, that she took her second chance at making a life for herself and fought for everything she wanted.

Even if in that everything there's no me.

"Enough questions, you guys just keep asking the same ole shit." Cam looks down the row of fighters. "Let's get to the announcements." He grumbles a quick introduction.

"Here we go," Laise whispers at my side.

I lean forward and adjust my UFL hat before meeting eyes with the crowd of reporters and journalists. "I spent a year in London training with this crew of incredible fighters. I was offered a five-year fighting contract to stay in London, but in order to make that decision, I wanted to come home to Vegas and get some perspective, and what I learned was—"

The back door swings open so hard it bangs against the wall, calling the attention of everyone in the room. It's too cramped and crowded for me to see who did it.

"What I learned was that after fighting for a year in London, I'm not ready—"

"Killian, no!"

My eyes dart to the cluster of reporters who're being shoved aside to clear a path.

"Ax?"

She bursts through the crowd, breathing like she ran here, only to get stopped by a rope that holds the media a healthy distance back. "Don't go, okay?" Her big blue eyes are glued to mine, as if we're the only people in the room. "Please, just . . . don't go."

"Axelle, honey?" Layla's standing off to the side, her eyes as wide as mine.

Ax doesn't acknowledge her mom. "Killian, I thought by letting you go I was doing what was best for you, but I was thinking about everything we've been through, and I'm so sick of fighting this pull between us. I'm sick of trying to do the right thing when the right thing feels so wrong."

"Ax, baby—"

"Because that's what a life apart from you is, Kill. It's wrong. We were on to something those few days before you left, and I thought sending you away was the right thing. I've spent the last five years searching for something, and all this time you've been right in front of me. You were my bright light, Kill. I didn't realize how bright until you were gone and the darkness was so thick I thought I'd never be free of it. But I got out, I did it, and doing it on my own didn't make me miss you any less."

"What're you saying?"

"It's like that story you told me, the one about the woman who jumped from the Eiffel Tower?" She laughs as a single tear rolls down her cheek. "I've jumped. I'm free falling, and I'm so scared you're not going to be there to catch me."

The room erupts in flash bulbs and whispers, but none of it matters.

My girl, my woman, Axelle . . . she wants me. She interrupted an international press conference to stop me from leaving. I would've settled for a text.

Without a coherent thought beyond getting closer to her, I hurdle the table and cross to her. I stop just shy of her, and my arms tense at my sides. "I'll always catch you, Ax."

She lunges at me with the force of a girl falling, and I easily lift her into my arms.

"Baby, I—"

Her lips crash against mine with an eagerness I've never felt from her before and one that matches my own. Cameras pop all around us along with whispers that remind me we're far from alone.

I kiss along her jaw to her neck. "We'll have to finish this later."

Her cheeks pink and she nods. I place her feet back to the ground and grip her hand, pulling her back to my seat with me.

"Killian, does this mean you're staying in Vegas?"

"Are you taking her with you to London?"

"Calm the hell down," Cam growls into the microphone. "Let the guy get to his seat, and I'm sure he'll answer your questions."

I step around the table, dragging Axelle behind me, and earn smiles of approval from everyone on my team, even Fleur. When I'm back to my spot, I drop down and pull Axelle into my lap. "Right, so as I was saying, I wanted to come back to Vegas to get some perspective, and what I learned was"—I lock eyes with Axelle and she shifts on my lap, her gaze unsure— "I'm not going anywhere."

Gasps are followed by murmurs and then questions, but I ignore them all and continue.

"I would never be where I am today if it weren't for my team here in Vegas." I shift my eyes around the room and find Jonah, his arms crossed over his chest and a knowing grin on his face. "Jonah believed in me before anyone else even knew I existed, and I mean anyone. I owe everything I have to him"—I squeeze Axelle tight and turn back to her—"and this woman right here. I loved my time in London, and I'm not saying I'll never go back, but my family is in Vegas, and this is where I'm staying."

A reporter stands. "Are you afraid the choice to stay will hurt your career?"

"Have you seen the kid fight?" Cam's eyes narrow at the guy. "He could be fighting in Timbuktu and dominate." He nods to another reporter.

"Killian, can you give us the name of this woman you're staying for?"

Cam growls into the mic. "Let's keep the questions to fighting—"

"Cam, it's okay." I stare at Axelle, who seems more than a little uncomfortable with all the eyes on her. "Can we make it official?"

Her face breaks into a brilliant smile and she nods. "Yes."

I lean close to the mic to make sure I'm heard. "This is Axelle Daniels, daughter of Blake and Layla Daniels. I'm gonna ask politely that you leave her alone. Any questions you have I'll be happy to answer, but she's off limits to—"

"You don't need to protect me, Kill." Her lips are at my ear. "I can handle a lot more than you give me credit for."

"I know you can, but that doesn't change the fact that I'm going to do whatever it takes to keep you safe. Fight me all you want, but you can't fight the inevitable."

"Quick Kill! Can you tell us who you're fighting next?"

"Is it true you're going to fight T-Rex?"

"Any plans on going for the title?"

Cameron introduces the London team, and they each get an opportunity to answer questions while I hold Axelle on my lap, praying this will end quickly so I can get her somewhere more private. There's still so much to say, and I can't wait another second to say it all.

Axelle

With the press finally satisfied, Cam wraps up the conference. Before the microphones are even turned off, Killian pulls me through the crowd, dodging reporters until we're in the hallway of the training center. He looks in both directions before hauling me off to the left.

"Where are we going?" I can't help but laugh as he frantically grabs at door handles until he finds one open.

He throws the door wide, pulls me in to a small office with a generic table and chairs, then closes and locks it behind us. It's then I notice he's not dressed in the fancy clothes I've seen him in before. He's wearing a pair of worn jeans that hug his lean thighs, paired with a brown T-shirt that says, *Come to the GEEK side. We have Pi.*

His eyes lock on mine, and it takes everything I have to not back up a step as he comes toward me.

"Killian?" I blink and unease slides through me. "You're not mad at me, are you?"

"You jumped for me." His voice is husky.

"I did." I can't take my eyes off his face. The firm set of his jaw and the bronze-color of his eyes almost twinkle with what I confused earlier with anger, but now I recognize as hunger.

"You know what today is, right?"

I don't answer because he knows I'm aware today is Valentine's Day, the most hated day of the year. Until now.

He tucks a strand of hair behind my ear. "We're making new memories, starting now, baby."

"You're really staying?"

"Of course. Don't act so surprised. You heard Cam. I could fight in Timbuktu."

"It's nice to see your ego's still intact."

He swipes his lips across my forehead. "You think it's something you can get used to?"

Killian has never been a confident guy, and with as much crap as I've been giving him, he's earned the right to be proud of his accomplishments. He's not just believing the hype. If he continues on like this, he'll be an MMA legend. I wrap my arms around his neck and smile up at him. "As long as you can get used to me not needing you to hold me together anymore."

"No joke." He sets his eyes on mine and his smile falls. "I loved holding you together."

"Now you hold my heart." It thumps heavily in my chest. "Don't break it."

"No fucking problem." His lips descend, and he takes my mouth in a gentle and slow kiss. He slides one hand down to the top of my ass, pulling me in deeper while his other hand cups my nape. My legs feel weak as he commands my body and possesses my mouth so beautifully it brings tears from my eyes. The saltiness mixes with our tongues, and he pulls back, pressing his forehead to mine.

"Don't cry, Ax. It kills me when you cry."

"I can't help it. I've been walking around for hours, regretting everything I said after we'd made love. I thought I lost you."

"Never. You can push, and I'll gladly take your fears and be your punching bag, but I meant what I said at that press conference. As long as you want me, I'm not livin' another day without you."

"Good. Because I want you." I press a soft kiss to his lips. "I have always wanted you, Killian."

"I was wondering, with today being Valentine's Day and all, if you'd let me take you to dinner."

The buzz of reporters filters through the walls. "You think there's a restaurant out there where we can find some privacy?"

He chews his lip then shakes his head. "Good point. How about my hotel, anything your gorgeous heart desires off the room-service menu, and we'll rent movies? Just like the old days but with more kissing and fewer clothes."

I sigh long and hard. "Now that sounds like the perfect Valentine's Day.

THIRTY-FIVE

Killian

I wonder if it's too late to change my mind about this morning's plan.

After we made it back to my hotel room last night, we made love until we worked up an appetite that couldn't be ignored. We ordered enough room service to last days then dialed up some romantic comedy she wanted to see. I tried to sway her to the blockbuster sci-fi movie, but all my best moves failed, and frankly, by the time I had my mouth all over her skin, I didn't give a fuck what was on the TV anyway. Turns out, after we hit "play" and our naked bodies were tangled together, she didn't care either.

It wasn't until after she'd fallen asleep in my arms that I was plagued with visions of what the last year of her life had been like. I couldn't lie there for another second without doing *something*, so I sent out the mass text with instructions to pass it on to anyone who might be interested.

It was enough to set my mind at ease so I could get some sleep.

This morning I woke up to a shit load of texts and was forced to peel my body away from hers and hit the shower. Thirty minutes until I'm supposed to be there and I'm finding it impossible to leave her.

Her legs shift beneath the single white sheet, kicking it further off her body so that the smooth, tanned skin of her hip is exposed to the light. I groan as she rolls from her side to her back, the full mounds of her breasts illuminated by the sun cascading through the window.

My shorts grow tight, and I make an adjustment so that I can cross to her without limping. Her thick black lashes flicker to life as I drop to the bed beside her.

"Good morning."

A slow, lazy smile pulls her lips, and her blue eyes are brighter than I ever remember seeing them. "Morning." Her voice is rough with sleep as her gaze rakes over me. She frowns. "You showered without me."

I run a hand through her silken hair and down her neck to rest against her breastbone. Her pulse flutters beneath my palm. "I considered dragging you in there with me, but you were sleeping so hard I didn't want to wake you."

She stretches, arching her back, and unable to resist the invitation, I dip my head to suck on her nipple until it forms a firm peak. Her hands sift into my damp hair and hold me in place. I chuckle at her eagerness, but reluctantly pull back and cover her with the sheet. She gathers the covers to her chest then rolls to her side. "You have somewhere you have to be?"

"Unfortunately." I smooth her hair back from her face. "Order breakfast. Take a long hot bath. I should be back by the time you're done."

She runs her teeth along her lower lip. "And then what?"

"As much as I'd love to spend the day in bed with you, I made plans for this afternoon."

Clouds of doubt pass through her sky-blue eyes. "I can just go home. I need to get my car anyw—"

I press my thumb to her lips. "You haven't even been up for five minutes and you're already at it." I run the pad of my finger along her lower lip. "Don't waste your breath; you can't push me away."

"I'm not pushing you away. If you have plans, I'll get out of your hair."

"My plans include you, if you're interested."

Her brows drop low, but the unease in her eyes is gone. "They do? What are they?"

"Turns out I'm staying in Vegas and have no place to live so . . ."

"You want me to help you find a place?"

Nerves coil in my gut, but I promised her honesty and that's what she's going to get. "No, I want you to help find *us* a place."

"You . . ." She blinks up at me. "You want me to move in with you?"

"I want you to marry me, but I figure living together is a good first step."

"But—"

"I know what you're thinking—this is me trying to take care of you—and your new empowered self can't stomach that, but just hear me out okay?"

She presses her lips together and nods.

"You were right; we've both changed over the last year. I look at you and I love what I see. You're making your own way, standing on your own two feet. I have no desire to get in the way of that." I lean over her, bracing my weight on one arm. "But I will continue to do everything in my power to protect you. It's in my nature. I can't change that just as I can't change my love for you." I dip down and press a kiss to her lips. "I don't want to smother you, Ax, but I can't back off either. I hope you can understand that."

"Hmm . . ." She chews her lip, and my skin prickles with worry. Shit, what if she tells me to go screw myself and leaves. *Then you'll chase her back down and make things right.*

"Okay fine." Her face breaks into a brilliant smile seconds before she throws herself into my chest, knocking the breath from my lungs. The sheet falls to her hips, and she pushes it away to crawl into my lap, and my arms wrap around her waist to hold her close. "Does this mean I get to be protective of you too?" Her hands cup my jaw, and she rests her forehead to mine. "Because I'm getting a little sick of watching women fall all over you, Kill."

I laugh and blush simultaneously. "Depends, am I going to have to start a bank account for your future bail funds?"

She purses her lips. "Maybe."

"Are you saying you'll move in with me?"

"Only if we split all our expenses fifty-fifty."

"I'll pay the rent; we'll split the expenses."

"We'll split the rent and the expenses."

"Why don't you just cut my dick off while you're at it?"

Her nose wrinkles in the most adorable way. "Eww, no, I happen to really like your dick."

"Then let me pay the rent so I can still call myself a man."

"We'll see."

I groan and nuzzle her neck. "Stubborn. Sexy . . . but stubborn." I breathe her in, allowing her scent to relax me. "We're making a go of this. I'm serious. No more fighting the inevitable."

She wraps herself around me. "I have everything I've ever wanted right here in my arms."

"Great thing about having everything you ever wanted is having everything you ever wanted. Bad part is being afraid of—"

"Losing it."

"Exactly." I rub my palms all over her naked skin. "That won't happen to us. I won't allow it."

"I won't either." She pulls back and makes a fist at her chest, using her thumb to cross an X at her heart. "Promise."

When she brings her fist to her mouth to kiss it, I snag it and bring it to mine. "Me too." The clock on the bedside table says if I don't pull my ass away I'm going to be late. "Shit, I gotta go." I pick her up off my lap and place her back on the bed, covering her up because walking away from the visual of her naked body is something I'm not strong enough to do. "I'll be back in an hour or so."

"Wait. Where are you going?"

I rub the back of my neck. "It's nothing, just something I need to do." I grab a keycard to the hotel room and head to the door. "I'll explain when I get back." Before I pass through the door, I turn around and grin because how the fuck did my life become perfect overnight? "I love you."

"I love you too."

~~~

The cab driver drops me off at the address Ryder texted me last night. I make a note to get my damn Jeep out of storage ASAP because relying on a taxi to cart my ass around is getting old.

Standing out in front of a rundown apartment complex are enough UFL fighters to make any man piss himself. I jog toward them, and they all turn to me as I approach.

Jonah, Rex, Blake, Mason, Wade, Caleb, Ryder, and Cameron.

"Thanks for coming on short notice."

"You send out a text at midnight, saying you want to rally the troops for my daughter. No fucking way I'm gonna miss it." Blake reaches out a hand to shake mine. "I appreciate you steppin' up."

I shake his hand. "I fucked up by leaving—"

"No, leaving was the right thing. I love my girl, but she needed to figure some shit out, and having you here wouldn't have done her any favors."

Caleb smacks me on the back. "He's right. You had to invest some time into your career. Now you're right where you need to be."

"We gonna sit around strokin' the man's balls or are we gonna do this?" Cameron's words don't match the proud, and subtle, grin on his face.

I lift my chin towards Ryder. "You know the place?"

"Yeah, number thirty-two." He motions to the building closest to us. "It's just around the corner from this one here."

"We gonna need to call in a favor so we don't go down for something or are you just here to send a message?" Jonah tilts his head, studying me through dark glasses. "I'm cool either way. I fucking hate this scumbag."

"Just won Ax back, and I promised her I wouldn't fuck us up, so . . . no, nothing to clean up. Just sending a message."

"Damn," Rex mumbles.

"I was kinda looking forward to getting a shot in myself." Ryder swings his gaze around the circle of fighters staring at him in disbelief. "What? Oh, just because I don't look like some WWF knockoff like the rest of you, doesn't mean I can't hold my own in a fight."

Cam claps his son on the back. "He's a pint-sized badass."

"No, if it comes to blows, his ass is mine." I don't tell them that I secretly hope it does. I wasn't kidding about not messing things up with Axelle, but if he throws the first punch, I can't be held accountable for defending myself.

"I got dibs on second," Blake holds up a hand to mark his place in line.

Jonah next. "Third."

"Fuck that. I get third." Ryder raises his hand.

Rex grins and lifts a hand. "Fourth."

"At this rate, we'll kill the poor bastard." Mason chuckles.

Jonah growls. "He deserves no less for what he put Axelle through." He glares at Ryder. "Third."

For a moment, I just sit back and watch as this group of men argue over who gets to exact retribution on the dickwad that put Axelle through hell, and it hits me that, although the two men who meant the most in her life left her, they've been replaced by this renegade team of fighters who would gladly get arrested for her. My heart swells at the show of support, and I wish I could capture it on video and show her just how loved she is.

"Mind if we do this before noon, boys? I've got a woman at home with two kids who all speak the same language, and I could've sworn they were plotting against me this morning." Mason narrows his eyes. "Either that or they were planning to go to the park. My Russian is mediocre at best."

"Here's the deal. I go in first and drop the warning; you guys back me up and keep me from doing anything stupid."

They all agree, and like a wave of menace, we descend on the apartment complex. Blake pulls up beside me. "Think he had to move here after I had my buddy at the LVPD pull a search warrant on his house. Turns out his roommate was selling crack. Ole Cliff weaseled out of any charges by squealing on his buddy, which pissed me off. I was hoping we could get the piece of trash locked up for a while."

I scan the door numbers in search of the right one. "She told me what he did, Blake. How could you keep from killing him?"

"I wanted to; trust me. But when you've got people who depend on you, you have to consider them too. Getting locked up won't do my family any good, ya know?"

"I'm starting to understand that, yeah." Because as much as I hate Clifford, I love Axelle more. Leaving her for any reason is no longer an option. I nod toward the door in front of me. "There it is."

"Good." His lips pull back from his teeth. "Now let's have some fun."

I close my fist and bang on the door. The heat of fighters at my back floods me with power, but more than that with security. There's no doubt they'll keep me from doing something I'd regret.

The door swings open to reveal Clifford in nothing but a pair of jeans. His eyes narrow on me, but then widen as he scans the wall of muscle behind me.

"What's up, Cliff." I push past him and into his pad. "Long time no see."

"Hey, wait. You guys can't just come in here."

Jonah knocks into Clifford's shoulder, accidentally on purpose, sending the guy back a few steps. "Sure we can, kid. We just did."

The cramped living room is littered with fast-food trash and empty pizza boxes. Beer cans and overflowing ashtrays cover the coffee table and the place stinks. Remorse turns my stomach to think of Axelle and a baby living here. For a year, I imagined them making house, but never considered it would be like this. I have to believe Blake would've never allowed it.

"I'll call the cops." Clifford grabs his phone off the couch only to have it snagged from his hand by Wade.

"Not so fast, Clit." He shoves the phone in his pocket.

"It's not Clit." Rex shakes his head. "It's Clifford, bro."

"Oh, my bad. Listen, Clitford, we're not gonna hurt you."

"Unless you want us to." Rex smiles wickedly.

"You guys come here to jump me? Is that it?" Cliff's fake bravery is so pathetic I almost feel sorry for him. Almost. "That's how you assholes fight, huh? Six against one."

Jonah pops out his bottom lip. "*Aww,* don't hurt him, guys. He can't count." His face turns damn near homicidal. "There are nine of us, and if you so much as raise your voice, we will fuck you up."

"Oh, nine against one. Freakin' cowards."

"Says the cocksucker who bullied a girl half his size." I close in. "Tripped her when she was . . ." I bite my tongue and growl. I don't have to finish the sentence. I can see that Clifford gets me.

"You can't do this; you can't break into my house—"

"I remember being invited over." Wade holds up Clifford's cellphone with an outgoing text that reads, *Come on over for a circle jerk. Let yourselves in.* "Kinky, but no thanks."

Clifford's eyes bounce between Blake and me. "I can't believe all this is about *her*. I was just fuckin' around, man."

I step into his space. "I'll give you credit for not saying her name, because you know if you did, I'd destroy you."

His eyes narrow, but I don't miss the way his dilated pupils dart back and forth in fear. "What do you want?"

"I want you to promise, right here and now in front of these witnesses, that you will never come near my woman again."

He laughs awkwardly. "Dude, she has a restraining order against me. Pretty sure that's already been settled. You'd have known that if you weren't busy banging bitches in Europe."

My arm flinches, but a firm hand steadies me. "I don't mean stay away from her because of the restraining order. I mean for the rest of your sad pathetic life. I mean if you ever run into her, five, ten, fifteen years from now, you turn and walk the other way. I mean if she comes home and says, 'You'll never believe who I saw at the grocery store . . .' we come back to pay you a visit."

"That's impossible! We live in the same city."

"Move." The single word comes from behind me, and I realize it must be Blake who steadied my arm.

"Don't care what you have to do or where you have to go, but know that if I find out you so much as pass her car in a parking lot, I will come back for you."

"Fine." His hand shakes as he pulls a smoke from the pack in his pocket. "You done here?"

"Not yet." Ryder steps up along with Caleb and Cam. "We delivered the message, but we need some insurance."

I stare at the boys, having no idea what they have in store but enjoying the idea anyway.

Cam pushes up to Clifford, intimidating him with his size, and the guy shifts on his feet like a little kid who needs to hit the bathroom and fast. "Seems you took some questionable photos of our girl without her permission."

"That's bullshit! She begged—"

I slap him in the face, not hard enough to leave a mark, but enough to get his attention. "Don't fucking talk about her."

Cam pulls out his phone. "I think you deserve to know what it's like to have your picture taken and posted for all your friends and family to see."

I swing my gaze to Blake, who's grinning in satisfaction.

"Come on, Clitford." Wade's voice coos. "It'll be fun. We'll strip you naked, tie you up, and play whack-a-mole with—oh, shit." He throws his hands up in the air. "He pissed himself. Real nice."

"I'm not touching that." Caleb steps back.

"Damn, that's a lot of piss for one man." Jonah pulls out his phone and snaps a few photos. "We can post these from a dummy account."

"Alright, okay?" Cliff's bottom lip trembles. "I'll stay away. I'll move. Whatever, just . . ." He sniffs and clears his throat. "I'll leave her alone, I swear."

"Do you believe him?" Blake's next to me, arms crossed over his chest.

"I do. Because he knows if he so much as thinks about her and we find out we're coming back for him."

Cliff exhales hard.

"Alright, boys." Cameron turns toward the door. "Let's blow."

"Aw, man, I was hoping we could get in at least one good hit." Rex pouts as Cameron ushers him and the others out while they grumble their complaints.

Once they all leave, I address Clifford for what I hope will be the last time in Axelle's long beautiful life. "I know what you did, and I know you saw my leaving as a chance to do it." I slam my fist into his gut, and he doubles over, gasping. "This is over. Do not make me come back."

I whirl around to leave and find Blake standing in the doorway. He nods in approval then turns, and I follow behind him, slamming Clifford's door so hard the wood snaps.

"I think that went well," Blake says with a smile in his voice.

"I'd say the message we came to deliver was received."

He nods. "It was a wet reception."

"Yeah, it was."

We chuckle, and once we're at the cars, everyone pats me on the back. Blake squeezes my shoulder. "Good job, Killer. You did the right thing to call us rather than go in there alone. You needed the back up."

I knock Blake's hand off my shoulder. "I didn't *need* you guys here. I just figured after what I'd seen the last few days, how much you all dig my girl, that you'd want the chance."

"Hey, until you make this shit official, she's still *my* girl." Blake pokes me in the chest.

"Oh, that reminds me. We're going house hunting this afternoon."

Blake seems genuinely shocked. "You tellin' or askin'?"

I shrug. "Um . . . both?"

"So this is it, huh? You two are finally done fucking around, and you're gonna give this thing a real chance?"

"Absolutely, although there's no *chance* about it. I've settled for less than all of her, but those days are over."

Blake's eyes study the ground, and when he looks up, they're shining. "I approve, Kill."

"Yeah?"

He nods. "Now let me take you to grab your car so you can take *my* girl house hunting."

I head to his Rubicon. "Nice of you, Blake, but I don't think Layla will be interested in house hunting with me."

He glares. "Don't you take Axelle away from me, Kill. I'll put the hurt down."

I glare back. "Same to you."

He groans and hops into the truck. "You two are obnoxious. Damn soul mates of annoyance."

"Can't argue that."

EPILOGUE

Four months later . . .

Axelle

"Axelle, don't."

I have to bite my lip to keep from laughing hysterically at Killian as he tries, once again, to tell me what to do. I can't see his eyebrows behind his sunglasses, but the tanned skin of his forehead is pinched in irritation, his lips held in a tight line that only makes me want to kiss him until they soften beneath mine.

"Kill, relax."

He swivels his head from left to right and back again as if the power of his thoughts could make everyone on this St. Tropez beach disappear before I do something stupid.

"It's my birthday and we're in Southern France!" I toss my crocheted beach bag onto the chic lounger the hotel has set up on the beach. When Kill said he was taking me on a trip for my birthday, I expected extravagance. I did not expect a *Lifestyles of the Rich and Famous* European vacation worthy of rock gods and Hollywood royalty: everything from the travel pods on our first-class flight to hotels where the bed sheets probably cost more than I make in a year. He's left me wanting for nothing.

Well, except this.

"No." He practically stomps his flip-flap-clad foot into the sand before he drops to the lounger, pouting. "I'll lose my shit, Ax, I swear to God."

He's adorable all the time, but when his big ole body is slumped over and he's sulking, he's irresistible. I step between his open legs and pull his head to my stomach. "Kill . . ." His arms wrap around me to lock around my thighs. "You're being ridiculous." I hold back the giggle that threatens to burst free and run my fingers through his hair until he loosens up. "It's just a bikini."

"It's *hardly* a bikini."

"In France you're supposed to be *free* with your body. Besides, all the important parts are covered."

"When you showed it to me this morning, you swore you'd keep your shorts on in public." The whine in his voice is more than I can handle, and I lose the battle with my laughter.

"Right before you stripped it off me and made love to me on the ice-cold marble countertop."

He sighs then tilts his head back to look up at me. "Yeah."

I push his sunglasses off his face to prop them on his head. His eyes are practically glinting with that internal struggle between giving me freedom and protecting me. "I got the bikini specifically for this experience. I mean, when will we ever be in St. Tropez again?"

"I'll bring you back every year if you promise to keep those shorts on this ass." He cups and squeezes my backside then groans and drops his forehead to my stomach.

"I didn't let you train me, grunt through an hour of weight lifting and one-hundred squats a day for the last thirty days, to keep my booty covered up in St. Tropez."

His shoulders drop in defeat. He knows I'm right. He also knows I'm going to do it anyway, but because I love him, I'll give him the chance to come to terms with it before I completely piss him off. It's a routine we've fallen into that seems to work well.

"When you become a McCreery, will you start listening to me?"

The mention of my future last name brings my eyes to the single princess-cut diamond set in platinum on my ring finger. He proposed three days ago at the Eiffel Tower, surrounded by candlelight, thanks to the prep work of Fleur and the boys. It was the single most romantic moment of my entire life, and even though the ring has only been on my finger for days, it feels as if it's part of me.

"You mean will I be a good little obedient wife?" I rake my nails along his scalp, and his answering groan vibrates in his chest. "Not on your life."

"Fine." He drops a kiss to my belly and pushes himself back to recline. "But if anyone stares too long, I'm throwing you over my shoulder and locking you in our room until you come to your senses."

My stomach tumbles at the threat in his words. I know exactly what he'll do to convince me, and having Kill's hands and mouth all over my body gives me a moment of pause. "So you're saying this is a win-win for me."

Finally, the corner of his mouth lifts in a half smile. "Can't deny the birthday girl." He pulls his T-shirt up over his head, and my mouth goes dry. No matter how many times I've seen him naked, I always get the butterflies as if it's the first. His pecs contract as he balls up his shirt and tosses it to my beach bag. And he's worried about me? Kill's body is like a dinner bell to the female gender, calling not only eyes but shameless flirting, which he's great at ignoring.

I turn my back on him and pull the drawstring on the cute linen shorts I bought while shopping with Fleur in Paris last week.

I wanted to hate her—I really did—but she's one of those girls who's impossible to dislike. I mean unless she's kissing the love of my life, which she hasn't done since Kill and I became official. She's funny, and I get the feeling that if we lived closer we'd be great friends. And for a girl who hangs out with dudes all day, she has amazing taste in clothes.

With a little wiggle, I push the shorts down over my hips, and the rumble of a growl sounds at my back. I shake my head and do a quick knee bend to snag the fabric from the sand rather than an at-the-waist bend that'll only irritate Killian more.

"So?" I turn and toss my shorts on the lounger then prop my hands on my hips and strike a pose. "What do you think?"

I already know what he thinks. He made it clear when I showed him the suit in the privacy of our room, but I'm hoping that, however indecent he felt my uber-expensive designer suit was then, he's seeing now it's not as bad as he thought.

It has a black triangle top with gold band embellishments at the ties. The bottoms are also black, but at the back, gold beads make a triangle pattern right above where the fabric disappears between the cheeks of my overly-toned and spray-tanned ass.

"*Fuck*, Ax!" He grabs a nearby towel that's been rolled and placed on each lounger. With a quick whip of his wrist, he shakes it out and places it over his hips. "You're killing me," he says through clenched teeth.

I shake my head at my incredibly protective, gorgeous, and sexy fiancé then put a knee to the lounger and crawl between his legs, pressing my body to his sun-warmed chest to rest my head on his shoulder. "Thank you."

He tosses one side of the long towel over my ass, making me laugh. "You thank me like I had a choice." His voice sounds less tense, and his arms slide around me. "You were gonna do it anyway."

"Yeah." I sigh and nuzzle his throat. "But that's not what I'm thanking you for."

"It's just money, Ax. It's your birthday, baby." He kisses the top of my head. "You deserve so much more. I plan on showing you just how much more for as long as we live."

368

I hum against his collarbone and kiss him there until he shivers. "I loved you when we were poor, Kill. As much as I've enjoyed these last ten days, I'd have loved them just as much if we were backpacking and sleeping in hostels."

"Is that right?" He's skeptical, rightly so. I've *really* been enjoying this life of luxury. Who wouldn't?

"Well, yeah." I peek up at him. "But even still, that's not what I was thanking you for."

He doesn't ask for more but sets those whiskey-colored eyes on mine, asking the silent question.

"Thank you for never giving up on me."

"Ax—"

I press my finger to his lips. "I'm serious. I was looking so hard for something, and you were there offering it to me for all those years. You stood by while I dated other guys. I . . ." I think of all the epic fuckups he had to stand by and witness, all the times I took my anger out on him just because he was available, made him pay for the sins of every man who walked away with a piece of my heart. "I don't know if I would've been strong enough to have done the same—to have been there while you burned through countless women. How did you do it? I wasn't always nice to you, and you never gave up on me."

He hooks my chin and brings my lips to his. "Because I love you."

"Is it that simple?"

"Nothing between us has ever been simple, but the choice to be there for you was. It still is."

I understand that now because I love Killian and have let go of all my hang-ups, all the voices that were telling me I wasn't what he needed or what he deserved. But the choice to stand by him through everything life brings—his fighting, the traveling, the press, the rumors, the women—*is* simple. I'll never leave his side, no matter what.

Pushing up to my elbows, I tilt my head to sink into a delicious kiss that has my toes curling as I rub myself against him. "I can't wait for the rest of our lives, Killian. I'm going to make you so happy." I dip in for another soft kiss, speaking against his lips. "Make it so you never regret choosing me."

He smiles against my lips. "Love your determination, but that's not necessary. I've got the sexiest woman alive stretched out against me. Her love, her loyalty, that's all I need—just you." He runs the tip of his tongue along my lower lip. "Now behave, or I'll slip that tiny piece of fabric between your legs to the side and we'll show the people of St. Tropez just how *free* with our bodies we can be."

I drop my forehead to his neck and force back the instant lust his words evoke. It's nearly impossible to keep our hands off each other when we're fully clothed, and something about the sun, sand, and skin combo heightens my desire—the hardening evidence between his legs only making it worse.

"You're right." I take a few calming breaths and then turn to move, only to have him grip me and pull me back so that I'm sitting between his legs.

"Not yet. I need, uh . . . a minute."

Fine by me; being surrounded by Killian is not a hardship. I lean back against his chest and wave over a beach attendant who takes our orders for two ridiculously fruity drinks from the bar. We sit for a while, allowing the sound of the surf to lull us into a comfortable silence. He absently runs his fingertips along my bare belly, drawing patterns that bring goose bumps to the surface.

In the distance, I watch a couple at the water's edge, hand in hand and talking about something only the other can hear. The sight before would've made me want to vomit in my mouth, but now I— My body stiffens when the woman turns around.

"Don't. Even. Think. About. It." Killian's words are growled against my neck.

I smile. Big. "Oh, I have to now."

"Not a fucking chance in hell, Ax."

"But—"

"No."

"It's—"

"No!"

I lick my lips, and excitement explodes in my chest. "You're right." I scoot away from him, hoping he doesn't catch my bluff. "Phew, it's hot out."

"Ax . . ." *Uh-oh . . . he's using his warning tone.*

I stifle a giggle. "I'm going to go get my feet wet."

"Axelle Rose Daniels, I swear to God if you—"

I take off running. A howl of laughter born deep in my gut bursts from my lips and electrifies the air. "I have to!"

"Dammit to hell."

I can hear his powerful footfalls in the sand behind me as I work frantically to untie my top. "I just want to be *free!*"

"Don't do it!"

"I have to!" My words are incoherent through my laughter as my feet hit the water.

"Axelle, no—"

But it's too late. The strings fall from my body, and the sun's heat hits my bare breasts. "I'm free—*omph!*"

Solid weight slams into me from behind. Warm arms wrap around me. Hands cup my breasts. I shriek when I become air-born. Flipped. I land backwards into the ocean with Killian to cushion the fall. He brings me to the surface, and I'm sputtering for air, but not from the water, from the laughing.

His arms, hands, and body stay in place as he vibrates with laughter too.

"You're too . . . fast . . ." I suck in air and allow him to take most of my weight as we stand waist deep in water, our backs toward the beach.

His breath is hot against my neck. "I can't believe you just did that."

"Sure you can." I push wet strands of hair from my face.

"I'm taking you back to the room now."

I press my palms over his hands still cupping my breasts. "It's okay, you big party pooper. I'll put my top back on. Besides, I've heard sunburned nipples are a bitch."

"That's not why. Watching your ass when you took off running did me in, Ax." He groans and flexes his hips into my ass. "I need you."

I gasp at the desperation in his voice and marvel at how it matches my own. "Okay, Kill." I wrap an arm up and behind me to pull his head down for a kiss that leaves us both breathless. "You can't walk me back to the beach like this." I motion to his hands on me. "I'll keep myself covered."

"I don't trust you. Wanting to be free and shit, fuck . . . Next trip we're going to Pennsylvania to shack up with the Amish."

I wiggle free, and he's forced to release me, but I quickly cover myself with my own hands. His eyes flare. "That's even worse." He looks behind him at my top lying abandoned on the beach then turns me back towards the horizon. "Stay."

"I love you, Killian McCreery," I yell over my shoulder as he jogs to get my top.

"You're a pain in my ass, but I love you too."

THE END

FIGHTING FATE PLAYLIST

Thunderstruck – AC/DC

Chandelier – Sia

Flashlight – Jessie J

Flavor of the Week – American Hi-Fi

I Can Wait Forever – Simple Plan

I'd Hate to Be You When People Find Out What This Song is About – Mayday Parade

It Girl – Jason Derulo

Lost with You – The Heyday

No Heroes Allowed – Mayday Parade

Red Light Pledge – Silverstein

Secret Valentine – We The Kings

So Soon – Marianas Trench

Thank You – Simple Plan

The Last Something That Meant Anything – Mayday Parade

Three Cheers for Five Years – Mayday Parade

When I'm Gone – Simple Plan

You Be the Anchor That Keeps My Feet on the Ground, I'll Be the Wings That Keep Your Head in the Clouds – Mayday Parade

ACKNOWLEDGMENTS

Writing a book is always a group effort, and I couldn't be more excited and overwhelmed by the amazing people who helped me bring Axelle and Killian's story to the page.

Amanda Simpson at Pixel Mischief Design . . . I don't even know where to start. What began as a business relationship quickly grew into friendship, and now you're even dipping your toes into beta reading. Is there anything you can't do? I think not. Your insight on this project was invaluable, and the fact that romance "isn't your thing" yet you help me anyway is a kindness I could never adequately repay. When we get to our private island, you can have the master house. I'll take the servants quarters. And those first few rum drinks are on me. From the bottom of my heart, I thank you.

I owe a huge thank you to Toshia Slade who has been through this series with a fine-toothed comb: editing audiobooks, proofing e-books, beta reading. I've managed to rob the girl of the enjoyment of The Fighting Series, and yet she's always anxiously awaiting more. Thank you, Tosh, for all that you've done both for me and for The Fighting Girls. From day one, you were there, and you've been a steady force ever since. I'm forever grateful.

To my favorite stalker, Kelly Fletcher, I'm forever grateful for your help on this book. It is because of you that none of my fighters sounds like Dick Van Dyke in *Mary Poppins*. I adore you, and I look forward to one day getting to give you a big ole hug to say thank you.

Thank you to my dear friend Claudia Connor, who took the time to blast through this book for me at the last minute and always ensures I'm putting my best work forward. I love you, Dia.

As always, a huge thank you to Elizabeth Reyes for encouraging me to write when I was terrified to try. I will always owe everything to you. Thank you for taking the time to invest in me. I will *never* forget you and remain more grateful than words could explain.

Huge thank you to my incredible agent MacKenzie Fraser-Bub, who's always fighting in my corner and believes in the writer I am and the writer I can become.

Thank you to Theresa Wegand for editing the entire Fighting Series. You've lived through all these books, and I'm forever grateful for your guidance.

I'm beyond grateful to my family, who've been my #1 fans. You've helped make this incredible ride so sweet. I love you all to death.

Ginormous thank you to all The Fighting Girls who've cheered me on, pushed me when I felt like giving up, and who constantly remind me that romance readers are the most beautiful, compassionate, and passionate women on earth. You've blown me away with your support and your love for each other. Every book I write I write for you.

Free to Fly . . .

ABOUT THE AUTHOR

JB Salsbury, New York Times Best Selling author of the Fighting series, lives in Phoenix, Arizona, with her husband and two kids. She spends the majority of her day lost in a world of battling alphas, budding romance, and impossible obstacles as stories claw away at her subconscious, begging to be released to the page.

Her love of good storytelling led her to earn a degree in Media Communications. With her journalistic background, writing has always been at the forefront, and her love of romance prompted her to write her first novel.

Since 2013 she has published six bestselling novels in The Fighting Series and won a RONE Award.

For more information on the series or just to say hello, visit JB on her website, Facebook, or Goodreads page.

http://www.jbsalsbury.com/

https://www.facebook.com/JBSalsburybooks

http://www.goodreads.com/author/show/6888697.Jamie_Salsbury

Made in the USA
Middletown, DE
11 August 2023